"HIS SECOND NOVEL CAN'T BE PUBLISHED SOON ENOUGH."
—Associated Press

"Mr. Lindsay's first novel is a delight. . . . He has lived and written with equal flair."
—*The New York Times Book Review*

"What makes Lindsay's story sizzle are his wry, dead-on sniping at Bureau mentality and, particularly, his intimate knowledge of cop's lives. . . . With action that accelerates to a stirring climax, Lindsay delivers a crime thriller to savor."
—*Kirkus Reviews*

"The plot is well-made, the writing superior and the characters are beautifully etched, especially Mike Devlin."
—*The Indianapolis Star*

"This is an amazing fast-paced action-packed novel which takes the reader into the guts of the world which is the FBI. Lindsay has broken new ground here by bringing the genre of the police novel to a new height."
—*The New England Review of Books*

Please turn the page for more reviews. . . .

WITNESS TO THE TRUTH

A Novel of the FBI

Paul Lindsay

FAWCETT GOLD MEDAL • NEW YORK

A Fawcett Gold Medal Book
Published by Ballantine Books
Copyright © 1992 by Paul Lindsay

All rights reserved under International and Pan-American Copyright Conventions. Published in the United States by Ballantine Books, a division of Random House, Inc., New York, and simultaneously in Canada by Random House of Canada Limited, Toronto.

Witness to the Truth is a work of fiction. Names, characters, and incidents are products of the author's imagination. Any resemblance to actual events or persons, living or dead, is entirely coincidental.

Grateful acknowledgment is made to EMI Music Publishing for permission to reprint an excerpt from "We Gotta Get Out of This Place" by Barry Mann and Cynthia Weil. Copyright © 1965 by Screen Gems-EMI Music, Inc. All rights reserved. International copyright secured. Reprinted by permission of EMI Music Publishing.

Library of Congress Catalog Card Number: 92-53639

ISBN 0-449-14794-0

Manufactured in the United States of America

First Ballantine Books Edition: June 1994

10 9 8 7 6 5 4 3 2 1

Because she always held down the fort
while I ran off on some small-boy's adventure,
this is for my wife, Patti.
Always.

gentle people

i know
we were
a gentle people
once,
but the rulers
have made us
fighters,
fighters better
than they;
and we will fight
so that we can become
gentle people
again.

—b. p. Flanigan
5/10/46–10/15/89 irish victor

". . . All of you are now witnesses of the truth. I am as sure of this as I am that the Bureau will endure."

—Unnamed Instructor
FBI Academy
New Agents Class #3, 1972

ACKNOWLEDGMENTS

THANKS TO:

Nettie Jones for her refusal to give up on my writing.

Joe and Janis Vallely for leading me through the minefields of New York and Hollywood.

David Rosenthal for his endurance in solving the puzzles of this book.

Diane Baldwin for a warm ear during cold doubts.

Neil Kirsten for solving a thousand Detroit mysteries.

Sgt. Dennis Richardson, whose police work reminds us all why we took the oath.

Sam Ruffino for his mob stories and the sometime folly of our pursuit.

Hayes Scott for his biggest fault, his generosity.

PROLOGUE

Although it was a familiar task, he took his time taping the sickening single-edged razor blades to the ends of his fingers. With intense precision, he set them to cut one-sixteenth of an inch deep into any surface that his hand contacted.

Ever so slowly he continued to wrap his fingers as he watched the terror burn through her. One by one, his fingers became horrifying weapons. It pleased him to hear the racing heartbeats in her breath.

When the right hand was finished, he stood over her and let it dangle close enough to her face that she could smell the tape's adhesive and even a frightening metallic hint of the honed steel blades. With his unarmed hand he checked the heavy gray tape that bound her and then tested the chain around her neck, ensuring it was anchored in the wall of the forsaken building. The girl's breathing became that of an accelerating locomotive, causing a soft smile of understanding in his eyes.

He sat again and started preparing his left hand. One of the blades cut the new hand. The blood ran impatiently into his palm and then down his arm. He positioned the flow so she could watch its course. Her eyes strained involuntarily toward the wound.

As each finger was taped, a new cut was made. When he was finished, his hand and forearm were heavily veined in red. Her vision glowed white; her head floated. Her senses became intoxicated as the arm turned into a kaleidoscopic swirl. He was pleased.

He put his hand to the flawless skin of her paralyzed face. She could smell the uninhibited odor of the thick, copper-rich fluid. She stiffened, realizing she did not know whose blood it was.

The police, when would they come? her silent prayer asked.

It was as if he could hear her thoughts. "This is Detroit," he answered. "No one is coming."

||| PART ONE |||

||| CHAPTER 1 |||

Because Mike Devlin knew that drug dealers who commit murders are not likely to be awake at six in the morning, he drove carelessly by the house looking for the killer's car. The sun had not yet risen, but the gray light warned of its immediacy. In Vietnam, the Marines had called it first light. For Devlin, it was a secret time, a valley hidden in the rush of Detroit's day. He had learned its use from the Viet Cong. It was their favorite time to attack: a time when they could see and not be seen, kill and not be killed. First light belonged to the hunter.

As Devlin slowed his dark blue Chevrolet to a stop, he searched the house's driveway. He was looking for a new black Mercedes-Benz with Alabama plates. At the end of the driveway, a car was angled around the back of the house barely visible from the street. A black Mercedes—but with a Michigan plate. Even in the dense light the car's silky newness humbled its surroundings. A curly telephone antenna rose from the top of the rear window. Devlin pulled an old pair of artillery binoculars from under the seat. They cut through the dimness between the two cars, allowing him to read not only the license plate but more important, the plate holder: "Dixie Motors, Birmingham, Alabama." He smiled. The plate had been changed, but not the holder.

He took his foot from the brake and silently coasted until he was out of sight of the house. Adjusting his side mirror

3

to watch the house behind him, he opened a pulpy tan folder. He took out a blue three-page document. The color demanded expeditious handling, but Devlin judged urgency by content, not color. This one was hot. The Birmingham, Alabama, office of the FBI had sent it to the Detroit office. The subject of the communication was Leroy Osgood Taylor, also known as Leroy Thomas, also known as "Lee." Wanted by the Birmingham Police Department, Taylor, a large-scale cocaine trafficker, was charged with a double homicide. Two of his dealers had "fucked up his money," so he summarily terminated their employment by shooting them each three times in the back of the head. Both victims were sixteen-year-old black males. One of Taylor's accomplices later confessed, naming Lee as the shooter. He also told the Birmingham police that immediately after the murders, Lee had fled to Detroit, leaving a telephone number where he could be contacted. Taylor had reasoned that he could easily hide in Detroit's lush forest of dope dealers and murderers. Also included in the communication was a detailed description of Taylor and his car. A mug shot was enclosed.

The last paragraph was captioned "Leads." It read, "Detroit will attempt to locate and apprehend the subject through telephone (313) 555-7113."

The last line on the page was underlined, warning, *"Consider the subject armed and dangerous."*

The telephone number came back to the house where the Mercedes was parked.

The house presented a variety of problems. It was a large old Victorian frame whose wooden exterior had long since turned a colorless gray from neglect. Doors and windows wrapped around the house endlessly. Cordoning off and searching it would require at least a squad of agents. A force that size would bring out the bosses with their usual assistants: Reluctance and Hindsight. Legally, the Supreme

Court, in one of its ivory-tower decisions, demanded a third-party residence search warrant if the ownership of the house was unknown. But the biggest drawback, which was every cop's nightmare, was the possibility of a barricaded gunman. Devlin had seen too many folded flags in Vietnam. He had secretly vowed he would let any and all fugitives slip away before he folded another one.

He made a decision. A decision he knew would later be challenged.

"DE Four-one to Central," Devlin said into his radio handset.

"This is Central; go ahead, Four-one."

"In ten minutes call the Fifth Precinct and advise them that an agent needs assistance arresting an individual wanted for murder in Alabama. The address is 7778 Ashland."

"7778 Ashland. That's ten-four, Four-one."

Quietly he got out of the car. Without shutting the door completely, he closed it far enough to extinguish the interior lights.

Abruptly a house door opened behind him. Devlin turned quickly. An older black man wearing freshly pressed tan work clothes came out on the porch for the morning paper. He glared at Devlin. After fifteen years, Detroit's militant eyes no longer offended Devlin. Without emotion, he stared back evenly. The man recognized the look. Cop's eyes. With his contempt thinly disguised, he looked at Devlin one last time before disappearing into the darkness of his house.

Devlin went back to his trunk and took out a screwdriver and two other items known to car thieves as a slim-jim and a slammer. With these three tools a thief could steal a car in less than sixty seconds. The slim-jim, made from a strip of flexible metal twenty-five inches long with a square notch cut at the side of one end, was a tool requiring patience and a certain touch. Conversely, the slammer, originally used for auto body repair, was a two-and-a-half-foot-long rod with a self-tapping screw device at one end and a heavy handle at the other. A five-pound free-floating metal weight slid along the rod. It was a tool requiring only strength.

Cautiously, Devlin walked to the house. He was relieved to see that all the windows were closed and dark. As he turned up the driveway, he reached inside his suit jacket and unsnapped his holster, raising his stainless-steel magnum an inch, then letting it drop loosely back into its leather casing. He lightened his footsteps, but they still seemed too loud. As he reached the driver's door of Taylor's car, he looked back toward the street protectively. He inserted the slim-jim between the window and door frame, pushing it down until he could feel the locking mechanism. In short, upsweeping arcs, he worked the metal strip until the notch caught the release arm of the lock. A quick pull, and the door was open. The interior had the smothering odor of dead cigarette smoke made more irritating by the residue of some syrupy cologne.

Devlin felt under the seat. No gun. If Taylor had one, it was in the house with him. The telephone was appended to the dashboard and appeared to be functional once the engine was started. He inserted the screw end of the slammer into the ignition, turning it stiffly until half of the case-hardened screw was anchored in the ignition lock. Holding the handle with his right hand, he threw the sliding weight hard into the handle. Twice more he slammed the weight away from the ignition, which popped out still attached to the tool. Working by feel only, he guided the screwdriver into the electrical circuits that had previously been protected by the ignition lock and turned the starting mechanism clockwise. The engine started inaudibly, and the phone lit up.

Quickly he dialed the number he had received from Birmingham. After six rings a drowsy black male answered with an irritated "Yeah."

In a black voice Devlin said, "Lee, day axed me ta call en tell ya dat da po-lice is comin. Day be der in fit-teen minute." He hung up.

The side door of the house exploded as Taylor came running out wearing pants, no shoes, and pulling on a shirt. His car keys in his teeth. He unlocked the car door and quickly got in, attempting to put the key in the ignition. When he could not find the keyhole with the usual thrust of the key, he realized the lock was gone.

"What the—?" he wondered out loud, but his unfinished question was answered when he felt the unmistakable hardness of Devlin's magnum pressed against the back of his head.

"Guess I'm a little early, Lee."

Scout car 5-22 rolled in slow motion along east Warren Boulevard. Its driver pushed the exhausted blue machine along without thinking or seeing. With an hour left on his midnight shift, he let the car wander the precinct aimlessly. Beyond the eclipsed eastern border of the city, daybreak gave its silvery warning. For the weather-beaten cop it was a flare, signaling that another night had been survived. All the felons were asleep or dead. Hopefully, the bodies would not be found until the day shift took over.

He drove past a school. In foot-high letters someone had neatly painted IS THERE LIFE BEFORE DEATH? Since the spelling and grammar were correct, he assumed it had been written by a teacher.

His partner had spent his entire six months as a Detroit police officer in the Fifth Precinct. The rookie searched the deserted streets, knowing he had only an hour left on his shift, wanting something to happen—something, as a cop, only he could handle. He looked at the speedometer. "You want me to drive?"

Without focusing his stare, the old cop answered, "To where?" The rookie knew what that meant. He had heard it all before. There was no place to go. Their job was as pointless as the direction of their car. He disagreed, but only silently.

The first night they had ridden together the veteran had made his feelings clear. "I'm going to tell you what I tell all the white guys with less than five years on the job—get out." Then he looked down at the sending light on the radio to ensure that his words were not being accidentally transmitted. Trusting his partner was not a concern. Even the newest rookie understood that the sanctity of the scout car was as sacred as a priest's confessional. "You married?"

"Yes," the rookie answered absentmindedly, still confused by the advice.

"Kids?"

"A boy and one on the way."

"Residency says you have to live in Detroit, which is *at least* eighty percent black. You can't send your kids to the public schools, and you can't let your wife go out at night. If you leave your house, the burglars will kick your door in because they know you're a cop, and cops keep lots of guns in their houses."

"But I don't keep guns in the house."

"Be sure and leave them a note."

Like all rookies, the young policeman did not want to be thought of as a rookie. He wanted to be accepted by the others as a cop. The sarcastic dart reminded him of his inexperience. He rolled down his window and turned his face into the streaming air.

"How about promotions? Think you're going to want to get promoted someday?" the veteran asked in a tone void of any further malice.

Still feeling the sting, the young man measured his answer. He had thought about promotion; all the recruits had. Some had thought of nothing else. But he decided he was not going to admit it. "I haven't really thought about it," he fibbed. "Maybe. Maybe someday."

"Have you met Eddie Thomas yet, works the desk days?"

"I don't think so," the rookie answered defensively out the window.

"Tall guy, built like a linebacker?" The driver's tone was unaffected by the rookie's coolness. The new cop shook the back of his head at the question. "Anyway, he took the sergeant's exam. Fifteen years on the job. Good cop. He did real good, wrote a ninety. They were going to make sixty-six sergeants. He placed thirtieth on the list. Should have been in the top half of the promotions, right? Ha!" The *Ha* sounded like an echoing rifle shot. "Because of affirmative action, they had to make eight white females, eight black females, twenty-five black males, and last and *certainly* least twenty-five white males. So with all that figured in, he's number seventy-two on the list, five below the cutoff. Out of the forty-one blacks and females that were promoted, only two had a higher test score than Eddie. None of them had ten years on the job. It's bad enough he didn't get promoted, but now these people are his bosses. He busted his ass on this job for fifteen years and now has to answer to bosses who will never be as qualified as he is. And do you know why they will never be as qualified?" The rookie didn't answer. He knew by the crescendo of the old cop's speech that the answer was unstoppable. "Because if you get something you didn't earn, you'll never do it honor. And every time that happens, the department suffers a loss. Do you think Eddie Thomas will ever really give a shit again? Ask him if he shouldn't have gotten out ten years ago."

The young policeman decided he had had enough. "Well, I'm not going to worry about that now. A promotion is at least ten years away."

The answer angered the vet. "I'll tell you what's ten years away. You'll be drinking more, a lot more. Things like dead bodies and raped kids won't be as important as where you're going to eat lunch. You'll have been shot at, assaulted, sued, investigated, and motherfucked until you're as numb as the junkies you lock up."

The recruit's frustration was turning to anger. "If I ever get that way, I'll quit."

The old-timer shook his head in mild disgust, like an impatient teacher whose student cannot see the answer because he really does not understand the problem. "Quit? It'll be too late. You won't be able to quit. You're a cop. Everyone else is either an asshole or a boring asshole. Only cops understand what's important, who's right and who's wrong, who should live and who should die. Being a cop in this life stinks, but it beats the hell out of whatever is left. You willingly—no, gladly—become addicted to your own misery. If you're married, you're cheating on your wife. If you're divorced, half your check is going to the Friend of the Court. And no matter how hard you work, no matter how much scum you lock up, Detroit will still be the most dangerous city in the world." He stopped. In a low voice that seemed involuntary he said, "If you don't believe it, kid, just look at me."

Both men rode in silence. The rookie looked at his partner's atrophied eyes and realized that the tirade was not a warning, but a confession. Like a worn, flickering movie, the old warrior's life was replaying itself in one of the back theaters of his mind. It had been a hell of a first night.

The scout car radio spoke. "Radio to Five-twenty-two."

"Shit," complained the driver.

The rookie grabbed the microphone, "This is Five-twenty-two. Go ahead."

"Five-twenty-two, the FBI needs assistance arresting an individual wanted on a murder warrant out of Alabama." The radio gave the address on Ashland.

"Five-twenty-two on the way." The young cop sat up and discreetly started checking the equipment on his belt, trying not to let his partner notice.

Without looking at him, the driver said, "Don't get a hard-on, kid; you won't need it. The FBI will do all the screwing."

He made a U-turn and headed for the address, increasing his speed slightly.

"Oh, you know all about the FBI," the rookie said with all the sarcasm available to a six-month veteran.

"Let me tell you about that great American myth." The young policeman again turned his attention to the insistent stream of air that rushed in through the window. Relentlessly the veteran continued, "In the early seventies the bank robbery gangs were killing us. Every Friday was National Bank Robbery Day, sometimes ten a day. In fact, one year Christmas Eve fell on a Friday, which made it twice as bad because everybody needed to pick up a little extra cash for that last-minute shopping. All we did that day was go from one robbery to the next, no time to do any investigating. Well, two of these fucks walk into a bank through opposite doors, both with guns drawn. But they don't know each other. They're both robbing the same bank at the same time."

The rookie laughed. "Who got the money?"

"Nobody. They each thought the other was a cop and started shooting. By the time I got there, they were both tits up." The old cop smiled into the distance. "The holidays have some wonderful memories." For a brief moment he let his mind swim back into the warm waters of a time when justice triumphed not only more frequently, but with unbridled certainty.

"Anyway, they decide to send some guys from patrol up to Holdup to help out. My commander didn't like me and sees an opportunity to dump me for six months. So I'm working out of the Armed Robbery Unit. Pretty good duty. Except every time you go to a bank job, here comes the fuck-*ing* FBI. With their white shirts, black wing tips, and smiling handshakes. Then you don't see them again until it's time to make the lockup. You bust your ass to solve the case, and the next thing you know you read how the FBI has arrested the bank robber."

"So we can add the FBI to that long list of things that have conspired to screw up your life."

The veteran laughed slowly, as though he had just tied the rookie to the railroad tracks. "You'll see. When we get there, he'll probably want us to kick the door in because he doesn't have a search warrant, so if anything goes wrong it'll be our ass."

"There he is," the rookie said and was out of the car before it stopped.

Devlin was standing next to his prisoner, who was handcuffed behind the back. He nodded to them as they got out of the scout car. "I'm Mike Devlin." He held up his black FBI credential case so they could see the gold badge pinned to the outside.

Resisting the urge to do the smiling handshake, the young policeman introduced himself while his partner examined the agent in silence. Devlin sensed his coolness. He had experienced it with other police officers.

"Sorry to drag you out here so close to a shift change, but I'm alone and could use a hand taking this prisoner down to the office," Devlin offered in an attempt to show that he had some understanding of the police and their priorities.

The silent cop took note. And, although he did not want to admit it, he was impressed that Devlin had arrested a murderer by himself. He knew how dangerous one-on-one arrests were. And looking closely at Taylor's size, decided, given the option, he would not have taken him on. "How come you're alone?"

Now Devlin knew what was bothering him. "Have you worked with the FBI before?"

"Yeah."

"Then you know why I'm alone."

The cop laughed at Devlin's honesty. Pointing at the prisoner, he asked, "Who's this?"

"Leroy Osgood Taylor. Wanted in Alabama for capping two of his own dealers."

Turning to Taylor with feigned concern, the cop said, "Too bad you didn't do it in Detroit, Leroy; it's only a misdemeanor."

Taylor did not laugh.

"How'd you get him?" the rookie asked.

"Just lucky. Got him leaving in his car."

The veteran police officer looked at Taylor's bare feet and knew that more than luck had been involved in the arrest.

"If you could transport him to our office, I would appreciate it. I'll radio ahead and have someone waiting."

"Sure," the young cop answered, sensing his partner's shift in attitude. "Are you going to follow us?"

"Ah—no, I have something to take care of here." The rookie did not detect the evasion in Devlin's tone; his partner's practiced ear did. As the younger officer put Taylor into the back of the police car, the veteran lowered his voice so only Devlin could hear him. "Alabama's got a real nice ride there."

Devlin felt a conspiratorial edge to the cop's words that was as valid as any two-handed sword. They served as a password, giving both men entrance into the other's locked storeroom of secrets. Seasoned eyes probed seasoned defenses. Hiding at the midnight of their souls was a beast of strength and fire, so mystical that only those who keep it chained within can identify it in others. *The Dragon of Vengeance*. Such dragons perched inside every good cop, ever ready to strike, no matter the consequence. To settle the score—whatever the cost.

Because nonowners would condemn its existence, the dragon's flights were always classified. But Devlin felt the bond that existed among such men and released his own dragon into the air between them. "Too nice."

The old cop recognized the all-but-forgotten warmth that hummed in his chest and realized that not all FBI agents were college boys playing detective; some were unfortunate enough to be cops.

As the police car left, Devlin ran his hand over the eight coats of paint that protected the perfect German steel of Taylor's $70,000 Mercedes-Benz. It felt powerful, capable of conquering the world's most demanding roads. But the streets of Detroit offered a challenge the Black Forest engineers had not anticipated.

Devlin knew the car would eventually find its way into the garage of Taylor's lawyer as payment for his defense. A defense filled with loud, empty voices. A defense costing just about the price of the Mercedes plus any other assets Taylor might have. No, Devlin decided, the dope giveth and the dope taketh away. The junkies paid for it, let the junkies enjoy it. Enjoy it the way they do everything—to death.

He restarted the car and drove it beyond his own car, close to a moderately busy intersection. Leaving the engine running, he walked back to his car. The morning air felt thick and cool. He smelled the sweet, smoky odor of bacon cooking.

As he radioed instructions to meet the prisoner, he watched a skinny black teenager wearing a black Gucci T-shirt and red high-top gym shoes without laces walk past the Mercedes for the second time. His head snapped from side to side, looking for the fool who had answered a life-long prayer. Another young black man walked around the corner and seemed blinded by the same target of opportunity. The vulture ants were on the march.

Devlin drove off without looking back.

Uneasily Lucius John Fauber, also known as L. John Fauber, also known as Yoda, waited in ambush for Mike Devlin. And he was determined not to take any prisoners. Especially a *mere* street agent.

Not very often during his time as Devlin's supervisor had he been in such a position. He was right. It was refreshing. But he swore not to become accustomed to the feeling. He had seen it in the past—managers destroying their careers by trying to be right. He would hold this inviting enemy at arm's length.

He stood outside the mug room, where prisoners were fingerprinted and photographed. An odd sensation calmed him—one of impeding victory, of perfect written rules over grimy, threadbare experience. He was tired of the coffee-machine talk about cases and arrests. Although he had never actually heard them, he knew there were whispers about his inexperience. There were reasons he had never made an arrest, important administrative reasons. But it did not matter. He knew all the Bureau arrest procedures. By heart.

Down the hallway, he heard the combination being typed into the cipher lock. He started toward the door, anxious to intercept Devlin at the earliest possible moment. But Devlin's prisoner was being escorted by two other C-4 agents, Bill Shanahan and a new agent whose name he could never remember. "Where's Devlin?" Fauber asked, embarrassed by his miscalculation.

"He'll be here in a few minutes," Shanahan answered.

Fueled by his embarrassment and the momentum of his mistimed attack, he turned on the prisoner. "What's your name, Shithead?"

Taylor looked at the odd-looking gnome in front of him and felt certain that he could lift him off the ground with a front snap kick to the testicles. But he felt equally certain that the big Irish-looking dude holding his arm would retaliate by surgically removing his vital organs with his huge black wing tips. Instead, Taylor defiantly sucked his teeth and said, "Yo mama know where you at?"

Fauber's eyes darted side to side to ensure that neither agent was enjoying Taylor's response. "Leave my *mama* out of this." Fauber emphasized "mama" sarcastically, mimicking Taylor's southern black pronunciation.

"Oh that's right, you sissies hate yo mamas."

This time Fauber caught the new agent grinning. "When Devlin gets in, I want to see him immediately. You understand?" The question was directed at the new agent, who was solemnly nodding his head. "Immediately!" Fauber reiterated.

Without waiting for further response, he spun around and stomped off, making a mental note to learn the new agent's name for the next time a volunteer was needed for a shitty job.

Taylor looked at Shanahan. "Devlin the dude who got me?"

"Yep."

"And that punk is his boss?"

"He's all our boss."

"Where you guys find someone like that?"

Shanahan's face became mischievous. "This is the government. We're committed to hiring the handicapped."

"Yeah, but do you got to promote them?"

L. John Fauber's career profile was becoming more common in the FBI management ranks. Out of training school he had been assigned to white-collar crime cases in Omaha, Nebraska. The *Manual of Administrative Operations and Procedures* states that, without exception, an agent must have two years' investigative experience before he or she becomes a Bureau supervisor. The only exception to this is if he or she is an exceptionally gifted ass-kisser which is the exception to every Bureau rule. So, after two years to the day, Fauber, not being especially gifted, requested transfer to FBI Headquarters in Washington, D.C., commonly referred to as "Disneyland East." His reason—he no longer wanted to be a "mere street agent." He wanted to get on with his career. In his new assignment at the Records Management Division, his boss was Roy Pilkington, who was subsequently promoted and transferred to Detroit as the Special Agent in Charge. SAC Pilkington had wanted Fauber in Detroit as a supervisor. Not only had Fauber displayed unblushing loyalty, but he had invariably arrived at the same conclusions as Pilkington, and almost as quickly. Six months after Pilkington's arrival in Michigan, Fauber was transferred to Detroit as the supervisor of Criminal Squad Four. C-4 investigated bank robberies, kidnappings, extortions and chased federal fugitives. Although Fauber had never worked any of these violations, he knew they were not as complicated as the white-collar cases he had had a brush with in Omaha. He had studied the manual and knew every reporting rule that would keep the Bureau happy. After all, the Bureau was—well—*The Bureau*. And this was just the field, at worst—temporary.

Pilkington welcomed Fauber and told him he needed strong leaders like him to control freewheeling agents, that ten percent who had caused him problems as long as he had been in the Bureau. They were forever trying to do something, never considering the effects on his career.

When Devlin arrived at the office, he entered through the back door, hoping to delay his confrontation with his supervisor. He carefully peeked into the mug room and was surprised that Fauber was not waiting for him there. Shanahan read Devlin's caution. "He's already been here, Mike. And you're right; he *is* looking for a piece of your ass." Shanahan nodded his you've-done-it-again smile.

"I suppose he wants to see me."

Shanahan gave him the same smile. "Maybe you should leave your gun here."

"Don't worry, I'll probably just wing him."

On his way to Fauber's office Devlin passed his desk and noticed a blue note, folded and stapled, sitting on his blotter. Within the Detroit office, the blue communiqué had the same effect as if it had been penned by the Black Hand. It was the SAC's personal memo. That it was folded and stapled precluded hopes of a silver lining. Devlin opened it. *See me. Ten A.M. R. K. Pilkington.* Evidently Fauber had already gone to the SAC with his complaints. The last time, Devlin recalled, he had been banished to Seattle for three months.

Another C-4 agent, Tom Anderson, was in Fauber's office with him, so Devlin took a seat outside the door. He could hear Anderson's voice and was surprised at the unshielded desperation in it. Whatever Anderson had become in recent years, despair was an unlikely companion. "John, I'm not some fucking nut calling in an Elvis sighting. You've got to help me. This is my daughter. She's missing, not run away."

Fauber's words came with a paralyzing coldness. "She's run away before."

"Yes, but . . ." was Anderson's condemned rebuttal.

"Let's give it a day or two and see if she doesn't turn up."

Anderson did not wait for Fauber's words to settle in the room before he stalked out in protest. When he saw Devlin, he started to ask him something but then seemed to remember their troubled relationship. His face went blank with hopelessness as he hurried out the door.

Devlin walked into the office with a calmness that seemed intentionally exaggerated to Fauber. He became more enraged. This was finally to be his triumph, his time of confirmation, and Devlin was stealing it by not being the least bit servile. Although his anger made him more determined than ever, he still avoided Devlin's eyes.

Devlin looked at Fauber and wondered what had happened to the FBI he had joined the year J. Edgar Hoover had died. He thought of his first supervisor, Allen "Wing 'em" Landis. A tall, handsome Texan, who was as easygoing as his drawl but made decisions as though the fate of the Alamo hung in the balance. He had earned both his supervisor's desk and his nickname one cold February day in a west side motel stairwell when he shot the gun out of a bank robber's hand. It made national news. The media heralded this FBI agent, who, although he had been trained to kill opposing pistolaros, opted to disarm him with Hollywood accuracy. They had nicknamed him "Wing 'em" and declared that the fair play that had made the Old West legendary was alive and well in Detroit, Michigan. His ascent was unstoppable. The Hoov personally saw to it.

But like many good news stories, the truth had undergone extensive plastic surgery in order to catch the eye of the public. One drunken night Landis let Devlin inside his personal myth. The occasion was the annual office tour of the Stroh's Brewery. It was the most popular function of the year. Free beer. Free food. And spouses were not allowed. No one ever took the tour; in fact, anyone who raised a hand to go was booed into reversal. Everyone sat in the

Stroh Haus trying to drink enough beer to last until the next year's "tour."

Devlin sat at a table with Landis. They had just finished their sixth pitcher of beer when Devlin asked him about the shoot-out.

"It was my first winter in Detroit. Like everyone else, I was fucking thrilled to be here." Uncharacteristically, Landis belched, and Devlin realized how drunk his supervisor was. "One of the guys had a subject who had done a bunch of Friday afternoon robberies, so we wanted to get him before he cut into any more of our weekends. I'm sent to cover the back of the motel. I didn't have a radio, so I had no idea what they were doing. It's cold. I mean, I'm from Texas and I haven't seen anything this cold since my first wife's diaphragm. I'm out there a long time and finally say the hell with it and duck into this stairwell. It's just as cold in there, but at least I'm out of the wind." He stopped and drained his glass and refilled it from pitcher number seven. "Suddenly the stairwell door flies open. Guess who?"

As if the truth were leaving a bitter taste, Landis was punctuating each sentence with a gulp of beer. "That's right, sports fans, it's the asshole we've got the warrant for. We look at each other, and we know exactly who's who."

Although Devlin was drunk himself, he hung on Landis's every word. New agents are mesmerized by tales of shoot-outs, mostly because they wonder if they could pass the final exam. Older agents, on the other hand, know two things about shootings: one, as many times as not, someone fucked up, and two, they're glad they weren't there.

"So we start screaming 'Motherfucker' at each other. I'm tearing at my coat, and I can hear buttons hitting the concrete floor. He's doing the same. I swear to God I don't know how I got to my shit first. We're four feet from each other. No time to fuck around, I hip shoot. I go low in the K-5 area, around the navel, but he has his gun in his belt, so he has to cross-draw. Because his hand is reaching across his stomach, my round hits him in the hand and his gun goes clanking down the stairs."

"Shooting team like it?" Devlin noticed that his sentences were getting shorter.

"You kidding? Thought it was wonderful. Was a good shoot, so all they had to worry about was packaging it. See, it was post-riot Detroit. The black extremists were claiming white law enforcement was attempting genocide. So this would demonstrate to the black community that although I was trained to shoot to kill, the FBI was not in the business of assassinating blacks. They didn't give a shit about the truth; they told the SAC to get some mileage out of it. At the press conference when one of the reporters asked if I had intended to shoot the gun out of his hand, the SAC smiled and said that some of the Bureau's best shots were from Texas. He didn't answer the question, but they didn't care. They had a quote to build a story around. J. Edgar liked it so much that he transferred my supervisor back to Washington with a promotion and gave me his job."

Landis had retired ten years earlier. Devlin had never repeated the confession to anyone. He could not. Like all other new agents leaving training school, he had sworn to maintain the Myth.

Now, he stood looking at his new Bureau supervisor, thinking about how he would have handled the stairwell confrontation. Graphically, he pictured Fauber being shot in the buttocks as he fled the bank robber. Such wounds were many times fatal for supervisory agents since they usually conducted the Bureau's business with their heads up their asses.

He found L. John Fauber to be almost comical. He had probably decided that using his first initial like J. Edgar Hoover would give the appearance of continuity with the old Bureau. But the old Bureau would not have hired him. He would have been three inches shorter than the five-foot-seven-inch requirement. His physique was best described as soft-edged. His sparse hair was the same lifeless color as his balding scalp. Deep premature creases lined his forehead horizontally in front of large artificial-looking ears. His complexion had the color of uncooked dough. Soon after his arrival in Detroit, he had been given the nickname Yoda. Oblivious to his resemblance to the *Star Wars* creature, he resented the name, believing agents were referring to his puppetish allegiance to the SAC. He also disliked the references to his most loyal men as the Jedi. He complained to the SAC, and eventually the nicknames stopped. For once he had defeated the agent conspiracy around him.

Fauber closed his office door. "It's completely against Bureau policy to make an arrest alone." His voice trembled slightly.

Devlin concentrated on sounding nonchalant. "Maybe you worry about Bureau policy too much."

Fauber glared at the wall behind Devlin. "Evidently you worry about it too little. I'm trying to bring this squad into the twentieth century."

"What do you consider the twentieth century?" Devlin appeared to be holding back a yawn.

"The way we do things at Headquarters."

"How many arrests did *we* make at Headquarters?"

That proved it, Fauber thought, they had talked behind his back. An unflattering color started to rise in his face. He had intended to reprimand this—this *agent*—to gain some sort of an advantage, but instead Devlin just stood there as if he were waiting for a commercial to end. Fauber was cornered. He had only one option left—*insubordination*. Its use indicated weakness. Demanding obedience strictly because of rank revealed a severe lack of leadership. But it was effective, because no matter how wrong the supervisor was or how right the agent was, the agent could be fired if insubordination could be substantiated. Throughout FBI history, it literally had been the last commandment for a number of unbending agents.

"Goddamn it, I'm giving you an order!" Devlin had heard this warning before. "No more arrests with less than four agents—in fact, you cannot make an arrest unless I am present to supervise you." Fauber surprised himself with the creativity of the last restriction. Not only would it restrain Devlin's work style, but Fauber's on-the-scene supervision would drive him to, and hopefully over, the edges of insubordination.

Fauber stepped back and leaned against his desk, the creases in his forehead smiling. Composed now, he could feel the gray returning to his face. He had Devlin where he wanted him. Any confrontational answer would only strengthen Fauber's case. Devlin knew it was not a question of if, but when, he would have to answer an insubordination charge.

Supremely confident, Fauber dared a glance at Devlin's eyes and saw controlled rage. He was pleased; he had finally won some control over this thorn in his command. It was clear now who was in charge.

With an electronic snap, the paging system, accessible through any one of the office's 150 telephones, came on. A couple of seconds of static preceded a full symphonic version of the *Star Wars* theme. As if it sensed something that Fauber did not, his forehead wilted into a frown. Over the music, the voice of Luke Skywalker said, "Yoda—Yoda, the farce is with you." The pager clicked off.

The extraterrestrial announcement pumped enough adrenaline into Fauber's bloodstream to pinken his face and melt the tremors in his speech. "You dirty bastard. You did that. You—" Devlin turned and left Fauber in mid son-of-a-bitch.

||| CHAPTER 2 |||

As Devlin reached the interrogation room, he could still hear Fauber's obscenities ricocheting off the walls. The distance helped him appreciate the comedy of it all. He smiled at Taylor as he waved the two agents guarding the prisoner out of the room.

Taylor had made up his mind before Devlin got there. He wasn't going to say a muthafuckin thing. Not even his name. Fuck em!

When Devlin walked in smiling, his prisoner became confused. He put his hand on Taylor's shoulder. "How you doing? How about a cigarette?" As he lit Taylor's cigarette, he could see uncertainty reshaping the man's face. It was something he always tried to orchestrate during an interview. Uncertainty was the waiting room of vulnerability.

"Lee." Devlin looked over his shoulder at the otherwise empty room; it gave the effect that secrecy was a priority, and he lowered his voice to further the drama. "Between you and me, I don't care if you tell me what happened in Birmingham or not. I'm not going to waste a lot of time on it." Devlin's whispered intimacy continued its effect on the prisoner. He looked over his shoulder again and lowered his voice further so Taylor had to strain to hear him. "See, if you don't make a statement, I don't have to do any paperwork. I hate paperwork. But I know one thing—I'm not the one who told you this—but they got you dead nuts.

One of your people at the shooting rolled over." Taylor became defensive. It was an old cop trick to say one of your partners confessed. He searched Devlin's face. He found no evidence of deception.

Devlin knew what he was thinking. "If it isn't true, then how did I find you?"

The question gnawed away at Taylor's defenses. Devlin watched as his prisoner's expression went from defiance to doubt. He was ready.

"I know they were shot because they were thieves." Taylor looked down at his hands and started wringing them. Devlin grabbed them, causing Taylor to look up at him. "Lee, as a man I can think of a lot of reasons for killing someone, but I can't think of one for stealing from him. You had better tell someone your side of it."

Taylor grasped for the salvation of Devlin's twisted theorem. He was not a murderer; he was a vigilante who had rid the earth of two heinous thieves. He searched Devlin's face one last time for hidden motives.

"Okay, what you want to know?"

During the next hour and a half Devlin wrote out a four-page confession that Taylor read and signed. Taylor was then turned over to the U.S. Marshal's Office pending extradition to Alabama.

Devlin returned to his desk and started his report detailing the arrest and subsequent confession. No mention of slim-jims, slammers, or vulture ants would be made.

The phone rang. It was Bill Shanahan talking in a low monotone. Devlin looked back across the squad area to where Shanahan sat at his desk with his back to Devlin and the rest of the squad, including the Jedi, who never seemed to leave the office.

"Mike, I notice you're spending a lot more time in Fauber's office lately. You haven't been putting your lips in his lap, have you?"

Devlin laughed. "You know, a talented guy like you really should get a job."

"And what, leave show biz?"

Devlin smiled at Shanahan's broad back. In a more serious tone Shanahan said, "I thought you should know, after you came out of Fauber's office, he had Sue take some dictation. She let me read it over her shoulder while she was typing. You are a challenger of authority, a disruptive influence, and a raving faggot."

"And he promised not to tell," Devlin said.

"What, about being disruptive?"

"You know, William, this story lacks credibility. You have never stood over Sue without going cross-eyed from focusing on her cleavage."

"Sure, that's it, rub it in. Just once they find a guy's binoculars in a girl's blouse, and you're branded a peeping Tom forever."

Two rookie Jedi walked into the squad area. Devlin and Shanahan sat in silence as if they were both listening and waited for the intruders to wander away from their conversation.

"Seriously, Mike, he's got you in the cross hairs. As soon as Sue was done typing the memo, he took it in to Pilkington. He's teeing you up for an insubordination charge."

Devlin checked his watch. "I know. I'm due in Pilkington's office in five minutes."

"That reminds me, don't go groping any of the stenos in the Xerox room." He paused. "They hid a video camera in the ceiling to see who's copying what."

Devlin waited for Shanahan to finish, but he was enjoying the sole ownership of his rumor. "Okay, why the camera in the ceiling?"

"There's supposed to be a leak. Here—in Detroit! Word is, a list of informants is floating around. One of the Organized Crime sources said he was told about it. One of the geniuses in the front office thought if it were true, whoever had it would Xerox it. Yeah, you'd probably want a file copy of something like that. What an idiot! Pilkington refused to believe it, because he knows he would have a major career problem if it was true."

"Is it true?"

"The source is very solid. You'd like to think it's someone's imagination, but supposedly some other sources are hearing the same thing."

"And just how did you find out about this?"

"The ASAC's secretary told me. In strictest confidence."

"Ah, another one of your sexual harassment victims."

"Victims! These young things are hired for their earthiness. If it wasn't for the sexual harassment, most of these girls would find honest work."

Devlin laughed. "So their solution is to put a camera in the ceiling?"

"It beats the hell out of admitting there's a problem."

Sue, the squad secretary, got up from her desk and walked away. Although his back was to her, Shanahan, alerted by some predator's instinct, turned in his chair and tracked her departure with steamy eyes. For the first time since the conversation had started Shanahan looked at Devlin. "The child does have a world-class exit."

"Well, since you've boarded the plane for Fantasy Island, I guess this conversation is over."

"Oh, yeah, there's a squad conference at four o'clock to plan an arrest."

"Why the whole squad?"

"Why else—it's Fauber's idea. Moorehead's case. Some pencil-necked accountant wanted out of Chicago for real estate fraud. They've got an address and an employment. It's a gimme, but that's why Moorehead's got it."

Duncan Moorehead was all-conference Jedi, tall and too

well dressed for an agent. Each of his facial features was flawless, but like decorating a house with the best furnishing from different periods, the composite effect was confusing.

He gave complete allegiance to Fauber and did not care who knew it or disliked him as a result. As soon as he got "this agent crap" out of the way he would be management, the next generation.

Shortly after arriving in Detroit, he had had the SAC present him with a plaque naming him one of "America's Most Successful Young Men." Thereafter the plaque was prominently displayed on his desk. While most people were casually impressed with Moorehead's selection, Shanahan, an infallible judge of people, doubted its validity. He clandestinely inspected the plaque but found no clue as to its origin. He started dialing the 110 U.S. area codes and asking directory assistance for "America's Most Successful." Finally, area code 212, New York City, produced the number. Upon reaching the company, Shanahan found that not only could you be the most successful young man, but woman, black, gypsy, collie, or Studebaker, providing the thirty-five-dollar fee was paid. The next day, after obtaining one of Moorehead's credit card numbers, Shanahan again called the company and in a low, moaning voice told them that he was Duncan Moorehead and ordered a new plaque. Two weeks later he intercepted it in the office mail and discreetly replaced the plaque on Moorehead's desk. A week later, after almost everyone in the office had seen it, Moorehead discovered his new forte—"Duncan Moorehead: One of America's Most Successful Young Homosexuals."

Displaying his innate crisis management skills, he permanently removed everything from his desk top, including the treasured photograph of his less-than-breathtaking wife. Before Moorehead had discovered the switch, Shanahan would, to any audience he could muster, nod at Mrs. Moorehead's stern face and say, "Don't be too hard on the guy. If you had a wife that looked like that, you'd probably switch too."

Shanahan had assumed he would react that way and took the precaution of photocopying the faceplate of the four-by-six-inch plaque before its "presentation." He then enlarged it on the copier to eight by ten. Whenever he felt Moorehead was becoming a little too taken with himself, he would discreetly post a copy in a public place. To Shanahan's delight, it drove Moorehead crazy.

Devlin turned to Shanahan, but he had turned his back again. "Why does Fauber need the whole squad for a guy you can call and have surrender?"

"That's probably your fault. After you made him feel like a puddle of piss this morning, he took this case into Pilkington and blew it out of proportion, telling him the guy's really dangerous. He's even talking about a SWAT team followed by a press conference."

"A SWAT team?" Devlin laughed. "You'll excuse me if I don't make the meeting."

"Mike, he told me to make sure you knew you had to be there."

"I guess I'm not going to have the last laugh after all. And what do you mean, this morning was my fault?"

In the breathless, miniature voice of Yoda, Shanahan answered, "May the force be with you, Luke Skywalker," and hung up.

Shanahan's ability to mimic voices had always impressed Devlin. That morning it had helped him out of a difficult situation with Fauber, but the inevitable was only being postponed. His right hand tightened into a fist. His differences with Fauber were intensifying, and he knew the humps never win. *Never.* Somewhere he had read that the

Irish were never at peace unless they were fighting. He cursed his heritage and headed for the SAC's office.

Devlin sat in the SAC's outer office. He checked his watch. For Pilkington, ASACs were required to wait five to seven minutes, depending on their seniority in the office, mere agents ten minutes, and agents in trouble at least fifteen minutes. Devlin checked his watch again—twelve minutes. His chronographical suspicions were confirmed by the SAC's tiny secretary, who gave him an any-last-requests look as she told him to go in. The ancient frog, who never seemed to move from behind her mahogany lily pad, knew everything.

The walls of Royal K. Pilkington's office were covered with reminders of a career filled with danger, bravery, and justice. Top Ten fugitive flyers with APPREHENDED hastily stamped across them. Stunning plaques presented in appreciation. Certificates, framed newspaper articles, and shooting trophies. Photos with every FBI director, celebrities, and sports figures. The veneer of importance reminded Devlin of the Irish natural loathing of pretense and hypocrisy.

Pilkington did not acknowledge Devlin's presence but instead appeared to be wearily concentrating on a memo, his forehead furrowed for effect. Devlin looked at the leather chair in front of Pilkington's desk. Once someone sat in it, regardless of their height, the SAC was able to look down at them. Without looking up, Pilkington slowly waved his hand at the chair. "Sit down."

Devlin had been watching his eyes. He was not reading the memo. He was using his best stuff on Devlin. Devlin knew he was in trouble.

When he found something that worked he stayed with it. Being obstinate had gotten him this far, so he sat on the arm of the chair and looked down at the SAC. He could see that Pilkington, without looking up, was immediately aware that Devlin was not below him.

Now he looked at Devlin. "Please don't sit on the arm."

Devlin's face never gave a hint that he had heard Pilkington or intended to do as he asked.

Pilkington's concentration was broken. He *read* the memo again to regain his escaping composure.

Finally he put the memo down. "I have a communication here from your supervisor, stating that you violated several Bureau rules: insubordination, making single-handed arrests, failure to notify your supervisor of the changing status of an investigation, et cetera, et cetera, et cetera . . ." The SAC looked at him, expecting some sort of defense. Again Devlin appeared not to have heard him. "Well?" Pilkington asked.

Devlin decided to end the charade. "Guilty."

Pilkington misinterpreted Devlin's admission as a weakening and decided to lecture him while the opportunity presented itself. "I know your intentions regarding the arrest were good, but the road to hell is paved with good intentions. You know, I like to think of my agents as my children, but you and John are starting to act like Cain and Abel. Are you familiar with the stories of the Bible?"

Devlin had had enough. "The only one I can remember is the ass in a lion's skin."

Pilkington could not place the Biblical reference, but he did sense the apocalyptical edge to Devlin's voice and as always chose discretion. "Anyway, it appears as though you and your supervisor need another cooling-off period. I'm going to strike a compromise. For the next thirty days I'm assigning you to work a Title III with C-Ten. They can use a man of your experience."

A man of my experience, thought Devlin, that was supposed to make sitting on a wiretap acceptable. Sitting under earphones, listening to mafiosi talk about who they were screwing on the side and wondering why their kids were doing so lousy in school. Their kids were a bunch of lazy, selfish, whining punks who had failed to inherit their parents' old world crime work ethic. It all worked out; having rotten kids was its own punishment. Devlin thought of one mob father who had found the ultimate method of disciplining his errant teenage son; he took his jewelry away. The diabolical mind of organized crime.

Now Pilkington leaned back in his chair and hid a smile. He grabbed on to the chair's padded arms and held on as if he were about to be electrocuted with pleasure. "Also, I'm assigning a new agent to you for training." He watched Devlin for a reaction. Devlin looked unemotionally into the SAC's eyes, forcing him to divert them down to the memo that lay next to the phone. He picked up the phone and pushed a button. "Send in the new man."

As he entered the SAC's office, Devlin turned only enough to recognize a black agent recently assigned to the squad. He had been there for about a week. Devlin had seen him with Duncan Moorehead and had assumed that he was the newest Jedi.

The new agent did not wait for Pilkington to introduce them. "Hi, I'm Edgar Livingston," he said, holding out his hand.

Devlin shook his hand. "Mike Devlin."

Pilkington said, "Agent Livingston was assigned to Duncan Moorehead for training, but John Fauber tells me he's far too busy. So I'm reassigning him to you."

Great, thought Devlin, the wiretap *and* a new agent. Handling a new agent was not about training but about doing a lot of extra paperwork during the evaluation period. Just another administrative pain in the ass. It was the real reason Duncan Moorehead was "too busy."

Devlin considered Livingston. Since Pilkington had taken such delight in reassigning him to Devlin, Livingston was evidently intended to be some sort of punishment. But how? Devlin looked closely at him. He guessed Livingston's age at twenty-five or -six. He was tall, athletically slender, and by any standards clean cut. But his most distinctive characteristic was his speech. Not only was he articulate to the point of distraction, but his rhythm and delivery were riveting.

Livingston smiled a crushing white smile. Devlin recognized it. Just happy as hell to be an FBI agent. An FBI AGENT! It was a smile of anticipation, of hope, mountains to climb, and then valleys to look down on, if there was time before the next mountain. It reminded Devlin of the smiles on the newly arrived Marines in Vietnam; the ones who thought they were going to kick some ass. A long time ago, Devlin had smiled that smile. Still, he decided, caution was in order.

Pilkington dismissed both men. As Devlin left, he took a last look at Pilkington's testimonial walls, a fitting tribute to an ass in a lion's skin.

Back in the squad area, Devlin asked, "Have you had any cases assigned to you yet?"

"Just one, sir!" came Livingston's eager answer.

Devlin wondered if his formality was genuine. Or had someone put him up to it? He glanced at the Jedi who were present. They were waiting for Devlin to treat the newcomer the way he had treated them—with contempt. Once his gaze caught theirs, they suddenly remembered overdue phone calls and began dialing the time and weather recordings.

"Okay, Edgar, there are no sirs in this outfit unless you're trying to get promoted." Devlin's look turned the statement into a question.

"Not me. I want to be a street agent. And please call me Ed. I'm just glad to get away from Moorehead. How long has he been with the Bureau, two or three years? He's already treating me like he's a supervisor: giving me orders, sending me routing slips, having me do his work for him. Yesterday I told him I didn't mind doing my own work, but I sure wasn't going to do his."

Now Devlin understood. Fauber and Pilkington thought Livingston was a malcontent and were going to give him and Devlin a dose of their own medicine by pairing them up. Devlin smiled at the possibilities.

"Okay, Ed. Let's take a look at that case."

Livingston handed him a three-page teletype from the New York office. It was dated a week earlier. The subject, John Thomas Washington, aka Alexander Johnson, Allen Johnson, aka Big Bad John. On December 24, the victim, Sheila North, black female, twenty-two years old, had last been seen leaving a Manhattan singles bar with Washington. The next day her body had been found in a Dumpster behind the subject's apartment building. She had been severely beaten, raped, sodomized, and manually strangled.

Devlin recognized the thick pumping in his chest. The dragon was anxious to take flight. Fauber's ravenous traps now seemed inconsequential. Only the hunt mattered. To be the messenger of justice, no matter how difficult the journey. *To prevent the next Sheila North.*

Yet, he had to consider Livingston's wide-eyed vulnerability. "Sit down, Ed." Devlin leaned toward him and quietly said, "Right now there are safer people to align yourself with."

Livingston had heard the argument that morning, and it was well known that Devlin and Fauber did not get along. Livingston summed up his priorities simply but unconditionally. "I try to make my decisions based on potential advantages, not disadvantages."

To Devlin, the declaration again revealed the quality of the man before him. "Where are you from?" It was more of a compliment than a question.

"A small town in New England that no one ever heard of."

"Hell, there are states in New England no one has ever heard of. Was there much of a black population?"

"Just my mother and myself. My dad died when I was twelve."

"Is your mother still there?"

"Yes. She'll never leave. She's the head surgical nurse at the hospital. She worked very hard and very long to get that position and wouldn't give it up for anything."

"So you've never been exposed to many blacks?"

"Just a few in college."

Devlin grinned, "You must find Detroit—ah—different."

"It's certainly different than New England." His smile seemed to wink at Devlin.

"Let me finish reading this teletype," Devlin said.

Washington was described as a black male, thirty years old, height six-foot-six, weight 250 pounds, with a long arrest record for assaultive crimes, including robbery, assault and battery, and rape.

His whereabouts were unknown, but his mother's phone records had been subpoenaed and revealed long-distance calls to several cities from Atlanta, Georgia, to Irvine, California. The New York office had methodically set out leads to all the cities listed. Devlin carefully read the long inventory of calls and then asked Livingston, "What's your best guess where he's at?"

Livingston had no idea where his fugitive was, but like all beginners, he felt compelled to prove himself. He scanned the list of calls. For him they were meaningless. "You can tell where he is by the phone calls?"

"Sometimes," Devlin answered. "In this case it looks like he's here." Livingston looked at the calls that were set out for Detroit. The thought of his first arrest excited him. He forced himself to concentrate on the Detroit phone calls.

There were three. All collect from Detroit. Each from a different phone, about a week apart. He had physically checked the phones. They were all pay phones. Of course! Who would be calling Washington's mother collect, once a week, from different pay phones? And there were no calls placed *to* Detroit, so even his mother did not know exactly where he was. Livingston explained his reasoning to Devlin.

"That's right, a smart fugitive must never let anyone know where he is, not even his mama."

The unusual warning at the bottom of the teletype caught Devlin's eye: SUBJECT IS FORMER NATIONAL HEAVYWEIGHT GOLDEN GLOVES CHAMPION; CONSIDER ARMED AND EXTREMELY DANGEROUS.

Devlin picked up Washington's mug shot. Regardless of their stature, most men appear to be the same size in arrest photos. Washington looked grotesquely oversized. His shoulders disappeared into the edges of the photograph. Though his broad neck was accented by the thick, smooth, black cables of muscle running from his shoulders to just under his jawline, his head looked menacingly large. But his most terrifying feature was his eyes. They seemed three-dimensional, overdilated, and moist with the insanity that boiled behind them. Devlin had seen the look before. This animal would go hard.

"Where are the phone booths?" Livingston handed him a sheet of lined paper. On it were printed the phone numbers and their locations. The handwriting was in thick black ink done with the elegant precision of a calligrapher. The locations were all in the Cass Corridor.

If Detroit had a highest-crime area, the Cass Corridor was it. It is bordered on the south by the McNamara Federal Building, on the north by Wayne State University, the west by white poverty, and the east by black desperation. Cass Avenue was in an unceasing state of decay. Housing projects, hour-rental motels, rescue missions, and bars made up the majority of the Corridor's legal business. The area was inhabited by nomadic scrums of junkies, who wandered sleeplessly, addicted to the hunt for their next score. Few escaped the Corridor's diseases. Fewer wanted to.

Devlin considered everything: the subject, the area, and especially Livingston's inexperience. "Ed, I'm going to be honest with you. This case may be over your head. It should never have been assigned to someone with your limited experience. Fauber assigned it to you because of *his* inexperience. Would you consider asking him to reassign it to another agent?"

"No." The single syllable rang with the permanence of a steel chisel on ancient granite.

Devlin thought of Fauber and knew he would now consider Livingston an enemy. "Okay, just remember, if you fly with crows you get shot at."

Livingston thought for a second and asked, "Do you know why crows are shot at?"

"Why?"

"Because they live life with such reckless abandon."

The two men stared at each other comfortably. Devlin felt an old, forgotten need. It glowed warmly inside him. It was something beyond camaraderie or friendship, even beyond devotion. It had been a long time since he had called someone *partner.*

He picked up the phone and dialed. "James. Can you meet me in thirty minutes? ... At Les's ... okay." He picked up Washington's photo. "I'll be back as soon as I can. Lunch?"

"Sure."

When he left, Livingston sat at Devlin's desk. He examined the items that covered it. The most interesting was his blotter-size calendar. There were names, license plates, phone numbers, and other information, along with coded initials of the informants who had provided them. To Livingston it had the look of craftsmanship, like a one-of-a-kind handmade tool, uniquely functional. The calendars were kept in the stockroom. He started to ask one of the Jedi where it was, but he thought of Devlin and decided to find it himself.

||| CHAPTER 3 |||

Devlin drove to Les's pawnshop to meet James, his longest-surviving informant. Informants are "closed" for one of three reasons: death, prison, or they simply dry up. They never retire. More than a survivor, James was an orchestrator. He could, through his contacts, mystically, almost musically, find the answers for Devlin. To ensure his longevity, Devlin never met with James unless it was absolutely necessary for the exchange of information or money. The rest of their business, contrary to Bureau policy, was conducted on the telephone. The less they were seen together, the smaller the risk was for James. That was why they liked to meet at Les's; Devlin went in the front door and James the back.

Les's was the busiest pawnshop in the Cass Corridor. It was part of a building that originally had contained three other stores and eight second-story apartments. The shop was the only remaining unit not boarded up or burned out. The building had been faced with expensive red wire-cut brick with stone windowsills and door frames. The accelerating list of landlords had covered the structure with endless coats of paint; the last, applied just before the riots, had been white. Time and neglect had turned it, along with the rest of the Corridor, an anonymous gray.

When closed, a worn, dented steel door rolled down the

front of the store, completing the building's abandoned motif.

When open, the store's windows were filled with wonderful, barely affordable things: watches, rings, radios, binoculars, a saxophone, even a microscope. Each had its own pet-store-puppy appeal: Take me home. High in the window hung a dusty pink neon sign silently confessing: CASH FOR GUNS, GOLD, SILVER.

Devlin walked in and, after exchanging a couple of short stories with the old pawnbroker, asked if he could use the office for half an hour. As the owner attended to a customer, Devlin unlocked the alley door from the inside. Then he walked out the front of the shop and sat on a concrete bus bench directly in front of the store. It was part of a long-standing signal he and James used. If Devlin was seated when James drove by, he was to park in the alley and enter through the back door. However, if Devlin stood behind the bench, something was wrong and the meeting was aborted.

Devlin sat on the bench enjoying his idle anonymity. No one knew who he was, and nothing was expected of him. To the wandering dead of the Corridor he was just another white dude, probably looking for a hooker or maybe actually waiting for a bus.

While his mind escaped, his eyes tracked two black teens walking across the street. They were too young and well built to be full-blown junkies, probably just learning. The taller of the two wore a long-sleeve Pistons sweatshirt. The shorter one seemed to follow the other's lead. The shorter one's head was the shape of a coffee can; his close-cut hair exposed small pretzel-knot ears. They both noticed Devlin at the same time. Instinctively, without a word, they cut across the street, slowing down and going into the traditional I'm-a-bad-motherfucker strut. The basketball fan gave pretzel ears the somebody-left-the-Mercedes-running look. Devlin's eyes warned his slumbering mind—*vulture ants*.

Basketball looked hard at Devlin. The lack of fear bothered him. Money was only the business part of robbery; power was the perk. He sat down next to Devlin. His partner stood three feet away, arms declaratively crossed. The metallic click of a switchblade locking into place caused Devlin to turn to the Piston ant beside him. With a deadly smile on his face, he was cleaning his fingernails with the point of the blade. "Say, man, you got a couple of bucks you could lend me?"

A concerned look washed across Devlin's face. He reached into his back pocket and pulled out a handkerchief, wiping his forehead.

"Did you hear me, man?" Still holding the handkerchief, Devlin reached back with his other hand. The ants looked at each other and smiled their let's-get-ready-to-smoke-some-crack smile. When they looked back at Devlin, he was using the handkerchief to wipe off the barrel of his magnum.

James drove by just as the two were leaving, knifeless, not taking the time to do the "bad motherfucker."

James was a fifty-five-year-old black man, tall and paper thin. His deep, smoky voice was part of his charm. He prided himself on being able to talk anyone into or out of anything. He was originally from Philadelphia but had left because of an outstanding homicide warrant. Six months later Devlin had arrested him for interstate flight. By that time, James had established himself among some of Detroit's more industrious felons. During the post-arrest interview, he told Devlin where he could find two bank robbers who were responsible for fourteen robberies. Out of appreciation, Devlin called the Philadelphia detective who was in charge of the homicide case and told him of the cooperation. The detective told him that the case was probably self-defense, but James had fled before telling his side of it. He promised Devlin he would do what he could to help with the charges.

A week after he was returned to Philadelphia, James phoned Devlin and told him that because of his call to the detective, the charges had been dropped. If he could ever do anything for Devlin, he said, Devlin just needed to call.

The FBI had always put an intense emphasis on developing and maintaining the best possible informants. A good portion of Bureau cases were solved by informants, and like James, many sources began as subjects of FBI investigations.

Because of the Detroit banking community's reward program, $1,000 a robber, James was entitled to $2,000. When Devlin showed up at his house unexpectedly and paid him, the partnership was formed.

That was twelve years earlier, and since that time James had helped solve dozens of cases and received many thousands of dollars. He was only one of several informants that Devlin operated, but he was the best. He supported himself by being a middleman. Brokering anything from false identification to truckloads of stolen televisions, he was never the buyer or seller, simply the *connect*. Devlin was apprised of every transaction and took the appropriate measures. The thing that Devlin appreciated the most about James was that he would never get involved in narcotics. However, he did know many dealers and users because drugs were the common thread running through the fabric of Detroit's crime.

As they shook hands, their friendship was remembered.

"How are you, James?"

"Just fine, Mike. Just fine."

Devlin handed him the mug shot of Washington.

James winced. "Yeah. He's been hanging around the Duffield every night for about a week." The Duffield was a black bar in the Cass Corridor. Tens of thousands of dollars' worth of dope changed hands there nightly. They had the "cleanest" dope at the best prices. Every Corridor junkie went there to cop. Shootings were not unusual, and knifings were so common that the police would not respond unless the victim could not find his or her way to the hospital.

"Mike, the dude is crazy. Whoever wrote 'Bad, Bad Leroy Brown' must have run into that motherfucker."

"I know. We want him for a rape-murder."

"Did he beat the girl to death?"

"She was badly beaten and then strangled."

"Yeah. He's real good with his hands. He took on some big dude the other night and fucked him up. I mean— fuuucked him up! I ain't bull-shittin. He would have felt better if he had been shot."

"Can you go to the Duffield tonight and call me if he comes in?"

"Sure, but if I call you'd better bring some people who ain't afraid to give it up. Leave the meek and mild at home."

"Okay. Anything else?"

"There are a couple of things. Did you hear about that guy they found last week, up on Fenkell, with his head cut off?"

Devlin nodded. Although many homicides are not reported in the newspapers in Detroit, beheadings are generally considered newsworthy.

"Do you know why they cut his head off?" James asked, not expecting anyone to be insane enough to guess the reason. Decapitation is usually done to prevent identification of the victim because the murderer can easily be detected once the victim is identified. However, the way James was shaking his head in disgust, Devlin suspected he was about to be introduced to a new level of barbarity.

"They shot him twice in the head. A guy named Slack

and his partner, Anthony Downs. See, the guy was dealing for them and fucked up their money, so they took care of business."

Money ... business ... just another day at the office. Like the old cop had said that morning, "It's only a misdemeanor in Detroit."

"Who was the shooter?"

"Slack. He's got this pistol he really loves, a chrome-plated Colt Python with a six-inch barrel with the ribbed vent along the top and pearl grips. A real gangster's gun. He's always taking pictures with it, with his dope and his money. But he knows if he keeps the gun, Ballistics could match it with the murder, so instead of dumping the gun, he cuts the guy's head off and buries it."

Devlin felt the dragon rumble in his chest, but the dragon did not fly for dope dealers.

James's value as an informant was not that he knew who or why; many sources could provide that information. He knew what was needed to prove it. Twelve years as an informant had taught him to think like a cop, knowing what was necessary for an arrest. Devlin knew James would have the required details. Taking out a small notebook, he said, "Okay, James, make me a star."

"These two guys are always together. They deal coke, eight balls on up. But I don't know Slack's real name." Devlin knew if the smallest quantity he dealt was an eighth of an ounce, DPD Narcotics would be able to identify the psychopath known only as Slack. "If you want to cop, call them on this beeper." He handed Devlin a piece of paper. Also listed on the paper were two addresses, one on Sorrento Street and one on Anglin. "The addresses are their crack houses. The head is buried in the backyard at the Sorrento address."

"Where's the Python?"

"They drive a black Jeep Renegade. You know how the

dealers stamp the name of their dope on the packets, theirs is 'Renegade.' They think they're slick. Have someone from Narcotics beep them, order up an ounce, and they'll deliver." James's eyes beamed in anticipation. "They'll deliver the dope in the Jeep. They always carry the gun in a briefcase with the dope."

What a legitimate businessman James would have made, thought Devlin. His simple plan would solve the murder, bring the killers into custody, cause the issuance of two dope house search warrants, and result in a hand-to-hand undercover buy of an ounce of cocaine, the seizure of the Jeep, the recovery of the murder weapon—and of course the victim's head. No one could accuse James of not taking care of business. Devlin shook his head in amazement, letting James know who the real star was.

"You're okay behind all of this?" Devlin asked.

"They can't trace anything back to me," James assured him.

"Good. I'll take care of this right away. You okay?"

"I am a little short right now."

From behind his credential case Devlin took out two fifty-dollar bills. He handed them to James, who appreciated the loan, knowing the hundred was Devlin's own money, which would be paid back when James received the authorized payment for his information.

Thinking their meeting was over, Devlin put his hand out to James, but he would not take it. He looked down at the two fifties and said guiltily, "I wasn't going to give you this because it involves my nephew, Dimitrius Stone. You know those Little Italy Pizza stickups?"

The Little Italy Pizza Corporation was a national chain that had started with one neighborhood store in the 1950s. In the last three months, a gang had robbed dozens of its Detroit stores. Detroit Holdup, which handled only armed robberies of businesses, was investigating the robberies.

Street robberies, because of their sheer volume, were considered a lesser priority and were given the once-over-lightly by overloaded precinct detectives. Holdup had some of the most talented detectives in the department, and they still felt armed robbery was a serious violation of state law. The Little Italy robberies had frustrated and embarrassed them. After each robbery the Detroit *Free Press* would print, on its locally important page three, the headline LITTLE ITALY ROBBERY NUMBER . . . , finishing with the latest total, as if it were as expected as the Dow Jones close. Many a dragon perched on the desks at Holdup, waiting for the Little Italy bandits.

"That's a real hot item down at Holdup," Devlin said.

"Hey, Dimitrius is just the wheelman. The guys with the guns inside are the James brothers."

"Frank and Jesse?" Devlin joked.

James gave a short laugh. "No, James is both their first names, and they're brothers, different fathers, same mother."

"Sounds like an ethnic joke."

"I know, but I don't know their last names. They both stay at their mama's, over on Plainview, just south of Grand River. They're driving a new silver Buick, the plate is EEE 031. The car is in one of their names. Mike, my nephew is just the driver."

"Do you think he'll cooperate?"

"I'll make sure he does."

If a getaway driver's testimony was needed, more often than not he would be allowed to plead to a probational offense or simply not charged. Devlin knew Holdup would cut Dimitrius Stone a deal that would ease his uncle's guilt.

"I'll do what I can," Devlin said.

James looked into his eyes and found the reassurance he needed. "I know you will."

• • •

Detroit Police Department headquarters has stood at 1300 Beaubien Street since 1922. The ancient gray stone building was overbuilt as a fortress against any future crime surge, as remote as the possibility seemed. The granite structure stood formidably, like a great heavyweight bare-knuckle champion, ready to bully and vanquish any and all challengers to the decency of the city. Seven decades later the ignored building, stained brown by the same progress that had witnessed twenty thousand homicides, was as fatigued as the cops who came daily, trying to keep the criminal justice system's losses to a minimum.

Except for three rooms belonging to the Narcotics Bureau, the entire north end of the fifth floor was occupied by Homicide. The walls and ceilings were painted one of the usual stale municipal pastels. A strange awareness filled the air. The rooms seemed darker than their lighting would dictate. The visitor's senses quickened, like a slow-motion camera clicking extra frames. Details became indelible, almost surrealistic. It was a place where laughs died before being heard, a place where experienced cops never dared to boast, "Now I've heard everything."

In the hallway outside the reception area, a bus-station-type row of chairs held witnesses and members of victims' families twenty-four hours a day. The eight chairs were welded into a single, immovable unit so they could be kept orderly and, more important, not be stolen one by one.

The night before, homicides 371 through 376 had been committed, but because it was already midday only two people remained in the chairs waiting to be interviewed by the investigators. The black middle-aged couple had dressed in a hurry. The woman wore a long brown raincoat over her nightgown; a scarf covered most of her hair. The man wore a dark suit with only a T-shirt under the jacket, and stiff-looking work shoes covered his sockless feet. Devlin guessed they were one of the six victims' families, parents who had worked hard their entire adult life, and now their success seemed of little consequence. They slumped in the impossible plastic seats, trying to sleep, willing to escape into any nightmare—which was preferable to the torturous prison of their reality.

Above the entrance a small, neglected wooden sign, yellowed by the smoke of a million cigarettes, hung perpendicular to the wall—HOMICIDE UNIT. Under it, taped on the wall, was what looked like a photocopied bumper sticker in black and white letters: WHEN YOUR DAY ENDS OURS IS JUST BEGINNING. HAVE A NICE DAY—DETROIT HOMICIDE. Years before it had been placed there as a joke. No one had laughed; no one had cared enough to take it down.

Before the mayor had realigned the department "for the good of the people," the Homicide Unit had had ninety investigators. Afterwards—sixty. Administrative assignments such as the morgue and the court, timekeepers, furloughs, sick, disabled, and the desk further reduced the number of detectives. On a good day, the unit was fortunate to have four two-man teams working on unsolved cases. After the initial crime scene investigation, most homicides were investigated by only two detectives for a single day.

As he walked in, Devlin waved to the two older sergeants manning the desk. They both had phones to their ears and were writing on pads of paper that lay next to the day's crossword puzzle. The morning news had said only that there had been six homicides the night before, and the reason that that was newsworthy was that six murders on a weeknight was unusual. Weeknights traditionally were two-, maybe three-homicide nights. Devlin knew the desk would be busy a good part of the day taking tips, tips that would solve a good number of homicides. Both sergeants absentmindedly waved back.

Devlin walked past the Special Assignment Squad, which handled cases involving police shootings. The door was open. A black detective was interviewing a young white girl. Devlin guessed her age at ten. He turned into the next office. The room was as spartan as the rest of the offices in the Homicide Unit. Only two items hanging on the walls identified the office: a frame containing photos of all the inspectors in charge of Homicide since 1922 and a year-by-year chart of the city's murder rate. On the lone desk in the room were six neat piles of reports detailing the night's homicides. Sitting upright behind the desk was Inspector Jerome Wicks, asleep. Quietly, Devlin sat in one of the chairs facing the desk and waited. He knew it would not be long. In all probability, Devlin calculated, Wicks had not been home or in bed during the last thirty-six hours. Devlin had found him like this before.

Wicks had grown up in Detroit and had been with the department for twenty-three years. When he was promoted to sergeant he was transferred to the newly formed Homicide Unit—Squad Six. The drug wars were wearing out the granite giant on Beaubien. Detroit effortlessly led the country in homicides per capita. The department felt that too many of them were dope dealers killing dope dealers. Squad Six was handpicked. Wicks was the only black. The talented investigators worked unending hours. They called their mission "The Ark of Justice": dealers were disappearing two at a time—one killed, the other sentenced to life imprisonment for the murder. The ark was filling two by two, but they soon realized it would never be full.

One of the cases assigned to Wicks during those days had involved a narcotics hit man named Ernest Griffith. Most sources estimated that Griffith had personally booked passage on the ark for at least twenty heroin dealers. Wicks eventually obtained a first-degree murder warrant for him and then learned he had fled the state. The FBI was asked for assistance and sent a brand-new agent out of training school, Mike Devlin. Within two weeks, he located Griffith in California and had the Los Angeles office make the arrest. Since then, Devlin and Wicks had worked together on dozens of cases. Devlin would find fugitives, and Wicks would turn over informants whom he could not afford to pay out of DPD's meager budget. The federal wallet was always full.

The inspector's eyes snapped open. He was instantly lucid. He smiled at Devlin and glanced at the piles of reports to ensure there were no more than six. "How are you, Mike?"

Devlin nodded. "Long night?"

Wicks waved his hand over his desk as an answer.

"Does Squad Six have the beheading?" Devlin asked nonchalantly, knowing Wicks would be greatly interested.

Fully conscious now, Wicks answered, "No, I gave it to Seven. Six was buried at the time. I know it was narcotics-related, but which one isn't? The media is all over our ass about it." Wicks's eyes had not left Devlin's face since he had said the word "beheading." "Have you got something?"

"You buying lunch?"

"Isn't extortion a federal crime?"

"That's what I like about you locals, you're so appreciative. I'll tell you what, I'll buy, but you have to promise not to fall asleep in your moussaka again. Besides, there's a new agent I want you to meet."

"Not another one."

"You'll like him, he's like you."

"He's black?"

"No, he's pretty."

For the next fifteen minutes Devlin and Wicks discussed the information regarding the homicide. When Wicks walked down to Squad Seven, Devlin called Livingston at the office.

"Do you know where Greektown is?" Devlin asked.

"I think so."

"Go to the Old Parthenon and ask for Artie. Tell him you work with me and we'd like the room upstairs if it isn't being used. Do you like pastitsio?"

"I don't know. What is it?"

"It's a Greek dish. Artie makes it better than anyone. Order for three. I'll see you there in about half an hour."

Wicks walked back into his office with Tim Moran and Ray Hansen, both of Squad Seven. They both looked as tired as Wicks. Devlin had known them for years and had worked with them before under similar circumstances. Moran listened while Hansen took notes. Devlin knew that Anthony Downs and Slack would soon be boarding the ark.

Wicks and Devlin arrived at the Old Parthenon about fifteen minutes late. Artie rushed to meet them. He ceremoniously greeted everyone at his restaurant, but for these two customers he was especially gracious. Twenty years earlier, he had come to the land of opportunity and found the fairy tale to be true. Because Greektown was adjacent to DPD headquarters, cops had always been a substantial share of his business, especially on payday night, when the ouzo flowed long after the liquor curfew. He had known Wicks since he was a uniformed patrolman walking a beat and was introduced to Devlin by Wicks fifteen years earlier. As always, he asked about both men's wives by name. Neither could ever remember telling Artie their names.

"Did my partner get here, Artie?"

"Yes. He's upstairs. The pastitsio is almost ready. I already took up some hors d'oeuvres. Wine today?"

"No, thanks," Devlin answered after looking into Wicks's sagging eyes.

Livingston sat at a table large enough to seat six. He seemed to be cornered by the three different appetizers Artie had brought up. His nostrils turned up as if threatened by the Mediterranean odors. Artie lit the cheese with the traditional *opah*.

"Ed, this is Jerome Wicks. He's in charge of Homicide."

"How do you do, Inspector. I saw you on the news a couple of nights ago. You were talking about that beheading case. Anything new on that?"

Wicks looked at Devlin. Devlin nodded, and Wicks explained in detail the information Devlin had provided an hour before. As he finished, Artie arrived with the pastitsio. Once he tried it, Livingston found that he liked the dish and impressed Artie by guessing that the unusual taste in it was cinnamon.

Just as Artie asked about dessert, Wicks's beeper went off. Artie took him to his office to use his private line and took him a cup of dense black coffee, shutting the door.

When the inspector reappeared, he no longer looked tired. "I've got to go."

"Fresh scene?" Devlin asked.

"Yeah, a triple. One of them is a three-year-old girl. All with their throats cut."

As if haste could somehow bring the three victims back to life, Wicks hurried desperately back to his office. Devlin lengthened his stride to remain abreast of the silent homicide detective, who was already organizing the investigation in his mind. As they walked by the Homicide desk, Wicks was handed a report with all the available information concerning homicides 377, 378, and 379. Wicks started reading it as he headed to his office. Remembering Devlin, he turned and gave him an apologetic wave, which he knew would be understood. Devlin did understand. The inspector's dragon was taking flight. And it never came home hungry. Homicide 379, the three-year-old girl whose throat had been cut as if she were an adult, could count on vengeance.

The Armed Robbery Unit was up two flights of stairs.

Devlin decided to walk up, hoping to burn off some of Artie's pastitsio, half of which he had left at the restaurant, where Artie was giving Livingston a tour of the kitchen.

The Holdup desk was being handled by Sergeant Sara Holmes, who was talking on the phone. Behind her a sign was taped to the wall, positioned so it could not be seen from the hallway: IF ASSHOLES COULD FLY, THIS WOULD BE THE WORLD'S BUSIEST AIRPORT. If a complainant made it as far as the desk, the sign usually tempered his demeanor.

The sergeant was trying to explain something to the person on the phone for the second time and rolled her eyes to let Devlin know that the caller was a pain in the ass. Without warning, she hung up midsentence. "Hi, Mike. What brings the Feebees here?"

Nodding at the sign behind her, he said, "I came for the culture."

With the practiced tongue of a boatswain's mate she said, "Go fuck a duck."

"Ah—I love poetry."

As Devlin stood in front of her, she lit a cigarette and directed a stream of smoke at his fly.

"Careful, you'll set off my smoke alarm."

"Don't get my hopes up."

The phone rang. It was the caller she had hung up on. "Just a minute." She hit the hold button. "I'd like to chat with you, but I got other perverts to talk to."

"Who has the pizza robberies?"

"They're scattered around, there's so many of them, but Brackoff has most of them."

Damn, thought Devlin, "Have you fed him yet today?"

"Yeah, but he wanted a Fed for dessert."

"Is he in?"

"He's back in his office. Should I announce you?"

"If you do, I'll have the IRS look at your charitable contributions."

Sergeant Holmes held up her hands in submission and hit the flashing button on her phone. "Yes, sir, I checked. That is a federal violation. You'll have to call the FBI. Ask for Special Agent Mike Devlin. He handles all of their animal sexual assault cases."

Devlin formally bowed in surrender and walked back to Brackoff's office.

Sergeant Gunnar Brackoff was the most menacing man Devlin had ever met. At a glance, he would be described as obese, a miscalculation that had cost more than one undiscerning individual a trip to the nearest emergency room. He stood five-foot-ten and weighed 300 pounds. His terrible face brought the realization that he was capable of taking and delivering great amounts of pain. His eyebrows were gone. In their place were zigzagging arcs of glowing white scar tissue. Numerous other scars bit into his hard face, leaving a permanent sneer.

When Brackoff was fifteen, his father, a construction worker of legendary strength, had been killed saving a fellow worker's life during a building collapse. His mother was left penniless with Gunnar and his three younger sisters to care for. Like many women of that time, she took in laundry and sewing. She also stayed up late at night cooking her delicious beef pasties, which Gunnar would dutifully carry from bar to bar after school and sell to the patrons.

One of his stops was Slim's, a popular but always rowdy black bar. Slim was an invalid and, although confined to a wheelchair, ran the daily operation. Because of the unruly customers, he always hired the toughest person available to manage the place.

Slim loved Mrs. Brackoff's pasties and was in the process of buying some when an ex–college football player walked up to the bar's manager and announced he wanted his job. The noisy saloon froze in silence until the two men headed for the alley. The bar emptied behind them. Uninterested, Slim sat eating the meat pie and explained his process of selection to Gunnar. It was good for the bar because the customers could see the manager's skills firsthand, which would ensure compliance with his future demands. In five minutes the *new* manager walked back in and introduced himself to Slim, who told him what his weekly salary would be. Brackoff could not believe the amount.

The next day Brackoff walked into Slim's without his kettle of pasties. Slim sensed something in the overdeveloped kid's face. He walked up to the manager and told him he wanted his job. The ex-footballer looked in disbelief at Slim, who simply gave a laissez-faire shrug of the shoulders.

Brackoff had always been able to withstand pain, so it took his opponent a long time to beat him into unconsciousness. By that time, Brackoff's nose was broken and the skin covering the top half of both eye sockets had been shredded, exposing bone in a dozen places.

The manager reentered the bar and bought the house a round. Many of the spectators clapped him on the back, telling him he would have the job forever. He accepted their congratulations but felt an unfamiliar burning of doubt in his stomach. The more he hit the kid, the more unyielding he became. He had fought a lot of men, but he had never experienced anything like that.

The burning in his belly rekindled itself the next day, when Brackoff, his face a maze of unstable scabs and swellings, walked up to the manager and simply nodded toward the door. Again Brackoff was badly beaten, but his opponent required seven stitches to close the cut over his left eye.

And so it went for a week, each "job interview" lasting a little longer, until on the sixth day, Brackoff, who could barely see through the swelling that had become his face, beat the former manager into unconsciousness. The crowd, which had been increasing in size daily to see the crazy white kid, yelled for Brackoff to stomp his opponent now that he finally had the upper hand. Through a mask of blood and exposed bone he leered at them, chilling them into silence.

Brackoff was never challenged for his job. Out of some sort of gladiator's pride, he had never allowed any of his wounds to be medically treated or stitched. The resulting keloids were wide and permanently swollen. People were hypnotized by his face. They could turn their heads, but their eyes remained fixed on the grotesque, angry object in front of them.

Many felt his threatening presence was the reason for his success as an interrogator. His confession rate was in the ninetieth percentile. The old detectives felt his success was due largely to his open-window policy. Even in the dead of Detroit's arctic winters, Brackoff's window was always wide open. If questioned, he simply attributed it to his Siberian heritage. Early in his career, a prisoner had jumped—so the reports read—handcuffed, from Holdup's seventh-story window. Brackoff obtained detailed photographs of the corpse. When an interview would hit an impasse, Brackoff would ask the prisoner to go to the open window and see if his car was still parked on the street. When the prisoner sat down again, the photos would be spread out on the desk facing him. After a few more questions, he would again ask the prisoner to check on his car. When he would decline to do so—and he always did—Brackoff would handcuff him and they would walk to the window. The last line Brackoff invariably wrote on a confession before it was signed was "no promises or threats were made to me." After all, the Fifth Amendment guarantees freedom from self-incrimination, and Brackoff *had* sworn to uphold the Constitution.

His tiny office, once a storage room, contained a desk, two chairs, and a filing cabinet, leaving little floor space to move around in. No other sergeant in Holdup had his own office. Officially it had been given to him as a reward for solving the robbery and shooting of the chief's brother in a blind pig. The chief's brother and a date were leaving when two of the neighborhood's young entrepreneurs robbed and shot him.

A week later Duane "Little Red" Harrison called Brackoff from his holding cell in the Wayne County Jail. Harrison was a forty-five-year-old felon who committed armed robberies between prison sentences. Most of his life since hair formed on his testicles was spent at the State Prison of Southern Michigan. When he called Brackoff, he was about to make his fourth and probably final trip to prison for an armed robbery of a dry cleaner's. Not satisfied with the thirty-eight dollars in the till, Little Red took the time to go through the cleaning to pick out a couple of new ensembles. The clerk had hit the silent alarm when Harrison had announced the robbery. The precinct scout car was waiting for him when he ran out, carrying clothing stacked so high he could not see the laughing cops.

Little Red knew Brackoff's reputation. With his record and the cop's recommendation, he knew he would be sentenced to twenty-five years on the robbery and possibly life imprisonment for being what the State of Michigan referred to as a "habitual offender."

His offer to Brackoff was simple: He would give up the names of the two who robbed and shot the chief's brother if the habitual offender charge was dropped. That left Little Red with the twenty-five-year armed robbery sentence, which meant in eight years he would be back visiting metropolitan Detroit dry cleaners'.

After the arrests had been made the chief called Brackoff to his office to thank him personally and ask if he needed anything. He said he would like his own office, so he could get away from his pinheaded lieutenant. The chief had heard all the Brackoff rumors and decided he should be kept separate from the sane. Besides, the chief knew the lieutenant was a pinhead. The chief arranged not only for Brackoff's office but also for a two-line telephone to be installed. One line was an Armed Robbery Unit extension. The other was a private line. No one knew the number except the chief, who would discreetly call it when special measures were needed.

Devlin had worked with Brackoff before. Holdup had concurrent jurisdiction with the FBI not only over bank robberies, but also over extortions and kidnappings.

Devlin carefully stuck his head in Brackoff's office. "Hello, Gunnar."

"Mike," the hulking detective answered.

Devlin sat down and looked into the policeman's eyes without noticing his scars, a technique not easily mastered.

"You have a lot of the pizza robberies, don't you?"

"Twenty-two of them. When I get those cocksuckers, I *will* throw them out the window."

Devlin smiled. "Don't do that. I made some promises."

Brackoff shot a look at Devlin and realized that he knew who was committing the robberies. "What's this going to cost me?" he asked with uncharacteristic lightheartedness.

"I'll tell you what, Gunnar, let's put it in the bank. I might need someone killed someday."

"Just let me know who." Devlin could not tell if he was kidding.

Devlin told him about the James brothers and, without telling him his uncle was an informant, about James's nephew. At Brackoff's instruction, he called James and made arrangements for him to bring his nephew to Brackoff's office as soon as possible.

Devlin looked at Brackoff's hungering window and wondered if it would accommodate both the James brothers at the same time.

||| CHAPTER 4 |||

The FBI's major-case room was a medium-sized room cluttered with long tables, chairs, radio equipment, and enough telephones to manage a small telethon. There were no windows, and the walls consisted mostly of blackboards and pinboards. The room had originally been designed as a control center for legitimate kidnappings, extortions, and other major, quick-breaking investigations that demanded a concentration of communication abilities for a brief time period. Since the room had been outfitted thirteen years earlier, not one major case had called for its use. Instead, it was used for very personal phone calls, homework, groping sessions, or any other unauthorized activity that needed seclusion.

The fact that Fauber had decided to hold the squad briefing in the major-case room indicated the type of importance he was trying to lend to Duncan Moorehead's fugitive. Devlin sat down and warned himself not to say a word no matter how bad it got.

As the squad members straggled in, they chuckled at the item that had been posted on the pinboard. At the front of the room, two thumbtacks held a larger-than-usual announcement, again naming Moorehead "One of America's Most Successful Young Homosexuals." Someone asked, "Who keeps putting these up?" Devlin looked around for Shanahan.

Fauber and Moorehead arrived and started to close the door when Shanahan pushed his way in and sat down.

Nice touch, thought Devlin. Shanahan would not be a leading suspect for the latest America's Most Successful hanging since he had arrived after Fauber and Moorehead. His eyebrows snapped up and down in a secret salute to Devlin, letting him know he had gotten Moorehead again.

Moorehead was trying to figure out where to stand because all the tables and chairs were turned in different directions. Then he noticed the pinup, which completely distracted him. Finally Fauber directed him to one end of the room, and the agents turned their chairs toward him. Shanahan was delighted. The announcement Moorehead was trying so desperately to ignore hung just over his right shoulder. Devlin glanced at Shanahan, his face pure angelic concentration.

Devlin checked his watch. It was three o'clock. The second hand seemed to drag. Moorehead started the briefing. He talked nonstop for thirty minutes. Mostly he offered evidence as to what a menace this five-foot-five-inch, 135-pound accountant was. Finally the arrest plan was presented. A neighbor, previously contacted, would call the office as soon as the fugitive got home from work. The squad would remain in the office on standby until the charge was sounded. Moorehead, enjoying his role as arrest leader, tried to continue, but even Fauber had had enough. He cut him off, made a few comments so everyone would remember who was really in charge, and called for questions. A few of the younger Jedi politely rolled Fauber the traditional softballs, which he easily answered. Then the meeting was dismissed.

At eight P.M. the squad was still waiting. Moorehead sat nervously in his chair. When Devlin's phone rang, Moorehead picked up his own and anxiously announced, "Special Agent Moorehead" to the dial tone.

Devlin picked up his phone; it was James. Big Bad John was at the Duffield. Devlin looked at Livingston and went to an empty interview room. Livingston followed.

"Washington?" Livingston's voice raced slightly.

"He's there now."

"Well, let's go."

"Wait a minute, Ed. Do you understand what you're doing? I know this has you excited, but Fauber won't stand for you siding with me. He may try to have you fired. You're still on probation."

Livingston considered Devlin's words. Calm and confident, he spoke two words as if they were expensive chocolates: "reckless abandon." As if this was what he had been born for, the young agent stood there unwaveringly like an ancient warrior about to storm the castle, knowing that the goal was not victory but the battle itself.

Devlin was hoping that Livingston would back off because he knew Fauber would try to have Devlin fired for insubordination. Fauber had given him an order not to make any arrests without him being present. But Devlin was so taken by Livingston's determination, he had to ignore his own problems. Still, he was curious about Livingston's single-mindedness. More prudent men would call it self-destructive. Devlin wondered if it was something else. "Are any of your ancestors Irish?"

With the seriousness of an ancient ritual he answered, "No. They were Vikings."

Great, thought Devlin, an Irish rebel and a black Viking were going to take on the Golden Gloves heavyweight champion, and a sniveling beaucrat named Yoda was going to have their asses for it.

The Duffield Bar was the deadliest 800 square feet in the Cass Corridor. Its design, both outside and in, was a model of simplicity. The exterior was classical post-riot architecture. Thick steel doors sealed off the front and back of the structure. All windows had been either bricked up or replaced with bazookaproof Plexiglas, and all building materials were at least fire-retardant. The outside was painted an ominous hospital green. The inside looked as though it had never been painted. The worn hardwood floors were a gritty tan. The original mahogany bar was marred by hundreds of black worms left by forgotten cigarettes. A few small tables were scattered around. Behind the bar stood four bottles of liquor: vodka, scotch, whiskey, and cognac. Beer was available only in lukewarm cans. Two coin-operated devices had been installed in the bar: a jukebox, which was normal, and a telephone, which was not. Businesses in high-crime areas rarely had telephones inside or immediately outside. The easiest way to case a place for a robbery was to go in and use the phone until the most opportune moment presented itself. But the Duffield, because of its customers' armament, was virtually robbery-proof.

Devlin and Livingston drove by the bar. Livingston felt four beats of thicker blood pump through his heart as he looked at two black men arguing on the sidewalk. Devlin searched for James and spotted him on the curb a block north of the tavern.

Devlin pulled the car around the corner, and James slid into the darkness of the backseat.

"James, this is Edgar." The two men shook hands.

"Is he still in there?" Devlin asked.

"I've been watching the front door from up here, and he hasn't come out. Unless he went out the back. He had a broad with him. He looked like he was going to party all night."

"What's he wearing?" Livingston asked.

"All-black leather suit, even has a leather tie. Don't worry, you'll know him when you see him. That's one big motherfucker."

"How many people are in there?" Devlin asked.

"Hmm. Maybe twenty. Even if you get a dozen cops, you're going to have trouble."

From under the dashboard a shrill voice demanded, "Central to DE Four-one." Livingston looked at Devlin, trying not to appear worried.

"I wonder who that could be this time of night," Devlin said sarcastically.

Again the voice came, a little more irritated, a little louder. "C-Four Supervisor to DE Four-one."

As if he were swatting a buzzing mosquito, Devlin turned off the Bureau radio with a snap of his wrist and asked James, "How'd your nephew do with Sergeant Brackoff?"

"Yeah, everything's cool. He even let Dimitrius go home. We thought he was going to lock him up. Scary dude. That's what you need to get that motherfucker in the bar."

"I'm glad it worked out. Want me to drop you somewhere?"

"No, man, I'm going back in. I got to see this." Devlin and Livingston stared at each other like two men who had climbed out on a building ledge and saw a crowd gathering to watch an unstoppable tragedy. James got out of the car and hurried toward the bar.

"Ready?" Devlin asked.

"Ready? Aren't we going to get some backup?"

"How? We can't use the radio because of Fauber, and the only phone around is in the Duffield. Caution is good only up to a certain point; after that it causes mistakes. We're at that point." Devlin waited, but Livingston did not respond.

Something dark enveloped Livingston. A nauseating surge rolled around in his stomach like a melting steel ball that became heavier as it melted. His skin was cold, and he was on the verge of shivering. In defense, he yawned. Devlin saw the yawn and understood his fear. He had seen the yawn before at times of anticipated danger. He fought back the urge himself.

"Do you want to live forever?" Devlin said. It was not a question, rather a demand.

For the first time, Livingston realized he was scared. He became angry with himself. If Devlin could handle it, he could handle it. "Let's do it," Livingston said.

Although he was acting cavalierly for this new agent, Devlin knew the risks that lay ahead. But then, what the hell, he had already lived forever.

Devlin's Bureau car was nice enough not to look like a police car but not attractive enough to be stolen in this neighborhood where no possession was permanent. He parked it three spaces south of the bar in front of a white BMW with all-gold trim, knowing if anything was stolen, it would be the Beamer.

"Give me a two-minute head start. Make sure your gun isn't visible through your coat. Take it out of your holster. It's not unusual to have a gun in there; it *is* unusual to carry it in a holster. When you come in, order a beer. Don't ask for a glass, and sit near the front door. Don't eyeball any-one; they'll know you're a cop if you do. And get rid of your tie."

Livingston took off his tie, unclipped his holster, and shoved his automatic deep into his waistband just below his right kidney. He watched Devlin go to the trunk and put on black horn-rimmed glasses, which, because of Devlin's light coloring, made him look dopey. He took off his hol-stered magnum and put it in the trunk. He took out two other objects. One looked to be about the size of a baseball, but Livingston could not tell what it was because Devlin slipped it into his bulging jacket pocket, adding to his klutzy look. He got back into the car with the other item in his hand. It was an ankle holster with a .38-caliber snubnose wedged into it. He bent over and strapped it tightly above his right ankle.

"Okay, Ed, just remember, that isn't the Elks Club in there. You're not looking to develop friendships, and if you show any fear or weakness they'll find you in the yellow pages next to Jimmy Hoffa, under 'Cement.' You understand?"

"Yes."

"One last thing. If things go wrong, don't be in a hurry to shoot anyone. If you have to shoot, try to wound them first. It's better that they sue the Bureau for a million dollars than put you in prison for killing one of them. If a cop shoots someone in this town, those are the possibilities."

Livingston nodded he understood the instructions, but he was puzzled about the sense of order, something he had been taught his whole life. Where was the respect for or fear of the law? The admiration for the FBI? In training school, they would have walked into the saloon, announced they were the FBI and had a warrant for John Thomas Washington for rape and murder. And if anyone made a false move, they would shoot them at least once through the heart. What about when they got him back to the office? Shouldn't there be applause? Instead, Fauber waited and schemed. If things went wrong, they could wind up in prison; if they went right, they might be fired. There was something to be said about not wanting to live forever. "How do we do this?"

"We're going to have to try and finesse him, get him out of there on some pretext. If that doesn't work, we'll have to try and be creative. What was your major?"

College curriculum seemed like a strange topic at this moment but Livingston answered quickly. "Music."

"Good. You must have some creative abilities. Use them in there. And Ed—"

"What?"

"Loosen up." Devlin got out of the car and walked into the Duffield, pushing his glasses up on the bridge of his nose.

Surprised to see a white man, the two men on the sidewalk stopped arguing, and one of them said something insulting to Devlin. He ignored it, and the two men resumed their argument.

As he walked into the Duffield, he smelled familiar stenches, the odor of fermenting urine and the stink of sour dampness that were so common in the old, dying buildings of Detroit. The jukebox played loudly, and the customers huddled lethargically in small packs. He spotted Washington wedged into a booth, his date pinned inside. Just as James had said, Big Bad John was in a black leather suit. Because of his size, the girl looked like an unsuspecting child. He looked back at Devlin. Washington's eyes seethed with a life full of hate as he glared at the white fool who was obviously lost and about to be given some very unfriendly directions. Devlin timidly leaned on the end of the bar and did not look at James, who sat at the opposite end of the U-shaped bar.

Behind the bartender was a volume control for the jukebox. He turned it down. Everyone, turning to the bar, now noticed Devlin. Without moving, the bartender spoke as if his words were soaked in bile. "What do you want?"

A few of the men started to stand up in search of some sport with the outsider. In a shaky voice Devlin said, "I want to buy a drink for the toughest man in the place." Everyone sat back down and looked at Washington, who seemed disappointed he was not going to have to beat someone to death to earn the drink. Then a nasty smile infected his face. Because of his size he had to wriggle out of the booth, shaking its structure as he did. The black leather accented his power. He moved with the ease of a professional athlete. His shoulders did not move as his feet glided across the straining floor.

Devlin felt the twenty-year-old shrapnel in his shoulder heating up, his own personal warning system. He doubted if five shots from his snubnose would stop Darth Vader of the Duffield. Almost unnoticed, Livingston walked in and sat at the nearest empty table. Involuntarily, he stared at Washington, awed by his physical presence.

Washington looked for fear in Devlin's eyes and thought he saw it. "My lady would like a drink too."

"Certainly, certainly," Devlin bumbled. "But I've got a business proposition for you. Is there somewhere we can go and talk?"

Without a word, Washington looked at the bartender and flicked his head. The bartender turned up the jukebox volume, so all conversations once again became private. Washington sat down on a bar stool and nodded to Devlin to do the same. Devlin glanced at Livingston. He looked stunned. He did not know whether it was fear or culture shock, but Livingston's help now seemed questionable. James might help. Devlin glanced at him. He was grinning, enjoying the show.

Devlin's only hope was to get Washington, himself, and the Nordic Warrior out of there as quickly as possible. "I married money. She inherited numerous pieces of property, one of which is a bar over on Second Avenue. I believe it is called the Midnight Hour. Do you know the place?"

"No, man."

"Well, in brief, because of my tax situation, it would be beneficial for me if the bar showed a loss of a hundred thousand dollars next year. I would need someone of your, say, forcefulness to manage it."

"Man, I ain't no fucking bartender."

"Oh, no, no. You could hire your own bartender, set your

own salary, make all the financial decisions. I repeat; I need to show a hundred-thousand-dollar loss."

Washington's mind was accelerating, fighting the effects of the pint of cognac he had already drunk. He did not know exactly how, but he was about to steal $100,000. "Man, you got a deal."

"Good, but I don't want to ever come down in this area again, so let's go over and take a look at the bar now."

"Naw, man, I can't. I got my lady here and—you know. I could meet you somewhere tomorrow."

Devlin knew after tonight Fauber would have him buried somewhere, so it had to be now. He casually glanced at Livingston. He was still in a trance, and the bartender was starting to stare at him. Devlin decided this was it. He noticed Washington's long leather tie hanging in the air as he leaned on his forearms against the bar.

"Okay, let me call my accountant and see if he can meet you tomorrow." Then Devlin, as if trying to teach Washington the technique, leaned back on the stool and, with great deliberation, thrust both hands into his pants pockets and meticulously searched their depths. "I'm sorry, I don't have any change for the phone. Do you have twenty cents?"

Devlin had counted on the tightness of Washington's pants to make the search difficult. Big Bad John leaned back and worked his hands into his constricted pockets. In an attempt to loosen them he straightened his legs, dangling them and balancing himself on the seat of the stool.

No one saw Devlin's hands move. He grabbed Washington's tie and in a single, fluid movement jumped off his stool and pulled the tie down with his entire body weight. In a blur, Washington's head ripped forward violently. The rounded edge of the mahogany bar top caught him just above the eyebrows. The resulting thud sounded like someone had exploded a melon with a baseball bat.

Devlin was not certain the blow would stop Washington.

Out of reflex, the fugitive straightened up and looked at Devlin with confused eyes. Devlin brought his ankle holster to his hand and drew his revolver. Washington's pupils disappeared into his eyelids, and he floated off the stool and crumpled to the floor.

The thud snapped Livingston out of his trance. He now stood next to Devlin, his gun drawn.

"Cuff him, Ed," Devlin ordered with urgency in his voice. Livingston quickly handcuffed him behind the back.

The bar crowd now realized what was happening. Some of the men started edging toward the agents. Washington started to move. He struggled to clear his head and stood up on disobedient legs. They each grabbed one of his arms and started backing toward the front door. The crowd advanced toward them. Both agents pointed their guns at the pursuers. The crowd froze. Washington staggered, and both the agents were whipped back and forth because of the almost dead weight of his lurching body.

Sensing their struggle, the crowd again inched toward the retreating men. Devlin knew they would never make it, because the crowd would turn into a mob the closer they got to the car, and they were beginning to suspect that the agents were not anxious to shoot.

Devlin stuck his snubnose in his belt and took out the object Livingston had failed to identify at the car. It was a green World War II hand grenade. Again the forward edge of the group froze. A female's voice rose from the back, "The muthafucker's bluffing."

Not giving anyone time to think, Devlin responded, "The Secret Service doesn't bluff." He pulled the pin on the grenade and rolled it, with the care of a professional bowler, at the crowd. The handle of the device sprung into the air, indicating that in five to seven seconds metallic pineapple would be served to all who stayed. Devlin heard James's voice. "Everybody out the back door."

While everybody stampeded out of the bar, Devlin
backed out the front door and looked at James, who sat
calmly at the end of the bar, smiling. He saluted Devlin
with a raised beer can. He had given Devlin the dummy
grenade two Christmases ago as a gag gift.

As they drove their prisoner back to the office, Devlin
reluctantly turned the radio back on. "DE Four-one to Central."

"Go, Four-one."

"Central, we are ten-fifteen with the subject of file
88-27713. We'll be there in five minutes. Will you have
someone bring the prisoner elevator to the basement."

"That's ten-four, Four-one."

Devlin took a deep, tranquilizing breath. "And Central,
notify the C-Four supervisor."

In the darkness of the car, the two partners looked at
each other. Devlin said, "Well, I guess the fun part of the
evening is over."

Livingston laughed the deep, hearty laugh of a Viking
triumph.

The prisoner elevator doors opened, yawning light into the
sleeping Federal Building basement. Tom, one of the night
clerks, stood inside holding a key in the override lock.

Devlin and Livingston stepped in with their prisoner.
Washington's forehead had begun to swell. Combined with
the excessive features, his face had the shocking attraction
of a horror-movie mask. Unwillingly, Tom stared at Washington.

"Where's Fauber?" Devlin asked, trying to interrupt the
clerk's gaze.

"Oh, he's out on Duncan Moorehead's arrest," Tom answered, still unable to take his eyes off the prisoner. Washington stared back at the clerk, finding him equally
mysterious. The weight of Washington's combative eyes fi-

nally forced Tom's attention elsewhere. "And you're supposed to report to the SAC."

"Why is he here so late on a Friday night?" Devlin asked.

"I think he wants to have a press conference when Moorehead makes his arrest."

Livingston took the statement as a personal insult. "America will sleep better tonight knowing that Ralph the Real Estate Ripper is off the street." He turned pleadingly to Devlin, who stared ahead calmly. Livingston realized that Devlin was not worrying about "whose was bigger" but wondering what the SAC had waiting for him. But this was Livingston's first arrest, and he was entitled to a little emotion. The rookie grabbed Washington by one of his frightening arms and stood next to him proudly, as if posing for a picture with a record-setting marlin.

Devlin liked Livingston's excitable pride. It would drive him on when there were no good reasons left. After the bureaucrats had neutralized all incentives, after his peers had given up, pride would get the job done.

Without knocking or invitation, Devlin walked into the SAC's darkened office and pulled a straight-back chair up to his desk.

Pilkington did not acknowledge his visitor. He continued writing on the lone piece of paper on his oversized wooden desk. The only other object on the sterile surface was a green-shaded bank lamp that held a foot-high cloud of light between itself and the desk top. The top edge of the cloud did not reach Pilkington's eyes. It enabled him to look at his seated guests from the safe distance of a sniper.

He put his pen down and looked down through the light at Devlin. In the dimness, Devlin could see tiny sparks of anxiety in his eyes.

"Your supervisor was in to see me again about *your* disregard for his orders." Pilkington's inflection used the word "your" like a finger poking into the chest. Devlin sat motionless, looking into the emptiness above the glossy desk.

With a hint of fluster, Pilkington continued, "Did he, or did he not tell you not to make an arrest without him?" This time "did" poked the finger.

"He did," Devlin answered without inflection.

Pilkington was surprised by Devlin's response. "Well, why did you make that arrest tonight without him?"

"Actually, I didn't. It wasn't my case. It was Edgar Livingston's. I was just helping him."

Technically Devlin was right. The case and arrest belong to the case agent alone. He is solely responsible for whatever happens or fails to happen during its investigation. Livingston had brought it to its logical conclusion, and Devlin had simply assisted him. Fauber had not said anything about helping other agents with their arrests; in fact, he had insisted that single-handed arrests not be made. It was Bureau policy. It was a technicality, but an irrefutable one. Pilkington realized that Devlin was right, but Devlin knew Pilkington would never admit it.

Devlin looked into Pilkington's foxhole of darkness with the curiosity of a marine biologist, trying to catalogue him into known strains. He was tall and thin, almost gaunt. He had an unremarkable face centered by a long, pointed nose. His graying hairstyle and lubricant were products of the 1950s. His suit and tie were funeral-home gray. As he contemplated Devlin's words, he sat erect, hands folded, like a minister who had given his blessing to a meal. In truth, his father had been a nondenominational minister, of limited success, in Omaha, Nebraska. As a result, Pilkington took a great deal of people's time boring them with his personal code of morality. He would not allow smoking, drinking, profanity, or sexual conversations in his presence, and his

ASACs, supervisors, and aspiring agents carefully observed those taboos.

The phone rang. Pilkington pushed the button for the speakerphone, leaned back in his chair and answered, "Yes."

"Hello, boss." It was Fauber. "It looks like Chicago screwed this one up. The subject turned himself in to local authorities in Chicago three days ago and was released on bond. Chicago never notified us."

"How do you know all of this, John?"

"He just finished telling me."

"Have you verified this with Chicago?"

"Ah—no, sir, but I will immediately."

"Where is the subject now, John?" "John" was now being used to poke Fauber in the chest.

"We let him go back to his apartment."

"Go and get him. Hold on to him. Verify his status." The three commands came with the agonizing patience of a parent teaching his child how to tie his shoes. "Are you on your car phone, *John*?"

"Yes, sir, we're right outside the subject's apartment."

"Fine, *John*. I'll hold while you round him up. And *John*, he'd better be there."

"Yes, sir."

Pilkington waited, outwardly calm, but Devlin knew he wanted that news conference. Instead of his usual in-office following, he could anesthetize an entire state.

"Boss, I'm sorry. He's gone. Out the back door. I told these idiots to watch him." Devlin knew it was a lie. First he blamed the Chicago agents and then his own. "What do you want us to do?"

Pilkington deliberately hesitated. He knew Fauber's blood pressure was heading north. Finally, thinking himself compassionate, he said, "John, I want you to come and see me first thing Monday."

"Boss, I have to come back to the office now anyway. I could—" Fauber pleaded.

"I don't want to see you until Monday, *John*." Pilkington leaned back contentedly, looking spent, as if he wanted to light an after-sex cigarette. Devlin wondered if he had ever smoked or for that matter, had had sex outside the office.

"Yes, sir," Fauber said with the enthusiasm of a person who had just been diagnosed as terminally ill.

Have a nice weekend, *John*, thought Devlin. But he knew come Monday, Fauber would perform the necessary amount of groveling to reenter Pilkington's good graces and it would be business as usual.

As though the thought had caused a disturbance in Pilkington's body, he sprang into an upright position. "Mike, how about the fugitive you arrested? Anything newsworthy there?"

The hypocrisy of management, which was exceeded only by its selfishness, never ceased to amaze Devlin. For the second time in twelve hours Pilkington had tried to punish him for the convenience of one of his supervisors, and now, as if the two were unrelated, he was asking Devlin to feed the piranha of his ego.

"Well, I don't know. The case originates in Omaha." Devlin knew Pilkington's hometown would get his attention. "The subject, who describes himself as a minister, and a group of about ten others, set up a church called 'The Assembly of Noah's Ark.' They would get members to donate animals, and then the minister and the elders would have sex with the animals."

Pilkington stiffened. "No, I don't think that's what the media are looking for."

"Say, aren't you from Omaha? Maybe you know this guy."

"I seriously doubt it, Agent Devlin."

Devlin walked out whistling "Talk to the Animals,"

knowing the embarrassed SAC would never check his story.

After lodging Washington at DPD's lockup, Devlin and Livingston stood on the front stairs of the headquarters building and watched the night's activity on the street. Devlin said, "It isn't New England."

"It is different."

"Have you had enough, or would you like to boldly go where no Viking has gone before?"

"Well, we do have a certain penchant for exploring."

"Penchant? If you use that word in Detroit, people will think you're retired. Never mind. I'm going to take you to a place that most Detroiters don't know exists."

||| CHAPTER 5 |||

The Tomfoolery was one of those downtown bars that attracted people who were between mistakes in their lives, people who needed the comfort of being alone in a crowd. They never planned to go there, but when their five-o'clock options were quickly dissolving, it was a safe bet.

Plenty of Kelly green formica, medium-stained oak, and shiny lacquered brass. The mirrors were all positioned so the customers could not watch themselves. The men wore gold necklaces under their shirts like disguised superheroes and ordered white wine by the glass. The women carried leather briefcases containing unread *Wall Street Journal*s and petrified condoms, smoked unfiltered cigarettes, and drank scotch or bourbon on the rocks. Sensitive men and decisive women.

Fauber had ordered four of his Jedi to accompany him to the bar. After his *careerus interruptus* phone call to Pilkington, he felt a racking need to surround himself with his most loyal men, to absorb the ambiance found only at the Tomfoolery.

Leading the *Star Wars* quintet, Duncan Moorehead held the door open for Fauber. Yoda positioned himself against a back wall and waited for the glow of the Formica People to soothe him. Moorehead appeared before him and handed him his favorite drink—a fuzzy navel. None of that white wine for a decision maker like him. Moorehead paid for the drinks and would continue to do so the entire evening. He appeared to be drinking the same drink, but since he ordered the drinks, only he and the bartender knew his drink had very little alcohol in it. His logic was simple: he could drink with Fauber all night and stay sober, keeping his judgment and memory intact in case an error on Fauber's part presented an advantage to him. The cost was irrelevant. Moorehead would blue-slip all the costs of the evening as some disguised expense relative to the case. Supervisors approved all blue slips, so—the Bureau was buying.

After two hours of drinking and homage by the Jedi, Yoda was feeling a warm, dreamy relaxation. His face started showing red splotches caused by the alcohol. "Duncan," he overenunciated to compensate for his now-fuzzy tongue, "do you think my ears are too big?"

Moorehead looked at him sincerely and said, "Were Clark Gable's too big?"

Silently Fauber congratulated himself on being such an astute judge of people and recognizing someone as full of promise as Moorehead. Like flowers seeking the sun, the creases in Fauber's forehead reached for the fluorescent ceiling. He no longer feared Monday.

Through the near east side of Detroit, Livingston followed Devlin closely. He had no idea where they were going. Devlin turned down a one-way street the wrong way, drove for a block, and pulled to the curb. Livingston parked behind him. Both men got out, and Livingston tried to figure out where they were. The entire neighborhood was residential except for the building on the corner where they had parked. The structure was a combination of apartments and a store on the first floor. Livingston guessed it had been either a grocery store or a dry cleaner's. The entire building was boarded up and painted a dark brown that caused it to fade into the urban night.

"Where are we going?"

Improbably, Devlin swept his hand back and indicated the brown building. "But first, we'd better protect the cars." Livingston had been so intent on not losing Devlin during the drive that he had not noticed the neighborhood. Although there were more than ten thousand abandoned buildings in Detroit, this street seemed to have more than its share. Semistripped cars rested on steel milk crates. Metal bars and bright security lamps accented the houses that lingered.

Devlin picked up a fast food napkin and wrote on it with a black marker: DON'T ROB CAR—PIGS WATCHING. He put it under the windshield wiper so the printing could easily be seen.

"Think that'll work?" Devlin asked.

"If the thieves can read."

"Congratulations, Edgar. You're becoming a real cynic."

Devlin knocked lightly on the door of the boarded-up store. The door opened a foot, and a huge brown face looked first at Devlin and then Livingston. "Hello, Mr. Devlin, how are you?" the face asked.

"I'm fine, Julius, how you feeling?"

"Fine. Is this gentleman with you?"

Devlin smiled. "So far, Julius. So far."

Julius opened the door, revealing the rest of his gigantic body. Devlin shook hands with him. "This is Edgar Livingston. We work together."

"How do you do, Mr. Livingston." The two shook hands. "Are you gentlemen carrying?"

"Always," Devlin answered for both men.

"Sorry. You'll have to check them."

Livingston was confused. In training school, he had been taught to never give up his gun. Here they were, in the middle of a tough Detroit neighborhood, and Devlin was peeling off his ankle holster and giving it to what looked like a hatcheck girl. He decided that Devlin knew best and did the same. The girl gave him a blue plastic claim disc with a white number thirty-eight on it. He wondered if he was the thirty-eighth person to check his gun that night. As Julius turned his back to open a second door, Livingston saw the familiar outline of a large-frame revolver through his suit coat. Livingston followed Devlin through the door.

The room opened into a cavernous nightclub. Livingston estimated that there were at least two hundred people sitting at tables watching the entertainment, drinking and enjoying themselves. Four older black men in casual attire were on the stage performing an old Four Tops song, "I Can't Help Myself."

Devlin and Livingston sat at the bar and watched the entertainers. Livingston tapped the bar rhythmically with both hands. "They're really good. Looks like the Four Tops might have some competition."

Devlin laughed. "Those *are* the Four Tops."

Livingston thought he was kidding. He watched the group closely. It *was* the Four Tops. Livingston was astonished. "What is this place?"

"It's a blind pig."

"Blind pig?"

"An after-hours joint. You know, no liquor license. Or any other kind of license. There's a hundred of them in the city. Most of them are for gambling, but this place is actually a nightclub—an illegal nightclub, but no dope, gambling, hookers, or guns are allowed."

"So the cops don't know about this place?"

"Oh, they know about it. I recognize at least three of them in here."

"They must spend a fortune on entertainment, if they have groups like the Four Tops."

"No, actually they all perform free of charge. Anyone

can perform, but they had better be good. This is a tough audience."

"I don't understand. Why free?"

"Ed, you have to understand Detroit—the city of the People Mover, the People's Bank, the People's Community this or that. No social barriers or even borders allowed. There's barely enough rules to prevent chaos, and sometimes they fail. Anyone with the price of admission can go anywhere and be as big a pain in the ass as they want and no one is going to stop them, because if they do, lawsuits for discrimination are as predictable as their lawyer's ethics. And then who is on the jury in these civil trials? The *people*."

"Let's hear it for the lawyers."

"The oldest profession."

The Four Tops finished the song and everyone applauded wildly.

Devlin said, "This place doesn't worry about being accused of discrimination or any other excuse for not following the rules. It's concerned only with its customers' deserved enjoyment. If someone doesn't act right, they're not allowed in here. It's that simple."

"Who decides what's right?"

"Big Julius."

"Whoa! It works for me."

"It works for everyone. That's why the entertainers work for free. They love to entertain, and the crowd appreciates them. It's something out of the past. There's probably not another place like this in the country."

"What's it called?"

"The Knock Knock Club. I guess because you have to knock to get in. Actually, the doorman has to know you. It's been here over thirty-five years. A lot of the Motown groups used to come here when they were starting out and sing for their supper. When they're in town, they'll come back as an ongoing thank-you to the owner."

"How do you know Julius?"

"Actually, I know the owner. I guess it was twelve years ago. A major heroin dealer named Buck Tom came here one night and liked it so much, he decided he should own it. He offered the owner peanuts. He said no. Buck Tom, having the gangster mentality, kidnapped the owner's daughter. She was only twelve. The Bureau got involved; I got the case and met Scrapiron Jemison."

"Was the girl okay?"

"You tell me," Devlin said, nodding at the young woman walking toward them.

Sydney Jemison's beauty would always be one of Devlin's treasures—something, a dozen years earlier, he had helped preserve. Because her mother was Australian, hence Sydney, her skin was bright and lush, like creamy porcelain. Her features gave only an exotic hint of her father's race. Her hair was medium brown and wavy. Like her mother, she was medium height with a willowy frame that was amply female. She hugged Devlin.

"Are you in trouble again, Mike?"

"Me? In trouble? Why would you think that?"

"The only time I see you anymore is when you're in trouble. The last time I think you were being sent to Seattle. You came in here and annihilated our Irish whiskey supply."

Devlin nodded toward Livingston. "Sydney, this is Ed Livingston." Her hand glided to him. He took it and held it.

"Hi."

"Hi."

"Ed's my new partner."

She took her hand back and said, "Since when do you work with a partner?"

"Hey, it wasn't my idea. I was ordered to," Devlin joked.

"Ordered to? Now you're going to tell me you follow orders. If you followed orders I'd still be in the trunk of Buck Tom's car." She pinched him affectionately on the arm.

"Speaking of orders, I'd like to order a drink."

"I'll have to go in the back. This isn't an Irish whiskey crowd."

Devlin considered Sydney's words. He decided he did come here when he was in trouble. Seeing Sydney again gave him reassurance. Reassurance that somewhere out there a grand plan did exist. He looked at Livingston, who was watching the door Sydney had disappeared through. "I guess you like."

"Are you kidding? Who wouldn't? I think I saw something in your eyes too."

"Yeah. You did."

Sydney walked back in and twisted the top off the Bushmill's bottle, breaking the tax stamp. "How about you, Ed, can I get you something?" she asked when she had finished pouring four ounces of the raw whiskey into an iceless glass.

"I'll have a beer, please."

Not knowing whether he could or not, Devlin said to Sydney, "Ed loves to dance."

She opened a bottle of beer, poured it into a glass, and placed it on a napkin.

"I don't get a napkin?" Devlin asked.

"You don't dance." She walked around the end of the bar and took Livingston's hand to lead him to the dance floor.

Devlin watched them for a moment and listened to the music and the colliding sounds of everyone enjoying themselves. He turned his attention to the Irishman's dance partner—whiskey.

Oblivious to everything, Sydney and Livingston danced until she whispered, "Hey, I got to get back to work."

"Sure. I'm sorry."

"I'll see you in a little bit." She disappeared again through the door behind the bar.

Livingston walked back to the bar and noticed the whiskey bottle was one-third empty. "Do you drink fast, or were we out there for a while?"

"Check your beer." It was flat. Livingston ordered a fresh one from a bartender who was not much smaller than Julius. He turned to Devlin. "Thanks, Mike. Today has had a lot of firsts in it."

Devlin held up his glass. "To beginnings."

"To beginnings," Livingston repeated.

For Livingston, things he had waited for and wondered about had peacefully marched by, leaving a delicious hunger. The anxiety of defeat no longer existed. He now had the privilege of fearlessness.

Devlin had toasted a different beginning, or maybe it was an ending. Were his days of hunting fugitives and bank robbers over? He had seen it happen to other agents. They were dumped into various office burial sites: wiretaps, night shifts, road trips, any other place where they could be left unattended and not further injure themselves or, more important, not injure the rungs higher up the ladder. Because not much was expected, the burial grounds soon became comfortable and the agents were never heard from again. Devlin drained his glass and vowed never to succumb to burial.

"Special Agent Devlin, as I live and breathe." Devlin turned around to find a thickly constructed black man slapping him on the back.

"Scrapiron!" They shook hands. "Scrapiron Jemison, this is my new partner, Edgar Livingston."

"How do you do, sir," Livingston answered formally. After shaking his hand, he had an idea about the nickname. Scrapiron was medium height and built like a bank safe, no neck or waist. His smooth, dark brown skin was drawn tightly against his jawbone. His energetic eyes searched Livingston's face longer than a casual introduction would necessitate. Livingston assumed Jemison had seen Sydney and him dancing. "How you doing, Edgar?"

The club piano started playing one of those piano bar songs that had no beginning or end.

"Mike, how do you like my new piano player? I have him play when no one wants to get up."

"If you need a musical opinion, you'll have to ask Ed. He majored in it in college."

Jemison looked at Livingston and waited for his answer.

"Well." The answer came cautiously. "He does seem to be dying out there."

Winking at Devlin, Jemison said to Livingston, "Maybe you could do better."

Livingston wondered if more than his musical talents were being scrutinized. Flashing a smile, he said, "I'll give it a try."

Jemison signaled the piano player to take a break. Livingston sat down at the piano and decided that some Scott Joplin songs might show off his skills and his sense of history. He started playing "The Entertainer."

When finished, he was surprised that he received no more applause than the club piano player. He wondered if there was some sort of Detroit aversion to Scott Joplin.

Sydney walked up on the stage, took a microphone from its stand, and sat down next to Livingston. "Do you know 'It Takes Two'?"

Livingston knew all the Motown hits. Marvin Gaye was one of his favorites. "It Takes Two" was a duet Gaye sang with Kim Weston. He started the song on the keyboard.

When they got to the chorus, Livingston looked out at the club and was delighted to see the customers clapping rhythmically and dancing next to their tables.

When they finished, the applause was enthusiastic and

the people continued it to force them to take a bow. Livingston knew most of it was for Sydney and her gifted voice, but he did not care because her father, standing next to Devlin, was smiling his approval.

The crowd wanted more, but Sydney, with a shrug of her shoulders, indicated she had to get back to work.

By the time Livingston got back to the bar, Scrapiron had disappeared and Devlin had turned his appreciation back to the Bushmill's.

"Not bad, rookie," Devlin smiled.

"Thanks. Where did Mr. Jemison go?"

"He had a phone call."

"Did he say anything about me?"

"He said you had bad taste."

"Yeah, I guess I shouldn't have played that Joplin piece."

"No, he meant working with me."

Livingston smiled, but Devlin did not. "Ed, you're already on Fauber's wrong side for that stunt we pulled tonight. When he finds out Monday that I wasn't given the death penalty, he's going to be looking to get a piece of you."

"You've survived him."

"Have I? I'm gone for at least thirty days. Fauber will try to make it permanent, and I've been around here for a while. You're brand new; you're still on probation. Within the first year, they can fire you on a whim."

"What can I do?"

"The best thing?"

"Yes."

"Stay away from me."

"I won't."

Livingston delivered his refusal with such finality that Devlin offered a compromise. "Okay, but let's keep it behind closed doors. You bring me your cases, and I'll try to steer you in the right direction. And don't tell anyone in the office. There is no one worse at keeping a secret than an FBI agent. Okay?"

"Yes, mighty Thor, god of thunder."

"That's it. I've tried to ignore this Viking stuff. Didn't you see *Roots*?"

In a patient voice that was answering the question for the hundredth time, Livingston said, "I actually descended from Viking royalty. I have traced *my* roots." Anticipating that Devlin would have the usual doubts, he added, "I have charts in my apartment to verify it."

Sensing Livingston's defensiveness, Devlin decided not to question the lineage further. "Do I call you 'your highness' or 'Prince Livingston' or what?"

With feigned condescension Livingston said, "You may call me Ed."

Devlin poured whiskey into his glass. "Why me, Odin?"

The piano played another anonymous song.

"Mike, I wanted to ask you about tonight, in the Duffield. When we were backing out of the bar and you said, 'The Secret Service doesn't bluff,' what was that all about?"

"If one of those lowlifes wanted to call in a complaint about federal agents throwing hand grenades in crowded bars, they'd call the Secret Service."

Livingston laughed and then, more serious, asked, "Were you scared in there?"

"Yeah. I was scared Washington was wearing a clip-on tie." Devlin held up his glass. "To the Secret Service."

Daily, Knox Devlin would rise at 5:30 and head for the basement, where she would practice her rowing in "dry dock" on a machine. On occasional Saturdays she was able to sneak out of the house, leaving her family to their own "decadent" schedules, and row single sculls among the high school athletes at the boat club. It was, as she put it, her only recollection of her previous life—her life before she had met and married Mike Devlin. Although their daughter, Kathleen, was already ten and their son, Patrick, eight, the rowing kept her unmistakably feminine figure lean and strong.

However, this morning, sensing her husband's absence, she unwillingly woke up a half hour earlier. Defensively, as is a mother's duty, she thought of her children and then remembered they were spending a couple of weeks in Chicago with her parents.

Her parents were Professor and Mrs. Lawrence Hughes. The University of Chicago mathematics professor and his wife had not been as enthralled as their daughter when she had met the unconventional son of an Irish bricklayer. Devlin had been working summers as a Lake Michigan lifeguard when he pulled her out of a raging northeaster after her scull had overturned. The Canadian wind traveled 270 miles and could, in a matter of minutes, turn frictionless glass into huge broken wedges of rolling blue-green concrete. The old sailors said the storms were God's reminder of who was really in charge. When Devlin's forceful hands had lifted Knox from the threat around her, she felt a reckless strength in him. There was a danger about him, and she became hypnotized by it, knowing she would never be afraid when she was with him. Although she was soaked and wearing the blue tinge that the lake could coat its victims with so quickly, he knew she was the most beautiful thing he would ever see.

He had just graduated from a small college in southern Illinois, and she was a junior at the University of Chicago, on her way, her parents thought, to a Ph.D. in history.

After that day, the only thing that would separate them was Knox's return to her senior year and Devlin's commission in the U.S. Marine Corps. Without telling her parents, they planned to marry after Knox had graduated. Devlin was reluctant to make plans any more specific, because he knew a commission in the Marines had only one address—WESTPAC. Probably the only time in the Corps's history that it allowed itself the use of a euphemism, it stood for Western Pacific Command—Vietnam.

That first separation had altered their timetable. Devlin finished his Basic School training after three months in Quantico and returned to Chicago for thirty days' leave before heading overseas. Knox Hughes and Second Lieutenant Devlin were married his first night home.

Knox graduated and waited for her husband to come home. Her parents joined the agonizing vigil and soon realized, through Devlin's long letters, that their son-in-law was, after all, worthy of their daughter. With newsreel clarity, the letters brought images of *his* men, mostly eighteen- and nineteen-year-olds, called on to perform daily miracles under hopeless conditions. And they succeeded, almost as if they did not realize that their bootprints had been left on the impossible. Their spirit was untrained in defeat. They would, Devlin wrote, keep America's future.

Three years later, Knox's parents could only give their bewildered okay when Devlin announced that he had accepted an appointment to the FBI and they were being sent to Detroit.

Knox's Vietnam experience had left her husband somehow invulnerable in her eyes. Anyway, invulnerably was the only way she could sanely send him daily to do the kind of work he did. So she did not allow herself to worry when he was out all night. He was either working or, if in trouble, drinking. Either way, he would not bother her with a call, because Vietnam had taught them both that a phone ringing in the middle of the night was never good news.

If he had been drinking, she knew what his priorities would be when he got home. The thought of it pounded through her heart. She pulled off her white cotton nightgown and searched her dresser for anything more romantic. Finding something barely black, she hurried to the shower.

As she was finishing, the shower door slid open. It was Devlin. He looked at her. Her durable beauty still distracted him. Her dripping black silk hair and those damn dark blue eyes. She was as fresh as the day he had pulled her out of that angry lake.

"Anyone call for a lifeguard?" he asked.

"Well, well, well. If it isn't the Chicago alley cat." She tried to manufacture coolness to heighten what she knew would be the unpreventable ending to their little drama.

Devlin looked between her breasts and watched her heart beat. He timed it against his own and knew she was becoming aroused. "What's wrong with a little alley cat once in a while?"

With the heat rising between them, she knew this would be her last parry. "They're dirty."

Without hesitation, Devlin stepped into the shower; the water darkened his suit. As if a vacuum existed between their mouths, their lips knotted in a violent crush. She tasted the Irish whiskey and knew there was trouble at work. The last time had been the night, or more accurately morning, he had been ordered to Seattle. She would not ask until they had slept, whenever that might be. He took off his sticky jacket as she impatiently tried to solve the knot of his wet silk tie.

His mouth was now biting at her neck. As it slid down past her collarbone, Knox's head shot back as if her very core had been struck by lightning.

Devlin looked into the blueness that poured from her eyes. "Do you know the funny thing about alley cats?"

Her "no" came breathlessly.

"They only attract their own."

"Yes," she pleaded.

He picked her up and carried her to their bedroom, leaving a trail wet with clothing.

Knox did not know if she was dreaming. Her heart seemed to be pounding irregularly as her consciousness struggled to surface through the euphoric haze that had lowered her into a vaporizing sleep.

She looked at the clock and, because it read noon, realized she was now awake. Knox put on her husband's robe and followed the unsteady rhythm to the garage.

Inside, Devlin's fists, wrapped in elastic bandages and light boxing gloves, dug unceasingly into a heavy punching bag. The vicious attack on the helpless object verified Knox's suspicions that her husband was again jeopardizing his job for the sake of uncompromised principles.

Shirtless, he wove around the black leather bag, aiming both hands low and high at imagined body parts. Tiny grunts ended with louder thuds. Sweat oiled his skin. He saw her as he circled his target and stopped. They exchanged an intimate smile. After a moment Devlin asked, "Is there something I can do for you?"

Knox considered the possibilities of her husband's offer and forced herself to control a rush as intense as the one she had felt in the shower. "I came out here to plead for the bag's life."

Devlin laughed. "It provoked me."

"How could a seventy-pound weakling provoke a stud like you?"

"By putting me on wiretap duty."

Knox was surprised to feel the anger rise within her. She knew how well he did his job and that his "reward" was simply for not playing the game. As Devlin took off the gloves, she could see blood on the elastic wrappings where he had split the skin over his knuckles. The intense workout had made his body look stronger, more alarming, reminding her of his dangerousness. And she knew, as always, there would be no retreat. "In that case, you'd better teach him a lesson."

He stared at her with that smile that turned up a corner of his mouth. She felt another shudder charge through her. He said, "I think I better teach *you* another lesson."

Devlin unwrapped his hands and pulled down the garage door from the inside. As the door closed slowly, the sunlight disappeared from the garage's interior. The last thing Devlin saw was his robe hitting the concrete floor.

III CHAPTER 6 III

The Lebanese desk clerk had been working at the Packard Motel for two weeks. Cultural differences aside, the most difficult part of the job was keeping the guests from abusing the rental rules. He had been instructed to keep the hookers from turning tricks in their rooms unless they paid the higher short-stay rate for each customer, and he was to make sure that no more people were in a room than had rented it.

Room 203 had been rented by a lone middle-aged white man. An hour later, a second man showed up and was quietly admitted to the room. The desk clerk decided if two men wanted to share the room, he was not going to worry about preferences. Fifteen minutes later two more men went into it. Enough was enough. The clerk picked up the phone to clear out the room. As he dialed, a fifth man started up the stairs and looked callously at the desk clerk through the bulletproof glass. The Arab felt an icy suffocation. He recognized the stare. He had seen it many times in Beirut. It was how the secret police identified themselves. He chose not to look at the last seven or so men who knocked at the door of Room 203.

Inside the room the agents sat waiting. It was an uncommon time, a time beyond the rules, a time of unencumbered action. Tonight they would be warriors. Their dark clothing bulged over bulletproof vests, reminding them that breaking and entering, whether authorized or not, was still dangerous. They sat reflectively, like troops waiting to parachute down to darkened enemy beaches.

The one exception to this desperate glow of camaraderie was Touchy Williams. The sixty-five-year-old man sat in the room's lone chair, aware only of the crossword puzzle he held in his eloquent hands. The long, unaged hands seemed to belong to someone half his age and twice his size. During his fifty-four years of committing burglaries, they were something he had been extremely proud of, as though they were his only child, a very gifted child.

What these men were about to do was described, at hushed levels, as a court-ordered break-in. For Touchy, it was still burglary. And when he did it, it kept his aging heart more regular than the world's finest pacemaker.

The night's target was the Bella Luna nightclub. Court-ordered bugs were to be installed. For years it had been a hangout and meeting place for local mafiosi.

The twelve agents were cramped in the small room. Touchy Williams sat comfortably in his chair with his legs carefully crossed so as not to injure the hard creases in his suit pants. Five of the agents sat on a lumpy, complaining bed. The rest sat on the floor along the walls.

It was two A.M., and the television channel was signing off with the national anthem. One of the agents did the patriotic thing: he stood up and turned the set off.

During the break-in, the other agents would perform their workman-type assignments. Devlin and Touchy Williams each had his own specialty. Devlin had discovered his in the Marine Corps. Williams had found his touch when he was eleven.

Jonathan Williams grew up in the downriver area of Detroit. In his neighborhood eleven-year-old burglars were not uncommon, but one who could bypass a lock was. As his prowess and reputation grew, so did his projects. In his prime, he was afforded the respect, and percentage, of a concert pianist.

In the days when major burglaries were an art form, Touchy Williams would wait safely outside the building until all barriers had been lowered by his criminal infantry. Then he would be taken to the safe. Once he had it opened, he would turn and leave, not concerning himself with the contents. Honor had also been part of the profession then. His services would have commanded a substantial flat fee for each campaign, but he always agreed to a percentage. It turned just another job into *a score*.

His favorite story, told only long after the statute of limitations had expired, was about a two-million-dollar burglary at a Chicago racetrack in the fifties. It was mob-sponsored. Touchy had been taken to Chicago in a private car aboard a passenger train. Picked up in a black limousine and taken to the roof of the racetrack, he was lowered on a rope chair through a large hole in the ceiling. Less than two hours later, he was pulled up through the hole and was headed back to Detroit in his private car before breakfast. His end was a quarter of a million dollars.

In the early 1980s, he started working with a group of young bank burglars. Their impatience and lack of professionalism worried Williams, but a man had to work. Their last job was a sleepy suburban bank that netted them just over a million dollars. Bureau informants identified the group. It was their eighth bank in three years. The cases were assigned to Bill Shanahan. Within a year the entire gang, minus Williams, was in prison.

Although Shanahan knew that Williams was the group's "box man," he had no evidence he could take to the prosecutor. Shanahan was instructed to interview Williams and, barring a confession, close the case.

Williams insisted that the interview be at a local bar. The

interview lasted four hours, during which both men became drunk and, liking each other, exchanged stories from his own side of the law. Shanahan physically applauded the racetrack score.

Suddenly somber, Williams asked, "Bill, are you going to arrest me?"

For the first time Shanahan realized his advantage. He paused for effect. "I'll make you a deal: you stop doing banks and I'll let you slide."

Williams ordered a round of drinks. "If there's ever anything?"

"You mean like if I lock myself out of my car?" Shanahan kidded.

Williams smiled politely and said, "I know you guys have to break into places occasionally. So if I can help—"

When the Bureau heard about Williams's offer, they were delighted. They could train agents to pick locks, but not even the best instructors in the world could bestow the touch.

Jack Hansen, the supervisor in charge of the break-in, finished a short briefing and, looking around the crowded room, asked for questions. There were none.

A coded radio on the table whispered that the last car had left the nightclub's parking lot. Hansen gave the order to move out. He was the last one to leave the room, ensuring that nothing was left behind except the key. No one would be back to check out.

Devlin rode in the backseat of a nondescript station wagon. Touchy Williams sat in the front. As soon as he made the front door lock, Devlin would enter the club alone. He would slip into the darkness of the building and search it before the others were allowed to enter.

They parked across Eight Mile Road in the shadow of an old printing company, about a hundred yards from the Bella

Luna. With a night scope, Devlin scanned the club and its parking lot. An unusual night fog sat low along the ground. It had a blue glow like smoke from burning wood, as if a secret fire seethed under the city's surface. The club seemed to be sitting on a cloud. Bella Luna indeed.

Other agents were half a mile away at the Bell box, the juncture of hundreds of phone lines including two that went from the club directly to the police department, which were activated when the club alarm was tripped.

When the alarm man went to the door, he would attempt to defeat the alarm before anyone worked on the lock. If the alarm was set off accidentally, the agents at the Bell box, who had already electronically blocked the two lines going to the police, would hold them up until all the agents had finished at the club. The lines would then be released, and when the officers responded, they would find nothing but an apparent false alarm.

Under a red-bulb flashlight Devlin studied a floor plan of the building. There were eleven rooms besides the main dining room. Three bathrooms, a kitchen, an office, two small storage rooms, the bar, an employees' room, a meeting room, and a locked room used for unknown purposes.

Devlin checked his equipment. A handheld radio with a scrambling capability hung on his belt. It had an earphone for privacy and a microphone the size of a pencil eraser that he clipped onto his shirt just below his chin. His Browning 9mm was completely encased in a special black nylon shoulder holster. He slipped an unauthorized blackjack into his back pocket and waited.

"C Nine-one-one to all units," Hansen said. "Looks like everyone is gone. C Nine-two-three, take your team in."

"On the way, One-one."

A dark van rolled up to the front door, stopped briefly, and pulled away. Devlin raised the night scope and watched the alarm man working on the door in the darker shadows. A second agent stood with his back to the door watching the street, his gun hand hidden behind his thigh. The alarm was the type that took a cylindrical key. The agent had what looked like an elaborate soldering gun that had a cylinder on the front. By pulling the trigger, the pins in the lock were moved, releasing the electrical shunt and turning off the alarm. The system was old and easy for the experienced agent. Within three minutes the small red light in the faceplate of the alarm went out. The covering agent spoke quietly into his chest: "The alarm's down."

Devlin's car was moving forward. Just ahead of them, the van pulled up to the front door and the two agents were gone. Williams went to work on the deadbolt. Devlin watched the street. He could not see any Bureau cars. He took it as a good sign. Their invisibility was an indication of how well they were doing their job.

A small voice spoke in Devlin's ear: "One-seven to all units, we have a roller nine bound on Eight Mile. Stand by." Devlin grabbed Williams, pulled him into the deeper shadows, and gave a one-word explanation: "Cops."

Both men watched as the scout car rolled by from the east, just as One-seven had reported. Another good sign. When the car disappeared, Williams turned back to the lock. Twenty more seconds and it was open.

In a low voice Devlin announced, "Four-one to all units—we're in."

As soon as Devlin closed the door, he heard the station wagon pick up Williams and drive away.

"Four-five to all units, we're in with no alarm. Repeat, no alarm," said the agent who was monitoring the lines at the Bell box.

To enhance his hearing, Devlin closed his eyes and opened his mouth slightly. It was a technique the Marines had taught him in Staging Battalion, that month in the hills of California used to make the final mental adjustments before the thirteen-month Vietnam tour began. The days were spent impatiently waiting to get to the war and its glories, and the nights, secretly praying that the war would end before those thirty days were up.

Devlin heard nothing except his echoing heart. He opened his eyes and waited for them to adjust to the darkness. He could no longer hear his slowing pulse. His unusual eyes gathered twice as much light as an average individual's, allowing him to see almost as well in the dark as in daylight. He had discovered his rare night vision in those raven black hills of California. In Vietnam, his vision had been a great weapon against the night, which was more feared than all of North Vietnam's regiments.

Because of his talent, he was ordered to be the lone surveyor on each Detroit break-in. Actually, no one else wanted to do it, which made it that much more appealing to Devlin. It could be dangerous and frightening. It was one of the few things left that took his breath away.

The interior of the club lightened. Devlin took off his shoes and because of his advantage glided from room to room quickly. He ticked off the floor plan in his head. No one else was there. He had gone full circle and was back at the front door. He keyed the mike: "Four-one to One-one, we're clear inside."

By 5:30 A.M. the Bella Luna again sat quietly on its cloud. Its intruders had gone.

Within the Detroit FBI Office existed a maze of rooms that could be entered through only one door, which was marked anonymously with a cipher lock. Only a handful of agents knew the combination. The innermost room was the tech room, where monitoring equipment for wiretaps was set up. Against the walls, tape recorders sat in booths, awaiting enemy voices.

It was seven A.M., and Devlin sat slumped in a chair in front of one of the tape recorders, dozing. After two A.M., when the club closed, there was little for the monitoring agent to do but sleep. Because he was not regularly assigned to the Organized Crime Squad, Devlin was not granted insider's rights and had been put on the midnight shift. In the three days since the installation of the bugs, not one criminal conversation had been recorded.

Earphones sat crookedly on his head, one side pulled behind his ear so he could hear noises around him, the other on his ear so he would wake up if anyone should reenter the club.

Through his uncovered ear he heard the hard, springy clicks of the combination being typed into the outer door lock. Edgar Livingston walked in with two cups of coffee. "How are the Italians treating you?"

Devlin gulped a mouthful of the hot black liquid and said, "I used to worry about the caliber of agents we were hiring in the 'New Bureau,' but after listening to the young, second-generation mafiosi, I feel better. Evidently the Mob recruiting board has lowered its standards too. These guys are exactly what their parents deserve: worthless daddy's boys, who would be a joke if it wasn't for their last names." Devlin's eyes set in deep resolve. "Ed, I want you to remember a name for as long as you're here—Joseph Pantatelli, Joey Pants. His old man is Anthony Pantatelli, a lieutenant with the outfit, gambling, extortion, drugs. He's Don Scantina's right hand. Very, very dangerous. Listen to son Joey, the sunshine of his life."

Devlin pushed a tape cassette into a handheld player. After a couple of seconds of electronic crackling, a phone rang and a little girls' voice answered, "Hello, Pierce residence, Amy speaking."

The slightly frenzied voice of Joe Pants said, "Hi, Amy, are your mom and dad home?"

"Yes, they're outside. Should I go get them?"

"In a minute. I want to see how you are doing. How was school today?"

"Fine. Thank you."

"What grade are you in now?"

"First."

"Oh yeah, that's right. What did you wear to school today?"

"My blue dress."

"Oh, how nice. What color shoes did you wear?"

"My white gym shoes."

"I'll bet they looked nice."

"Yes."

"And what color were your panties?"

"Ah, I think pink."

Pantatelli's voice became more breathless. "Oh, you're not sure. Do you still have them on?"

"Yes."

His voice came quicker. "Well, pull up your dress and look at them."

A man's voice was suddenly heard in the background: "Amy, who's on the phone?"

"It's for you, Daddy."

"Hello," the father said to a dead line.

Devlin turned the tape player off. Almost imperceptibly, the dragon stirred.

"That dirty son of a bitch!" said Livingston. "Are we going to get him?"

"Ed, when you watch all of this for a few years, you'll come to realize that if things are left alone, sooner or later justice will prevail." Livingston's stare questioned Devlin's apparent apathy. Before Livingston could ask, Devlin changed the subject. "What have you been doing?"

"Fauber assigned me an old bank robbery." Livingston's confusion was obvious.

"And?"

"And. I don't know what to do. I thought I had it solved, but I don't know."

Now Devlin looked confused. "Let me back up," Livingston said. "The problem started with the Bureau calling Fauber and telling him the bank robbery solution rate in Detroit was down twelve percent. Scared his beloved Bureau might think him a failure, he panics and has all the unsolved robbery photographs run in the paper. We get two calls on the same guy on my robbery. Here, take a look." Livingston handed Devlin the bank robbery surveillance photo and mug shot of the suspect.

Devlin compared the photos. "The surveillance photo isn't very clear. I suppose it could be the same guy. What has he been arrested for?"

"He's got arrests for B and E, drugs, and right now he's out on bond for robbery and assault."

"Sounds like a good candidate."

"That's what I thought. So I went to the bank and showed the victim teller a photo spread and she tentatively picks out my suspect. Since the robbery is a year and a half old, I'm happy to get any kind of an ID. I tell Fauber about it, and he gets all excited and tells me to call the United States attorney and get a warrant. Here's where it starts getting complicated. The assistant United States attorney says because the case is shaky he'll call the local prosecutor on the assault and robbery case and see how good his case is, because if he's going to do a lot of state time there's no need to prosecute him federally since the federal judge would probably give him a sentence to be served concurrently with his state sentence. Yesterday morning, he calls me back. He and the local prosecutor and the suspect's attorney have it all worked out. The guy has agreed to plead guilty to unarmed bank robbery with a seven-year maximum sentence. I'm happy. I tell Fauber; he's happy. Then yesterday afternoon, I'm writing everything up, and I see that eighteen months ago he did three months in the county jail for one of the B and Es. At the time of the bank robbery, he was locked up in the Wayne County Jail. I verified it with Wayne County. I called the assistant United States attorney, and at first he's telling me don't worry about it. When I press him, he tells me that although this guy may not have committed this robbery, it's best for everyone. The suspect wants to go to federal prison rather than state prison. His court-appointed attorney will get his fee without a trial. The state prosecutor will get a conviction and a concurrent sentence, and the state does not have to pay for the incarceration. The assistant United States attorney will get a conviction without the anxiety and work of a trial. I'll get credit for solving the bank robbery, and Fauber's solution rate goes up."

Devlin wanted to test Livingston. "If everybody is happy, what's the problem?"

Livingston searched the circumstances and then said, "I guess *I'm* not happy?"

"Why?"

"Because it just isn't right. Is it?"

"When I went through training school, there was this Constitutional Law instructor named Charlie Donlan. He was one of those people who could explain anything. One day, almost at the end of training, someone asks him if we should write our reports to favor prosecution. I'll never forget what he said: 'There will be times when the answer will lie at the end of a maze so complicated by the law and circumstances that if we try to guess the next turn, we will be lost forever. No. We simply report what we have seen, clearly, honestly, without regard for the consequence. We are witnesses of the truth. It is our foremost priority. Truth is a splendid, wild stallion whose presence will give us unparalleled strength. If we try to saddle it with our own purpose, its power and satisfaction will never ride our way again.'"

Livingston sipped his coffee, understanding the responsibility of the tool that had been handed to him. He also considered its weight. "How do I break up this conspiracy of convenience?"

"One sentence to the assistant United States attorney: 'If you don't dismiss the charges against this man, I will inform the chief judge.' They're afraid of the judges. That'll be the end of it."

"Any idea what I should tell Fauber?"

"Tell him the truth. The assistant United States attorney found out about the suspect being in jail at the time of the robbery and decided to keep it out of the courts. Charlie Donlan never said anything about letting that horse stomp you to death."

Without another word, the two men finished their coffee. As Livingston started to leave, Devlin asked, "Have you heard anything about Tom Anderson's daughter?" Livingston looked at him, surprised that Devlin knew about the problem. "I overheard Anderson and Fauber talking the other day."

"Anderson went to Fauber again this morning. He begged him to do something. Fauber didn't want to, but because Anderson is one of his boys, he knows he has to act concerned. So he goes to Pilkington and gets half a dozen extra agents for a day to run out the routine leads: canvass the neighborhood, interview the boyfriend and acquaintances. Basically just covering his tail. I guess she's run away before."

Devlin thought about Tom Anderson and wondered why they were no longer friends. Years ago they had been alike, maybe too much alike, constantly competing with each other to arrest the most fugitives, the most dangerous fugitives. Friends, but competitors first. Only when they had found themselves, out of necessity, side by side, kicking in the same menacing door, would they expose, in the wake of an adrenaline rush, their friendship. Once a year, at the insistence of his first wife, Anderson would host a squad barbecue, during which he and Devlin would abandon the games of the Bureau and act like the friends that they really were.

Devlin recalled the last time he had been to their home. Anderson's tiny daughter ambled into the room, and her father's face was flooded with undiverted worship. Devlin never forgot it. The moment helped him to understand Anderson, a man who put a great deal of energy into his work and into loving his family.

His daughter's beauty captured everyone's breath in the room. Any one of them would have been proud to have had her attention.

Unabashed, little Vanessa walked directly to Devlin and asked, "Do you have a little girl?"

Devlin picked her up, put her on his lap, and said, "I do now." She gave him an unsolicited hug and then struggled to explain her ABCs. She finished stealing his heart when she wrapped her hand around his finger and pulled him to the basement to share her greatest treasure—her new puppy sleeping in his cardboard "house." She held her abbreviated finger to her lips, indicating the dog needed quiet.

Shortly after Anderson remarried he got in the management program and now seemed interested only in being promoted to supervisor. He was the oldest, and probably the most unlikely, Jedi.

"Do you know his daughter?" Livingston asked.

"A long time ago. When her mother was alive."

"How'd she die?"

"Cerebral hemorrhage. It was tragic. She was a hell of a gal."

"What's his new wife like?"

"I don't know; I've never met her."

"I've got to get going. Fauber's having a briefing two minutes ago."

As Livingston left, the tape recorders snapped on, indicating that someone had picked up the phone at the residence of Anthony Pantatelli. Devlin put on the earphones. It was old man Pants himself. He dialed a local number. After two rings a middle-aged male answered, "Hello."

"Tommy, did I wake you?"

"Ah, Tony, no. I guess not. What's up?"

"Did you get out and see that guy last night?"

"Yeah. Lou and I leaned on him real good. He was shaking like a motherfucker when we left." Devlin made the appropriate entry in the wiretap log, noting the telephone number called, the time, and the footage on the tape recorder's counter. Then, in the block marked "Type of Call," he marked a "V" for a violation call. It sounded as though the men were discussing collection of a loan-sharking or gambling debt.

"Good. I'll have Julio call him today and offer him twenty thousand for the list. How much does he owe you?"

"A couple of hundred less than twenty K." Devlin suddenly became curious as to what list could possibly be worth $20,000.

"Tony, let me ask you, what are you going to do with a list of the FBI's snitches?"

Anthony Pantatelli exploded: "I should kill you, you *stupid* motherfucker." Tony Pants slammed the phone down.

Even though Bill Shanahan had alerted him about the possibility of a leak, Devlin could not believe what he had heard. A list of FBI informants: it would be catastrophic.

Devlin rewound the tape and played it again. Because of Pantatelli's well-known reluctance to discuss details on the telephone, the abrupt, violent ending to the conversation seemed to validate the existence of the list.

Devlin knew if this call was reported to Pilkington, his main investigative thrust would be to prove that there was no such list. Devlin thought about his own informants. He would not leave their future in the hands of the SAC and those who would be like him.

As if the air was thick with reason, he drew it deep into his lungs, holding it long, as though he expected a narcotic effect to take command of the impulse that throbbed inside him. Slowly, reluctantly, Devlin let the air escape. He knew he had no more control over it than he did over what he was about to do.

First, he rewrote the wiretap log and noted Pantatelli's call as personal. That way the case agent would not review it for weeks because the priority was always to review violation calls first. Then, in hopes of finding other clues, Devlin reviewed all the logs. He found nothing until his eyes fell on the entry noting Joey Pants's obscene phone call. Because other sources were picking up rumors of the list and Joey worked with his father, it was reasonable to assume that Joey Pantatelli would also have knowledge of the list. He would be Devlin's target.

Devlin turned off the pen register. It was connected to the telephone lines and automatically printed out numbers of all outgoing calls on the tapped phone. Attached to it was a large reel-to-reel tape recorder that automatically activated as soon as the tapped phone was taken off the hook. By turning off the pen register, the entire system was deactivated. Any calls on that line would not be recorded. And Devlin did not want the next call recorded.

Devlin dialed one of Joey Pantatelli's home phones, the one that corresponded with the pen register he had just shut off. Devlin looked at his watch: 7:30 A.M. Pantatelli had been at the club when it closed at two A.M., so Devlin knew he would be home sleeping.

" 'Lo," a thick voice mumbled.

"Joey. How are you?"

"Who the fuck is this?" Pantatelli demanded, his voice gaining clarity.

"Joey, Joey. You've got to work on your telephone manners. You were much nicer to Amy Pierce yesterday."

"Who the fuck is Amy Pierce?"

"Let me refresh your memory." Devlin turned on his tape player.

As soon as Pantatelli recognized both voices, he hung up. Devlin quickly redialed. The phone was off the hook.

"Joey, Joey, Joey," Devlin said to the empty room. He leaned over and turned off the pen register for Pantatelli's other home phone and dialed it.

"Hello," Pantatelli answered cautiously.

"Hang up again, and the next time you hear that tape will be at your arraignment. Do you understand?"

"Yes. What do you want?" Devlin could hear the fear and confusion in his voice. Ironic, thought Devlin: Pantatelli was now the victim of the anonymity of the telephone.

"Tonight, ten o'clock, meet me on the third floor of the Whitney, at the bar. You'll find out then."

"Okay," Pantatelli answered obediently.

"And do yourself a lifetime favor and don't tell anyone about this. You do and I'll drop this tape off at police head-quarters. I know everything about you."

"Okay, but how will I know you?"

Devlin hung up and said, "Have a nice day."

III CHAPTER 7 III

At the turn of the century, lumber baron David Whitney built his Victorian mansion on fashionable Woodward Avenue. Its three-story exterior, constructed of fortress-thick pink stone, stood virtually unaffected by the swirling wreckage of time and events. In the mid-1980s, four million dollars transformed it into a three-star restaurant. Visually overwhelming, each room had been constructed to excess, with stained glass, hardwood paneling, hand-carved fireplaces as big and detailed as small European cathedrals. The structure's restoration was accomplished by patient artisans who understood the pink stone anachronism that stood blushing on Woodward Avenue.

The Whitney's third floor consisted of a dining room with a piano bar and several smaller rooms for overflow. In the main room customers listened to the piano, drank, and could order an eight-dollar hamburger.

Purposely arriving a half hour before Joey Pants, Devlin took a table in the back of the main room facing the door and watched the arriving customers to ensure Pants had heeded his come-alone warning.

Just before ten, Joseph Pantatelli arrived and took a seat at the bar. His head twisted nervously at every new voice or movement, making his short, fat body more animated than usual.

After ten minutes, Devlin felt confident that his appoint-

111

ment was alone. He sat down next to him at the bar. Pantatelli stared at him anxiously. "Hello, Joey."

"Hi." Pantatelli's answer was more of a physical reaction than a verbal response.

"Bring your drink." Devlin walked to one of the empty overflow rooms, and Pantatelli followed like a bloated puppy. The two men sat down at a small table. Devlin watched Pants squirm under his stare.

"Who are you, and what do you want?" Pantatelli asked with surprising politeness.

Devlin did not answer. He let his memory replay Pants's question. His tone bothered Devlin. He had listened to him for hours through the earphones. He knew the rhythm of his voice, his vocabulary, and his enunciation. His speech was now louder, more distinct, like it had been when he called little Amy Pierce.

Devlin stood up and snapped, "Get up!"

"I'm not going to take—"

"Get up," Devlin said calmly. Too calmly for Pantatelli; he had seen this muzzling of anger before. To Sicilians, it served as a warning, a precursor of overwhelming violence. Like most Sicilians, Pantatelli had learned it from his father. He stood up and, sensing what was coming next, he raised his arms to the sides. He did not know who Devlin was, but he knew he was dealing with a cop.

Devlin patted him down and found a microcassette tape recorder in his inside jacket pocket. It was the voice-activated type. "Joey, what am I going to do with you?" Devlin took it and slipped it into his own pocket.

"Who—who are you?"

"Mike Devlin," he said and showed his credentials—Pantatelli's five-foot-four frame seemed to shrink into the chair. He looked like a lost child, ready to cry.

With resignation he asked, "Why is the FBI busting my balls?"

"Ah. That sounds more like the Joey Pants I know."

"Come on, what do you want from me?"

"This is your lucky night. I'm going to let you work off your little problem."

"Oh, no. I ain't no fucking snitch."

"I've got a tape recording that says you are."

"Go ahead, give it to the police. It's only a misdemeanor."

"You misunderstand." Devlin had that dangerous calm in his voice again. "Do you think I'm some do-gooder spending all my time to right some wrong? You see the letters F-B-I and figure I have to live by some code. I'm not interested in legal justice; I'm interested in *farsi giustizia da sè*." Pantatelli knew the words—take the law into one's own hands. Devlin knew more than the words. He had grown up in a tough Irish-Italian neighborhood on the west side of Chicago. "I'm not going to give this to the police; I'm sending it to your father. And all his friends. To your wife and, of course, a copy to your kids, *farsi giustizia da sè*."

The life went out of little Joey's face. He forced himself to breathe. Devlin knew he owned Joey Pants.

"They'll kill me," Pantatelli said.

"Don't get my hopes up."

"I'm serious. It would kill my old man if he found out I was working with the FBI."

It was obvious to Devlin that Pantatelli was ready. But certain techniques had to be utilized when dealing with informants. If an agent was not careful or became too trusting, a clever source could elicit more information than he or she gave. If Pantatelli was forced to bring up the list, instead of Devlin getting minimal and possibly misleading answers to his questions, it would be a much better gauge of his truthfulness. Once Pantatelli opened up, Devlin planned to continue the pressure to ensure he had as much information as Pantatelli did. Then he would leave his informant scared enough to call as other information became available. Devlin began. "Give me something that won't come back to you."

Devlin knew Pantatelli had to speak next. He must not be given any way out. He stared at his hands as if they were troublesome strangers, then at Devlin, then at his hands again. Finally he drew in an uneven breath and said, "Okay. What I'm going to give you is big, really big. If you want me dead, just give me up on this." Pants lit a quivering cigarette. Its glowing tip sped toward his mouth as he dragged fiercely on its filter. "There's somebody dirty in your office. They're going to sell my father a list of all the FBI informants in Detroit."

"Okay, give me the rest of it."

"I don't know much more. I know it's costing my old man twenty grand."

"Is it a man or woman?"

"He said an FBI guy."

"Agent or clerk?"

"He didn't say."

"When is this supposed to happen?"

"I don't know." Pantatelli was starting to sound as though he thought he was off the hook.

"Sorry, Joey, this isn't good enough. You could be making this up. If it is true, the exchange could have already taken place. And if it hasn't, you haven't given me enough to prevent it. No, you'll have to give me something else," Devlin bluffed.

"There isn't anything else."

"What about the Molini hit?"

The question paralyzed Pantatelli. Alfonso Molini had been a rising star in the Detroit family, but not fast enough for his own liking. He decided to take a little extra territory: territory belonging to Vincenzo Scantina, the Don, a most vindictive person. He pushed Anthony Pantatelli's button.

Molini's body was found in an abandoned factory, where he had been beaten into semiconsciousness. Then, according to the medical examiner, he was tied in a standing position among some scaffolding, at which time an eight-foot-long steel reinforcing rod was rammed into his mouth from above. While one man held it, another used a sledgehammer to drive it down through the torso, exiting just behind the scrotum. Devlin had seen the crime scene photos. Even though Molini's face was swollen with trauma and the gases released by death, his eyes bulged grotesquely with the last surprise of his life.

When the Organized Crime agents finally caught up with old man Pantatelli and asked him what he knew about the killing, he answered with old-country guile, "From what I hear, his eyes were bigger than his stomach." Then he would not answer any more questions. The answer revealed not only why and how Molini was killed, but indicated that Pantatelli was present to see Molini's incredulous look.

Most of this Devlin had learned from reading the 120-page affidavit for the wiretap. He looked at Joey Pants and knew he was trying to remember if he had said anything on the telephone about the murder.

Pantatelli silently cursed his undisciplined use of the telephone, something his father had lectured him about endlessly. Devlin knew he had not talked about the murder but thought the bluff was worth a try.

"Listen, I'll know when the exchange is going down. I'll let you know where and when."

It was exactly what Devlin wanted, but he stared off as if pondering Pants's fate. "How soon is it supposed to go?"

"Within a week."

Devlin stared off again. "Okay. I'll give you one week. Then I'm going to start mailing packages. Understand? One week."

A low, defeated "Yes" ended the meeting.

• • •

*J. Edgar Hoover was more brilliant than most people real-
ized. He set up systems and procedures which would always
be the bellwether of law enforcement. But the smartest decision he ever made was to die in May of 1972. On that
cool Washington night, the Gods of Power sent a visitor to
awaken him from his always troubled sleep.*

*"John, I am Mediocrites, recently appointed undergod of
Justice. I have been sent to show you what will happen to
the Bureau in the next ten years and to see if you want to
continue as director."*

*Hoover did not like what Mediocrites said. He liked his
appearance less. He wore wire-rimmed glasses and offen-
sively long hair, and his mouth curled in a sneering arrogance that reminded Hoover of a number of congressmen.
He did not answer except with his infamous bulldog stare
of impatience.*

*Even against the undergod of Justice, the leer was effec-
tive. He rushed on with his presentation; he knew he was
to have the last laugh. "Later this year the first female FBI
agents will strap on guns. And every year thereafter more
and more of them will be hired. Congress will mandate it."
The director's sallow face darkened. "Also, minorities will
be actively recruited and hired in unprecedented numbers."
Mediocrites was pleased; Hoover's face now glowed red.
"Now let me tell you about Watergate, which will ultimately
lead to the election of a peanut farmer as president."*

*When Mediocrites finished telling Mr. Hoover exactly
what that president would do to the Department of Justice
and the federal judges he would appoint, the director said,
"I've heard enough. It's obviously time for me to go. Before we leave, I want to leave a note of instruction for
my assistants. They're considering a major revamping of
the management program. With these changes you've de-*

scribed, the new management system would be a disaster. It must be left the same, for continuity."

"Certainly," Mediocrites said too easily.

The memorandum read as follows:

To: All Assistant Directors
From: JEH
Subject: Field Supervisors

Presently there is a popular proposal to have Bureau supervisors, who have little or no street experience, take over field supervisory positions as part of a career path. Further proposed is the idea that all managers would transfer on an average of every two years between the field and Headquarters. This notion is obviously put forth by individuals more concerned with promotion than the mission of the Bureau, which, I remind you, is to successfully investigate violations of federal law. It has been my experience that the best supervisors are the ones who have come up through the ranks, know their city and violations, and know if they do their job well, they will be doing it until retirement.

To help offset great, unsettling changes I foresee in the future, I feel continuing present policy is absolutely critical to the maintenance of the high standards of the Bureau.

Finally, under the proposed system, good managers would have to choose between their family and a promotion that would regularly disrupt that family. The Bureau has been built on the magnificent efforts of men who believe in God, country, but most of all, family.

This proposal is denied indefinitely.

H.

Satisfied, J. Edgar Hoover scowled into Mediocrites's wire-rimmed glasses and said with characteristic resolution, "Let's go."

"After you," Mediocrites said with all the respect due the director. Hoover laid his final edict on his nightstand and departed.

Mediocrites knew his future work would be made even more difficult by Hoover's last communication, so he slipped it under his robe and followed the Bulldog at a safe distance.

Because Detroit was one of the larger FBI offices, it was allotted two Assistant Special Agents in Charge. ASAC number one, so designated because he had been in Detroit longer than number two, was David Dewson. He was the missing link between Pilkington and Fauber. Magnificently deceptive but astonishingly incompetent, one day he would be an SAC; Mediocrites would see to it.

Number two was Tom O'Hare. Of the dozen or so ASACs Devlin had seen come and go, O'Hare was the most highly regarded by the street humps. He was a good manager who had enough agent time to make good decisions. He was never fooled by the deceivers, so they rarely went to his office to attempt sexual acts. Contrary to managerial dictum, his family was one of his priorities. In spite of Pilkington's orders, O'Hare could get things done. Devlin grudgingly admired that in him.

About an hour after he left Joey Pants drinking double vodkas at the Whitney, Devlin called O'Hare from the tech room.

"Tom. Mike Devlin."

"Hello, Mike, what's up?"

"I'm working the Title III and can't leave, otherwise I'd come out to the house to talk to you."

"That important?"

"We have a security problem."

"With what?"

"One-thirty-sevens."

"What do you know about that?"

"Enough to get you down here."

"I'm on my way."

Forty-five minutes later, O'Hare walked into the tech room, his face urgent.

"Shoot," he said before sitting down. Devlin explained the information he had received without telling him the source. In essence, he had let Pants know that the FBI had wiretaps on his family. Serious consequences for Devlin existed if that fact ever became known.

However, Devlin knew that no matter who they convicted as a result of the wiretap, it would never be as important as the compromising of the entire informant program. If the list did fall into the hands of organized crime, all informants, past and present, would have to be advised for their own safety. Notification of the media would be only one outraged phone call away. Once exposed, the recruitment of informants not only in Detroit, but nationwide, would be next to impossible. And anyone who understood the Bureau, really understood it all the way down into the boiler room, knew that would greatly damage the FBI.

When Devlin finished, O'Hare sat shaking his head. With the heart of a street agent, he realized the consequences. He also knew he would be sent back to the Bureau and buried. He did not care for himself, but his family had been whiplashed enough in his career. "Any ideas?"

"I think I've got an idea how to find out who the leak is," said Devlin. O'Hare straightened in his chair. "Can you keep this to yourself?"

"I should tell Pilkington."

"If you do, he'll either say it cannot be true, or there's no evidence, or he'll put one of Fauber's windups on it and old man Pantatelli will beat them to the list anyhow." The anguish pulling back the ASAC's lips told Devlin that O'Hare knew he was right.

"Okay, what do you want to do?"

"First, there are four clerks who have keys to the informant file room. They're all *females*. We know they're not involved because the information is that it's a male."

O'Hare noticed something was bothering Devlin. "What is it, Mike?"

"There's one other person who has a key."

"Who?"

"Frank Sumpter." O'Hare had forgotten about Sumpter. As the informant coordinator, he was responsible for the overall supervision of the program's day-to-day operation. The girls handled all the work, and Sumpter did not get involved unless there was a problem. That's the way he liked it. He had asked to become the informant coordinator because it offered a quiet ride to retirement.

Sumpter had been assigned there because of a drinking problem. He had once been tall and thin. Now he never seemed to stand erect, and his once-handsome face had a gray pallor that left him now unnoticed. Like many drunks, he lived from hour to hour.

Both men hated the thought that an FBI employee would sell out but, probably because they were agents, feared even more that an agent was involved.

"Christ, I forgot about him. He does have his problems."

Devlin remembered Sumpter before his problems. He had been a good agent with an impressive number of convictions for truck hijackings. Then, one day, he ran out of desire. When his wife finally divorced him, he gave up any pretense of self-respect and surrendered completely to alcohol. Since he had never been caught drinking on duty, the Bureau never chose to make an issue of it. He was conveniently sentenced to burial. "Let's just make him one of the five people who have a key. One of the four girls could have lent a key to whoever is selling the list. If our unknown did borrow the key, that means he had to duplicate it because he would have needed hours alone in the room, probably in the middle of the night, to obtain the names and copy them. It's reasonable to believe that he had his own key made."

"That sounds reasonable, but how do we know which one?"

"Here's your part in this. First thing tomorrow morning, have the lock changed on the door. Call the girls and Sumpter in one at a time and tell them the Bureau is starting a new security procedure for the 137 rooms, that is, to change locks without notice, and these changes are not to be discussed. As you collect the keys, place them each in a separate, marked envelope. Tell them that as part of the new procedure, they must answer a routine list of questions, and they may be subject to polygraphs, so they must be candid. Give them some camouflage questions like, Have you ever divulged any sensitive information? The question you're trying to get to is: Who have you lent the key to in the last year?"

"So we'll have the keys and a list of the people who borrowed them. What then?"

"Then I'm going to need some help. I'll give you a list of people I know I can trust to keep this quiet. You'll have to tell their supervisors they're doing something for you and to keep it confidential."

"That's no problem. How many will you need?"

"I won't know until the keys are collected. Initially I'll need only one, and you'll have to get me out from under these earmuffs."

For the first time, Devlin saw O'Hare's expression lighten. "Don't care for wiretap duty?" Devlin's look answered the question. "No problem. Who do you want?"

"Edgar Livingston."

• • •

In the morning, Livingston found Devlin scanning an office personnel roster and making notes. He handed him a dripping cup of coffee and asked, "New hobby?"

"*We* have a new hobby." Devlin explained the situation to Livingston, leaving out the source of the information.

Livingston smiled. "Life is full of coincidence. Just yesterday you tell me to remember the name Pantatelli and today—it comes up again. Ever wonder why coincidences seem so arranged?"

"I guess that's why they call them coincidences." The two men smiled at the secret they shared.

Devlin outlined the key-collecting procedure to Livingston but did not mention Sumpter.

"What are you going to do with the keys?"

"You're flying them to Washington this morning."

"I am?"

"O'Hare is going to call Fauber and tell him you're doing something hush-hush for him. You'll take the keys to an old friend of mine, Danny Jennings. He's in the Latent Fingerprint Section but has a contact in the Microanalysis Unit. I called him this morning. When you get a flight, call him, he'll have someone pick you up. Microanalysis will examine the key on the sly. As soon as you get the results, call me."

"What can be found on the keys?"

"When a key's made, it's clamped into a viselike instrument. Under the microscope, especially the electronic ones in the lab, they'll be able to pick up the vise marks."

"But won't all the keys have those vise marks?"

"Yes. But the key we want to isolate will have two sets of marks: one when it was made, and one when it was copied. And since all the informant room keys are stamped with 'DO NOT DUPLICATE,' only the key in question should show duping marks."

A look of appreciation swept across Livingston's face. "Then you take the list of borrowers for that key and our man will be on that list."

"That's the way it looks on the drawing board."

"What if none of them has been copied?" Livingston asked.

Devlin knew if the lab tests were negative, Frank Sumpter would become a prime suspect, but he decided not to tell Livingston. "We'll worry about that when the time comes."

"If it has been copied, how will you identify which borrower it is?"

"Maybe we'll get lucky and there'll only be one male borrower. If there's more than one, I think I know how to identify him. I'll explain that to you later, if we need it. You'd better make your reservations and call Jennings."

"Do you think I'll be back tonight?"

"You should be. Why?"

Livingston smiled at the chance to tell Devlin. "I have a date with Sydney."

"Well, well, well. I'm glad, but you might have to put it on hold until we take care of this. You'll have a long time to sing those old Motown songs together."

"We were pretty good."

"She was good. You almost restarted the sixty-seven riots."

Laughing, Livingston said, "I'll call her."

"Before you go, what happened with Anderson's daughter?"

Livingston's mood changed. He became uncomfortable, not looking at Devlin when he answered, "It looks like she's a runaway. At least the SAC has declared she is and has ordered no more agent-hours be spent looking for her."

"What makes Mr. Indecision so sure?"

"Because her boyfriend is black." Livingston emphasized only the first and last word in the sentence.

"And you're going to take it personally."

"No, I just thought the FBI was supposed to be different."

"If you're looking for justice, you're in the wrong outfit. Injustice is very popular these days. There's no patience for real justice. Don't get me wrong; I don't have the patience either, but the way I deal with it is by not taking it personally."

"I guess I am taking it personally, but it's the reasons he gave. Because she had run away before and recently had a fight with Anderson *and* there were no facts to the contrary, she, in all likelihood, had run away again and would probably show up in a few days."

"When they don't want to do something, they can find a dozen reasons. But if they wanted to look for her, they could give a dozen reasons, and some of the reasons would be the same. In this case, Pilkington, for whatever reason, decides he doesn't want to get involved, so he gets out his excuses chart and selects number three, seven, and the overused number eleven. Case closed."

"I kind of feel sorry for Anderson. Fauber and Pilkington have abandoned him when he really needs them. The Jedi are loving it, though, compassionate bunch that they are. With Anderson out of the way, they each move up a notch with Fauber."

"That's what the management food chain is all about. If there weren't Jedi to kiss the rod, there wouldn't be any Faubers or Pilkingtons."

After Livingston left, the phone rang. It was Tom Anderson. "Mike, can I come back and talk to you?"

Both men had grown to dislike each other equally, but, feeling he knew the answer, Devlin asked, "Why?"

"I need your help," he whispered, a truce sounding in his words.

Surprised by Anderson's honesty, Devlin sent a message of mixed feelings. "I guess so. I can't leave here until eight o'clock anyhow."

Within a minute, Devlin heard someone repeatedly mistype the combination at the outer door. Devlin opened it and found Anderson looking at the cipher keys in disbelief. His suit was badly wrinkled, his red eyes were balanced on top of dark half-moons, tiny clumps had been unknowingly twisted into his hair.

They sat down in the tech room.

"Mike, I don't know what to do. I haven't slept in three days. My daughter is missing. I think she's been kidnapped. But that cocksucker Pilkington will not do anything about it."

Cocksucker. The word was to show Devlin that he and Anderson were now on the same side. He was sure that a week earlier, Pilkington would have been "Boss," and he would have been the cocksucker. "What do you want *me* to do about it?"

"See if you can find her. I'd try and do something, but I can't even think straight."

Devlin wondered if this was Fauber's idea, this time setting him up for insubordination against Pilkington's orders. "The SAC has given orders to lay off."

"I know, I know. But, if anyone can find her, it's you. Besides, you've never worried about the front office before."

"And that's why I'm now locked up in this closet."

As if it were too large, the word struggled out of

Anderson's mouth: "Please." Its strains were exhausted, pathetic.

"If I do look into it, how do I know you won't dime me out to Fauber?"

"I know you and I have different priorities now, but this is my daughter. That's all that is important to me."

Devlin hesitated, letting Anderson know that his plea was suspect.

All the bells and lights Devlin had developed to warn him of bureaucratic intentions were overwhelming him. His mind rushed back, looking for an answer.

He was aboard an airplane with 250 other Marines flying from Honolulu to Da Nang. They were dressed in plain green stateside utilities, full leather boots and innocent white underwear. Their bodies unscarred; their weights normal. Their only concerns were their silly high school girlfriends.

In thirteen months, they would fly in the opposite direction—with luck. The satanic elements of Vietnam marring their uniforms and jungle boots. Underwear, if worn, would be a dark, survival green. Jungle rot, malaria, shrapnel, and bullets leaving lifelong reminders of their foolish pride. At first they would think of comrades lost, then the miracle of their survival, and, as they landed, silly high school girlfriends.

Then he thought about the Marines left behind. When they had departed Hawaii for Vietnam, two of the men had refused to board the plane. They were court-martialed and given brig time to exceed the thirteen-month Vietnam tour they had chosen to avoid. The men Devlin had left in Vietnam had died heroically, even if they had not been decorated. En route to Vietnam, Devlin decided that he feared only one thing—to die ingloriously. To be killed by friendly fire or a bursting appendix. If it were to be, he needed a hero's death.

He remembered little Vanessa leading him to her puppy. He looked around the tech room and thought—better a glorious death than this prison. He stared at Anderson, hoping he was not making a mistake, and said, "Okay."

||| CHAPTER 8 |||

Troy, Michigan, was a typical Midwestern suburban community. Six miles of less expensive suburbs buffered it from the televised horrors of Detroit. Most residents were families and considered Troy a good place to raise kids. The schools were more than adequate, and the community activities were substantial. Property values, though directly dependent on the automobile industry, were usually rising. It was not for any of these reasons that Tom Anderson had relocated in Troy. His house was the closest one his wife could find to John Fauber's, only three blocks away. She decided being that close would facilitate a friendship between the two families, which in turn would enhance her husband's career.

As he parked in front of Anderson's house, Devlin heard the Bureau radio operator announce, "KEX Seven-six-zero, it's twelve o'clock." He estimated that Livingston's plane would be landing at Dulles Airport in Washington. O'Hare had collected the keys and obtained the lists without any problems until he had called in Frank Sumpter. O'Hare thought the informant coordinator appeared to be in a stupor when he told the ASAC that he had lost his key, time and place unknown. Furthermore, he could not recall if anyone had borrowed his key. O'Hare felt the memory lapses were suspicious and was going to take a closer look at Sumpter's life.

The Anderson house was a brick-and-aluminum colonial on a street monotonously lined with similar homes. Dark, thickset green lawns, maintained with Astroturf perfection, joined an occasional immature tree to complete a Lionel-train-village illusion.

All of Anderson's window shades were drawn, giving the impression that no one was home. Devlin knew better. Anderson had called his wife and told her to expect Devlin.

She opened the door and introduced herself, "I am Judith Anderson," extending her hand. She looked at his clothes and seemed annoyed he was not wearing a suit.

"Mike Devlin," he replied, shaking her hand.

"I appreciate your help. Thomas has told me you're very experienced in finding people." Somehow the words were more condescending than complimentary, as if being able to find someone was an unfortunate side effect of working at a common trade, like the grease on an auto mechanic's hands. Devlin chalked it up to the crisis she was going through.

"We'll see what can be done. I'd like to ask you some questions and then look around if it's all right?"

"Certainly. We can go into the family room. Can I get you some coffee?"

"Black, please."

The family room was separated from the kitchen by a waist-high counter. Devlin watched her make fresh coffee. She was older than her husband, somewhere in her late thirties. Her hair, severely short and solid brown, looked younger than the face it surrounded. Devlin guessed it was dyed regularly. The dress she wore was more appropriate for dining out than kidnap waiting. All of the other victim parents he had encountered looked like an earthquake's rubble. Her formality was completed by her high-heeled shoes, which brought little or no definition to her sinking calves. But it was her tinted glasses in the darkened house that cautioned

Devlin. They gave her an air of evasion, as if she waited in ambush for people's mistakes.

The only light in the family room was a floor lamp next to the chair Judith Anderson had been sitting in, reading. On the table next to it was a half-empty coffee cup with lipstick prints, a cordless telephone, and a biography of Eleanor Roosevelt. The wall behind the chair was taken up by two bookshelves. One was filled with sports biographies and crime books, the other with women's biographies and self-improvement books.

Mrs. Anderson came back in and handed Devlin his coffee. "I hope it's not too strong."

"I don't think it could be too strong today."

"Oh, yes, Thomas said you worked all night."

"I guess it depends on your definition of work."

"I'm sorry. I don't understand."

He thought about telling her. Telling her about Fauber and those who aspire to become his replacement, like her husband. But if he judged her correctly, she was the one with the aspirations. Again he considered her situation and said, "The work is not my first choice, but that's not why I'm here. I knew Vanessa when she was little. She introduced me to her dog once." Devlin smiled.

"Yes. We had to get rid of him. He shed too much."

Devlin felt somehow disappointed about the dog. "Vanessa's sixteen?" he continued.

"Yes. She'll be seventeen in September."

"Where does she go to school?"

"Troy Athens High School. She's a junior."

"How have her grades been lately?"

"Well, to tell you the truth, her final grades this year did slip."

"Any other problems or behavior changes?"

Her eyes dropped behind the darkened glasses. "I suppose Thomas told you. He and Vanessa have had a couple of arguments about the boy she's dating." Now she lowered her voice. "He's—black."

"Where did she meet him?"

"A friend of hers used to date him, then he became interested in Vanessa. They started going out about a month ago."

"What's his name?"

"I think it's Alvan Stand. He lives in Detroit." She pronounced *Detroit* with the same contempt as she did when she described Stand as *black*.

"What were the arguments about?"

"She started coming home late. Cutting classes. Just generally out of control. She used to be such a good girl."

"I'm sure she still is. I have to ask these questions; I'm sorry. Any indication of drug use?"

"I really don't think so, but Thomas wanted to have her tested. He suggested it to her the night she disappeared. She became very upset and ran up to her room. She came down a little later. She was calm and asked if she could use the car to run to the store. That was the last time we saw her."

Devlin waited a moment. "She ran away once before?"

"Yes, but that was just overnight. She stayed at a friend's house and called us first thing in the morning."

"What kind of guy is Alvan Stand?"

"We don't know. We've never met him. I guess the other agents talked to him. He said he hadn't seen Vanessa."

"Besides her room, where else in the house does Vanessa have her belongings?"

"Nowhere. Her winter clothes are stored in boxes in the basement. Other than that, everything she owns is in her room."

"How about things you or Tom might share with her, like books or toiletries?"

Without hesitation she said, "Nothing. To the best of my knowledge we don't share anything."

Devlin was trying to keep an open mind about what had happened to the girl, but he was tired, and her stepmother's answers were making a good case for the runaway theory.

"Judy—" he started.

"Judith."

"Judith. I want to go up and look at her room. If you don't mind, I'd like to do it alone. I'm able to concentrate better."

"Certainly. It's the room at the end of the hall."

Devlin climbed the stairs and noticed a pine-scented odor in the air. He shut the bedroom door, hoping it would keep him from thinking about the woman downstairs. The room was as meticulous as the rest of the house. The bed was made with ironed neatness. The lines in the carpet indicated it had been recently vacuumed. Vanessa's makeup was neatly arranged on her dresser. It was evident to Devlin that *Judith* spent a lot of time in Vanessa's room. If anything was to be hidden from her stepmother, it would have to be hidden well.

Devlin slipped off his shoes and lay on the bed amid a dozen stuffed animals that looked at him with bored faces. He examined the room. The walls were devoid of the normal teenage decorations: posters, photos, signs, banners. It felt as though someone had moved out, or maybe had never moved in. The furniture consisted of the bed, a dresser, a desk, and a chair. A single short, white bookshelf hung conspicuously over the desk.

First he searched the closet, including all the clothes and shoes. Then under the mattress, the dresser, and the desk. He found nothing.

On the bookshelves were a dozen books, including Vanessa's latest high school yearbook. One by one, Devlin flipped through the books. In the yearbook he found a loose photograph of two girls hugging each other warmly. One girl, with dishwater blond hair and a cute face, was Vanessa

Anderson. The other had very long, dark hair, classic bone structure, and stunning eyes. The contrast between the girls was as though different photographers had taken each girl's picture, one amateur, one professional. On the page was the same girl's class photo—Nancy Pappas. Next to it in a female's handwriting was: "To Van, You're always there when I need someone. Love, Nan. Van and Nan forever."

Devlin thumbed through the rest of the book. On the inside of the back cover two pieces of masking tape held three new twenty-dollar bills.

Devlin searched the entire room again and found nothing more. When he came downstairs, Judith was reading in her chair. "Did you find anything?" she asked.

"Nothing out of the ordinary. Who is Nancy Pappas?"

The question seemed to slap her across the face. "How do you know about her?"

Devlin was losing patience with *Judith's* priorities. Unemotionally he looked at her, letting her know he wanted an answer to his question.

Judith decided she did not like this man. His threatening presence reached at her with a scolding stare. She was forced to treat him as an equal. "I'm sorry. That girl has caused this family serious problems. We have forbidden Vanessa ever to see her again. About a year ago Miss Pappas got herself in trouble and decided to have an abortion. She dragged Vanessa along with her. We didn't know anything about it until Mr. Pappas called up here accusing us of knowing about it and urging Nancy to do it behind their backs. Vanessa was forbidden ever to talk to her again."

"Evidently she did, because Vanessa's yearbook has a note from Nancy. Didn't she just receive her yearbook within the last few months?"

"Right. In May. About two months ago."

"Where can I find Nancy Pappas?"

"Not that I go there, but I saw her working at the Island

Cleaners at the beginning of the summer. It's at the corner of Crooks and Maple."

"One last question: when she left the other night, what did she take with her?"

"She was wearing jeans and a sweatshirt and carrying a small black purse."

"Okay. I'm going to talk to Nancy."

"May I ask you something?" Devlin looked at her and waited. He knew what the question was. "Do you think she was kidnapped?"

"At this point I can't answer that."

Frustration welled up in her. "How could Mr. Pilkington abandon us at a time like this? What kind of man is he?"

As Devlin left, he considered the irony of her question.

As Devlin drove to the Island Cleaners, he received a radio message to phone the ASAC. "Mike, guess who's in hock up to his ass—has a ten-thousand-dollar loan with our contact in Dearborn and hasn't paid them a dime in six months."

Devlin hated to admit it, but Sumpter was opening up quite a lead on the other suspects. "Well, we should hear soon about the keys. If none of them has been duplicated, it looks like we found our leak."

O'Hare spoke almost reluctantly. "There's more. During the last three months C-Ten has had periodic surveillance on the Bella Luna. They've spotted Sumpter going in there on three different occasions. They didn't think anything about it. You know agents are always wandering through surveillances unintentionally."

Devlin knew the betrayal would be bitter if it was Sumpter, but he had little time to consider the consequences. "I've got an interview to do. I'll call you when I'm done."

"I'm going to keep working on Sumpter."

• • •

Devlin found Nancy Pappas working behind the counter at the Island Cleaners. She was as attractive as her photo.

"Can I help you?" Without a word, Devlin held up his credentials and watched her reaction. It was the normal confusion. "Yes?"

"I'm looking for Vanessa Anderson."

"What do you mean—looking?"

"She's been missing from home for a few days. When did you last see her?"

"Is she all right?" The question was emotional, not logical. Her face, now distorted with fear, seemed older. Devlin judged the girl's affection for Vanessa as genuine. "Ah, let me think— I think it was four or five nights ago; it was the night she had a fight with her father. Ever since she started dating this black guy, he's been coming down on her. That night he accused her of being on drugs."

"Why did she come to see you?"

"Just to talk. We're very close. I went through some tough times awhile back, and she stood with me the whole way." She looked warily at Devlin. "Did you talk to her mother?"

"I'm sorry, Nancy. She told me about the abortion."

A small sting pierced her. "Vanessa was a real friend through it."

"So what did you talk about?"

"She did most of the talking. She said her father and stepmother were smothering her. Her father has been worse since she started going out with Alvan. Giving her a real guilt trip. Telling her that he does everything for her and she repays him by jeopardizing his career. She said she couldn't handle it anymore. She was going to tell Alvan she didn't want to see him anymore."

"Did you hear from her after that?"

"No. Not a word. I figured she was grounded or sick or something. Because of her parents, I can't call her."

"What's Alvan like?"

"Well, I guess he's all right. Do you think he has something to do with this?"

"There is some thought that she's simply run away."

"I doubt it. She ran away for a night once before and was grounded for two months. Besides, she would have told me. And she would have called me by now."

"You don't think she might be staying with Alvan?"

"No. She never liked the guy that way. She just went out with him to bug her parents."

"Did you give her any money that night?"

"No. When she left she said she had to hurry because her parents thought she was at the store."

Devlin handed her his business card. "If you hear anything, give me a call. If she has run away, that's between her and her parents, and I can stop wasting my time."

"Can I call you to find out what's going on?"

"Twenty-four hours a day through that number."

Devlin stopped at the first pay phone he saw and called Anderson at the office. "When Alvan Stand was interviewed yesterday, what did he say?"

"Basically he hadn't seen her since the night before she disappeared. Have you found out anything?"

"Not yet," Devlin lied. "How much money does Vanessa normally carry with her?"

"Very little, less than five dollars. Why?"

"Just trying to fill in some blanks. Switch me up to Sue."

The squad secretary came on the line. "Hello, stranger."

"Hi. Did I get any calls?"

"Just from Ed. He said number two had been duped, you'd know what that means."

"Yes. I think so." For a moment Devlin felt relieved that Sumpter might not be the leak but then became angry with himself for allowing his personal feelings to enter into the investigation. "Do me a favor—make sure no one sees that."

"Okay."

"Thanks. Switch me up to O'Hare."

"John O'Hare."

"John, it's Mike. The lab got a hit on key number two."
O'Hare was silent. "So you don't think it's Sumpter?"

"I don't know. Let's just proceed with the investigation."

"Yeah, you're right."

"How many borrowers on that key?"

Devlin could hear O'Hare's drawer opening. "Damn, that's the longest list—six people, only two females."

Devlin wasted no time. "Here's what we'll need. First, your secretary, Diane, she's been trained in the photo lab. Have her pull the personnel files on those males *plus* Sumpter's and make ten copies each of their photos. Have her do it after hours, when the photo clerks are gone."

"I'll make sure she tells no one. What else?"

"I'm going to need four or five more agents for as long as it takes."

"That many? Okay."

"I'll call you with a list in the morning, so you can notify their supervisors. We'll have to work out of another location. How long can we keep this a secret?"

"Well, Pilkington is leaving tomorrow for an SAC conference in San Diego. He's taking his wife along, so they're going to stay awhile. Tomorrow, just have your people come in here in the morning and then disappear. Chances are no one will notice. I'll tell the supervisors. The SAC won't be back until the following Monday, so you've got about ten days."

Ten days. Devlin wondered if it was long enough to prevent the leak *and* find Vanessa Anderson—if she wanted to be found.

• • •

Devlin drove over the railroad tracks and turned into the yard. The operation covered twenty-five acres in an area of Detroit where no one went unless they were in the scrap metal business. As he got out of the car, he watched another four tons of scrap being silently released from a huge electromagnetic disk, then heard the metallic explosion as it joined the thousands of other tons on the ground. He could taste the rust in the air. Devlin liked the honesty of the yard. Workers in muddy rubber boots, trucks momentarily parked on unerring scales, only first names used, and the boss could not be distinguished from the laborers by the clothing he wore. Unadorned tonnage simply equaled dollars.

"Is Jeff in?" Devlin asked the receptionist. She said he was in a meeting that should end shortly. Devlin sat and waited. Jeff Ross had been working for his uncle at Les's pawnshop when Devlin had met him. He had just graduated from Cornell University and wanted to try something besides his father's scrap metal business, where he had worked summers since the age of ten. Devlin was investigating a large bank robbery that had led him to the pawnshop.

The robbery occurred shortly after Fauber's transfer to Detroit and had taken place in the city of Hamtramck, an ancient Polish community lost in time. The square-shaped municipality was completely surrounded by the urban blur of Detroit, a city within a city. Early one morning, three black males in coveralls and ski masks entered the Hamtramck Community Bank and introduced the first-generation Poles to the modern magnificence of armed bank robbery. At gunpoint, they held thirty people frozen on the floor for over an hour, impatiently waiting for the vault's time lock to expire. Once it did, they fled with its contents. An hour later they were in a housing project, having their pictures taken with half a million in cash stacked on a twenty-five-dollar kitchen table.

Normally supervisors do not respond to bank robberies, but because of its size Fauber reluctantly left the sanctuary of his office for the mysteries of the street. He doubted if the street, unlike his subordinate agents, would take into account his now-elevated position.

When Fauber arrived at the bank, it was closed to customers. Bewildered, non-English-speaking Poles stood outside the front door displaying their historical stubbornness, refusing to leave, fearing their money was lost forever. A black, non-Polish-speaking security guard was trying to explain the problem to them, unable to understand their tenacity. It was their strength, the reason why, although surrounded by the decay of Detroit, they would not run. A lot of people talked about standing and fighting, but only the Poles did it.

Fauber showed his FBI credentials to the guard, who appeared to read them one letter at a time. The guard opened the door, and Fauber sneered at him for disrupting the flow of his entrance.

"Pollocks and pricks," the guard mumbled, opening his newspaper to the want ads, taking a solemn oath that this would be his last workday in Hamtramck, or maybe anywhere else.

The bank's lobby was chaotic. Thirty employees, ten agents, half a dozen police, a tracking dog, and two languages swirled Fauber's equilibrium. He needed sanctuary; where was Duncan Moorehead?

Although he had only three years with the Bureau, Fauber had made Duncan Moorehead, because of his commitment to the squad's twentieth-century mission, the bank robbery coordinator, a job usually held by a senior agent.

When Fauber found him, he was in a small room attempting to organize dozens of pieces of evidence. With characteristic bravado, Fauber told Moorehead to have Devlin handle the evidence so Moorehead could follow Fauber around and carry out his orders.

The evidence assignment, which would take Devlin back to the office and out of Fauber's way, would entail many hours of paperwork ensuring chain of custody and transmittal of the evidence to the FBI laboratories in Washington. Devlin would be tied to his desk for days. Perfect, thought Fauber: who says I can't make on-the-scene decisions?

With Devlin on his way back to the office, the Bank Robbery Supervisor, as he introduced himself to everyone, wandered happily around the bank, giving orders to policemen who ignored him and telling agents to do things they were already doing. He even found time to have a cup of coffee with the president of the bank, assuring him that he and his men would solve the robbery soon; it was just a matter of organization and leadership.

Devlin sat in front of his desk, which was piled high and wide with evidence oozing over the top like some great bureaucratic mushroom spawned on the deep, dark bullshit of FBI procedure.

As if trying to find the perfect apple at a fruit stand, he searched the heap, looking for something to catch his interest. The rifle. It was wrapped in a large clear plastic bag to, hopefully, preserve latent fingerprints. The hope was dependent on who had handled the evidence. Unpracticed agents made too many mistakes. They used handkerchiefs to pick up evidence, thereby wiping away the latents, or they clumsily put their own prints on the item. In the second case, the fingerprint examiners took great delight in sending back reports to the agents' supervisor stating, "The only latent print of value found on Q1 was the right index of Special Agent Dom Shitticus, Detroit Division." Agents never made that mistake twice.

Not wanting to be a Dom Shitticus, Devlin took a pair of milky-colored rubber gloves from his drawer.

Devlin examined the rifle. When the bank robbers had fled, they had dumped it in a Dumpster, where a tracking dog had found it. It was unusual. Most firearms he had taken from criminals looked like they belonged to criminals, barrels and stocks cut to concealable lengths, serial numbers filed away, broken parts taped, manufacturers' finishes eaten away by sweaty hands. But this rifle was flawless with the exception of two long, parallel scratches along the top of the receiver. Devlin guessed a scope had once been mounted on it but removed for the robbery.

He had the computer clerk run the serial number, but the weapon had not been reported stolen.

He held the rifle up so the overhead light banked off its dark blue metal. A partial latent print stopped his eye. He would not dust it. The latent fingerprint examiners would do that. It was part of their sorcery. As miraculous as the Myth itself

Since the weapon had not been stolen and the robbers had not intended to leave it behind, Devlin reasoned that it might have been purchased legitimately. He dialed ATF.

At 3:30 ATF called back. The manufacturer had shipped it three months earlier to Les's Loan, 7731 Cass Avenue, Detroit.

Devlin considered the mushroom. Fauber's purpose was to control him. A tremor of resentment was set off deep inside of him, resentment that would not allow self-protecting decisions, resentment for the weak being bullied and the unjust being allowed to continue. The curse of the Irish: to never be at peace. He headed to the garage.

When he entered the pawnshop, he saw a man whom he assumed was Les with a customer. He looked at Devlin briefly. With those survivor's eyes, a quick and accurate assessment of Devlin's intentions had been made. Veteran shopkeepers in Detroit had that ability; if not, they never became veterans. Les nodded at his nephew Jeff Ross to help Devlin after he opened his credentials.

Devlin said, "I'm tracing a rifle that was shipped here three months ago."

"Come on in the back. If we have the records, that's where they'll be," Ross answered.

At four o'clock Fauber and most of the squad returned to the office. Duncan Moorehead had been made the case agent for the robbery, responsible for its logical conclusion. "Logical conclusion" was another Bureau phrase filled with designed vagueness to later answer managerial need. Moorehead had handed out the standard leads: neighborhood canvasses along the escape route, interviews of recently fired employees, contact with DPD's Armed Robbery Unit for suspects. ARU came up with a few unlikely suspects. Everything else failed to provide any promising information. Fauber was worried. He may not have been experienced in bank robberies, but he knew an old-dog case when he saw one. This became more agonizing when Sue told him the SAC wanted to see him. He went into his office and closed the door.

Composure, he told himself. Composure was nothing more than a deception. He had spent years back at the Bureau learning to deal with crises such as this. At Headquarters deception was sacred, a guidepost of the daily routine.

Composed, Fauber walked into Pilkington's office. "Boss, we're still working on it. We got some decent suspects from Holdup. They're contacting their sources; we're doing the same. These guys were real pros, didn't make a mistake. But we'll get them. I've given this case to Duncan Moorehead. He's young but an excellent agent. If anyone can find these guys, he can." Fauber finished by briefing Pilkington about the bandits' M.O.

Pilkington had heard enough to satisfy his curiosity and answer any questions that might come from the media. If there were any facts he did not know, he could always call on deception. Who was going to say he was wrong, the bank robbers? He stared at Fauber and said, "Let's get it solved." Fauber thought it sounded like a warning. He backed out of the room.

Fauber walked by Moorehead's desk. "In my office, now!" Fauber shut the door. "This robbery has to be solved, and I mean now. Do you understand?"

"Yes, sir," Moorehead answered, but he did not understand. His mentor, to whom he had been so demeaningly loyal, was chewing his ass. He, Duncan Moorehead, had become a victim of managerial sex.

"I want this solved, or you can find yourself another squad. Do you understand?"

"Yes, sir." Fauber's yelling had him standing at attention.

"Well, you can't get anything done standing here." Moorehead hurried out the door and considered committing career suicide by screaming "Fuck You, Yoda." Instead he composed himself and vowed to pay someone back when he became a supervisor.

Still angry, Fauber stood outside his office. He now realized the squad had heard his outburst with Moorehead. He leered at them. Again the time and weather numbers were flooded with calls. Fauber's eyes landed on the mushroom.

"Where's Devlin?" he demanded of the back wall. Multiple voices started talking back to the time and weather recordings. When no one responded, Fauber turned to the squad secretary. "Where is he?"

Not knowing but ever loyal, she answered, "I think he had an emergency call and left about an hour ago. He called in about ten minutes before you got in and asked if anyone was here."

"Where was he?"

"He didn't say."

"That son of a bitch!"

Phones started hanging up now that the real culprit had been identified. Devlin! That *son of a bitch*!

"Ricardo Green?"

"Who's this?"

"Ricardo, this is Jeff Ross. I work at Les's pawnshop."

"So what?"

"So the FBI just left here. They wanted to know who I sold a certain rifle to. It seems this rifle was used in a half-million-dollar bank robbery today. I told them I couldn't find the records but would keep looking."

"What do you want from me?"

"Well, I thought you would be appreciative, especially if I lost the records permanently. You make the choice, either you're a hunted FBI fugitive with five hundred thousand dollars or you're cool, with say, four hundred seventy-five."

"It's going to cost me twenty-five grand to keep you from telling the FBI who bought the rifle?"

"Uh-huh. The agent told me the only leads they have are the rifle and the marked money."

"The fucking money's marked?"

"That's right."

"How do I know you won't turn me in after I pay you?"

"Tonight, after I close, bring the five hundred thousand. I'll launder it for another twenty-five. You get four hundred fifty clean and no worries about the rifle. You're getting a lot for ten percent. Think of me as your agent. After I accept the money I'll be a coconspirator and couldn't turn you in without involving myself."

"How do I know you're not setting me up?"

"For who? The FBI? If I'd given them your name, they would've been there an hour ago. And I'm certainly not stupid enough to rip you off. The FBI said you had at least two partners in the robbery, and if anything happens to you I know I'd have to deal with them. No, Ricardo, I'm a poor boy who sees a chance to help you and turn a profit. Nothing more."

"What time?"

"Seven o'clock. I'll leave the alley door open."

The next morning Fauber got up an hour earlier than usual. He wanted to reach the office a half hour before Pilkington so he could put the finishing touches on his indictment of Devlin. He did not like getting up early, but Pilkington was an early riser because, in his words, "Only the devil's disciples sleep past sunrise."

The squad area was empty. The pile of evidence on Devlin's desk looked even larger in the deserted office. Fauber felt more stimulated. Maybe he would invite the SAC over to see *the evidence* for himself.

Fauber tried to open the door to his office, but someone was sleeping on the floor so the door could not be opened without waking him.

"Hold it." It was Devlin. He got up and opened the door.

"What are you doing sleeping in my—" On his desk, stacked neatly, was the half-million dollars. Fauber dropped into his chair, speechless.

Devlin explained his plan and Ross's cooperation. When Green had walked into the back of the pawnshop, Devlin had arrested him and seized the money. Finally, Devlin handed Fauber Green's signed confession.

Fauber sat in his chair, pretending to read the confession. His mind, three hundred words behind Devlin's voice, was trying to understand exactly how the seventy pounds of currency had wound up in front of him. Later he would have Moorehead help him figure out what had happened and exactly which rules Devlin had violated. But first there were bows to be taken.

"Sue, get me the SAC and then the president of the Hamtramck Community Bank."

Devlin walked out and looked at the evidence on his desk. He decided to get some sleep; Fauber would not be looking for him today.

For the next two days the SAC held news conferences. When asked how the case had been solved, he would say only that an FBI undercover operation had been responsible and therefore was not open to discussion. During that time Fauber allowed the president of the bank to take him to lunch. Fauber not only explained, and reexplained, how he and his men had outwitted the bank robbers but gave a detailed account of his FBI career. By that time, the other two robbers and the driver were in custody. The president thought about how nice and quiet their cell must have been.

And during those two brilliant, heroic days, Devlin remained at his desk, tediously disposing of the mushroom.

On the third day, Devlin was summoned to the SAC's office. After reading him a list of charges Fauber had brought against him, Pilkington decided that the two men needed a cooling-off period.

Pilkington asked, "Have you heard of the case code name Soundmurs?"

"The Puget Sound murders in Seattle?"

"That's right. The Bureau is putting together a ten-man task force, all handpicked. A man of your experience would—"

"How long?" Devlin interrupted.

"Ninety days."

"Good morning, gentlemen. I'm Captain Al Brockman, King County Police. I have the dubious honor of being the Puget Sound Task Force Commander. We'll be seeing a lot of each other for the next ninety days, so feel free . . ." Devlin started reading the thick stack of documents on his desk. The other nine agents had identical piles in front of them.

Forty-one females, mostly white, had been murdered or reported missing in a twenty-month period. Of the twenty-nine murdered, twenty-two had been dumped into Seattle's Puget Sound. The press, with voyeuristic simplicity, gave birth to the "Puget Sound Killer." The victims, ages fifteen to twenty-five, had all been prostitutes or frequent hitchhikers who did not mind paying their fare with sex. All had succumbed to ligature strangulation, usually with an item of their own clothing.

Captain Brockman had finished his greeting and was starting to talk about the specifics of the investigation. "There has not been a murder or a girl missing in almost two years. Your people at the Behavioral Science Unit tell us that serial killers don't stop; if anything, their killing rate accelerates. So they figure this guy is either dead, in prison, or has moved to another state."

Devlin read the Criminal Personality Profile prepared by Behavioral Science.

"One last thing," Brockman said. "You won't find this printed anywhere, and for good reason; this must not leave the room." He paused and scanned the group for emphasis. "Every victim had a cross carved between her breasts." He stepped to the blackboard behind him and drew a simple cross of two intersecting lines. "The crosses are almost identical in size and method. They're an inch and a half high and an inch wide. They're not just two cuts; the skin is actually notched out and removed, like carving your initials in a tree. I know what you're going to ask; the BSU doesn't have any idea what it means other than he's possibly a religious nut." Devlin made a mental note to check on Pilkington's whereabouts two years earlier.

For the next hour, the captain answered questions from the agents. Many of them had already developed theories and possible courses of investigation, most of which had already been conducted by the King County Police. In closing, Brockman said, "Suspects, gentlemen, we have ten thousand uninvestigated tips. One of the television stations has offered a hundred-thousand-dollar reward, so the tips came in faster than we could organize them. That's one of the reasons you're here, to help us form some sort of plan of attack and then investigate and eliminate them. Only one of these suspects is the right one."

Great, thought Devlin, ten thousand suspects. We're looking for a guy who hasn't hit in two years, who may be in prison, dead, or elsewhere. And I'm three light-years from my family. Fidelity, Bravery, Integrity.

Eighty-nine days later Devlin and the other nine weary "volunteers" boarded their planes and headed home. And in all probability, thought Devlin, were leaving the Puget Sound Killer unaware of their visit.

During the flight, Devlin slept but was awakened by a nightmare. He was back in Detroit and had solved another bank robbery.

"Mike." Jeff Ross walked out of his office, warmly extending his hand. Shortly after the Hamtramck robbery Ross's father had died, necessitating his taking over the business. Devlin shook his hand and remembered Ross's strength, a by-product of endless summers spent wrestling cast-iron bathtubs and steel automobile frames. Devlin had shown up unexpectedly at Ross's father's funeral, and they had remained friends ever since.

They walked into his office, which had recently been remodeled. "Very nice." Devlin said, looking around.

"Not bad for a Jewish kid from Oak Park."

"Jeff, I'm sorry. I don't have a lot of time, and I need a big favor."

"Just ask," Ross said.

Devlin told him about the missing girl and the leak. He explained the SAC's position and his own banishment to the wiretap. "Do you still own that old warehouse on West Jefferson?"

"The one you used to hide the witness that weekend? Yes."

"I'd like to use it for about ten days. There will be about a half dozen of us. Because of the SAC, we need a discreet place to work out of."

"What'll you need?" Ross picked up a pen.

Devlin saw the look in Ross's eyes. It was the same exhilarated look he had had when they had recovered the half-million dollars. "Telephones, two lines, three extensions. Three or four tables, a dozen chairs. Six army cots. Does the shower still work?"

"If not, it will by tomorrow morning."

"Good. I'll need extra keys for the door. And a copying machine."

"When will you need to get in there?"

"Tomorrow morning for the group, but I'd like to go over there now and make some calls."

Ross gave Devlin a spare key and said, "I'll see you there at seven A.M. How about a drink?"

"No, thanks. I've got some recruiting to do."

||| CHAPTER 9 |||

East Jefferson Avenue was the main street along the Detroit River, leading drivers past Cobo Hall, Ford Auditorium, and the gleaming height of the Renaissance Center. West Jefferson, however, vanished into warehouses, marine shipping terminals, and a ghost town of long-deserted businesses and factories. Even with an address in hand, buildings were difficult to find. The street itself was overgrown with anarchistic weeds and debris, unnegotiable because of the mine field of potholes. Devlin turned his car into what looked like a dead-end alley. Left at the back of the building and left again. The narrow lane opened into a small parking lot, isolated on all sides by structures similar to the one owned by Jeff Ross.

The warehouse had only one entrance, a single steel door accessed from the parking lot. The loading doors were on the Jefferson Avenue side of the building and had not been opened since the days of Prohibition. Ross had taken the building in trade for a business debt from the man who had it built to hide the Canadian whiskey he smuggled from across the river. Ross did not need the building but had fallen in love with its infamous history. Secret rooms for rebottling, storage, or personal security honeycombed the basement. On the second floor was a functional apartment, and the roof was surrounded by six-foot walls, along which was a continuous step, two feet high, so armed lookouts could walk the entire perimeter.

Devlin went inside. He could smell the dampness of its disuse. It had a small office in a corner of the first floor. He sat at a worn wooden desk and took out an office personnel list from his briefcase, and studied it. Aside from Livingston and himself, he listed five others. They were men he had worked with for years, men who were not intimidated by the seemingly unsolvable enigmas of major investigations. Men of a variety of skills who had a common dissatisfaction with the direction of the present-day Bureau. Men Devlin had worked with on impossible cases under desperate circumstances and with whom he had formed the unbreakable bonds of success. Simply, men who could—and would—get the job done, in spite of obstacles foreign or domestic.

Devlin picked up the phone and checked for a dial tone. It was working. He dialed the office.

"C-Four, Shanahan."

"Feel like tipping over some windmills?"

"How much trouble is this going to get me into?"

"The usual."

"How can I turn down such an attractive offer?"

"Get ahold of Al Humphrey, too."

"Okay. Are you getting anyone else?"

"Agash, Riley Smith, and maybe one more."

"Christ, you've got every mutineer in the office."

"Would you want anyone else?"

"Must be serious."

"Yeah, I think we're going to need some of the old days to survive this one."

Shanahan thought about how rewarding the work used to be and wondered if things had changed that much or if all the fires had gone out. There was one way to find out. "Where and when?"

"Tomorrow morning, sign in and then come to that warehouse on West Jeff where we stashed that witness."

"We'll be there."

Devlin placed a toll call. "Good afternoon, FBI Ann Arbor."

"Hi, Sandy, Mike Devlin. Is Riley Smith in?"

"Yes he is, Mike. Hold on."

Riley Smith had always amazed Devlin. He worked in the Ann Arbor Resident Agency, one of the ten small branch offices throughout the State of Michigan. RAs were generally thought to handle low-priority cases and a lot of busy work. But Smith always seemed to be wrapping up a major case. In his easygoing, down-home Kentucky manner, he plodded and prodded until the case was solved.

Devlin had worked on a number of major cases with him and knew that behind that bluegrass square dance was one hell of an investigator. Devlin would invite no other resident agent. They had a tendency to be more loyal to their territory than to the matter at hand. However, Smith's personal loyalty was a Bureau landmark.

Ten years earlier a fellow resident agent had had a son who had died of Reye's syndrome, a childhood disease peculiar to the Midwest. The agent was devastated and requested an emergency hardship transfer back to his native New Jersey for the safety of his other son. Predictably, the Bureau dragged its feet, and when his surviving son came down with the same symptoms, the agent immediately flew back to New Jersey with his child. He did not care what the consequences were. For one year, Riley Smith signed him in and out and worked every one of his cases, never saying a word about it. Everyone in the RA knew and a few in Detroit knew, but no one at the Bureau ever found out. Eventually they granted the hardship transfer to Newark. There were three things agents were taught not to question:

that Dillinger had shot first, J. Edgar Hoover's heterosexuality, and Riley Smith's loyalty.

"Mike Devlin. I didn't know that they had restored your telephone privileges. Are you allowed visitors?"

"You hicks in the RAs aren't supposed to know what's going on in the big city."

"Hell, I was just guessing. You're always in trouble. I know I'm going to be sorry, but is there anything I can do for you?"

"You're right. You are going to be sorry." Devlin explained the situation.

"Well. I haven't been in trouble since that time we got drunk celebrating the Ypsilanti bank extortion and smashed up the Bureau car."

"I remember *you* getting drunk and totaling that car. And *me* getting blamed for it."

"Proof, Michael. In this country, you must have proof."

Devlin called the office again and asked for Theo Agash. Most of his admirers called him Doc, which was short for Doctor Dick, so named for his understanding of women. A tireless hunter, he never accepted a woman's refusal. Though not particularly handsome, he had the eyes and mouth that women secretly understood as sensual; his glance set off chemical reactions in women. And as for undercover work, his Mediterranean features allowed him to pass for anything from black to Puerto Rican, from Italian to Arab. Devlin needed him in the group. The Doctor had been known to use his gifts for "the good of the service."

On one occasion, a local bank had cut off free checking for the FBI, a near-catastrophe for the penny-wise agents. The bank was being reorganized, and the person responsible for that decision was a new vice president named Sandra Borrman. She had been made a vice president at a very young age because of the innovations she was bringing to the bank. Besides the elimination of the Bureau's free checking, she developed an ingenious system known as VILEP, Visual In-Line Educational Programs. Different banking programs, such as college funds and home equity loans, were discussed in two-minute-long segments on videotape. The closed-circuit monitors were placed so customers who were in the teller lines could learn about the bank's latest services. Borrman took it one step further and put small monitors at each of the tellers' stations, so they could, with half an ear, learn the program at the same time and answer customers' questions. Using this system educated the customer and eliminated training time for the tellers. Justifiably, Borrman was very proud of her system; in fact, other banks had already started to adopt the procedure.

The Doctor was called in to "reason" with Borrman in hopes of reinstating the agents' lost benefit. After a month of his best stuff, she turned him down, flatly stating that sex was sex, business was business, and one would never influence the other. The refusal made him more determined.

On their next date, he took her to the apartment of "an out-of-town friend." It was very luxurious, furnished with liquor, stereo, and a large-screen TV in every room. After making love in some new ways, he took her home and left abruptly. He returned to the apartment, poured himself a drink, and replayed the tape taken by the video camera hidden in the big-screen TV. The apartment was part of an FBI undercover project that utilized video cameras to record narcotics transactions. His favorite scene was when, as Vice President Borrman occupied herself below his waist, he flashed a smile and the okay sign to the camera.

Agash went to see her once more to ask for reinstatement of the free checking. With the true heart of an administrator, she refused the request. As he left, he passed the video recorder that played the VILEP tapes. Unnoticed, into the pile of that day's tapes, he slipped in one whose typed title read "Prudent Banking—How to Get Ahead."

Two hours later, Borrman sat paralyzed as Doctor Dick flashed her the okay sign from the screen of the monitor on her desk.

She called Agash at the office, where he was waiting for her call. Unceremoniously, she called him a motherfucker, which he agreed he was. Then he asked her if she thought any of the other banks would be interested in "Prudent Banking."

After a very long silence, she told him free checking would resume immediately.

"CI-Two. Agash."

"Doc. Mike Devlin."

"Mike, where have you been hiding?"

"You know me. Just trying to fit in."

"Yeah. I always try to fit in."

"Doc, how would you like to step into the breach one more time?"

"Ahhh. You know me. The breach is my life."

That was six people. He again considered his final choice. In Detroit, one could not always depend on technique, luck, or being right. The city was dangerous, filled with violent people. Devlin knew he needed intimidation. He needed terror. He dialed Gunnar Brackoff's confidential line.

Devlin drove home. He did not like what he was about to do. He would tell Knox about the investigations and their importance. Then he would tell her he was not going to be around much—with the long hours he would stay at the warehouse apartment. She had endured Vietnam, Sound-murs, and a hundred other cases that had kidnapped his attention and priorities during their time with the Bureau. Now this. She did not deserve it. But she would smile her support and shrug her shoulders. She had once said it was "simply part of the Devlin package." She never asked about cases and never got to feel the high her husband brought home after each success.

When Devlin walked through the door, Knox looked at the clock defensively, then at him, searching his face for trouble. "Everything's fine," he assured her. She kept her eyes on him, waiting to find out what "everything" was.

He told her about Vanessa and the leak, reluctantly exposing his prominent role in the coming conspiracy. She seemed almost relieved. She knew his caution was another apology to her for the latest wrong he always seemed to be called upon to right. Part of the Devlin package.

"Mike, did you ever wonder why it's always you?"

"Just lucky, I guess," he said facetiously. But she knew he was proud as hell that it was always him.

"If they catch you, what are the chances you'll be fired?" Now Knox's "if" sounded facetious, as though it was only a matter of time before "they" discovered the subplot.

"Hey, I just promised to love, honor, and obey. I never said anything about keeping you in all this luxury."

Knox laughed. She knew if she had wanted predictability, she would have gotten her Ph.D. in history. Actually, she had become a spellbound passenger on the roller coaster that roared and soared through their lives. "How much do you think I'll see you during this one?"

"I should probably stay down there the first few days until we get organized."

"You haven't got a girlfriend down there, do you?" Knox asked with mock suspicion.

Devlin held out his hand and looked at his fingernails,

feigning a womanizer's arrogance. "I'm going to have to take the Fifth on that."

"I'll pack a suitcase for you."

Devlin smiled warmly. "I guess I *am* just lucky."

||| PART TWO |||

III CHAPTER 10 III

By eight the next morning, Jeff Ross's warehouse was ready for the investigators, who now sat in their chairs facing Devlin. Along the walls, six army cots lay unobtrusively. A large, white secondhand refrigerator sat near the briefing area, quietly humming. Next to it, a table held a microwave oven. The refrigerator had been stocked with frozen microwavables, cold cuts, cheeses, bread, and a lion's share of beer. A small rented copying machine sat nearby, with an annex table loaded with paper. The phones would be installed no later than two P.M. A fifty-cup urn chugged away, and the smell of fresh coffee overrode the building's damp chill. Most of the men were drinking sleepily from Styrofoam cups.

The group was listening to Bill Shanahan. He was a storyteller in the finest tradition of the Irish. No matter how unbelievable his stories seemed, his Boston accent lent them credibility.

"You know Judge O'Malley over at Recorder's Court." It was not a question, merely Shanahan's version of "Once upon a time." "Well, you know how that guy likes to drink. His wife's out of town for the night, so he goes out and gets completely bombed. He gets so drunk he passes out. When he wakes up, he finds he's thrown up all over his suit. He goes home, strips, takes a shower, dresses, and goes to work. That afternoon his wife calls after coming

161

home and finding his clothes. But he's ready for her. He tells her a drunk came before him in court and threw up all over him. To add credibility to the story, he tells her he took care of the drunk, giving him five days in the county jail. Calmly, she says to him, 'Pat, if he ever comes before you again, you'd better give him thirty days because he shit in your pants too.' " Shanahan pumped his right hand in the air to prove the story was true.

When the laughter stopped, Devlin started the briefing. "I appreciate everyone coming. Jeff, can you come out here a second?" Ross trotted in for an introduction. "This is Jeff Ross, a good friend of the Bureau. He's responsible for all of this. In general terms, he knows what we're doing here. If you need anything, give him a call. His number's in your envelopes."

Shanahan sneezed, "Donutsss!" Ross smiled and made a mental note.

Devlin continued, "Let's give Jeff one of our traditional FBI greetings."

In slowly enunciated unison came their voices: "Hell-o, ass-hole." Ross knew the humor was a display of acceptance. The smile on his face was that of a minor-league ballplayer who had gotten called up to play in the World Series. Even riding the bench, he still had the best seat in the house.

Devlin became more serious. "We have one other non-Bureau person with us. For those of you who do not know him, this is Sergeant Gunnar Brackoff from DPD Holdup." Brackoff stood up and solemnly nodded to the group.

Again Devlin said, "How about a big FBI hello."

To the man, everyone chose discretion over valor and chimed in with "Hell-o, Ser-geant Brack-off." Devlin congratulated himself on choosing a group filled with such wisdom.

"As I see it, we have three problems," Devlin started.

"First, Tom Anderson's daughter is missing. SAC Pilkington feels she has run away and has outlawed any further investigation, which brings us to our second problem. This operation is against SAC orders, and we all know the consequences of insubordination. And, third, I have what I believe to be reliable information that an unknown male employee is about to sell a complete list of our informants to Anthony Pantatelli. You can all appreciate what damage that would do.

"ASAC John O'Hare is aware of the leak. He's agreed not to let Pilkington know for ten days and has authorized us to do whatever is necessary to resolve the problem. He has no idea about our investigation into Vanessa's disappearance. I gave him a list of your names, and he's telling your supervisors to excuse you. During these ten days, do not go to the office, and have your families screen your calls, so you don't have to lie to your supervisors. It'll be one less charge in the end. There's no good that can come of this for any of us. At best we can solve both matters and no one will ever know. We'll just go back to what we were doing. And you know what the worst is."

No one said a word. They sat stoically, remembering the Bureau they had joined and worked so hard for. And in return, they had been given an unmatched sureness that their lives had taken all the right turns. Now that feeling was being dusted off. It might prove expensive, but they all wanted to feel its touch once more.

Bill Shanahan spoke up. "I don't think much of Tom Anderson these days. I'd be surprised if anyone in this room did, but Vanessa is an FBI daughter, and if we don't take care of our own, no matter what the cost, then we become part of the farce we've complained about for so long. In the immortal words of my Irish ancestors—Fuck management."

Devlin polled the other faces and again decided he had chosen well.

Devlin took the next thirty minutes to discuss the search of Vanessa's room and his interview with Nancy Pappas. The group agreed that it was not likely she would have left the three twenty-dollar bills if she had planned to run away. Her visit to the Pappas girl reinforced their feelings, and each felt that Stand was the best lead.

Then Livingston explained the collection and examination of the informant room keys. Not only had the lab found a second set of vise marks on key number two, but they were able to determine that the marks had been made by different vises, verifying Devlin's theory.

Devlin gave a short explanation of the suspicions that had been raised about Sumpter and said, "In your envelopes you should have the following—" Devlin hesitated as everyone emptied his envelope. "A key for the door of this place. A black-and-white photo of Vanessa Anderson. Five Polaroids, one shot each of the four clerks who borrowed key number two plus one of Sumpter. A black-and-white DPD mug shot of Alvan Stand. Photocopies of the yellow pages of the approximately one hundred locksmiths in Detroit. Background sheets on Vanessa, Stand, Sumpter, and the four clerks. The last thing is an index card with everyone's new call sign on it. We're not going to use our Bureau call signs. If anyone decides to listen, they'll have to recognize our voices to identify us, and I think it'll make communications a little quicker and less confusing. Since we're working out of a warehouse, I picked the letters W.H. The military phonetic alphabet converts that to Whiskey Hotel, which will be the call sign for this operation. I assigned numbers more or less in the order that each of you became involved in this case. I will be Whiskey Hotel One, Livingston—Two, Shanahan—Three, Humphrey—Four, Smith—Five, the Doctor is Six, and Gunnar Brackoff is

Whiskey Hotel Seven. Jeff Ross is Whiskey Hotel Eight. The building will be referred to as Whiskey Hotel. You can stick these cards in your cars' visors as a quick reference. Here are the assignments: Riley Smith and Al Humphrey, split up the lock shops geographically and start showing photos. Ed, give them each a key—not number two, put that into evidence." Livingston handed the two agents keys. "Each key has DO NOT DUPLICATE stamped into it, so it should stand out in the locksmith's memory. Don't forget other places that make keys: hardware stores, department stores, et cetera."

Al Humphrey, a thorough, persistent bank robbery agent, asked, "How did they get around the DO NOT DUPLICATE warning?"

"A story wouldn't be hard to make up. Locksmiths make money duping keys, not asking questions. If you find the locksmith, note the make of the key machine and the serial number. We'll have to seize it as evidence and ship it back to the lab so the vise marks can be matched. Okay, communications. Use channel A-Three in private. But remember, the office can descramble it, so watch what you say. Any questions?" There were none.

Smith and Humphrey took out a map of Detroit and started dividing the hundred locksmiths into two geographical lists.

Devlin addressed the remainder of the group: "At least initially, the rest of us will work on finding the girl. We're going to concentrate on Alvan Stand. Theo Agash and Bill Shanahan, you'll surveil him. His address and car are on his background sheet. Gunnar Brackoff is going to check Stand's neighborhood for Vanessa's car. It's still missing. It's been entered into NCIC by the Troy Police Department. The car's description is on her background sheet. Ed Livingston will man the phones and radio, and I'll be here if you need me."

After the others had left, Devlin plugged in a large porta-mobile radio and switched it into the scan mode. Momentarily it locked on channel A-3. "Whiskey Hotel Five to Whiskey Hotel Four, how do you hear me?" Smith was checking his scrambler.

"I've got you, Lima Charlie," Humphrey answered. Loud and Clear.

It was nine A.M. For the last hour, Tom Anderson had been looking for Devlin. When he walked into the tech room at eight o'clock, a C-Ten agent explained that his supervisor had told him Devlin was not working the wiretap any longer. The supervisor had told him that ASAC O'Hare had called and said Devlin was doing something for him and was to be taken off the shift.

Back in the squad area, Anderson thought Livingston might know where Devlin was; they had been close ever since they had gotten lucky and arrested that murderer in the Duffield bar. Livingston was not around. Anderson checked his three-card slot—there was no locator card. Sue said she had no idea where Livingston was. He doubted she would tell him even if she did know.

He decided to ask Fauber, even though he had been icy toward him since his daughter's disappearance. "Excuse me, sir." Anderson's voice was adequately subservient. "Do you know where Livingston is?"

"No. Not that it's any of your business, he and Shanahan are doing something for O'Hare. The ASAC called and cleared it with me this morning."

Yeah, I'll bet he did, thought Anderson, and thanks for asking about my daughter, Supervisory Special Agent Cocksucker. "Thank you, sir."

Fauber made a mental note of Anderson's inquiry. Two of his men were missing, and despite what he had told

Anderson, he had not been offered a satisfactory explanation. He promised himself he would look into it.

By 9:30 the surveillance team had set up on Stand's residence. His chocolate-colored BMW sat in the driveway. The dew on the windshield indicated it had not been moved that morning. The house also showed no signs of life.

"Whiskey Hotel Six to Whiskey Hotel One." Agash was calling Devlin.

"Go ahead, Six," Devlin answered, his voice hollow in the empty warehouse.

"We're at the roost. Looks like our man is still inside."

"Stay on it, Six."

At noon, Stand was still at his residence. The warehouse had received periodic radio messages from Smith and Humphrey. After each locksmith interview, they called in so Livingston could line them off a master list. By noon, they had eliminated twenty-two shops.

At 1:30 Agash called Devlin. "Our man's firing up his chopper right now. He's carrying a large soft-sided brief case which is bulging. He's got a big, mean-looking mulatto with him. The mulatto came out first and really eyeballed the area. Then he called our man out. He looks to be packing."

Agash was streetwise. Before the Bureau, he had been a Los Angeles narcotics officer. Because of his blending appearance, he had extensive undercover experience. Devlin sensed the hunt turning in their favor. The smell of blood reduced the formality of the radio procedure.

"Doc, do you think our man is holding?"

"Tell you what, Mike, I'm sure he's holding, but I think the white shadow is going to light up anyone who gets near him."

A shudder of adrenaline fell endlessly through Devlin's stomach. If Agash was right, the mulatto, whose job it was to protect the narcotics Stand was carrying, would start shooting at the slightest indication of trouble. Any shooting would bring the police and an end to their investigation. "Six, give him lots of room, but don't lose him or that briefcase. I'm on my way."

As he reached the door, Devlin heard the radio. "We're rolling." In his car, he switched his radio to A-3 just in time to hear Agash. "Southbound on the main, just crossing the ditch. I'm going to give him some action. Three, can you get up here and take the eye?"

Shanahan answered, "Yeah, I got him, Doc. Go ahead and make your turn."

Once Agash had made the turn to avert suspicion, he made a hard U-turn, then turned again quickly and was again southbound a quarter mile behind Shanahan, who was now responsible for the eyeball on Stand. Devlin's vehicle wove in and out of expressway traffic at ninety miles an hour.

Shanahan spoke again. "We're held at a ruby. I'm two behind him."

Good, thought Devlin, with Stand stopped at a red light he would have more time to catch up.

"Shit," Shanahan spit into the mike. "He's busting the light. I'm stuck behind another car." Shanahan had no reservations about his next move. He stomped the gas pedal and cut the wheel hard to the right. The car slammed up and onto the sidewalk. Once around the car in front of him he turned hard left and bounced back into the street, heading after the vanishing BMW. "I'm on him again, but he's really got his foot into it."

"Bill, has he made you?" Devlin asked, wondering if Stand's tactics were the result of spotting the surveillance.

"I don't think so. Sometimes these clowns just drive like this. But, we're doing sixty in a thirty. He's going to make me before much longer."

"Try and stay with him. I'm almost there. As soon as we

can get you some help, we'll stop him." Devlin could not bother with the call signs anymore. "Doc, are you close?"

"No. I'm stuck at that light, at least a half a mile behind Bill."

Devlin turned off the expressway and saw Agash scream by. He ground the accelerator into the floor, trying to catch up. "Bill, have you still got him?"

There was silence. Damn, thought Devlin, hoping Shanahan had not crashed. Then: "Mike, I think I lost him. I'm doubling back heading west on Plymouth. Someone head east."

Devlin said, "Doc, you head east. I'm going to continue south."

For the next five minutes the radio maintained its aching silence.

Finally Devlin asked, "Anybody got anything?"

The answers came:

"Whiskey Hotel Six, negative."

"Three is negative."

Devlin slammed his fist on the dashboard. He was about to call off the search when he heard Brackoff casually call, "Whiskey Hotel Seven to Whiskey Hotel One. I have something I think you might be interested in. I'm at Sorrento where it dead-ends into the tracks behind an abandoned factory."

"We're on our way," Devlin answered. He was only three blocks from Brackoff's location and arrived first. He had questioned his selection of Brackoff to work on such a sensitive operation because of the cop's reputation as a bulldozer. When Devlin turned behind the factory, he questioned his choice no longer. Brackoff, holding an illegal sawed-off double-barrelled shotgun, stood over a spread-eagled Alvan Stand and his bodyguard.

Devlin gave Brackoff a questioning look. Brackoff simply answered, "I heard the surveillance. I was close by and thought I could help."

Devlin knew what Brackoff had done was much more difficult and dangerous than his explanation. He gave Brackoff a quick look of disbelief, telling him he knew otherwise and appreciated it. In the next thirty seconds, the other two Bureau cars slid around the back of the factory.

Agash got out first, smiling. "Hey, Brackoff, if you need any more help on surveillances, just let me know."

Devlin said, "Doc, I think Mr. Stand needs some help with his briefcase."

Agash asked Brackoff, "Was I right about the white shadow packing?"

"I didn't check." Brackoff's explanation had no apology in it. Agash knew Brackoff was too good a cop not to have searched for a weapon. He reached under the bodyguard's jacket and pulled a 9mm automatic from his belt. Agash looked into Brackoff's terrible eyes, then at Devlin. They realized that Brackoff wanted the bodyguard to try to use the gun. It was well known that "Gunner" Brackoff had shot and killed nine men and had never been wounded. Brackoff lowered the shotgun and let his shoulder and neck muscles relax, disappointed this wouldn't be the day his total would go into double figures.

Agash opened the briefcase. "Hair-on," he deliberately mispronounced heroin in black street vernacular. "We're going to have to arrest you for dealing drugs that are out of style, Al-van. Crack is the thang, mah man."

Letting his professional pride cloud his legal sense, Stand shot back, "You know, huh? Mixed jive is what's happening. I'da sold all hundred packs by dark." Each bundle contained ten dime packs, selling for thirteen dollars apiece. Heroin was making a comeback in Detroit, a city of infinite tradition.

"Quite the entrepreneur," Agash said.

The best technique was to separate the two dope dealers before they started talking to each other. Once separated, they could be questioned about Vanessa, and later their stories compared.

"Gunnar, take Alvan's friend for a drive," Devlin said as Brackoff's smile changed the mulatto's face from hate to fear. "Doc, go with them and see what he knows." The bodyguard was relieved to see the disappointment on Brackoff's face.

Devlin asked Stand, "How much weight have you got here?"

Again without considering the consequences, Stand said, "About fifty grams."

"You know the law, that's enough for a mandatory twenty-year sentence."

Stand's silence indicated he did, and he realized that he had better start measuring his answers.

"We're going to make this real easy for you. Twenty years as the Jackson Prison homecoming queen, or you tell us what we want to know."

With usual dope dealer integrity, Stand said, "Whatever you want to know. I can tell you who's dealing what and when."

"Uh-oh," Devlin said, "this man thinks we're from Narcotics."

Stand was confused. "Who the fuck are you?" Devlin opened his credentials. Immediately Stand understood the situation. "I don't know nothing about the bitch." Stand immediately realized he had chosen the wrong word to describe Vanessa.

Devlin drew close to him, close enough for Stand to envision the dragon's impending sortie. "I don't give a fuck about you; I don't give a fuck about dope; and I certainly don't give a fuck if you leave here alive. I want the girl. She was seen going into your place the night she disappeared," Devlin lied, "so if you won't help us, I'll have to assume you killed her, and we'll sentence you right here."

The two men stared at each other. Stand was trying to decide if Devlin would carry out his threat. Stand was tough-minded. As a dealer, he had been involved in this exact negotiation many times before. In this agent's eyes he saw the flecks of insanity he had seen in the deals he had backed down from, but this was a cop who, unlike dope dealers, was bound by conscience and law. But a certain impatient determination registered in Devlin's words, leaving Stand uncertain.

Devlin walked to his car and spoke into the mike. "Whiskey Hotel Seven, return to our location." Within moments the Bureau car pulled back into the parking lot. Brackoff lumbered out of the car, shotgun in hand, leaving a sweaty bodyguard behind.

Getting into his car, Devlin pronounced their sentence. "They're all yours, Brackoff."

The only measure of success in the narcotics trade was survival. Money was a constant. Surviving the competition and the cops was the bottom line. Many millionaire dope dealers occupied prison cells or expensive caskets. Stand's "success" to date had been a result of his ability to size up his opponents' strengths and weaknesses, then react appropriately. There was only one way to read the psychopath they called Brackoff. "No. Wait, I sent her to the airport to pick up a shipment from L.A. She never came back."

Devlin got out of the car and walked back to Stand. "Start over—when she came to your house that night."

"Okay. She comes over and tells me she can't see me anymore. I could care less. I didn't like her or anything and I wasn't—ah—sleeping with her." Brackoff's stern hand around the shotgun reminded Stand to choose his words carefully.

"Why were you going out with her?"

"I was trying to set her up to mule one load for me. I know about the profiles at the airports. They look for young blacks picking up suitcases. They run the dope dogs by you, and you're gone. So I figure out this scam for getting a suitcase full of dope here, but I needed a young white broad to pick it up."

"Go ahead," Devlin said.

Proudly, Stand explained, "My man in L.A. checked his woman, under Vanessa's name, onto an American Airlines flight to Detroit. Even though the flight wasn't until late in the afternoon, he checked her in with her suitcase early in the morning. He took the baggage tickets and Federal Expressed them to my house. Same-day delivery. Then I conned Vanessa into picking up the bag when the flight gets in. That way there's an innocent young white girl picking up the suitcase and if anyone checks, her old man's an FBI agent. And I don't have to touch the dope."

"That's pretty sophisticated," Devlin said.

"Yeah, except Vanessa gets in a fight with her old man and gets here two hours late and has to go to the lost-baggage counter to claim the bag. Really screwed up the appearance of just getting off the flight."

"Sure you thought this all up yourself?" Devlin asked.

"Well. I do have a senior partner, so to speak."

"What's his name?"

"Man, I can't tell you," Stand said weakly.

Devlin turned and looked at Brackoff.

"Okay, it's Frankie Williams."

"Ooh, Alvan, I think you might be out of your league," Agash said.

"How much contact did Frankie have with Vanessa?" Devlin asked.

"None, man. He never met her, didn't even know her name. He does now, though, cause it looks like she boogied with our shit."

"Why do you say that?"

"She left my place at eight o'clock. Half hour to the airport. Half hour there. Half hour back. She never showed. The FBI's at my house the next day, saying she disappeared. So she took off with the dope. If Frankie finds her, he'll have her whacked."

"Did you check after she didn't show up to see if the suitcase had been picked up?"

"No, after the FBI showed I wasn't going anywhere near that airport."

Walking out of earshot, Devlin asked Brackoff, "What did the mulatto say?"

"Same thing. Sent the girl to pick up the suitcase. She didn't come back. They were afraid she'd been busted, so they didn't want to call the airport. The next day you guys say she's gone, so they figure she took off with the dope. Seems logical, at least the way they think."

"Alvan, we're keeping your dope and guns. If anything you've told me is not true or if you hear anything and don't call me, the sergeant here will be coming for you."

"Man, I ain't bullshittin'."

"If you are, I'll see Frankie and let him know who his friends aren't."

The four men got into their cars and headed to the Detroit Metropolitan Airport.

As he sped west, Devlin radioed Livingston at the warehouse. "Anything on the key?"

"Negative. They've covered about forty locations. Still no luck."

"Okay. We're all heading to Metro Airport. When I get there I'll give you a landline and fill you in."

Reluctantly Devlin drove toward the airport, afraid all leads there would disappear as quickly as an outbound jet.

Although her day was not yet half over, the girl at the lost-baggage counter had had her fill of everybody else's problems. Her mussed blond hair and wrinkled uniform both hung on her disobediently. An alien Band-Aid sat crookedly on a just-broken fingernail, and her eyes blinked semaphorically: e-n-o-u-g-h. "Hi, we're with the FBI," Devlin said, opening his identification. Her expression showed she was not impressed. She challenged her latest problem with an unfriendly "Yes."

Devlin realized he had misjudged her and said, "Excuse me." He turned to Agash and said, "I'd better call Livingston. You can handle this." He gave Agash a relief-pitcher nod.

"Ed, how are you doing back there?"

"I would be better if I were out with you, doing something. Oh, yeah, the phones have been put in."

"Okay, tomorrow I'll rotate someone in there so you can work the street. How are they doing with the locksmiths?"

"Okay. Most of them close at five, so they'll have to quit then."

"Have them come back to the warehouse." Devlin then told him about Vanessa being sent to the airport to pick up the suitcase, and that he and Agash were trying to get it without a court order. "The rest of the crew is combing the airport parking lots for Anderson's car. I hope we're not running into a dead end here. I'll radio you when I figure out if there's anything else to be done today."

As Devlin walked back to the lost-baggage area, the smiling girl was pushing a suitcase over the counter to Agash, who made it appear that he was less interested in the suitcase than he was in her company. "What time do you work until?"

"This week, ten every night," she said with a disgusted moan as if she expected Agash to be as disappointed as she was.

Devlin took over. "You were here until ten o'clock Monday night?"

She answered with an annoyed "Yes."

Showing a photograph of Vanessa, he asked, "Was she here that night?"

"Yes, she was," the blonde answered slowly, trying to focus through her gauzy memory. "Yes, that's right. She came in. Said she was—" The girl looked again at the tag on the suitcase in front of her. "—Vanessa Anderson and wanted her suitcase. She had the claim check but had forgotten her identification in the car. She never came back, so I figured she was lying."

"What time was that?"

"Just before I got off." Looking to Agash, she finished, "At ten o'clock."

"Did she have anyone with her, or did anybody seem to be waiting for her?"

"No." She searched her memory further. "No. No one."

Devlin pulled the suitcase off the countertop. "Thank you very much. Doc, give her a receipt and make sure she knows how to get ahold of us if she remembers anything else. I'll be at the sheriff's office."

As he walked away, Devlin heard the girl ask, "Why do they call you Doc?" Devlin suspected that at ten o'clock, if they were not still working, all her questions would be answered.

Devlin walked outside to his car and radioed Bill Shanahan. Over the years, because he had been his contacting agent, Shanahan had learned about locks from Touchy Williams. Touchy had taught him to be patient with them, search them, stroke them. Once Shanahan understood it was like handling a woman, he became deft at their solution. "Meet me in the sheriff's office and bring your bag." Devlin did not have to ask if Anderson's car had been found. It would have been the first thing on the radio.

The Wayne County Sheriff's Office maintained a unit at the airport. Its personnel handled a full spectrum of cases, everything from stewardesses being pinched to smuggling guns, money, and narcotics. They were overworked and understaffed. They were also reasonable and helpful.

The sergeant on duty let Devlin use a room and lent him a narcotics testing kit.

Devlin called Alvan Stand. "Can you talk?"

"Yeah." The resignation in his voice told Devlin he knew who the caller was.

"I've got the bag, Alvan." There was no answer. "Where are the keys?"

"Frankie."

"It doesn't matter. I'm going to open it. You call Frankie and tell him you called the airport and the sheriff's office got the suitcase because the dog hit on it. Tell him to forget about Vanessa."

"Okay, but he ain't going to like it."

Devlin hung up. Agash and Shanahan walked in. "It's all yours." Devlin gestured at the suitcase.

From his small black canvas satchel, Shanahan took out a thin black metal bar bent in an L shape and a short, stubby pick. He inserted them both into each of the suitcase's locks and, with the speed of a key, opened them. Among some old clothes used as packing were four bundles, each approximately the size of a small loaf of bread, wrapped heavily with gray duct tape.

Agash hefted each package. "They're each a key." He cut into one of the packages with a pocketknife and drew out a small amount of brownish red powder on the blade of the knife. Talking to himself, he said, "Mexican." He tapped the granules into a testing tube, capped it, and broke the section holding the reagent. Almost immediately, it turned a deep blue. Agash flicked the tube with the fingernail of his little finger to ensure that all the heroin had dissolved. "For Mexican, it's really clean. As fast as it popped, I'd guess maybe forty percent pure."

"What's it worth?" Devlin asked.

"Which value do you want, what Frankie paid for it or what the SAC would tell the newspapers it's worth?"

"What Frankie lost on it."

"He probably paid eighty to a hundred grand a key, so anywhere up to four hundred thousand."

Shanahan asked, "What would it go for on the street?"

"Without a calculator I could give you a ballpark figure. Since you have about forty percent, and that's kind of a wild guess, you divide that by the street strength. In Detroit, that's about two percent. So you can whack this load about twenty times. So—roughly four million. As it goes from the Bureau to the media it'll be reported as six to eight million."

Shanahan laughed. "Boy, will Frankie be pissed."

Agash ripped a piece of tape off of one of the packages and put it over the puncture he had made.

"We're going back to the warehouse," Devlin said. "Doc, take the testing kit back to the sergeant and thank him. Then you can take off from here." Agash gave him a nod of appreciation. He hoped he had made his bed; he did not want Miss Lust Luggage to think he was a typical bachelor living in squalor.

At the warehouse, Livingston had nailed a sheet of plywood onto one of the warehouse's aged wooden columns. Using it as a briefing board, he had pinned up charts and lists he had constructed. At one end was a map of the metropolitan area, already stuck with pins locating Stand's house, the airport, and Vanessa's home.

Riley Smith gave the locksmith briefing. They had contacted the downtown locksmiths first, theorizing that the guilty person had probably had the key duplicated during a short, daytime loan. Time being of the essence, it would have been copied downtown, close to the office. But that theory had yielded nothing. Next, they had gone to the neighborhoods of the five suspects, thinking the person would duplicate it out of convenience or familiarity with the locksmith to avoid any question about the DO NOT DUPLI-CATE stamp. When that idea washed out, they split up the remaining shops and wore out shoe leather. At day's end, they had interviewed seventy-two locksmiths without a hint of success. Starting at nine A.M. the next day, they would start interviewing the rest.

"What do you think, Riley, are we heading in the right direction?" Devlin was asking a question that could be answered only by an investigator's instinct.

"I don't know. Somehow this approach feels right to me. I think we still got a shot."

That was good enough for Devlin. Smith's intuition had solved as many cases as his determination had.

Devlin gave a brief rundown of Stand's interview and what had been found at the airport. He asked for questions. Mischievously, Shanahan, an admirer of the Agash mystique, asked, "Where's the Doctor?"

Looking at his watch, Devlin answered, "By now, he's probably in surgery."

The warehouse door flew open and banged against the wall behind it. Jeff Ross balanced three large brown bags. "I hope you guys like Chinese." Cops have a natural distrust of outsiders, but Ross was becoming an exception.

Ross was allowed to stay and listen to the crew discuss the investigations as they ate. Vanessa had been at the airport. She had tried to claim the suitcase and was last seen going to her car. According to her stepmother, she had her purse and identification. Did she go back to Stand and refuse to pick up the suitcase, causing Stand to do something to her? If so, why didn't he attempt to pick up the suitcase? The only theory that answered all the questions was that when she had gone to the parking lot for her purse, someone had abducted her.

The next day's investigative plan was decided. Smith and Humphrey would finish the locksmiths. Livingston and Devlin would start at the airport, contacting different police departments regarding abductions, sexual assaults, and any other related incidents. Shanahan would man the communications at the warehouse. Agash and Shanahan switched cars with Humphrey and Smith for a new look while surveilling Stand.

The day had been disheartening for the group. The best leads had ended without promise. And although Vanessa's trail had been tracked further, it had abruptly disappeared into an empty parking lot. Devlin knew the crew would be more effective the next day if their minds were diverted for a while. He opened the refrigerator and started passing out the beer.

Bill Shanahan drank half a can with his first swallow. With a fresh pint in his fist, he started a story. "Did you ever hear what the good Doctor did to the woman who broke up his marriage?" Not waiting, he went on, "He had been screwing this nurse for about a month. She knew about his wife and decides she wants the Doctor all to herself. She calls up his wife and tells her everything, every little detail, even describes the Doctor's duggan, which leaves no doubt in Mrs. Dick's mind that the lady has had a dose of the Doctor's medicine. When he gets home that night, there are all these garbage bags in the driveway. He can't figure it out. He knows it's not garbage day. Inside the bags are all of his clothes and a note telling him about the call and that his wife is leaving him. The Master is pissed. He goes to the girl's apartment and literally drinks her unconscious. He then takes off her panties and dry-shaves all of her pubic hair. Then he puts her panties back on and stuffs all the hair back in them. Can you imagine what she thought the next morning? She gets up hung over, takes her panties off and her beaver falls on the floor."

The laughter was more intoxicating for Shanahan than the alcohol. Even Brackoff was smiling. Shanahan started his next story. The more he told, the more he drank, and little by little, a brogue crept into his voice.

It was crude and noisy, but Devlin had seen it before. An unspoken rule was in effect: no further discussions of the cases that night. The alcohol and stories were a buffer, separating the day's failures from tomorrow's renewed effort. As this case went on and on, the end-of-day sessions would get longer and longer.

‖‖ CHAPTER 11 ‖‖

Low across the flat, inky water of the Detroit River, a freighter's foghorn moaned its tired loneliness. It groaned again. Devlin judged it to be moving upriver. He could not sleep. It was almost one A.M. The others had left around eleven. Until midnight he had sat reviewing everything, but something was whispering to be noticed, something he had missed. When he finally turned out the warehouse lights and went to bed, the darkness intensified his apprehension. The foghorn gave a waning complaint from the northeast. His consciousness remained unsettled.

He got dressed and went to his car. Forcing himself not to pick a destination, he drove off, diverting his mind intentionally by reading every sign he could. Street signs, billboards, business names, bumper stickers. A large green truck, filthy from work, chugged slowly in front of him. On the tailgate was the company's logo: CADILLAC WRECKING: DEMOLITION IS PROGRESS. It could be the mayor's next campaign slogan, thought Devlin.

He let his mind focus and found he was westbound on the Ford Expressway, heading toward the airport. The whisper got louder.

He pulled off the expressway and drove slowly into the deserted airport, which at two A.M. was a much less complicated place. He drove the main road that looped within the airport for half an hour, trying not to focus on anything in particular, just seeing everything again and again. He decided to retrace Vanessa's probable route. He pulled up to the parking lot that was adjacent to the lost-baggage counter. The black-and-white diagonally striped gate refused him access until he pulled a parking ticket from the machine that triggered the raising of the gate. He parked as far away from the terminal as possible, reasoning he would then have to walk past where Vanessa had parked, wherever that was. Zigzagging through the parking lanes, Devlin checked the ground for any evidence of the girl. At the end of the lot, he walked directly to the lost-baggage counter, which was closed. Back in his car, he sat bewildered. He closed his eyes. Nothing.

He drove through the parking lot, then to the lone, sleepy parking attendant and handed her his ticket.

"One dollar." Devlin paid and drove around the airport for another half hour. He heard the whisper no more and drove back to the warehouse. When he lay down, exhaustion crept over him like a thick, warm quilt.

For the next few hours Devlin's mind slept, but then it rose and started working. The dream itself was exhausting. Devlin kept pulling up to the airport parking attendant, but Vanessa was the attendant. He would give her the ticket and she would say, "One dollar, Agent Devlin." He would hand her the money, and then he would be pulling up to the booth again, handing her the ticket. Again and again and again. Finally he pulled up and was out of cash. Vanessa was gone from the booth, and the gate was open. Devlin drove through the gate and snapped awake.

That was it! The parking tickets. Whoever left in Vanessa's car had to use a parking ticket to get out of the lot. Her prints would be pressed onto it as she took it from the machine, and if someone had abducted her, he might then have driven the car and handed the ticket to the attendant. Both their prints could be on the same ticket. All the tickets were dated and stamped with times in and out.

Devlin wondered if Anderson had a copy of his daughter's fingerprints. He looked at his watch—6:30. He dialed Anderson at home and calmed his voice. "Tom, just wanted to let you know I'm still working on this, but so far I haven't found much."

"Have Shanahan and Livingston been helping you?"

Devlin was caught off guard by Anderson's priorities. "Why would you think that?"

"They weren't around today, and Fauber didn't know exactly where they were." As soon as Anderson said it, he realized he had made a mistake. He could feel Devlin freeze on the other end of the line. Any conversation with Fauber, about anything or anybody remotely related to what Devlin was doing, would be interpreted as a breach of their unspoken agreement. Quickly he changed the subject. "What did that Nancy Pappas have to say?"

"Your wife told you about that?"

"Yes. Of course."

"Obviously you don't like her either."

"No. I don't."

"Before I forget, Tom, I thought it might be good to have a set of Vanessa's fingerprints, if you've got them."

"As a matter of fact, I do. When she ran away before, it occurred to me they might come in handy in the future, so I took her down to the office one Saturday and printed her."

"Good. Leave them in my mail folder and I'll pick them up this morning."

"Mike, how come you're not working the tech anymore?"

"The ASAC has me doing something for him. I've got to go. I'll call you tomorrow."

Anderson sat with the dead phone in his hand. Devlin, Shanahan, and Livingston were all doing something for the

ASAC. Anderson knew Devlin was hiding something. He had not answered one of his questions.

Next, Devlin called Allan Humphrey. Humphrey, like everyone else on the warehouse crew, had his idiosyncrasies. But Devlin had found that quirks were usually the balancing end of exceptional abilities. In Humphrey's case, he was considered a bookworm. While most agents had a tendency not to enhance their mental abilities beyond their job, Humphrey read incessantly. His two great loves were scientific journals and science fiction. He was the absentminded scientist type, capable of flighty behavior and, if interested, intense concentration. Normally if an agent went to a bank robbery and was told to dust for fingerprints, he would ask the victim teller where the bandit had touched and process those areas, not going a fingerprint further. Humphrey approached it as if he had discovered a tomb of the Pharaohs and was responsible for exploring every inch. He would dust every square millimeter of the teller's station, the chrome poles that held the customer line ropes, the glass doors leading in and out of the bank. Without exception, he would bring a large garbage bag back to the office and dump onto his desk every piece of paper from the customer-area wastebaskets because the robber might have touched one of them. Other agents were less patient, especially during golf season, and would leave Humphrey at the bank, where he would obliviously spend additional hours collecting his data. The other agents thought of him as a little offbeat until an important case broke and they needed unmatched thoroughness. Then they would call for that "genius" Humphrey. Devlin admired his abilities and enjoyed watching his aloof precision.

And he knew that, to the man, the crew would shelve their personal likes and dislikes for the purpose of solving the matters at hand. They had one common characteristic: they were all addicted to the hunt. Some of them had been derailed by the red-tapeists, but give them a good case, and they were hooked.

Humphrey yawned into the phone, "What's up, Mike?"

"I want to run something by you." Devlin then explained his parking ticket theory. There was a pause. Devlin waited. He knew the microchips in Humphrey's head were heating up.

Typical of Humphrey, his mind had accepted the theory and was already organizing the steps for the collection of evidence. "I'll need two other guys who can take good major-case prints. One of them should go by the office and pick up the following." Devlin was writing. "Fingerprint cards, ten blank cards for rolling the palms, the palm-roller box, ink, ink roller, and waterless soap for cleaning the hands. I've got all the latent equipment and collection bags I need in my car. Who'll do the latent exams?"

"I've got a friend in the Latent Print Section; I'll call him. You can fly the tickets and elimination prints back there as soon as you're done."

"What about my list of locksmiths?"

"Smith can finish them."

"Okay. Anything else?"

"What do you think our chances are, Al?"

"*If* the girl was abducted, and *if* the person who abducted her drove the car out of the airport, and *if* the tickets are re-trievable and untainted, and *if* we get real, real lucky, I think our chances are lousy."

"So?" asked Devlin.

"I like it. A lot."

Ever the dreamer, thought Devlin, looking for the lost galaxy through a pair of cheap binoculars. Devlin guessed that's why he liked him. He hung up, still unsure of his idea's chances. For the first time he noticed the stale beer taste in his mouth. He headed for the shower. He spent half an hour ridding himself of the previous day's residues.

As he walked into the crew's area, he smelled coffee brewing. Jeff Ross sat at one of the tables, reading the morning paper and eating one of the dozen and a half sweet rolls he had picked up at a Polish bakery in Hamtramck. "Good morning, Mike," Ross offered with the enthusiasm of a lottery winner.

Picking up a danish, Devlin said, "Just keep feeding us, Jeff. If this case goes long enough, we'll have to start coming in and out through the loading dock."

In a Yiddish accent, Ross said, "Eh, a little kugel. It shouldn't hoit."

Devlin laughed. "You'd have made a good Jewish mother."

"Funny you should say that; just the other day, a union guy called me a Jewish mutha." Both men smiled. "So—what happened yesterday?"

In a terse language, free of the usual adjectives, adverbs, and conjunctions, Devlin outlined both investigations and his dream. He wanted Ross's input. He may have been a scrap metal dealer, but his Ivy league–trained legal mind was as shearingly incisive as the giant metal shredders that made him wealthy.

"Explain the purpose of elimination prints," Ross asked.

"Put yourself in the latent examiner's shoes. He'll process all the parking tickets with chemicals, probably fuming them with iodine. Now, for the sake of explanation, let's say he finds two different latents on one ticket and one of them turns out to be Vanessa's. Who belongs to the other one? The only other people that could have handled the ticket are the parking lot employees or the kidnapper. So we take a full set of prints, including palms, sides, and tips, from the employees. We call them major-case prints. The examiner compares these against the unidentified print on the ticket, and if it's matched with an employee's, we're out of luck. But if it's not matched, there's a chance it belongs to the kidnapper."

Ross's mind cut right to the flaw. "Say the examiner finds the kidnapper's print, what then? Can you identify someone from one print?"

"No. Television's wrong. Only if you have the name of a suspect and his fingerprints are on file can the examiner match the latent to one of his inked prints."

"So unless you have a suspect, the latent won't do you any good?"

"Well, that used to be true, but enter the computer. Two years ago, the Michigan State Police instituted what they call AFIS, Automated Fingerprint Identification System. It's a computer that codes and searches latent prints. So if our lab can come up with a latent, we'll feed it into AFIS."

"If AFIS can identify the kidnapper, what then? Do you think she—" Ross stopped, hesitating to finish the question Devlin knew he was going to ask, a question Devlin had not allowed himself to ask. "Is she still alive?"

Like the night before, something was rolling around loose in Devlin's head, something he had forgotten. He thought his dream had solved the loose end, but this was something new. Devlin knew it was only a sliver in his sense of order right now, but like most unattended slivers, it would become infected and painfully demand more attention day by day.

The contemplative silence answered Ross's question. "Mike." Devlin looked at his friend. "You'll find her."

Ross filled his coffee cup and left Devlin alone with his thoughts. What was it he had forgotten? Again he decided not to press the feeling. Maybe the answer would come like the parking tickets.

Devlin called Theo Agash and instructed him to swing by the office and discreetly pick up Vanessa's fingerprints and the equipment Humphrey wanted.

He knew he had to call the ASAC and update him. He took a minute to prepare a mental maze to throw O'Hare into if he asked too many questions.

"Mike, where are you?"

"On the street."

"I tried to get you on the radio yesterday."

"Sorry. We were working on a different channel."

"Which one?"

"B-Two," Devlin lied. "But I think we're going to change that today. I'll let you know what it is," he lied again.

"Well. What's going on?"

"Do you think this line is secure?" Devlin knew it was, but if O'Hare thought Devlin was that paranoid he would not probe his vague answers.

"Ah—I guess so."

Devlin returned his oral pause with equal doubt. "Ah—well, we're working on it. We're checking every one of those places that copies those things. We started down by your location and are working our way out. There are about a hundred listed in the phone book, but we've found out there are a lot of independents not listed, so we're picking up a lot by word of mouth. By the time we're done we'll have three to four hundred." Devlin did not like lying to someone he respected, but if O'Hare thought there were three to four times as many locksmiths, he would not be as likely to question what the crew was doing with its time.

"And nothing so far?" O'Hare asked a simple question, trying to clear Devlin's vagueness from his head.

"No, but we're giving it a full-court press. Let me worry about it. Just keep the enemy off our back, John."

O'Hare was aware that by enemy Devlin meant management. He was pleased not to be considered one of them. "Maybe we could get together and talk."

"I'll come in and see you the moment we get some breathing room."

"Promise?"

"Trust me." Both men laughed at the two-word answer, which was recognized as the biggest lie in management-hump relations.

Outside, Devlin heard a car's engine idling. In that neighborhood, he knew it could be anything. He picked up his magnum and held it behind his thigh as he opened the door slowly. Livingston was getting out of a medium-priced Mercedes that Sydney Jemison was driving. He gave her a going-off-to-war kiss. She rolled down her window and looked at Devlin and then the warehouse. "Very nice, Agent Devlin, very nice. You've come a long way since I've known you."

"Sydney, that was very nice of you to drive all the way out to Ed's apartment and then drive him all the way down here so early in the morning. You're a terrific friend." He looked at Livingston, whose head was down with embarrassment. "I want to know what your intentions are, Miss."

"To get Ed to stop hanging around with you."

Livingston showed his relaxed smile and told her, "I'll call you later."

Devlin grabbed Livingston's arm, pulling him into the warehouse. "I'm sorry, it's time for Eddie to come in now." Sydney sped off, taking the hairpin turns around the building like a test pilot.

"Well, stud, what are *your* intentions?" Devlin saw his choice of words had stung Livingston.

"She's very special to me," he answered defensively.

"Whoa, I was just kidding. Other than her taste in men, I think a great deal of her myself. I'm just concerned that you might be trying to make decisions with brains that have dropped below your waist. From what I can see, you haven't spent a lot of time trying to understand the urban black female. If something permanent develops with Sydney, no one will be happier for you than me, but make sure it's for the right reason."

"I understand what you're saying. Believe me, I see more in her than sex. She's bright; she's a CPA. A CPA! Do you know how many black female CPAs there are in the country—hell, the world? She's funny and makes the best out of the worst. She wants kids. She wants what's best for me."

"You'd be great together."

"Is that part of being my training agent, sticking your nose in my love life?" Livingston joked.

"Oh, so now the rookie has a love life."

"I hope you don't mean rookie in the biblical sense?"

"Absolutely not—stud." Livingston broke into his recently learned impression of the bad motherfucker's strut.

"Did you tell her why we're here?"

"Well—yeah. Was that wrong?"

"No. Not at all." Devlin knew that, better than anyone. Sydney Jemison realized the importance of discretion during a kidnapping.

Of the various secret oaths an FBI agent takes, only one has remained undefiled throughout history: Never pass up anything free. So after all the sweet rolls but one were gone, the investigators sat down and waited for Devlin to begin.

Devlin explained briefly about the parking tickets. The leads did not have to be enumerated. They were all good investigators and could develop the logical investigative paths on their own. "Today's assignments. Shanahan will stay here and guard the refrigerator." To protest the group's chuckling, Shanahan took the final danish and pushed it into his mouth unbroken. The group applauded his performance once but questioned Devlin's decision to leave Shanahan and the bulging Frigidaire unchaperoned. Devlin felt additional instructions were necessary. "And Bill, notice how neat and clean and organized this place is." Shanahan was an unrelenting investigator but had no concept of order. He often returned to the office after a difficult case having to search his pockets for napkins or matchbooks on which the identity of the criminal had been scribbled.

"No problem, Mike," he answered, letting the entire danish fall from his mouth onto the floor.

Attempting to regain control of the briefing, Devlin continued, "Al Humphrey, along with Gunnar and Theo, will go to the airport and handle the parking tickets. Al will fly them back to Washington on the first available flight. I'll call Ident and have someone meet him at the airport. Ed Livingston and I will get on Stand as soon as we leave here, and Gunnar and Theo will join us when they're done at the airport. If we get a good latent print, Al will take it to the MSP lab. Al, do you know where the nearest terminal for the fingerprint scanner is?"

"Michigan State Police has seven AFIS terminals throughout the state. The closest to the airport is at the Northville Post," Humphrey said.

"Do you know anyone there that could help us?"

"Yes. I know a sergeant I took a class with. I think he's still there."

"Good. Get ahold of him and lay the groundwork. Does anyone have any questions?"

When he saw no one had any serious questions, Shanahan asked, "Yeah. Doc, how was that girl last night?"

It was a question he had been asked many times before. "Which one?" he answered, his face unreadable.

By noon, Devlin and Livingston had not seen any activity at Alvan Stand's house. Devlin radioed Shanahan. "Anything going on?"

"Yeah, we're getting low on cold cuts."

"Anything else?"

"Whiskey Hotel Four called. He's just about done at the airport. Said he should be able to make the two o'clock flight to D.C. Hold on." Devlin could hear the warehouse phone ringing, then silence as Shanahan temporarily quit transmitting.

As abruptly as he had quit, Shanahan resumed radio traffic. "Mike. Guess what." The words came in short, excited releases.

"You found more cold cuts."

Shanahan had regained his storyteller control. "No. But Riley found something." He let the transmission die and waited for Devlin to insist that he continue.

Devlin knew that could mean only one thing. Riley Smith had found the locksmith. "You're kidding. Where is he now?"

Disappointed he could not string Devlin along, Shanahan said, "He's on his way in."

"And so am I." Devlin looked over at Livingston in his car. "Love that Kentucky bloodhound. You stay here, Brackoff and Agash should be on their way."

When Devlin got to the warehouse, Smith's car was already in the lot.

"As usual, outstanding Riley." Devlin saw him blush slightly. "Who is it?"

"Sprinkler."

John Sprinkler was the least likely of the four suspects. He was a hard-working employee with ten years in the Bureau. He had worked his way up slowly but deservedly. Starting as a mail clerk, he was later reassigned to the night shift, where his organizational skills and hard work earned him the opportunity to be a radio maintenance technician. He took a night school course and worked before and after the bell. He became very good at his job and always had time to help with a problem. Within the office, he had an excellent reputation. Devlin checked his list. Sprinkler had borrowed the key when he was running some electrical lines for new computers in the informant room. He had worked during a lunch hour, which was not unusual for him. Innocently, the key was lent to him.

"Okay, Riley, tell us how you did it."

Smith momentarily dropped his head in embarrassment. "It wasn't anything special," he warbled in a voice that had, over the years, spliced his native southern accent with the flat, quick speech of the Midwest.

"Well, I finished the list this morning and started going through the yellow pages for the suburbs. There was this ad for the Keymobile—*Don't Have Time? I'll Drive To Your Lock.* So I call the guy, tell him who I am and he drives over and meets me. I show him the key and he remembers copying it because of the DO NOT DUPLICATE. He even remembers the number two stamped on it. I show him the photo spread and in a heartbeat he picks out Sprinkler."

"Did he ask him about the DO NOT DUPLICATE?"

"Yeah. Sprinkler tells him it was a key for his business and he had two of them engraved so his employees couldn't have copies made. But then he lost his so he needed this one duplicated."

"Pretty smart."

"Oh, that boy's smart all right." Smith's accent started drifting south. At that point, it was somewhere around southern Ohio. "He was smart enough to know that the warning on the key would draw attention to him, so he decides to go to a suburban locksmith. But he doesn't have time, so he has the Keymobile drive to a couple of blocks from the office, where Sprinkler walks over and has the key copied. He's out of the office for fifteen minutes. Very smart."

"But not as smart as Riley Smith," Devlin said with admiration. Smith went into a full blush. "I've got to make a quiet call," Devlin excused himself and went back to the warehouse office.

"Yeah," said Joey Pants.

"Joey, what do you hear?"

Pantatelli did not like jumping through FBI hoops, but he liked the alternative less. "The buy is Wednesday night."

"What time and where?"

"Wednesday night," Pantatelli answered as though he had more than completed his end of the bargain.

His reluctance angered Devlin. "Okay, Joey, I'm going to run this up one time. One *last* time. I want that list. I want it real bad. But I want it just a hair more than I want to walk in to your old man and play this tape. So if we don't get the list, I am going to be real upset and make plenty of copies. You can leave Detroit, but I will find you and so will those tapes. So stop with the Bogart, because you are nothing but a telephonic pedophile. You understand?"

A cornered "Yes" was his answer.

"Now, where and when?"

"Honest to God, I don't know. My old man never discusses details. He says that's the way to prison."

"Well, Joey, you'd better go to that church you donate so much money to and pray the buy never happens."

"If I find out anything, I'll call you right away, okay?"

To emphasize his threat, Devlin hung up without answering.

Devlin announced to the group, "The exchange is supposed to be Wednesday night. But we don't know where or when."

"We could get C-Nine to follow him until the meet and then take him off," Shanahan offered.

"I'm afraid he'd be too surveillance-conscious. If he went to all that trouble to copy the key, he's going to be hinky and he knows all of us. We can't follow Tony Pants.

He's been tagged so many times, he'll make us right out of the chute. Any other ideas?"

Riley Smith said, "There's a good chance he's got the list at home. When he goes to work Monday, we'll make his place and take a look. Tomorrow's Saturday. We could get into his desk at work."

"Sounds reasonable. Everybody agree?" Devlin had to ask. This time they were conspiring to commit an unauthorized burglary. No one objected.

The radio scratched the air. "Whiskey Hotel Six to Whiskey Hotel One." Agash was calling from the airport.

"This is One, go ahead."

"We're done here, and Four is in the air."

"Good. Swing by that surveillance location and check with Two. If nothing's going on, come back here."

Two hours later the surveillance team returned to the warehouse. As they walked in the door, Shanahan sprang to the refrigerator and passed out beer. He started telling a story about a police tracking dog that was accused by a captured bank robber of being "a muthafuckin liar." Shanahan was impersonating all the voices, including the German shepherd's.

It gave Devlin an idea.

||| CHAPTER 12 |||

By the time they left at one in the morning, everyone but Devlin and Brackoff was drunk. Devlin was not drinking, and alcohol seemingly had no effect on the big detective. Devlin felt the others needed to unwind. They had worked hard, taken risks, and solved one of the mysteries facing them. But Devlin feared the easy part was over.

He studied the briefing board. To his amazement, Edgar Livingston had managed to neatly organize and record the day's investigation. His craftsman's handwriting reported where everyone had been the entire day and at what time. Devlin did not know how Livingston had gotten some of the information he had: Humphrey's flight schedule; detailed information about the locksmith, including the manufacturer and serial number of the duplicating machine; everything was there. And Devlin could not remember Livingston doing anything but drinking beer, eating the pizza Ross had delivered, and sunning himself in the warm camaraderie that comes from alcohol, war stories, and success. He set a mental tickler to watch Livingston more closely the next day.

He turned his thoughts to Sprinkler. If they searched his desk and house and did not find the list, their choices were limited. They could confront him, but if he requested a lawyer, they were doomed. There was no evidence against him, and their only advantage, surprise, would be lost. Later, at a time advantageous to him, he could take the list anywhere and make the exchange undetected. Surveillance was another possibility. But more times than not, critical surveillances were unsuccessful, especially if the targets were wary. Devlin decided he would try the idea Shanahan had given him.

Driving to the FBI office, he switched his radio to the main channel to find out if any unusual Bureau activity was taking place. A deserted silence had taken over the FBI in Detroit.

Devlin typed the combination into the lock and looked up at the security camera so the night clerk would recognize him.

In the tech room, he found an Organized Crime agent with the earphones draped over his head. The tape reels were turning, recording a conversation. He switched the machine off when he saw Devlin. "What are you doing here, Mike?"

"Working midnight-to-eight surveillance. We lost the guy right out of the gate. So I'm hiding out for a couple of hours until he heads home and we can call it a night. What's going on here?"

"Man, this Pantatelli family is something. Old man Pants just got done boffing—are you ready—the Godfather's wife. If Scantina ever found out. . . . Old man Pants must have nuts the size of grapefruits. We picked it up off the bug at the nightclub. I got it on tape. Want to hear it?"

"No, thanks, I just ate. How about you, you got anything you need to do?"

"Well, I've got to Xerox all these logs from yesterday. It'll take half an hour, but then I won't have to do it in the morning, and I'll be able to get out of here at eight for a change."

"Sure. Take your time. And don't worry, if Pants *mounts* another attack, I'll get it on tape for you."

As soon as the agent left, Devlin shut down the machines so he would not have to witness the second coming of Pantatelli. He scanned the master list of the interception logs. He was looking for a lengthy conversation involving the older Pantatelli. A twenty-two-minute call to New Jersey ended his search. The synopsis of the call indicated Pants had done most of the talking. In an unlocked filing cabinet he found the administrative copy of the tape.

On a tape recorder used to review tapes, Devlin mounted the tape and ran it forward to the footage indicated for the New Jersey call, then copied it onto a standard cassette. He also made a copy of a tape of old man Pants and Mrs. Scantina.

When he heard the agent returning, Devlin switched the machines back on. The agent thanked him as Devlin left.

He returned to the warehouse and called the ASAC, hoping he would be asleep and not very inquisitive. "Did I wake you?"

"Christ, Mike, it's almost three A.M. When do you sleep?"

"John, it's Sprinkler."

"Sprinkler? You sure?"

"The locksmith gave us a positive ID."

"What do we do from here?"

"We're going to run surveillance on him. Today we'll bag his desk at the office. He's not supposed to work, is he?"

"Not that I know of, but I guess he works a lot of Saturdays on his own. What if you don't find it there?"

Devlin avoided the question. "I need you to do two things Monday. First, review last week's wiretap logs on old man Pants. Make sure we're not missing something between him and Sprinkler. And then find some ruse to keep Sprinkler working in your office for the rest of the day, so you can keep an eye on him."

"Okay, but why?"

"John. Have faith in us."

O'Hare understood. His question was not being answered for his own protection. He was out on a limb, but evidently Devlin's group was taking much greater risks. "I do, Mike. I really do."

At seven A.M., Devlin was awakened by Ross. The morning's offering was fresh-baked bagels and cream cheese. Ross handed Devlin coffee. "Congratulations. I see you found the leak."

"Been nosing around our briefing board?"

"I forgot my newspaper. I needed something to read while I was making coffee. What about the list itself?"

"I don't know. It could be anywhere."

"Without it you haven't got much, do you?"

"You're looking at it from a prosecutive standpoint. Of course we would like to prosecute him, but most important is getting that list, whether we do it in a way that produces admissible evidence or—by other means."

"Other means" was evasive enough for Ross. He would ask no more questions about the group's investigative direction.

Devlin trusted Ross without reservation, but that he had been able to learn the status of the investigations so easily was both a tribute to Livingston's organizational skills and a security concern for Devlin. With the exception of Bill Shanahan, he decided to keep everyone else in the dark about the Pantatelli tape.

By nine, all the bagels had disappeared into the hungry investigators. Devlin started making the day's assignments. "Shanahan will stay here again today."

Some of the agents started chanting, "Clerk! Clerk! Clerk!" With the controlled grace of a tai chi master, Shanahan slowly stood and lifted a leg, tunefully releasing the final liter of the previous night's carbonation. Cigarette lighters lit the air amidst pleas for mercy.

"Brackoff and Agash. Surveillance on Stand. Riley, go meet the ASAC at the office; he has the key for Sprinkler's work space and desk. He'll help you if you need anything. Livingston and I will be here for a while. Any questions?"

Someone asked, "Have you heard from Humphrey?"

"Not yet. I'll call Ident if I don't hear something by this afternoon. Anything else?" There was no response.

"Okay, channel B-Nine today. Don't give specific information over the air, not even with the scrambler," Devlin said.

When Ross heard the briefing breaking up, he came out of his office.

Shanahan said, "Hey, Jeff, I think the beer fairies were in here last night and cleaned out your fridge."

With mock seriousness, Ross asked, "What can we do about it, Bill?"

"I'll tell you what. If you bring in some more beer, I'll stay late and set a trap."

Ross laughed and indicated he was leaving. Devlin asked, "Where are you going?"

"To work. Someone has to pay the bar tab."

Livingston, Shanahan, and Devlin remained. Although he had not seen Livingston make a single note, Devlin knew he would be able to update the briefing board. "Ed, how about listing the assignments on the board for Bill. I've got to show him something up in the apartment."

Livingston started writing while they went upstairs. He sensed a conspiratorial air between them. When they came back down, Livingston was hanging up the phone. "Mike, that was Doc. When he got to Stand's house, DPD was all over the place. Stand's dead. Two in the back of the head. They figure somewhere around two A.M."

As soon as Devlin started his car, the radio spoke, "Central to Four-one."

"Four-one," Devlin said, remembering his Bureau call sign.

"Be advised that an individual has been trying to contact you all morning. He says it's urgent. Do you want the name and number over the air?"

Because the caller sounded as though he was a source, Devlin did not want his name broadcast and said, "No, I'll landline you."

Two blocks later Devlin found a phone.

"Radio room."

"Mary Ann, Mike Devlin. Let me have that name and number."

"L. C. Sanders. Said he didn't know if you would remember him. He helped you with a fugitive about five years ago." Devlin remembered him. He wrote down the number.

Love Child Sanders. When he had told Devlin what the "L.C." stood for, he understood why Sanders used initials. A friend of Sanders had been wanted for an armed robbery in Atlanta. When Devlin interviewed him, he, as always was the case, stated that he did not have the slightest idea where the fugitive was. Devlin went to work.

On L.C.'s walls were pictures, plaques, and awards noting his high school baseball accomplishments. At the center of the wall, prominently displayed by spacing, was a plaque naming him to the All-State team. Devlin, too, had played high school ball. For an hour, they discussed everything from the split-finger fastball to the hitch Devlin could never seem to eliminate from his swing. They exchanged stories, each laughing at the other's examples of adolescent priorities and their consequences. As Devlin was leaving, Sanders wrote a phone number on a scrap of paper and handed it to him. He offered no explanation.

Early the next morning, Devlin arrested the fugitive at the phone number L.C. had provided. Devlin knew that Sanders believed that he had not turned in his friend. He had simply written a phone number on a piece of paper, and justice followed its certain course. That afternoon Devlin had rung L.C.'s doorbell. When he came to the door, Devlin, without a word, handed him two box seat tickets to the next Tigers game and left.

Sanders's phone was ringing. "Hello."

"L.C., Mike Devlin."

"Oh, man! I've been trying to get ahold of you." His tone was desperate.

"What can I do for you?"

Sanders hesitated, then said, "I know something about a homicide." He said it as though the listener should be shocked.

"Do you mean you know in the overheard sense or the I-pulled-the-trigger sense?"

"Fuck no, man! I just drove. I didn't know the muthafuckers were going to check him in."

"Easy, L.C. If you weren't the shooter, you can deal. Where was it?"

"Detroit."

"That's good. You can deal with those people. Who was hit?"

"Dude named Alvan Stand."

As improbable as it seemed, Devlin had seen these coincidences before. Every hundred interviews someone like Sanders came along, someone who could solve crimes on a regular basis. An informant. He fit the profile of the productive informant. Above all else, he was tough. In Detroit's streets, only one thing ruled—fear. Not money, not influence, only fear, because unless a man was regarded as dangerous, everything else could and would be taken from him. Paradoxically, Sanders had a disarming smile and was easy to get along with, if boundaries were respectfully observed. The contradictory combination led him to the fringes of a number of criminal groups. When Devlin had met him five years earlier, he recognized his potential as an informant, but at the time he had more sources than he could handle. Another reason existed, probably the same reason that had ended L.C.'s promising baseball career—his hands. They were grotesquely swollen, a telltale side effect of the impurities in Detroit's heroin.

Devlin knew he had to get Sanders in tow for Homicide. "Where are you?"

"At home. Do you remember the address?"

"I'll be there in fifteen minutes."

When Devlin got back into the car, Livingston asked, "Anything important?"

"Only for Detroit Homicide."

When they pulled up to Alvan Stand's house, Devlin told Livingston and Sanders to wait in the car. His lingering glance told Livingston to keep an eye on L.C.

The uniformed officer was about to stop Devlin when he flashed his credentials. The officer waved him into the living room. Jerome Wicks knelt over the body, studying it as though it were an intricately balanced puzzle that at the slightest disturbance would come crashing down, destroying its own solution.

When Wicks stood up, Devlin said, "Inspector, when are you going to learn, the head of Homicide is supposed to go to seminars, give speeches, and look pretty for the TV cameras."

Wicks noticed Devlin for the first time. "Mike. Working murders these days? Anyway, I thought you were being, shall we say, *punished*."

"In the Bureau, that's how we punish people. We make

them go to homicide scenes." Two detectives who knew Devlin came into the room and nodded hello.

"Did I ever call and thank you when we closed that beheading case?"

"Of course not."

"Thanks."

"You're welcome."

"What brings you here?"

"We have an interest in Alvan Stand."

"What do you know about him?"

"Everything you want to know." Wicks understood Devlin's implication.

"Okay. Who killed him?"

"Oh, no! Not this time. When it comes to thanking someone for solving your case, you leave a lot to be desired. This time you've got to thank me first, then I'll talk. And make it genuine. Since being punished, I've become quite sensitive."

Wicks looked at the two detectives, letting them know not to be amused. "Thank you." Then Wicks smiled himself.

"Talk about sincerity. Okay, it was Frankie Williams and Haygood White."

"Frankie Williams doesn't surprise me in the least, but I thought Haygood White was Stand's bodyguard. We're talking about the big mulatto, right?" Wicks asked.

"That's right. He *was* Stand's bodyguard. What better way to get close enough to kill a guy than to buy off his teeth? According to my information, White sleeps where his next dollar is, loyal only to the moment."

"And how do you know all this?"

"The wheelman is sitting outside in my car." Devlin explained his investigation of Stand and Sanders's witnessing the murder.

"Are you going to need Sanders?" Wicks asked.

"He's all yours. I do need a favor. When the evidence techs are done, I'd like to search the house concerning our case."

"I don't think Alvan will object."

For three hours they searched and researched Stand's house. The only thing they found that related to Vanessa was her telephone number in his telephone book. With Stand's death, the chances of finding Vanessa seemed diminished. Devlin felt emotionally battered. He dialed the warehouse. "Bill, anything going on?"

"You want the good news or the bad news first?"

"Always the bad news first."

"Riley searched Sprinkler's desk and work area. Absolutely zero."

"Have Riley go and sit on Sprinkler's house and make sure he gets a full description of his car. Then run DMV. I want the VIN on the car." Shanahan knew why Devlin wanted the vehicle identification number for Sprinkler's car and chided himself for not thinking of it.

"Now give me the good news."

"Humphrey's on his way back." Shanahan hesitated, trying to draw the question from Devlin.

"And?"

"And. He's got a parking ticket with two latents on it." He hesitated again. "One doesn't match any of the employees'."

"And the other?"

"It's Vanessa's!"

A rush of adrenaline cleared Devlin's head. There was still a chance.

They drove back to the warehouse.

"Is Riley on Sprinkler?" Devlin asked. While Shanahan shuffled through papers in front of him, Livingston said, "Yes."

Devlin called Smith. "Whiskey Hotel One to Whiskey Hotel Five."

"Go ahead, One."

"Anything moving?"

"No, he just went to the store and brought back two cases of beer. He must be expecting company. The cases were different brands."

Devlin wondered if any detail ever escaped Smith. "Very good. Hold on there a little longer. See if company starts showing up. I'm going to try and find out what the buyer is up to." Devlin called the tech room and was told that Tony Pants had had an earlier conversation in which he had discussed plans to be out of town until Monday. Devlin looked at his watch—Saturday. It did not appear that Pantatelli and Sprinkler would be meeting that night. "Whiskey Hotel Five, why don't you hang loose out there and plan to be back here around five."

"Ten-four."

"What time is Humphrey's flight due in?" Devlin asked.

Shanahan checked his watch. "Should be in already."

"Did he call ahead to MSP?"

"Yeah, he talked to his buddy out there. All he has to do is drop off the print. They'll do the rest. Because it's the weekend, the computer is slow with all the weekend arrests. What else?"

"Double-check. Make sure everyone knows to be back around five." Devlin noticed Livingston updating the briefing board. He felt better now that he knew the rookie wasn't really a sorcerer.

Fauber sat at his desk, shaking his head. Duncan Moorehead, his number one Jedi, stood dutifully close. A large portable Bureau radio sat between them, turned to channel B-Nine. Obediently they waited for the device to speak again. Treating it with professorial respect, Fauber waited ten minutes for its truant broadcast and then switched it off.

"I don't understand what they're doing." Fauber seemed to be asking a question, directed at the radio as if it were some sort of oracle.

When it didn't answer, Moorehead offered, "I think they're surveilling someone."

"No shit!" Fauber thrust the poison words at Moorehead and watched his reaction. The young agent absorbed them fully, without an attack of self-respect. Moorehead would go far, Fauber thought, then, remembering the nature of the beast, thought, maybe too far. As soon as he had finished with Devlin, he would make sure Moorehead's climb was slowed. But first, Devlin. Fauber was encouraged. He had heard Devlin giving orders to other agents. He knew Devlin's style. With an operation that hush-hush, some rule or law was being ravaged by Devlin's headlong compulsion to get results. However, because the ASAC had apparently given his approval to the group, Fauber had to proceed with political surefootedness. But the trophy was certainly worth the trouble.

Devlin argued with himself over calling Anderson with the latent fingerprint information. He still did not trust Anderson. He also considered Judith Anderson, cold and manipulative, the real driver of her husband's goals. He felt no compulsion to give her refuge from her fears. But finally, he thought of Vanessa, cute, vulnerable, sixteen. Illogically, for Vanessa's sake, he decided to call.

When Devlin called the office, the squad secretary told him Anderson was out but was expected any minute. Devlin left his number. Fifteen minutes later Anderson called back.

"Tom, Alvan Stand has been murdered," Devlin said.

"Who did it?"

"A guy named Frankie Williams and one of his dummies."

"Did it have anything to do with Vanessa?"

"I don't think so. Have you heard anything?"

"Not a thing."

"Don't get too excited, but we've come up with a latent fingerprint on a parking ticket that also had Vanessa's print on it."

Anderson couldn't believe it. From the cases he had worked, he knew latent exams, because of backlog, could take months. In a matter of days, Devlin had somehow traced his daughter and come up with solid physical evidence. Involuntarily, he asked, "But how?"

Devoid of any details connecting him or the crew to any illegality, Devlin gave Anderson a sanitized version of the investigative trail that was presently marking time at MSP's fingerprint scanner.

"That's great! That proves she was kidnapped."

"That proves she was at the airport. Nothing else. That print could belong to anyone."

"I'll bet if I went to the SAC with this he would allow the case to be reopened."

"You still don't get it, do you? Sure, the SAC doesn't like the fact that Vanessa was dating a black. He doesn't like it that she's run away before, but that has nothing to do with why he's not working this. Those are his excuses. You've been around the Bureau long enough to know that big cases mean big problems. No cases mean no problems. You don't become an SAC by breaking cases. You get there by kissing the right rings. He doesn't look at this case and see an agent's sixteen-year-old daughter that may have been kidnapped; he sees career suicide."

Anderson knew Devlin was right. But Devlin, because he had never been interested in advancement, did not understand that promotion without compromise was a luxury no longer affordable in the priorities of Bureau management. Anderson decided that Devlin was right about not telling the SAC, at least for now.

"You'll let me know if anything happens?" Anderson asked, deciding to end the conversation and limit his complicity.

"I'll call you when I can."

Anderson hung up.

Devlin looked at the phone in his hand. It felt cold, reminding him that he should not trust Anderson. The second line lit up. Cautiously Devlin answered, "Hello."

"Mike, how are you?" It was Knox. Devlin gave her a quick summary. "Is there anything I can do?"

"Not over the phone."

"Anything else?"

In a distracted voice, Devlin said, "How about a month in the Greek islands?"

"Mike?"

"Yeah?"

"Take care, huh?"

"Thanks. Sorry about the lack of conversation, but there are some walls closing in."

"Don't worry about it. Just hang in there."

By 5:30, all the investigators were at the warehouse. Devlin recounted Stand's murder and the coincidence of its solution. Riley Smith reported his search of Sprinkler's work area and then Humphrey took too long explaining the discovery of the latents on the parking tickets. With scholarly detail, he started a lecture on fingerprint deltas and ridge counts. Devlin stopped him mid-sentence in an attempt to remove the glaze forming collectively over the crew's eyes. Then he asked him to brief the group about the Michigan State Police fingerprint scanner.

"How much detail do you want?"

"We want to know how accurate the scanner is, and if he's in the file, will it find him?"

"Okay, I'll keep it as brief as possible." Devlin peeked at Livingston. He was still not taking notes. "The computer they have is the latest high-tech fingerprint scanner. It's made by Nippon Electronics Company. Earlier systems, from other manufacturers, have a fifty percent success rate. The NEC system works differently. The latent is photographed on a separate computer. The photo is five times larger than the actual print. It's then traced onto a clear overlay, making sure all the points of identification are marked. The tracing is fed into the NEC, scanned, and then reproduced on the computer's screen. The examiner then edits the computer's image of the print, ensuring that all the available characteristics are in place. Once he's satisfied, he hits a button and the computer places a dot at every identification point. Again it's edited. Another button, and all the dots are connected into a complex geometric figure. Simultaneously, a geometric equation is calculated for that print. Our print, for example, may have an equation with forty characters in its equation. All ten million inked fingerprints on file at Lansing have a geometric equation which has been previously determined by the computer. Our equation is run through, and the machine provides the examiner with the ten equations which most closely resemble our latent. The screen at Northville splits. On one side is our latent. On the other, the ten suspect prints are called up, one at a time, and compared. If our boy's print is in the files at Lansing, we have a better than ninety percent chance of identifying him. We should know late tomorrow, early Monday."

The crew was encouraged by Humphrey's briefing. For them, a 10 percent failure possibility was almost negligible. For the first time the group's voices hummed with the anticipation of success.

"Tomorrow," said Devlin, "should be a light day, unless we get a call from MSP. Tony Pants is out of town until Monday. We won't search Sprinkler's house until Monday, when he's at work. Bill, did you get the numbers on his car?"

"Yeah, it's an '85 Dodge Daytona. I've got the VIN."

"Call our contact at Chrysler and get the key codes for the VIN. Can you cut the keys yourself?"

"No problem."

"Good. While you're working on the locks at his house, we can get into his car. Riley can do that search. Bill will get the keys to you tomorrow." Devlin did not ask for questions; he knew there would be none. They were tired but optimistic. They had had enough. "Bill, is there any beer?"

"There's a round or two, but I think reinforcements are on the way."

Shanahan started his first story while passing out the beer. Two DPD evidence techs had been called to a suicide scene. Because it was their fourth scene that day, they had not eaten. They ordered a pizza, and when it arrived, they told the delivery man to get the money from the guy on the couch. Only after he had told the still figure on the couch how much was owed did the delivery man notice the trickle of blood from the neat, dark red hole in his right temple. Dinner was free that night.

The crew laughed too hard, trying to unwind: an indication that the pressure was building.

A soft knock echoed from the hollow steel door. The warehouse became silent. Livingston pulled a sheet over the briefing board. Devlin went to the door. It was Knox.

"What are you doing here?"

"I brought some diversion." Behind her two men and two women were unloading a paneled truck.

She had everything set up on the warehouse's walled roof. It was one of those rare evenings in Detroit when the

weather was perfect, turning the roof into an island somewhere in the South Pacific.

The caterers were from Zocalo's Mexican Restaurant.
The owner was a longtime friend of the Devlins. The
agents helped carry chairs, tables, and insulated containers
to the roof. Knox had even thought to bring a large radio-
tape player. No expense had been spared. Three cases of the
best liquor were opened. The tables were covered with
white linen. Plates, silverware, and glasses were set out.
Large coolers held ice, beer, and mix. The agents, knowing
the best value, started opening the Glenfiddich scotch and
the Absolut vodka. One of the caterers was bent over a cutting board, slicing limes and lemons.

Devlin walked over to Knox, who was fiddling with the
burly radio, trying to find some music. Finally she found a
station that had the mariachi sound and turned it up slightly.

"This is really nice of you."

"After I talked to you, it sounded like you needed a little
cheering up. So I called Jeff Ross and asked him if it would
be all right. He said only if he could pay for everything."

"Well, nothing makes cops happier than free liquor."

Ross walked up onto the roof. He got a drink and walked
over to Devlin, who said, "Thanks, Jeff, I think this is exactly what we needed."

Ross looked at him and said, "Mike, I've worked hard
for my money, damn hard. But I never work hard at spending it. This whole thing—me being part of it—is something
I'm going to enjoy the rest of my life. Believe me, spending this money is very selfish."

Devlin held up his glass. "Here's to those who know
when the grass is greenest."

The caterers were serving hors d'oeuvres: quesadillas,
nachos, and miniature shredded beef tostados. The agents
stood around the tables with the eager concentration of
young heart surgeons.

Brackoff sat off in a corner. An iceless glass was half full of Wild Turkey bourbon. The bottle sat on the roof within reach of his thick fingers. He had his suit coat off. His immense shoulders and arms strained at his shirt.

Devlin sat down next to him. "Gunnar, I appreciate your help. Without it we wouldn't have come as far as we have. Is anyone at work asking where you've been?"

"No" was his simple answer.

Devlin knew that no one would question Gunnar Brackoff's work schedule. They might be curious, but they would not dare question it. For one reason, he was Brackoff. That in itself eliminated questions. But also, it was well known that he worked seven days a week, healthy or sick. Since going to Holdup, he had missed only one day, the day his mother was buried. People tried to guess the motivation for his work ethic but never could. He had been awarded dozens of personal commendations but had never showed up for the presentations. The cops with the union mentality simply explained him as "nuts." No one would ask Brackoff where he had been, not even the chief.

"Mike, do you think we'll find her?"

Devlin knew Brackoff meant—*alive*? But he avoided the word, as if it would jinx the success they seemed to be having. The question was one of unlikely innocence. It surprised Devlin.

In Brackoff's eyes, Devlin saw a look which in anyone else's, he would have described as desperate. "Just once," Brackoff said. He swallowed the warm, stinging whiskey and filled his glass again.

Devlin got a plate of food. Agash was speaking Spanish to the prettier of the two female caterers.

Like the bootleg lookouts of sixty years earlier, Livingston stood on the two-foot-high stoop that ringed the inside of the roof walls and watched the river. A large white boat, under sail, slid west down the river. Devlin and Livingston followed its course, occasionally sipping their drinks.

"What's the name of your boat?" Devlin asked.

"The *Valhalla*," Livingston answered absentmindedly, still tracking the white sailboat below.

"You look like you're aboard her right now."

"I am. *Valhalla* was heaven for the Vikings, a place where they fought all day and partied all night." Smiling, he said, "This is my destiny. But what about you? Why are you doing this? There's a chance we'll all be fired."

Devlin hesitated and gathered reasons whose reassurance had deserted him long ago. "I guess to be free. To do something that everyone tells me is wrong. It may cost me everything. But I know it's right. And if I'm the only one that does? What better truth? When a man can do that, nothing can own him or defeat him. Then, no matter what happens, that truth can always be called on as a man's worth. Truth is the greatest freedom."

Livingston finished watching the white triangle disappear into the distant edge of the river. He understood the serenity he was feeling.

Sunset brought the damp smells of the river to the roof. Dozens of candles were lit and placed every few feet along the stoop. They lent a strange glow to the dusk.

The food ran out at midnight. The liquor never did.

⏐⏐⏐ CHAPTER 13 ⏐⏐⏐

Bill Shanahan was the last to leave the warehouse. That was at five. Devlin slept until ten. He expected a terrible hangover, but remembered thankfully that single-malt scotches are kinder in the morning. He opened a Coke and inhaled its burning coolness.

At midnight, Knox had seen the direction the party was taking, so she kissed Devlin good-bye and reminded him that she was going to Chicago for a couple of days to see the kids. One of the last things Devlin could remember was Shanahan challenging Brackoff to arm wrestle. When Brackoff did not respond to the challenge, the big Irishman called him a cunt. Seeing it was only going to get worse, Brackoff, with all the concentration and effort of a sneeze, slammed Shanahan's hand on the table, breaking his wrist. That happened at two A.M. For the next three hours Shanahan drank and entertained everyone, including Brackoff. He felt no animosity towards the cop, but rather considered his injury one of the hazards of his approach to life. However, Devlin knew something Brackoff did not. As soon as Shanahan's wrist was healthy, he would challenge Brackoff again—and again—regardless of the consequences. It would end only when Brackoff no longer had the heart to hurt Shanahan. It was the Irish notion of victory.

Devlin swallowed another medicinal gulp of Coke. None

of the crew had wanted to leave the party. Even the Doctor had sent his young cateress unhappily on her way. Instead of exhausting everyone, the alcohol seemed to charge the group. They felt invincible. They felt that no one else could have turned risk and improbability into justice. A certain destiny prevailed, as if they were kamikazes and this was their last night to ride the divine wind.

Devlin checked the board. Other than Shanahan getting the codes for Sprinkler's car and cutting the keys, there were no other assignments. After a few phone calls, he would have the day to himself.

He finished the Coke and concentrated on the kidnapping. What had he missed? What other explanation would answer all the facts? He could not think of any. He had to continue to assume she had been kidnapped and was somehow alive. Again he felt the disruption in his sense of order. Something was turned the wrong way, begging to be noticed.

A key turned in the door. It was Livingston. He was dressed for sailing in a blue nylon pullover, white cotton trousers, boat shoes, and sunglasses that he did not bother to take off in the cool darkness of the building. He had brought coffee and doughnuts. "Some party. I think I took a Louisville Slugger in the back of the head. How do you feel?"

"Like the Louisville Slugger."

"That's why I came to get you. We'll sail. We'll swim. A few Bloody Marys, and you'll be ready to rock and roll."

"Sounds good. I've got to make some calls first."

"While you're doing that, I'll straighten up a little."

"Ed, let me ask you something. I've been watching you. I never see you make any notes, but when we come back here you're able to recall everything and organize it onto paper. How are you doing it? I can't figure it out, and it's driving me crazy."

Livingston laughed. "I guess it started with my mom. She's a very regimented person. She figured out early that being a good nurse requires good records. In the hospital, everything was noted on charts and reports. You never did anything unless you wrote it down, often before you did it. Of course, when she worked, I was with a baby-sitter. She insisted that the baby-sitter do the same, you know, meals, naps, medication. When I started first grade she found a great baby-sitter. Close to the house. Cheap. And did a lot of things with me. But she couldn't read or write, so I took over the duties. And I still do it. I keep daily journals. They're pretty detailed."

"Well, you've kept this Band-Aid operation organized."

"Thanks." Livingston laughed. "It *has* been a challenge." He started throwing leftovers into a large plastic garbage bag that dragged behind him.

Devlin called Humphrey first to see if he had heard anything about the latent prints. His line was busy.

He called Anderson at home.

"Hello."

"Tom, it's Mike. Anything going on?"

"Nothing. Did you hear anything on that print?"

"No, but we probably won't until tomorrow. Just remember, it's a long shot, so keep it in perspective. Is there anything else you think we should be doing?"

"I can't think of anything, but you know what bothers me? There's no sign of the car. You would think if something serious had happened, the car would have been found by now." Devlin knew that "something serious" was a euphemism for Vanessa being murdered. He guessed Judith Anderson was within earshot.

"I think you're right. As long as that car is missing, there's a little more hope. I'll call you tomorrow."

Devlin ran and reran the car question through his mind to see if it was the cause of the irritation. If it were found anywhere in the country, the Troy PD would be immediately notified. The car was last known to be at the airport. They had searched all the parking lots. Why had the crime been committed at the airport? Had the kidnapper gotten off a plane and simply needed a ride? Devlin felt a seepage of recognition in "at the airport," but nothing else clung to it. On a three-by-five card he wrote AT THE AIRPORT and pushed it into his pants pocket unfolded. It was a memory trick he used. Every time he put his hand into that pocket, the obtrusive card would remind him—AT THE AIRPORT. He called Humphrey again.

"Yeah, Mike, I just hung up with them. The latent is kind of tricky. He thinks they're going to have to play with it because the ridge quality is poor. He's going to draw four or five different overlays trying different combinations and run them all. Definitely tomorrow at the earliest."

Devlin had one more call to make to the ASAC. He called O'Hare's home, and his wife said he was at the office.

The weekend duty agent answered the phone. "Mike, you've gotten a couple of calls from Inspector Wicks at Homicide. He said he had tried you at home, but there was no answer."

"Thanks. Put me into O'Hare's office." The phone rang twice before the ASAC answered. "O'Hare."

"John. Don't you know management is not supposed to work weekends? It reveals a lack of organizational skills. Very bad for the image."

"You've got a lot of nerve busting my balls. You're the reason I'm here. I'm on the floor trying to screw up the wiring in here so Sprinkler will have something to do tomorrow. I hope I don't electrocute myself."

"Don't worry. If you do, we'll make him a pallbearer and you can keep an eye on him that way."

"Always trying to make my life easier, aren't you? So—anything new?"

"We checked his work area. Nothing."

"Damn. Probably has it at the house."

Devlin waited a moment and then slowly said, "Maybe."

O'Hare detected the reluctance and knew not to ask. "Oh, yeah, Mike. I had a long talk with Frank Sumpter. I asked him about being in the Bella Luna all the time. He said when he worked Organized Crime, he developed a source that was a bartender there on Wednesday nights. When he was working, he would let Sumpter drink free. I checked—all the surveillances had him there on Wednesday night. Anyway, we talked for a couple of hours and he's agreed to go to camp for thirty days and dry out."

"Good. I think he's worth it."

"Yeah, I think so too, now."

He hung up and dialed Wicks's private line at Homicide. "Hello."

"Jerry. Mike."

"L. C. Sanders was murdered last night."

"I'm on my way."

Devlin did not bother waving to the two sergeants at the desk as he and Livingston hurried back to the inspector's office. An extra copy of the preliminary report sat on Wicks's desk, waiting for Devlin.

At approximately two A.M. a neighbor reported hearing gunshots at above residence. Scout car 16-5 responding to the call found the front door wide open and interior lights on. Search of premises revealed bodies of three victims identified as follows:

1. Bessie Sanders B/F/52
2. Joshua Sanders B/M/56
3. L. C. Sanders B/M/35

Victims 1 and 2 believed to be parents of 3. All victims suffered multiple gunshot wounds to upper body and head. Homicide and evidence techs notified.

Devlin dropped into a chair and handed the report to Livingston. "They killed his parents too," Devlin said in disbelief.

"Probably because they were witnesses. They couldn't be bothered getting L.C. out of the house, so they just killed the parents. The bottom line was the same to them: no witnesses."

"Do you have anything?"

"Not really. The neighbor that called in caught a glimpse of them, not long enough for an ID. She thought it was a black guy and a white guy."

"Frankie and Whitey."

"Yep."

"How did they know L.C. had talked to us?"

"I had some people out looking for them. They probably heard that Homicide was asking around and just in case, decided to hit L.C."

"Can we get them?"

"Without L.C., we've got zip on the Stand murder, and we've got nothing on this one. No witnesses, and I'm sure the guns are already at the bottom of the river."

"There must be something we can get them on," Livingston said.

Wicks pushed back in his chair and said, "Let me tell you about the time I had a case on Frankie. I was a brand-new sergeant. The heroin wars were at their peak. Two of Frankie's dealers were found executed. Frankie was young then, did all his own hits. He wasn't as smart either. He used a .45 automatic. The shell casings that were ejected at the scene had his fingerprints on them. Also, when we go to arrest him, he's carrying the .45. We've got him dead nuts. I went into the trial the first day ready for jury selection, and his lawyer says he wants a bench trial. You know what that means."

Livingston asked, "What?"

Devlin answered, "What it means is, if you're being prosecuted for murder and there's a solid case against you, the last thing you want is a judge determining your guilt or innocence. A judge who has seen all the sleazy tricks of lawyers, all the false alibis and defendants' lies. What you want is a jury, especially a Detroit Recorders Court jury with their proven dislike of the police or any other authority. When you ask for a bench trial under those conditions it means only one thing."

Livingston shrugged.

Wicks finished, "The judge has been bought off." Livingston nodded. "And Frankie walked. That's why these people kill with such utter disregard for consequence. They think they'll never be punished." Wicks looked as tired as Devlin had ever seen him, as though his load was finally taking the life out of him. "I'm beginning to think they're right."

Almost to himself, Devlin said, "Sooner or later justice prevails."

In a voice swollen with resignation, Wicks said, "Later was a long time ago."

The *Valhalla* dolphined through the sun-beaded waters of Lake St. Clair. Livingston stood at attention at the rudder, full-faced into the wind and its freshwater spray. He looked possessed. The ride rejuvenated him. He sailed the five-foot waves so skillfully that Devlin didn't even notice them. Devlin admired the pleasure that Livingston derived from piloting his "longboat." He had sailed it to Detroit from the Atlantic Ocean. It had taken him two weeks, up the Hudson River, through the Erie Barge Canal's twenty-seven locks, onto Lake Erie, and finally up the Detroit River. He truly believed his Viking ancestry. Even the boat reflected his passion. It was wooden, completely rebuilt. In the age of fiberglass, a man spending his time currying such a timeless craft was unheard of, but that was who he was.

Devlin leaned back and sipped his second Bloody Mary. Livingston had not had a drink. He did not need one. Pushing his boat through the open water was the only drug he wanted. Like an ancient mariner, he belonged there.

"Has Sydney been out here?" Devlin asked.

"Oh, she loves it."

"What about the two of you?"

"We're pretty serious. As soon as we're finished at the warehouse, I'm going to request some leave and take her back to meet my mother."

"Does your mother know about her?"

"Of course."

"Does she know what Sydney does for a living?"

"No. That's a big sticking point for us. I want her to get out of there and get a straight job, but she's resisting. She's caught up in that urban black, stay-true-to-your-disadvantage life-style. I tell her she's too black. Then she tells me I'm too white. Am I?"

"You two are different, but you're right for each other. All the rest of it will work out."

Livingston considered Devlin's words and let his thoughts slip into the gray-blue waves ahead of the *Valhalla*'s bow.

Devlin remembered L. C. Sanders's face when he had given him the Tigers tickets. Sooner or later, justice would prevail.

III CHAPTER 14 III

Two things struck Devlin as unusual that morning. Everyone was early, and there were doughnuts, which Ross had dropped off an hour earlier, that had not been eaten. At first, he considered the possibility that after Saturday night's brain and liver massacre, everyone had made Monday morning health resolutions. But then he saw it, first in Riley Smith's face, then in each man he looked at—a rush toward the ultimate prize in any case: a human life. The reason. The hope that long ago had caused every one of them to put his right hand into the air and swear to be a witness of the truth.

But until the results of the fingerprint scan were available, they would continue their investigation of Sprinkler. From in front of the briefing board, Devlin spoke. "Today we're entering some legally gray areas." The crew looked impatiently at Devlin, letting him know he did not have to finish his leave-with-no-hard-feelings speech. "Okay. Okay. Assignments. Doc, you'll have the entry into Sprinkler's house. Have you done the neighborhood survey and checked the locks?"

"Yes. I did it yesterday. He lives on a dead-end street, only one neighbor, and he leaves for work at six A.M. The lock is an old Schlage. Nice and worn. I can open it with a credit card."

"Sure you can do it by yourself?"

"I'd rather work alone."

"Okay. Riley, you have the car. The ASAC found out he parks it in the early-bird lot on Second and Bagley, third or fourth level. Did you get the keys from Bill?"

"Yes."

"Don't search the car over there. Just drive it away. Take it to this address." He handed Smith a three-by-five card. "It's a bump shop. A guy named Sweetpea owns it. He puts secret compartments in dope dealer's cars. If Sprinkler has one, you'll never find it without him. Don't tell him anything about the case. If he becomes uncooperative, ask him if the stolen-auto warrant is still outstanding for him in Alabama. There shouldn't be any problems." Devlin picked up the phone and called the ASAC.

"O'Hare."

"Is he there?"

"Absolutely."

"Can you keep him there until noon?"

"Shouldn't be a problem."

Devlin hung up and said, "You've got until noon." The agents headed out the door. "Al, how about heading up to Northville and seeing what the status is on the latent."

"I'll call you when I get there."

"Bill, will you man the phones again?" Shanahan stood up and saluted with his newly casted hand.

That left Brackoff. "Gunnar, can I see you in the office for a minute?" Brackoff knew what that meant; he was going to be asked to do something illegal. He did not mind. That seemed to be what he did best. Sometimes it was the only remaining course. "I want you to get on Whitey. I want to know where he's living, what he's driving, and his daily routine. This is just between us."

Brackoff had a vague idea where Devlin was heading. He knew revenge was the goal. He knew it well. Previously, he alone had originated and executed all such plans.

But now he was being asked to trust someone else with his fate. He asked himself, Is revenge worth it? He answered Devlin and himself. "Of course."

After Brackoff left, Devlin asked Shanahan, "How's that assignment coming?"

"Good. Want to see?"

"In a minute."

Livingston checked his charts and notes, trying to determine what assignment had been given to Shanahan. Devlin knew he would not ask.

Riley Smith was the first to call on the radio. "Whiskey Hotel Five to Whiskey Hotel One."

"Go ahead, Five."

"I'm away in the chopper heading for Sweetpea's."

"Any problems?"

"None. The keys were perfect."

"Keep me advised."

The phone rang. It was Humphrey at the MSP lab. "So far they've run two of the four overlays and have eliminated the ten suspects for each."

"Can you tell anything yet?" Devlin asked.

"No, there's no warning. We'll only know something if the right print pops up. We've got twenty more chances."

The second line rang. "Let me know when they're done."

"It's probably going to take a couple of hours to finish."

"I've got my fingers crossed." Devlin hit the flashing button.

It was Agash. "I'm in without any problems. It shouldn't be too bad. Small place, only one bedroom."

"How long?"

"Two hours."

"No longer."

"I understand." They hung up.

Devlin and Shanahan asked Livingston to take over while they went up to the apartment.

For the next hour the radio was still. There was only one phone call, and that was from the phone company checking the line.

Devlin came down and asked about activity. Livingston told him about the lone telephone call.

"What exactly did they say?"

"They said, 'Michigan Bell calling. We've had reports of trouble on your line. Have you been having any problems?' I said no. They said, 'It was probably people calling into your location who were having problems. We'll send someone out to check the line. What is your address?' I told them I didn't know, but I would get it and call them back. They said they were on the road and couldn't be reached, they'd call back in half an hour."

Somberness shadowed Devlin's face. "Was there anything familiar about the voice?"

Livingston said, "Sorry, I can't remember. Why? What's wrong?"

"You've just received what we refer to as a pretext phone call. Someone had the phone number, but because it's unlisted, it's not in any reverse directories. So they were trying to scam the address from you."

"Who?"

"I've given this number to only one person."

Livingston thought and studied the board briefly. Then he remembered Devlin's Saturday afternoon call. "Anderson."

"You're learning. But I'm not sure it was him." Devlin called the squad secretary. "Sue. Mike. The other day when I left that number for Anderson. What did you do with it?"

"I put it in his message slot. Why? Didn't he call you?"

"Yeah. He called, but I think someone else might have gotten ahold of the number."

"Well, right after I left the message I had to go to Xeroxing. When I came back Fauber was flipping through everyone's messages like he always does."

"Thanks, Sue." Devlin cursed his carelessness. He had seen Fauber do that before and should have been more cautious.

Devlin looked at Livingston. "It's Fauber. He intercepted the message. He must sense something is going on. Now that he knows I'm involved, he won't stop until he gets in our way. Anderson didn't tell him. If he had, Fauber would have known what we're doing and been out here shutting us down. The next thing he'll try to do is put us under surveillance."

"I'm sorry, Mike; I didn't know."

"Don't apologize. In fact, I think we'll give our supervisor some help." Devlin dialed Jeff Ross.

"Do you still own that other warehouse on Vernor?"

"Yes, but it's vacant, all the utilities are turned off. What's up?"

"Trying to buy some time. Give me the address." Devlin wrote down the address and hung up.

Devlin handed the address to Livingston. "When they call back, give them this."

Livingston checked his watch. "That should be soon."

Devlin called Shanahan to come down and told him about the call. When the phone rang, Devlin and Shanahan picked up an extension and listened. It was the same caller. Livingston gave him the address and was told a repairman would be out in a day or so. He hung up.

Devlin and Shanahan looked at each other and said simultaneously, "Dawson." Alex Dawson was an office investigative clerk whose main duty was to obtain and deliver subpoenas to the phone company. Over the years he had developed the pretext call to lessen his workload. Fauber had probably gone to him to get the address for the number.

Devlin picked up the radio mike. "Whiskey Hotel One to Whiskey Hotel Seven."

"Go ahead, One." Brackoff's voice sawed through the air.

"Give me a landline." If Fauber was scanning their broadcasts, Devlin did not want him to hear his instructions to Brackoff. Within minutes, Brackoff called. Devlin said, "When you get done out there, go by an address on Vernor, it's another warehouse, and see if it's under surveillance." Devlin knew the surveillance squad would not make Brackoff.

"I'll be awhile."

"That's fine." Devlin gave him the address and then told Shanahan, "Follow me over there in your car. It'll look good if they see my car outside."

When they got to the Vernor Street warehouse, Devlin looked for the best vantage points for surveillance of the building. He parked his car strategically so it could be seen easily from those locations. On the way back, Shanahan's radio spoke. "Whiskey Hotel Five to Whiskey Hotel One."

"Go ahead, Five," Devlin said.

"The chopper's back in place. We found nothing. Sweetpea was also negative."

"We'll see you back at Whiskey Hotel."

When Devlin and Shanahan pulled into the parking lot, Livingston came running out the door, his eyes confused with the miracle of Christmas morning. "I didn't want to call you on the radio," he said, trying to be calm. But then, as if the words demanded their freedom, they burst into the air, exploding. "They matched the print!"

Shanahan and Livingston clasped each other on the shoulder.

Devlin felt something very private, an almost biblical sign that good shall triumph, that justice will prevail. The last time he had felt anything like that was when he had limped off the plane from Vietnam and been bear-hugged by his family. Withdrawn, he walked up to the apartment as Livingston and Shanahan watched in surprise.

He took out a bottle of cheap bourbon. The cheaper, he felt, the better. He poured two ounces into a glass and drank the first half ounce. He kept the bourbon, which he did not like, close at hand in times of urgency. He called it his reality grenade. The raw, artificial taste reminded him that emotional victories are usually lined with dangerous realities. The second half ounce started the reality implosion. He could taste the fear of defeat in the thorny whiskey. Playing cops and robbers, boys in their tree house repelling phantom pirates, was over. A mistake or a wrong guess could now end a life. He didn't know if he wanted to go on. Maybe it was time to turn the case over to officialdom. The third quarter of bourbon went down. If the SAC was in charge and something went wrong, he would nonetheless claim credit for solving the case and never look back. If something went wrong for Devlin, it would be a weight to be carried forever, like the six Marine lives he had left in Vietnam.

When he tipped his head up and drained the glass, he saw Brackoff standing quietly in front of him. "The fools are already watching the other warehouse," the detective said.

Trying not to be distracted by Brackoff's sureness, Devlin stared into his empty glass. Brackoff took the glass out of his hand and poured another two ounces of whiskey into it. "You know, I've been scared so many times this shit is starting to taste good." He threw all the bourbon back into his throat with one defiant gulp and left. But his words stayed—*the fools*.

Devlin came down the stairs quickly. Before he got to the bottom, he was asking Livingston, "Who's still out?"

"Agash should be back any minute from Sprinkler's.

Humphrey just left Northville, probably twenty minutes. The rest of us are here."

"Did Al give you any details?"

Livingston read from a sheet of paper. "The print is the number two finger—I guess that's the right index—of Marion Lee Tungworth, white male, thirty-six years old. He's wanted by the state police for escaping from Jackson Prison two months ago while serving five to fifteen years for kidnapping."

"Is that it?"

"So far."

"Riley," Devlin said. Smith was slipping his jacket on. "You know your way around Jackson. Get everything they got. Everything." Smith hurried out the door.

Devlin studied the board. Agash walked in.

"Did you find it?" Devlin asked the Doctor.

"No, but I think I found out why Sprinkler's flipped. I found a lot of signs that he's gambling heavy duty. Racing forms, line sheets, his phone bills show dozens of calls to sports touting services. His bills are all overdue. I think his gas has already been turned off. There were even a couple of pawn tickets. I photographed his phone book. Guess who's in there. Julio Pompassi." Pompassi was a mob lawyer; in fact, if there were such a thing, he would have been considered its *consigliare*. Agash was implying that Pompassi might have gotten Sprinkler and Pantatelli together.

Devlin recalled old man Pants's phone call that had first discussed the leak. What Agash found at Sprinkler's house seemed to verify everything—the gambling debt, Julio Pompassi, and the leak. "Good. Did you leave everything the way it was?" Devlin asked.

"We should be cool."

"I'm going to call the ASAC. Ed will fill you in on the

kidnapping." Devlin closed the office door and dialed the office. "John, is Sprinkler still there?"

"No. He left a half an hour ago."

"We struck out at the house." Devlin then explained about what they had found, including Pompassi's name.

"Now what?"

Even though, according to Joey Pants, the exchange was supposed to be Wednesday, which was two days away, Devlin said, "I've received some information that the exchange is supposed to be Saturday." He thought the lie would give them three more days to work the kidnapping. "Let us surveil him until then. If we don't come up with something, we'll confront him and hope for the best."

"I guess that's all we can do."

"John, there's one other problem. Fauber's snooping around. He has some surveillance people trying to watch us, but he doesn't really know where we're at. How about making up some wild-goose chases for him and the surveillance squad for the next couple of days?"

"I'll take care of that little fucking weasel."

"I know you're a big boy, but don't give him a clean shot. You have exposure on this, and he wouldn't hesitate to give you up to Pilkington."

"It's been awhile, but I'm ready to stand up and say 'enough.' "

Devlin laughed. "You'll look good with those earphones on."

Ten minutes later, Al Humphrey returned and started briefing the group immediately. "First of all, this is a positive ID. There is no question that Marion Lee Tungworth's fingerprint is on the same parking ticket as Vanessa's. On April 30, this year, he escaped from Jackson Prison, a minimum-security area, and fled to parts unknown. His home of record is in the Delray section of Detroit. Because there are several hundred escapees at any given time, the state police are not able to do any in-depth fugitive investigations. Their file on Tungworth is at the Livonia post. One last interesting item—in the case he was serving time for, he abducted his victim from the Detroit City Airport." Devlin reached into his pocket and ran his finger along the edge of the card: AT THE AIRPORT.

Devlin felt the panic of time evaporating, like oxygen from a coffin. So far to go. No mistakes allowed. "Ed, give everyone a copy of Tungworth's background." Livingston went to the copier and fed his notes in.

"Gunnar, can you cover DPD, get mug shots, fingerprints, and get their report on the kidnapping. Theo and Al. I want twenty-four-hour surveillance on his last address." Devlin looked at Livingston and smiled. The young agent was writing furiously. "By now you all know Fauber is trying to locate us. Temporarily we've thrown him a head fake. Watch your rearview mirrors and be circumspect on the radio. When you get a chance, call your families and tell them that they're not going to see much of you until we find Tungworth." Then, in a tone of certainty, he added, "And Vanessa."

The crew sat quietly for a few moments, assessing their responsibilities. Someone asked, "What about Sprinkler?"

Devlin took a deep, loud breath that warned that his answer was going to be distasteful to both him and the group. "All of you were asked into this thing because you're the best investigators I know. The fact that you've risked so much to work under these conditions shows me you're the best *men* I know. But as exceptional as all of you are, you cannot handle two things at once. Each and every one of you must focus solely on Vanessa. She's the only thing. I ask that you think of nothing but her and Tungworth. Day and night. Every assignment, no matter how tedious, must be handled with complete and total concentration. We're Vanessa's only chance, and that chance is extremely slim.

We may get only one shot at this. If you're thinking about Sprinkler or your kids' baseball game or anything else, it might give Tungworth the edge that beats us. Vanessa Anderson is certainly more important than the leak. Let me worry about the leak." Devlin took another deep, anesthetizing breath. "Although it's our practice not to use informants' names, even among ourselves, unless it has a purpose, this is one of those exceptions. The informant for the leak is old man Pantatelli's kid—Joey Pants." The group seemed impressed. "So let him and me work this out."

The warehouse crew seemed satisfied. Although they knew the importance of preventing the list from getting to Pantatelli, to the man they knew that rescuing Vanessa was their only real priority. They hurried to their assignments.

Hidden like a disfigured child in an old Victorian mansion was the Delray section of Detroit. All the unglamorous industries of Detroit were exiled long ago to that area along the Detroit River. Even Detroit, amid its infamy, refused to acknowledge the leprous community. As an apparent afterthought, its residential lots were cut and trimmed with jigsaw-puzzle irregularity, fitting around their industrial sponsors.

Because of the location, the turn of the century brought the poorest to live there. They came and named their streets with hope and pride: Yale, Vanderbilt, Du Pont, even Fortune. They began with nothing more than a work ethic, and as they earned the American dream, they relocated accordingly. They left behind the irresolute, the powerless, the vulnerable.

As time went on, the wrecking ball melted the community as if it were a warming glacier. In the last ten years, the only new construction has been a Department of Social Services building, reflecting Delray's current work ethic.

It had become a place where pride had sent more men to prison than any drug addiction, a place where only those too contemptuous of life survived.

At the south end of Day Street stood a six-foot-high cinder block wall. It separated the ugliness of the cement factory from the ugliness of Delray. The Delray side of the wall was covered with neatly organized graffiti, proclaiming everything from pride in the current high school class to the true love T-bone felt for at least three different girls. The largest notice contained four-foot letters proclaiming that the reader was standing on the turf of the Forman Fellas, a gang that hung out at nearby Forman Park.

Marion Tungworth had grown up around that park. He had tried to join the Forman Fellas, but, like most street gangs, you were not accepted unless you could kick someone's ass. Even the girlfriends of the Forman Fellas could kick Marion's ass. A boy named Marion growing up in Delray either became very tough or became very good at avoiding the wrong people. Of everything he had done in the last seven years, he had been caught only once, and that was the kidnapping that had sent him to prison. He was very good at avoiding the law.

When he decided to escape from the prison camp, he vowed he would never tell anyone where he was. And now he felt he had a place no one could find, a small apartment over a boarded-up store. It was at the very end of a street upon which only a few houses had survived. A long time ago, Tungworth had been a stock boy for Mr. Tome. When the owner fired him for stealing, Tungworth kept his key to the storage sheds. The key opened every lock in the building. After that, late in the night, he stole from Tome's sheds, but with much greater care. The old man never noticed the small losses and never thought to change the locks. Just before Tungworth escaped, Tome had had a stroke. Tungworth knew no one would bother him during the final cleansing this time. *No one.*

He sat at a dinette table eating tuna from a can. He loved tuna. They did not have it often in prison, and when they did, it was more mayonnaise and celery than tuna. The boarded-up apartment reeked of tuna. Tungworth did not mind; in fact, he preferred its smell to the ever-present stench of Zug Island, where the industrial belchings caused bypassers' car windows to be rolled up.

Vanessa Anderson sat on the floor dazed, occasionally testing the case-hardened chain that was padlocked around her neck. The other end of the steel tether was locked around an exposed stud in the wall that separated the bedroom from the rest of the tiny apartment.

She carefully ran her fingertips along her face, being careful not to disturb the long, thin scabs Tungworth's razor blades had left. She guessed they would leave no scars. Then she remembered that in a few days scars would be of little consequence.

It had been four days since she had cried. She had realized that crying was a device that had no use or importance within the horror of that apartment.

In the middle of the night, Tungworth would leave for hours. She would hear her father's car start and drive away slowly, squeaking as it rocked across the irregular ground in old man Tome's backyard. When he returned, Tungworth would park the car between two storage sheds attached to the rear of the building, leaving the white Thunderbird hidden from the street. Even though he had replaced the license plate with one he had stolen from an auto salvage company, he felt parking between the sheds was a necessary precaution.

When he was gone, she would test and retest the locks and chain. Using any thin metal object, she would poke blindly into the tumblers, praying for a miracle. She had tested the stud. Surrounded by plaster and lath, it was as immovable as a petrified tree. The first night he left, she screamed herself mute. No one heard her. And if they had, it was still Delray, where screams in the night served only as a reminder to lock the door.

She had considered physically attacking him in an effort to get the key he kept tied around his neck, but he always carried a gun in his belt, the same gun he had pointed at her when he had climbed behind the steering wheel of her car that night at the airport.

By ten P.M. everyone but the surveillance team watching Tungworth's last known address had covered their leads and returned to the warehouse. Riley Smith was the last to arrive. Jackson Prison was an hour and a half away, and getting through the security was also time consuming. But it had been worthwhile because of all the information collected. The prison file, full of presentencing reports, monthly reports, and psychological profiles, had the most complete background information.

As each investigator arrived, his information was given to Livingston, who transformed it into one comprehensive report. When he finished, he copied and distributed it to the crew.

Livingston read it out loud. "Marion Lee Tungworth, white male, thirty-six years old, five-foot-five, 130 pounds, hair brown, eyes brown, scar: six-inch knife scar on stomach, two-inch round birthmark in front of right ear, religion: Catholic, blood type O positive, residence at time of arrest: 6318 Cobalt, Detroit, lived in the house since birth. Education: tenth grade, quit to help support family. At that time, he went to work for the Mr. Tome grocery store at an unrecalled address on Barron Street. Worked there two years until fired for stealing groceries. He joined the U.S. Army but was given an unsuitable discharge after two months.

The Army cited inadaptability and nonconformity. Every night after taps, he would loudly masturbate in his bunk, which resulted in numerous fights with the other recruits. When interviewed by the Army psychiatrist, he vehemently denied it, claiming a conspiracy against him."

"Maybe I could use that to get a section eight out of the Bureau," Shanahan interrupted.

"It hasn't worked for you all these years," Devlin said.

Livingston continued, "After the Army, Tungworth returned home and went to work for Ford Motor Company at the Rouge Plant. He worked there for almost nine years as a solderer. His work reports show high absenteeism. Without warning or notice, he took off for parts unknown. He said he had gotten a girl in trouble. DPD says he was a good suspect in an abduction that happened in neighboring River Rouge. He would never tell the prison people exactly where he went, only that he was out west with an Army buddy who was a taxi driver and he got him a job driving a cab. About two years later he returned to Detroit and reapplied at Ford. Because of his work record, he was not rehired. He got a job at the River Packing Company. He told the prison psychologist it was the best job he ever had. He worked ten at night until six in the morning. He was responsible for the security of the building. He had his own key, and there was no one to boss him around. After six months, the company closed down. While he was collecting unemployment compensation, he was arrested for kidnapping and given a five-to-fifteen-year sentence. The first year he spent inside the walls of Jackson and was then transferred to a minimum-security camp. While there, he was knifed in the stomach. The wound took 150 stitches. After three months he simply walked away from the camp. No one has seen him since. His mother lives in the same house that we're on. Two sisters, Carla and Elizabeth, both married, one divorced. The divorced one, Carla, is living with the mother. The father ran off when Tungworth was ten. The only visitors at the prison were his mother and Elizabeth. He refused to see Carla, because she was the one who turned him in on the abduction. And that's about it."

"Anything jump out?" Devlin asked the group. The slowly turning pages of their reports quietly rattled in response.

Brackoff spoke first. "I don't know if any of you have ever worked Delray before, but we'll get no help down there. It's a tough place to survive, but the people who grow up there never want to leave. It's crazy, but they always go back there. When Tungworth ran after the kidnapping, he was smart enough to realize he had to get as far away as possible, otherwise he'd be drawn right back to the old neighborhood. He's in Delray."

The crew considered Brackoff's insights. They wanted Tungworth to be that close, where they could get their hands on him. But maybe that was why Brackoff thought he was there. The thought of Brackoff handling Tungworth, one on one, warmed them all.

Shanahan said, "Why don't you have Doc go see the sister that turned him in before? See if she knows where he's at."

"Good idea. He can tell her he's just working on him as an escapee in case she's not as helpful this time."

Devlin went to the radio. "Whiskey Hotel One to Whiskey Hotel Six."

"Go, One," Agash answered.

"What's going on down there?"

"Absolutely nothing. No one moving. No cars. But there are lights on in the house."

Devlin looked at the group. A nervous resolve wove its way through them. He took out the eight-by-ten color photo of Vanessa from which the small black-and-whites had been made and pinned it onto the briefing board. Vanessa stared back at the crew. Her expression was puzzled, as if the photographer had taken it before she was ready. She seemed to be anticipating something, waiting impatiently. Devlin said, "Okay, let's go find her."

||| CHAPTER 15 |||

As they crossed into Delray, a forbidding calm waited. Not a sound, not a twist of wind, just the darkness that had to be outlasted. In Delray it was a time of retreat, a reach to dawn. As he got out of the car, Devlin was warned by it. The eye of a hurricane crossed his mind. Was it him, or did the neighborhood sense the law enforcement storm descending on it? He wondered. He had seen stranger things.

The Holy Cross Church's cornerstone explained that it was a Hungarian Catholic church erected in 1924. It was after midnight when the crew pulled into its parking lot. Agash had left Humphrey watching Tungworth's last known address. When he pulled into the lot, Devlin and the remaining investigators were out of their cars. Agash was told about the sister. They decided she should not be interviewed until morning. If Agash showed up in the middle of the night, she would know it was more than a routine fugitive case.

"I keep a suit in the car for just such occasions," Agash said, indicating he understood everything that was being asked of him.

"Right now we're going to divide up Delray and search for the car." Devlin assigned a sector to each of the men, including himself. "Look for the car, not the plate. We'll have to assume it's been changed. Meet here in an hour."

Devlin had taken a section south of Jefferson Avenue. It

was eight square blocks bounded by the Rouge River and the Detroit River. Half of the structures were residential, the other half industrial. Many of them were boarded up or burned out. He noticed that garages where the car could be hidden were scarce. At least that was in their favor.

An hour later they met again in the church parking lot. No one had seen the white Thunderbird.

Devlin rotated the search sectors so that each area was searched a second time by a different agent. After another hour, they reported the same results.

Their faces conceded that the adrenaline had subsided long ago and, as it always did, had left them that much more fatigued. Devlin's own body felt thick with exhaustion. Since leads would need to be covered in the morning, Devlin decided that the group should get a few hours' sleep. He asked for a volunteer to watch the house. Unceremoniously, Brackoff raised his hand. He never seemed to need sleep. Everyone else headed for the warehouse.

Of the lessons Devlin had learned in Vietnam, sharing hardships with the troops was one of the most valuable. Whether eating enlisted men's food or walking point for an *expendable* private, Lieutenant Devlin had sent the message to his men: *We're in this shit together.*

As the crew settled into their cots and sleeping bags, Devlin was reminded of the defiant camaraderie he and his troops had shared for thirteen months. It was them against the VC, NVA, officers, the Marine Corps, and anyone else who expected them to surrender without a fight. Some things never change, he thought, as he lay down on a sleeping bag. Through the floor he heard a sound—or was it a vibration—coming from below. Was he hearing—or remembering?

It was November 10, the Marine Corps's birthday, 1968, for all present a most holy day. The day, every year, when Marines, past and present, stopped everything and celebrated being part of the proudest fighting force history has ever known. Some colonel had wanted a most traditional birthday, so Devlin's battalion was to land, World War II–style, on the beaches of some unremembered Vietnamese coastal village. The operation was named Daring Endeavor. During the preinvasion briefing, the colonel had tried to motivate his officers by telling them, "It isn't much of a war, but it's the only one we've got. Let's make the most of it."

As first light billowed over the gunnels of Devlin's landing craft, a somberness took over the troops. He felt the same fears. They had all seen the movies: Tarawa, Iwo Jima, thousands of Marine bodies like green herringbone driftwood, floating in the foamy surf.

The boat no longer bobbed aimlessly; it picked up speed, heading toward shore. Behind him, Devlin heard a bolt go home on one M-16, then twenty more. Silently, they all faced forward, waiting for the craft to ram the sand. Everyone lurched forward. As if by some evil magician's trick, the thick forward wall separating them from death disappeared. Lieutenant Devlin was the first to charge ashore. "Come on, you sons of bitches. Do you want to live forever?" He had remembered that Gunnery Sergeant Dan Daly had yelled it in Belleau Wood while earning his second Medal of Honor in World War I. Eighteen-year-old Marines responded to emotional leadership. Besides, Devlin knew a secret of combat, a secret so illogical that it refused to be passed along: The more aggressive a unit was, the fewer casualties it took. After six months in country, minimizing casualties had become Devlin's predominant mission. In Danang, he had watched tiny South Vietnamese soldiers walk hand in hand, oblivious to the consequences surrounding them; they knew the big Americans would win the war. They were as unconcerned as children at recess. Devlin knew between the war protests at home and the politicians caving in to them, the war would never be won. The only commitment he had felt was to his men, to take as few casualties as possible.

As his platoon ran onto the beach, they found themselves in the vortex of the enemy's machine-gun fire. The entire unit was pinned down behind a long, shallow berm of sand. "Who has a grenade?" Devlin said, tactfully asking for a volunteer. The response was immediate—a dozen hand grenades, the pins still in, thumped into the sand around him. He started laughing. Their thin, bone-sharp faces smiled back, hoping he would be the volunteer. From his shrunken 170-pound body, he slipped off all his equipment. He loaded the countless pockets of his jungle utilities with the donated hand grenades.

He raised his head above the berm and was greeted by a machine gun splintering the sand. If they were going to get off that beach alive, the machine-gun emplacement had to be destroyed. Machine-gun crews were usually at least four men. He had his right flank ready to fire when he took off, then he would angle left and the left flank could open up. He lay there a moment, trying to gather the courage to commit suicide.

Finally, he said to himself, "C'mon, ya son of a bitch, you want to live forever?" and was gone, right flank blazing. He got outside the enemy's flank and worked left to right, throwing grenades and firing his .45 automatic. As his men heard the grenades explode, they stopped firing, afraid of hitting their lieutenant. After ten minutes, there was no more enemy fire. The platoon sergeant had the squads leapfrog forward until they were on the enemy's lines. They counted twelve North Vietnamese regulars dead. The last two were found in a trench with Devlin. One had died midscream, the handle of Devlin's heavy-bladed Randall combat knife sticking out of his crooked neck. The other had been beaten to death by Devlin's empty sidearm.

Devlin laid under the one with the knife in his neck. Devlin had been shot in the shoulder and chest. His eyes were shut.

The platoon sergeant said, "Lieutenant, Lieutenant!"

Devlin opened his eyes and looked at the chronically exhausted faces of his men, their eyes wide with fear, and said weakly, "This leadership-by-example crap is really overrated."

As is required by regulations, five of Devlin's troops had written statements recommending him for the Medal of Honor. The last example of his devotion to duty they noted was "Although gravely wounded, Lt. Devlin refused to be medivaced that night in order to ensure the safety of his men." While it was true that he was not medivaced that night, the real reason was weather. The choppers could not find his unit in the heavy fog. He laid on the ground in a morphine stupor, unable to sleep. He could hear digging under him. They had camped on top of a large NVA tunnel complex, and the enemy was trying to dig its way to safety. No Marine slept that night, waiting for enemy helmets to spring from the ground.

Because of its reluctance to give the Medal of Honor to living Marines, the Corps presented Devlin with the nation's second highest medal for valor—the Navy Cross, for his "daring endeavor."

Devlin put the Bureau radio next to his sleeping bag in case Brackoff needed something during the night. As he drifted off, he could hear someone tunneling. *The enemy.*

At eight A.M., Devlin called Tom Anderson.

"Why didn't you call yesterday?" Anderson asked.

Quietly, Devlin filled his lungs before answering, "I don't want you to get too excited, but we've identified the latent print. It belongs to a prison escapee who was doing time for kidnapping. His name is Marion Lee Tungworth. We're looking for him now."

"Let me get the whole office out, and we can find him faster."

"Whoa. The area we think he's in is difficult to penetrate. If he's in there with Vanessa, it might spook him into doing something drastic."

"Well, then, can I come out and help you?"

"I've got enough help. As soon as there's anything positive, I'll give you a call."

"You sure?"

"I'm sure."

Devlin hoped Anderson was not weakening. Something else sucking the air out of his coffin.

Devlin sent Riley Smith to relieve Brackoff. Agash came down from the apartment in a navy blue suit and striped red tie. His hair was combed back. He looked more like a European model than a federal agent.

"Theo, you know what we need. When you're done, we'll be waiting at the church."

When Agash drove into the lot two hours later, the crew was waiting for him anxiously. Afraid his fatigue might cause him to forget some fact, Livingston sat next to Devlin, taking notes. When they had left the warehouse, Devlin, with a mysterious tone, had again told Shanahan to "keep at it."

Agash took out his notes from the interview of Carla Tungworth. Before he started, Riley Smith asked, "How penetrating an interview was it, Doc?"

With mock indignation, Agash blinked heavily, raised his chin, and demanded, "Please. I'm a trained professional." Silently everyone wondered if the Doctor had acted beyond the call of duty.

Agash started reading. "She said her brother was pretty

much a loner and has not talked to her since she turned him in almost three years ago. She has tried to visit and write him, but he wouldn't acknowledge that she existed. Growing up, he was always kind of a weird kid, no friends, other kids picked on him. A lot of times, the other kids' pets would be found dead. He was never caught, but she knew it was him doing it. He was thrown out of high school, thrown out of the Army, fired from the grocery store, got in trouble, went out west, worked as a cabbie, came back, and worked as a night watchman at the slaughterhouse on Cary Street until it closed. Only dated a few girls. The only one that's still around is a Mary Sue Ashley, lives on Yale, address unknown. The only friend he ever had was a Billy Rhodes. In fact, it was Rhodes's place he was arrested at on the abduction. Rhodes was out of town at the time. A witness got the tag and called it in to the police. They went to the sister, she sent them to Rhodes's."

"Where does he live?" Devlin asked.

"He lives on the corner of Harbaugh and Copeland. But that's not where Tungworth was arrested. That place has been torn down."

"Has she heard from him since he escaped?" Devlin asked.

"She says no," Agash answered.

"But?"

"But I asked her if her mother had, and again she said no. But it was a different no. She was lying. Probably to protect the mother. The mother *has* heard from him."

"Think she'll call you if she hears something?"

"I think so."

Devlin turned to Humphrey. "Al, I know we can't run a hard wire for a full tap, but do you think you could put a recorder on that line at the box?"

"Sure. I'll have to go back to the office and get some equipment."

"Gunnar, you want to go get some sleep?" Devlin asked.

"No." The answer was as convincing as a paragraph from anyone else.

"Okay, you and Doc go interview Billy Rhodes. You shouldn't have any trouble finding him. Ed and myself will interview Mary Sue Ashley. The interviews should be conducted under the escapee guise."

Devlin noticed someone across the street holding back a dingy white curtain, watching them. "We better not meet here anymore. Gunnar, do you know anyplace?"

"The Delray Cafe. It's on Jefferson, just past Westend. There's an upstairs. The owner loves cops."

"Good. How about lunch there at one o'clock?"

"I'll take care of it," Brackoff said.

"Everyone remember—this is Delray. Be as inconspicuous as possible," Devlin warned.

As the crew started getting into their cars, a DPD scout car bounced slowly into the parking lot. The two older white officers stayed in the car when they saw Brackoff walking towards them. He did not identify himself. Both cops knew him by sight. And reputation. Brackoff simply said, "We're working." The car cut a tight circle and left.

Mary Sue Ashley was not hard to find. Actually, no one in Delray was hard to find unless they wanted to be. Yale Street was only two short blocks. On those two blocks were eight abandoned houses. Devlin started knocking on doors. The third one was opened by a male in his early twenties. His dark, matted hair hung below the shoulders of his black Grateful Dead T-shirt. He was impressed that he was talking to an FBI agent. His first question was the usual: "What do you want me for?"

"This has nothing to do with you," Devlin said for the millionth time. "I'm looking for Mary Sue Ashley."

"What did she do?"

"She didn't do anything. Someone applied for a job with the FBI and listed her as a reference, that's all," Devlin lied.

"Oh," he answered slowly, while he decided if Devlin was lying. "Well, she lives on the corner in the white aluminum job. Can I get a job with the FBI?"

"I'll send you an application," Devlin lied again.

Mary Sue Ashley did not fit the jeans-and-T-shirt mold of the Delray girls Devlin had seen. She graciously invited the agents into her house. The furnishings were not expensive, but were impeccably matched in a traditional style. The tan wall-to-wall carpeting had been recently vacuumed. Original drawings and paintings hung everywhere, the kind that could be bought at art fairs for less than fifty dollars.

She had an easy grace about her, an almost southern charm. "Would you like coffee?"

"That would be great," Devlin answered for both of them. Long ago, he had learned that if you accept a person's hospitality, that person more readily accepts you. And without exception, the interview becomes more productive. Maybe one interview in a hundred was truly enjoyable. Devlin knew this was going to be one of those.

She walked back in balancing coffee, cups, saucers, spoons, cream, and sugar on a tray. She was in her early thirties, plain, well groomed, and wearing a print dress with a high collar and long sleeves. The long sleeves were the first thing that alerted Devlin. It was summer, and this girl, so fashionably correct, was covering her arms. When she poured the coffee, he noticed why. Her left hand—and by the way she held it, her arm—were artificial. Devlin immediately diverted his eyes. She saw him look away. It was always a relief when someone discovered her malady. She could be open about it, which was much more comfortable for her and everyone else.

It was unusual that she had not asked one question about

the agents' contacting her. Devlin wanted to reciprocate her hospitality by being direct, to relieve any apprehension she might have. "We're looking for Marion Tungworth."

She nodded, indicating that she had wondered what the purpose of their visit was. "We're interviewing old acquaintances. Nothing more."

She nodded again and waited a moment, ensuring she would not interrupt him. "That was a long time ago. We dated for a couple of months. We were definitely an odd couple: me because of my arm and him because of his peculiar behavior." Livingston stared at her left hand. Without looking at him, she felt his stare and gracefully hid her left hand in her right.

"Do you know why we're looking for him?"

"I know he went to prison for kidnapping a girl. Did he do it again?"

"I'm afraid he's escaped from prison," Devlin told the half-truth.

"That's terrible. Do you think he's around here?"

"We have no idea. We're just covering the bases. You mentioned his peculiar behavior."

"Yes. For one thing, he had no sense of humor. Everything was very serious with him. When we went out, we never did the fun things like movies, dancing, or restaurants. He always wanted to do something intense, like drive to Port Huron, which is a good hour away. He'd drive eighty miles an hour, make a U-turn and drive eighty miles an hour back. He'd be in a cold sweat when we got back."

"Anything else?"

"Probably the worst thing, the thing that caused me to stop seeing him, was that he became obsessed with me not wearing my prosthesis when we went out. He said it was phony and I would be more attractive to him without it."

"When was that?"

"Not long before he went out west. When he came back

he got a night watchman's job. He really liked that. He always was a night owl. Up all night, sleep all day. Very strange."

"When was the last time you saw him?"

"Just before he went to prison."

"Did he ask you out then?"

"No. I wouldn't have gone anyway. If it's possible, he seemed even more strange. But maybe I'm reading something into it now because of what he did."

"Is there anybody or anyplace he might go to for help?"

"Did you try Billy Rhodes?"

"Yes, we did."

"Other than his mom, that's about all I know."

"Thanks very much for your help," Devlin said and wrote the warehouse phone number on the back of his card. "If you think of anything, we'd appreciate a call. It's always confidential."

She offered them another cup of coffee, and when they declined, she delicately extended her right hand like the vulnerable neck of a swan. Both men shook her hand gently and thanked her again.

The Delray Cafe was the most vibrant place in the community. Outside, large, brightly colored murals covered the walls; inside, the illusion was Down South rather than disreputable Downriver. The lunch crowds were to capacity daily. Hundreds of truck drivers and plant workers jammed the old saloon, enjoying the down-home cooking and the waitresses, who still had a few good, lusty miles left. It was an exclusive club—blue collar only. So when the white collars walked in, the owner quickly took them upstairs. After they had eaten and the bill was paid, Devlin told the waitress they would not need her anymore and gave her an extra ten dollars. She understood. She had dated more than one cop.

Livingston read his notes from the interview of Mary Ashley. Then Agash reported his interview of Billy Rhodes. "This guy is burned out. He's been popped a couple of times for possession of PCP. Once did six months in Wayne County for B and E. He was loaded when we were talking to him. He started to fire up a joint in front of us until he caught Gunnar's face. He wasn't *that* stoned. Anyway, he tells us he and Tungworth used to hang out together. He couldn't figure out why because they had nothing in common, other than neither of them had any friends. I guess they became friends by default. He said Tungworth never did drugs or even drank. They'd work on cars together or occasionally go to a movie. Tungworth wrote him from prison and apologized for getting into trouble in his apartment. I asked him if he had seen him since the escape. This is where it entered the Twilight Zone. He said he was smoking weed the other night and ran out, so he drove over to the other side of Delray to cop. By his own admission, he was stoned. When he was coming back, he saw a guy coming at him in a white car, wearing a baseball cap and sunglasses. For a split second, he thought it was Tungworth, not by his face, but the way he leaned into the driver's door. He said Tungworth had that habit."

"Did you ask him if it was a T-bird?" someone asked.

"He wasn't sure. He said it could have been."

Devlin looked at a blowup of the Delray area. Livingston had somehow made it on the small desktop copier at the warehouse. "Show me where," he said to Agash.

"That's where it breaks down. He was so wired, he's not sure where it was. He's not even sure what route he took."

"Did you get his connect's address?"

"I asked him, and he refused." Agash smiled. "Then Gunnar asked him. Some guy named Eddie, lives on Vinewood. It's only a block long, and we got a description." He pointed to it on the blowup.

"You and Gunnar find Eddie. Ask him exactly when Rhodes was there. Then go back to the warehouse and get some sleep. Al, did you get that recorder hooked up?"

"About an hour ago. It's voice activated. I should check it every four hours."

"Good. I want to hear all the tapes. Tomorrow we'll have Doc go talk to the sister again and then see who she calls afterward."

"I wish there was some way we could run a trace, but the phone company would have my ass if they knew what I was doing."

"A trace would make this whole thing easier, but Michigan Bell is the only one that can do that, so we go with what we got. Riley, get back on the mother's house. If she goes anywhere, go with her, real loose. The rest of us should familiarize ourselves with Delray. Learn all the dead-end and one-way streets. Then everybody get some sleep. Gunnar, on your way back go by the other warehouse and see if they still have it under surveillance."

Devlin sat in a cloak of self-hypnosis. His mind, undistracted, raced through the investigation, start to present. They were getting close, very close. But it was like looking for a booby trap in Vietnam; the closer you got to it, the more deadly it became. To save Vanessa, if she was still alive, they were going to have to be good. Very, very good. Devlin heard Livingston's voice ask a question, but the words were out of focus. "I'm sorry, what?"

"What do you want me to do?" Livingston repeated.

"Go back and use this blowup of the area to plot out everything we know about Tungworth—addresses, girlfriend, both of Rhodes's places, employment, everything."

"Should I cruise Delray first?"

Devlin looked around. Everyone else had left. "No. You won't be coming back here tonight." Livingston wanted to ask why, but he knew Devlin was trying to answer too many questions already. Besides, he liked surprises. Training school had never promised anything like this.

Devlin drove over every street in Delray. He let the microcosm's culture sink in. Its overhead was crisscrossed with thick silver power lines. No home was out of eyeshot of a commercial building. Trucks outnumbered cars. Bars outnumbered grocery stores. Rusty playgrounds were wedged between unsympathetic industrial properties. Vacant lots were hidden by sentinel weeds, and tire tracks disappeared into them as though old cars, like elephants into rumored graveyards, went there to die. The sounds of the railroad were Delray's obtrusive clock. Abandoned railway spurs cut through the ground like a scarred butcher block. Plain black-and-white bumper stickers, as plain as their owner's life-styles, announced DELRAY—OUR PLACE. The clannishness was reemphasized by the young children, who stopped and glared at anyone who was not one of their own. *If you haven't survived Delray, you haven't earned the right to be here.*

When Devlin arrived at the warehouse, Shanahan was the only one there. "Are you making progress?" Devlin asked.

"I'm ready."

The others straggled in. The last were Brackoff and Agash.

"Did you find Eddie?" Devlin asked.

"Yes," Agash said. "He really liked Gunnar. Tried real hard to please him. He remembered Rhodes coming over that night, because he woke him up. He couldn't remember whether it was Thursday or Friday. You know junkies and time. Didn't recognize Tungworth's mug shot. He's only lived there about a year."

"There's no one watching the other warehouse, Mike," Brackoff said.

"Good. Try to check it once a day. It's a good indicator of how hard they're working to find us."

Al Humphrey was using headphones to listen to a portable tape player. He hit the stop button. "Nothing, Mike. She doesn't even talk about the FBI looking for her son. Her phone is not very active. Reviewing the tapes every four hours should be plenty."

"Okay, every four hours starting at eight o'clock tonight. No matter what's going on, get there. Is the Bell box in view of the house?"

"No. I can get there without them seeing me."

The warehouse grew quiet. The crew was settling into their cots, trying to get some sleep before the nine-thirty briefing. Livingston had made an even larger blowup of the Delray area. The only sound now was Livingston stapling its sections onto the briefing board. He studied and lined up the edges with the patience of a diamond cutter. As quietly as possible, he pushed the staples through the paper and into the plywood. Devlin found Livingston's precision soothing, something dependable, perfect amid the chaos stampeding through his ability to reason.

While the others slept, he studied the blowup. Livingston had color-coded all the locations of significance. Devlin plotted possible routes Rhodes could have taken to Eddie's and then placed pins in the map to mark where the investigators were to set up.

By nine-thirty no one needed to be awakened. They sat sipping fresh coffee, although they knew it would cause a biological inconvenience during the long surveillance.

Devlin gave them their positions. "If you spot Tungworth, give him lots of room. We don't want to get burned. We've got to take him back to where he's lying down. We don't want him; we want Vanessa. If we lose him, we can get him again, but if he spots us, we may as well strike tents." He hesitated for emphasis. "You're going to be tired out there. Remember what we talked about; you've got to turn it up a notch. Full concentration on Vanessa. We've got to be better than we've ever been before."

At ten-thirty P.M. John Sprinkler's phone rang. "Hello," he said.

"Do you know who this is?"

Although he had talked to him only once on the telephone, Sprinkler recognized the raspy, breathless voice of Anthony Pantatelli. "Yes."

"Something's come up. I've got to leave town again in the morning, so we're moving up the sale. Tonight at three A.M., at the Bella Luna. Park in the back, and come in through the front door. I'll leave it open. Small bills all right?"

"Yes, sir. I'll be there."

III CHAPTER 16 III

John Sprinkler sat in his car, shrouded by the dark silence at the rear of the Bella Luna. He asked himself, "Is Tony Pants going to kill me?" His mind slipped into a haunting scene: Pantatelli taking the list from him and, while laughing, shooting him to death. Sprinkler lying there listening to the rhythmic laughter, enjoying the warm, flexible anesthesia of death. "No! Not over a list of informants. Besides, now I'm his informant. He'll need me for things in the future. New informants will be opened; he'll need to know who they are." Now he envisioned Pantatelli laughing again, waving to Sprinkler to bring in the new group of informants so the old man could shoot them himself. "No!" Sprinkler yelled to himself. He sat and composed his thoughts, reeling them back to the shores of reality. "He'll have to pay me tonight if he expects help in the future. I have no choice, anyway. I owe the books too much. They're looking to hurt me. I have no choice."

With the list of every Detroit informant in his damp hand, Sprinkler got out of his car and looked around. There were no cars in the parking lot. He wondered where Pantatelli had parked his car. He walked to the front door and tried it. It was open. Quickly he reviewed his options again and, with a hopeless "Fuck it," went in.

The inside smelled of smoke and spilled beer. Only one light was on, at the back of the bar. He walked to the back

257

and stood in front of the door marked MANAGER. He felt sick. He cursed his weakness. The doorknob seemed stiff in his hand, as if it were warning him that the door separated him from a different life and stepping through it would preclude a return trip to innocence. Involuntarily, he knocked.

From deep inside, he heard Tony Pants. "C'mon in, kid. I'm in the can. I'll be out in a minute."

Sprinkler walked in and sat down at a chair in front of the desk. He heard the toilet flush. How appropriate, he thought.

From behind him, without warning, he heard, "Hello, John." Startled, he turned and found Devlin standing in the doorway.

At the same time, he heard Pantatelli say, "It's all over, kid." He turned back to face Tony Pants but instead saw Bill Shanahan standing there. "I hope you don't mind small bills."

Behind Devlin, Livingston came into the room. Sprinkler collapsed deep into the chair as if his spine had suddenly been stripped from his body. On his face, defeat waved its victorious shadow. "I'm glad. I really didn't want to do this, but the bookies were through fucking around. They were looking to do some serious damage—I'm sorry."

Devlin took the list from his hand and verified its contents. He leaned on the desk in front of Sprinkler and spoke to him calmly, as an equal, not taking advantage of the situation. "John, I'm going to tell you what would have happened. Tomorrow night when you met the old man, he would have had at least one broken nose with him. And when you showed up, they would have simply taken the list from you. Who were you going to tell? They wouldn't have given you a dime. And the next time he needed some information, he would have threatened you with exposure. The list is in your handwriting." While Sprinkler considered the evidence, Devlin said, "Don't you realize those bookies work for him?"

"I guess there's a lot of things I don't realize."

"I want you to give us a signed statement."

"Okay. Then what?"

Devlin knew he had to let him go home. If Sprinkler was arrested, the ASAC would expect the crew to resume its normal duties, which would, at the least, hamper the search for Vanessa. But he wanted to be sure there were no other copies of the list. "You give me all the copies of the list, and we'll let you go home."

"Are you kidding? I was scared enough just having this one. I was even afraid to keep it at my house. I hid it at my mom's until an hour ago."

"We're going to a place we've been using. We will take your statement there and then cut you loose."

Sprinkler looked at him. He knew Devlin was telling the truth.

As they left the Bella Luna, Devlin locked the door with the key that had been made during the court-ordered break-in. He considered the full circle of events that had started and ended at the nightclub's front door. This time justice had prevailed sooner rather than later.

Riley Smith sat in his car, fighting off sleep. He rolled down the car window to allow the industrial stench in unblocked, hoping for a smelling-salts effect. His eyelids dispensed the burning acids of fatigue. He rubbed his eyes until his vision blurred.

A white car passed him. His brain went to full alert. He was sure it was a Thunderbird. He started his car and slammed it into gear. He left his lights off, staying a block behind.

As he passed under a street light, he held the radio mike below the dashboard, hiding his transmission. "All units, this is Whiskey Hotel Five. I think I got him. We're west on Melville just passing—" He waited until he saw the next street sign. "—Yale. Can someone get up here and give me a hand?"

The other agents, jolted out of their own drowsiness, tried to respond at the same time, garbling one another's transmission. Finally, Smith took charge. "Break, break, break, cease your transmissions. I'll call out my position. Get to me as fast as you can."

Devlin marveled at the almost aristocratic calm of Smith's voice. Devlin and Livingston had finished with Sprinkler and were heading for Delray but were too far away to help.

"Crossing Harbaugh," Smith said.

"Whiskey Hotel Five, tap your brake lights twice. I think I'm about two blocks behind you." It was Agash. Smith made the signal.

"Yeah. I'm coming up on your six. Where is he?"

"He just took a right on Dearborn. I got to get off of him; he may have made me." Smith turned left and could see the taillights he had been tracking in his rearview mirror. The lights jerked up and down as the white car drove over railroad tracks without braking. The driver was in a hurry. "Doc, he's hinky. He's got his foot in it." Smith rounded a curve and lost sight of the car. He made a sharp U-turn and headed back.

Agash screamed up to the right-hand turn, then slowed to a normal speed to disguise the chase. As he took the turn, Smith was a block behind him.

Immediately Agash cut in. "I don't have him. There must be six small streets right here he could have taken. Everybody better get up here and help."

"Damn," Devlin said. He keyed his microphone. "Doc, stop right there and give out search sectors. Have everyone note which buildings have lights on. There shouldn't be many at this time of the morning. I'm about five away."

When Devlin got there, Agash sat in his car with Smith, studying a blowup of the area. Devlin got into the backseat. "Do you have enough help?"

"Yeah, I think so. Here, look at the map. This is a small pocket of Delray, the only part of it that's north of I-75," Agash said.

Devlin looked at the map. There were about ten streets, most of which were only a block long. The area was bounded on two sides by the curving highway; on the third side was Fort Street and on the fourth, the Rouge River. If he were hiding in that area, it would cut their search to one tenth of Delray.

"Riley, why do you think it was him?"

"At first I just saw a white car. That last right turn he made, I finally got a broadside view. It was a Thunderbird."

"Plates?"

"I never got close enough, and I had my lights off."

"Anything else?"

Smith's eyes grinned. "He was leaning against the door." As welcome as the identification was, they knew they had no time to celebrate.

"What makes you think he might have made you?" Devlin asked.

"After I was on him for a couple of blocks, he sat up straight and drove a little faster. I don't know if he spotted my car without headlights or not. That last turn up Dearborn, he ran the stop and flew over the tracks. The only thing that might have convinced him otherwise was when I gave him action and turned left."

"Show me on the map where he got hinky."

Smith traced their route with his finger and finally said, "Here, just past Harbaugh."

For a full minute, Devlin studied the blowup. "Okay,

let's assume he turned right as a decoy. If he were to turn left, it would give us another eight blocks to search. From Harbaugh to the expressway to the river. Let's go check it."

Marion Lee Tungworth sat low in the front seat of the white Thunderbird, breathing hard. The car sat between the two storage sheds behind the grocery store.

After waiting ten minutes, listening for cars on the dead-end street, he unlocked the back door of the grocery store and climbed the stairs to the apartment. When he had moved in, he had used sheets of plywood that had been stored on the first floor of the building to board up the apartment windows from the inside. There were three windows: living room, bedroom, bathroom. Feeling secure in the darkness, he lit a candle in the living room.

He went downstairs, through the shed, and into the store. He stood on a stool in the front, looking through a transom window, which, because it was so narrow, had not been boarded up. For half an hour he watched for traffic on Barron Street. Only one car drove down the street. It drove slowly, made a U-turn, and drove away. It looked like an unmarked police car, but the driver, who was huge, reminded Tungworth of a guy he had been in prison with. Was he followed earlier, or was he imagining things? That car had been behind him without lights, but it had turned the opposite way on Dearborn. Probably nothing, but he would be more careful in the future.

He went back upstairs and, in the bedroom, lit another candle. The flame writhed over the figure seeking refuge in the corner. "Wake up, Vanessa Anderson. It's another day of your attrition. The day after tomorrow will be your final liberation."

The girl sat up and pushed her back firmly into the corner. He handed her a dirty porcelain cup full of water. She drank it quickly, being careful not to spill any. She no longer begged for food. She knew she was going to die. When she was twelve she had watched her aunt die, inch by inch, of cancer. She had felt the hopelessness of the insidious death. She felt the same hopelessness now.

She heard metal softly ripping and smelled the penetrating odor of tuna fish again.

The first two days she had begged for her release. When she was not raped during that time, she realized her captivity could have only one end. He kept counting down days until her final cleansing, whatever that was. Whatever it meant, Vanessa Anderson knew that in two days her life would be over.

By the time everyone returned to the warehouse, the sun had risen. The daylight reminded them that the night's effort, however intense, had not been enough to reach their dire goal.

Devlin knew they were exhausted, but their attitude was one of quiet, angry resolve. They would never give up. Neither must he. "This will be brief. I want you to go home, get some sleep, and a real meal. See which of your kids are still living at home. Be back here at four. Tonight, all of us will be on the street. If he moves, we should have him. But everyone has to be fresh. Al, don't worry about changing tapes until four, just bring it in then. Questions?"

Brackoff's voice rumbled, "On my way in, I checked the other warehouse. They're set up on it again."

"I forgot about that problem. I'll take care of it. Anything else?"

Someone asked, "Can't we go in and start checking garages? There aren't that many."

"I considered that, but if Tungworth saw us in the neighborhood, we'd be finished. Agreed?"

One or two tired heads nodded.

"Before you go, give your list of garages and buildings

that had lights on last night to Ed. He'll make a master list of all of them. They may help later, if we can get this narrowed down to a smaller area." Devlin waited while the lists were handed to Livingston and then reached into the inside pocket of his suit coat and pulled out a thick envelope. "There is *some* good news. We got the list from Sprinkler." He held it up.

For a moment the group forgot the fatigue and congratulated one another.

Devlin explained how it had been recovered and then added, "Now we can focus on Vanessa."

After they all left, Devlin climbed heavily to the apartment and lay on the bed. In his pocket he felt the card—AT THE AIRPORT. Not now, he begged. A giant whirlpool pulled him down into a warm, dissolving sleep.

When he awoke, he could not remember if he had dreamt. He concluded he must have slept soundly. The dank air of the warehouse had been displaced by the congenial smell of brewing coffee. Devlin found Ross storing sandwiches, pop, and beer in the refrigerator. It was almost two-thirty in the afternoon.

"Jeff," Devlin said.

"Mike! Nice job on the list. The board also says you spotted Tungworth."

"Yes. But we lost him."

"You'll get him. Is there anything I can do?"

"It looks like you've already done your usual too much."

"You know Jews. We love to overdo."

Devlin thought of the other warehouse. "There is something you can do. When you leave, stop at the Vernor warehouse. Go in and spend about ten minutes inside. When you leave, stand outside with the door open and act like you're talking to someone inside for a couple of minutes."

"Who's watching it?"

"Some of our people."

"It's hard to believe you guys ever get anything done."

"The only thing we seem to get done anymore is reporting to Congress the figures they want to hear. Of course, the people who can reshape those figures the best, along with the surrounding truths, are promoted accordingly. We are but a shadow of our former myth."

Ross laughed. "You fucking Irish malcontent."

Al Humphrey arrived at three-thirty with the latest tape. "Mike, I listened to this in the car. I think our boy called Mama."

Ross excused himself. "Mike, I'll make that stop for you."

As Devlin listened to the electronic garble of the tape recorder rewinding, Humphrey watched the footage counter. He stopped it at the desired number and pushed the play button.

"Hello." It was the voice of a woman old enough to be Tungworth's mother.

"Hi, how are you?" There was nothing unusual about the voice, but Devlin felt his heart quicken, as if Tungworth had unexpectedly stepped into the room.

"I'm fine. How are you getting along?"

"Okay. Anything going on?" The male voice sounded matter-of-fact.

"The FBI was here yesterday."

"Did they give you a hard time?"

"No. It was only one agent. Real nice looking, really seemed to like Carla."

"That bitch. Did she tell him anything?"

"Not really. And you know I don't like that kind of talk. You used to be such a good boy. Church every Sunday. You were even an altar boy. You were such a good Catholic."

The voice seemed to smile. "I still am, Mama. I still am."

A long silence ran on the tape.

"You need anything?" he finally asked.

"I could use some soup and coffee. Oh, and a couple of jars of those peppers stuffed with cabbage."

"Okay, I'll drop them off tonight. Do you think that guy is watching the house?"

"I doubt it. He seemed more interested in Carla than catching you." Good job, Doc, Devlin thought. He had Humphrey play it again.

When he turned the tape player off, Humphrey said, "I guess I know where we'll be tonight."

Humphrey played the tape at the four o'clock briefing.

"It looks like we've got a shot at him tonight. One caution, though. Doc, could that caller be some other family member?"

"I don't think so. I think Tungworth is the only brother, but I'm not positive."

Devlin thought about Sprinkler and what assuming the identity of a voice had cost him. "Ed, take the tape over to Mary Sue Ashley and see if she can recognize the voice. Make sure she doesn't tell anyone about it."

Livingston nodded.

"Tonight I want four cars covering the mother's house. Remember, she's going to be looking for surveillance, so stay away. If we get on him, we have to take him back to where he's lying down. He is going to be tail-conscious. If you're on him, expect him to dry-clean; you'll have to give him some different looks to throw him off. Here's how we'll set up—" Devlin gave individual assignments. The main thrust of the plan was to intercept Tungworth as he left his mother's house. Each of the four primary vehicles would sit a block from the mother's house, each facing in one of the four possible directions that Tungworth might take after leaving. When he left the residence and his direction was determined by one of the primary units, the secondary vehicles would shift over to flood the area in which he was headed. He would be more surveillance-conscious when first leaving his mother's and, Devlin calculated, would relax as he got further away. If the move was executed properly, Tungworth, at least initially, would drive by units that were stationary, making discovery impossible. As he drove by the cars, they would fall in behind him at an undetectable distance, relying on directions being given by the cars being passed. Later in the surveillance, moving cars would have to track him, but it would be at a safe distance from his mother's house. Once all the cars were moving, the "eye" vehicle could change every block or so.

Devlin had spent half an hour studying Delray and all the relevant locations their investigation had uncovered. The shifting surveillance, designed specifically for the circumstance, was appreciated by the crew. It was something they had never considered before and felt was a logical innovation. It was a difficult maneuver, and the crew was apprehensive about being able to do it successfully. But Devlin knew the men and had built their abilities into the complexity of the plan. They had to succeed.

"I want to be on those locations by nine P.M.; it should be dark by then. In the meantime, just hang loose."

Livingston picked up the tape of the telephone call and left.

Shanahan started entertaining everyone. He was doing his greatest impersonation to date—Tony Pants. Although their night promised to be difficult, the crew felt good. For the first time since they had started, they had the luxury of time. They knew where Tungworth was going to be and approximately when. A manhunt is always run from behind, trying to catch up with the prey. For once they would be in front, waiting.

Times of such optimism always caused Devlin to cut back across the grain of the plan, searching for its failing. It was an unwanted trait the Sappers had branded into him twenty years earlier.

For American troops, the North Vietnamese Sapper Battalions had been the most feared enemy units in the war. Although very few would actually experience the crushing attack of the Sappers, everyone feared them.

They were the kamikazes of the Vietnam War. They knew their important psychological mission would probably be their last. Their attacks always came when they seemed least likely, when, as then in the warehouse, one was in a state of apparent well-being.

Only once had they been repelled before getting inside the inner perimeter of defense. It was Echo Company, Second Battalion, Seventh Marines. On the day Devlin had reported to that unit to take over as its company commander, a lieutenant general had arrived to personally decorate the men involved in the unprecedented action. A dozen men stood in a single row in order of descending rank. After the commanding officer was decorated, he attempted to tell the general just how the attack had been thwarted. The general held up a hand to quiet him. He then continued down the ranks, pinning on medals and congratulating junior officers, noncommissioned officers, and lastly a skinny private first class from Oklahoma. After he pinned a bronze star on the young Marine, he asked him what had happened. The Marine's answer was simple and honest. "I could feel them in the wire, Sir." The general knew the private was the one who had saved the company—why else would a PFC be decorated?

Now Devlin could feel them in the wire. Fauber and Pilkington, wending their way through the barbed wire of his deceptions, ready to throw a satchel charge into the investigation. The Sappers! Appropriately named.

After studying the map again, Devlin called Riley Smith aside. "Go check the old employments at the grocery store and the packing house. They're both closed down, but see if you can find any numbers or locations for the owners." Experience had taught both men that all leads have to be investigated, no matter how unimportant or illogical they seemed. They had each solved as many cases covering the tiny, obscure leads as they had chasing the overpoweringly obvious ones. "If you can, interview them about Tungworth. We've interviewed everyone else."

Smith drove to the slaughterhouse. It was on Cary Street, part of a four-square-block area south of Jefferson. Although the section was bordered by the Rouge River, it was a mix of residential and commercial property. Only a few houses remained occupied.

All the windows of the slaughterhouse were boarded over. The building's double front doors were boarded over with a large white sign: FOR LEASE. Smith estimated that at least two years of dirt covered the sign. He copied the phone number of the leasing company.

The stink from Zug Island had attached itself to the bricks and mortar of the building, turning it a darker brown. The entire four blocks seemed darker brown; even the grass, which cowered low beneath mutant weeds, was dyed brown.

Smith drove around the back of the building. The only two windows on the back wall were boarded over. A small loading platform hung under a wide steel overhead door and a heavy metal access door. Around the doors, white chicken feathers waved in the light wind. Smith remembered the farm he had grown up on. When he was nine, his mother had taught him how to wring the life out of the beasts. The feathers reminded him of that unpleasant task.

Smith had to drive out of Delray to find a telephone. Michigan Bell had long since stopped installing public phones in Delray. Perhaps the most obvious symbols of corporate America, the phones simply disappeared shortly after being installed. He dialed the number for Perennial Realty. The number had been disconnected. He knew it would take City Hall research to find the owners. He turned his car around and headed for Tome's Grocery.

Tungworth heard the crunch of Smith's tires coming down Barron Street. He yanked the girl into the bedroom and chained her, taping her hands and mouth. In stocking feet, he hurried down the stairs into the store and stood looking out the filthy transom window. It was not the same man he had seen the night before. Although he was tall, he was not nearly as big.

Smith got out of the car and walked to the door. He stopped and wrote down the building's address. Tungworth jumped off his stool and hid in the darkness.

Unlike at the packinghouse, there was no real estate sign. Experience had taught Smith that companies that specialized in boarding up buildings usually had small advertising stamps or plates on the plywood. He examined it without any luck. He stepped up onto the windowsill next to the doorway and looked in through the transom. He could see only the abandoned shadows inside. From behind an unused freezer, Tungworth looked up at the dirt-streaked face of Smith. He decided that if Smith went around the back of the store and saw the car, he would kill him.

Quickly, Tungworth slipped out the back door and knelt down behind the white Thunderbird. He thumbed back the hammer on his 9mm and waited to end Riley Smith's life.

Smith walked to the side of the building, checking the plywood covers for markings. As he got to the side of the shed, he heard a car trunk slam closed. He looked back up

Barron Street and saw an elderly woman carrying grocery bags from her car. Smith hurried to intercept her before she reached the safety of her house: a sanctuary most elderly Detroiters would not relinquish, no matter how many badges they are shown.

When Tungworth heard Smith's vehicle drive over to the neighbor's, he thumbed the hammer of his weapon forward. He decided his mother would have to do without her groceries for at least another day, because he was not chancing any travel tonight. Back inside the store, he watched as the tall cop finished talking to old lady Tompkins and drove off.

At a few minutes before eight, Devlin briefly covered the surveillance assignments again. "Ed tried to get ahold of the girl to confirm Tungworth's voice, but she was not home. A neighbor said she works afternoons but didn't know where. He'll get her first thing in the morning, if we still need to." Everyone picked up on the optimistic "if."

"Riley, why don't you give us a rundown on the employments."

"First, I went to the slaughterhouse on Cary. The only thing moving there was chicken feathers. I tried to run down the owners, but it was a dead end. The grocery store was also boarded up." Without warning Smith stopped, lost in thought. He got a look in his eye that caused Devlin to thumb the edge of the card in his pocket unconsciously. Something he had missed was bothering Smith, something like Devlin's AT THE AIRPORT.

Smith forced himself to continue. "Talked to a neighbor. She said old man Tome had a stroke a year or so ago and is living with a daughter in Dearborn. She remembers Tungworth when he worked there, but hasn't seen him in years. I looked up the name Tome in the Dearborn phone book, there weren't any. So for now, that's also a dead end."

As the crew got ready to leave, Devlin said to Smith, "Something was bothering you."

"Yeah. It's something I overlooked at the grocery store. I think. When I was talking about being there, that freight train that tells you you're missing something came rushing through my head."

"Does it have anything to do with the airport?" Devlin asked, hoping Smith would solve his mystery.

Smith thought for a second. "No, I don't think so."

By eight o'clock the warehouse crew was heading south, full of hope. But hope was not a flower that flourished in Delray.

||| CHAPTER 17 |||

First light extinguished their flickering hopes. No one had seen a car that even resembled a white Thunderbird. Devlin wondered if their surveillance had been detected, or if something else had scared off Tungworth. He decided he needed everyone to review yesterday's activities. "Let's break it off and meet back at Whiskey Hotel," he said over the radio. "Whiskey Hotel Four, how about stopping by our friend on the way in and see if anything is new."

"On my way," Humphrey answered.

"Whiskey Hotel Two, can you try to contact the girl again," Devlin said.

"Ten-four," Livingston answered.

Two blocks from the Bell box, Al Humphrey pulled his car to the curb. From the trunk he took a Michigan Bell Telephone hard hat and put it on, then a lineman's utility belt, which he wrapped around his waist. He walked quickly to the box, pulled it open, and checked the recorder. Thirty feet of tape had been used. He changed tapes and left.

In his car he listened to the calls on his tape deck. None of them was from Tungworth.

With everyone back at the warehouse but Livingston, the investigators discussed why Tungworth had failed to visit his mother. They tried to translate it into assumptions about his hideout. Humphrey said, "Wherever he's staying, there's probably no telephone. If he had a phone and wasn't going to make it to his mother's, he would have called her." Everyone agreed.

Devlin added, "If that's true, then for some reason he didn't go out at all last night. If he had, he would have called her on a public phone. Evidently, he got hinky and decided to stay holed up. Now, what did we do yesterday between the time of his call and last night?"

As each of the crew started to mentally retrace his steps of the day before, Jeff Ross walked in with three dozen bagels and cream cheese. With the critical selectiveness of locusts, the agents turned on the food.

Livingston rushed in. Devlin could tell by his face that he thought he had something, but he wasn't experienced enough to be sure. "Mike, I played the tape for Mary Sue. She said it was definitely Tungworth. Then she heard the part about bringing soup, coffee, and stuffed peppers. She said he must still be stealing from Mr. Tome's grocery store. I asked her why, and she said he used to brag about still having the keys to the place and regularly pilfering things. The bottled cabbage-stuffed peppers are a Hungarian specialty. Tome's was the only place in Delray you could get them."

Devlin looked at Smith. "What do you think?"

"I suppose he could have been in there."

"Was there a garage?"

"No."

"Did you get around the back?"

Smith thought about the question, but something else was registering. "No, I didn't. I went around to the side, but Mrs. Tompkins came home and I left to interview her." Devlin hesitated; Smith was still searching for the answer. "That's it! Goddamn it, that's it! There were tire tracks on the weeds at the side of the house. They went around back.

I remember because the weeds were knee-high and I walked in the tracks. How could I have missed that?"

"All those lots have tracks cutting through them. You had no way of knowing. Did you see anything else?" Devlin asked.

Thinking out loud, Smith answered, "I climbed up and looked in a small window above the door. Couldn't see anything." Then his skin lightened and he whispered "Jesus Christ" at the floor as he realized the danger he had unknowingly brushed against.

Devlin spoke for the group. "That would explain why he didn't come out last night. Did anyone else go by there since we started?"

Brackoff spoke. "I did. The other night when we lost him during the surveillance." Brackoff thumbed through a small notebook. "There were no lights on that I could see."

Devlin spun around to the map and confronted it as an enemy. "What's behind the store?"

Smith said, "It's basically an open field, a little shrubbery. There's a fence at the back of the field."

"What is the fence for?" Smith didn't know.

Brackoff answered, "I think it's a city sewage plant." He knew that because his was a city badge, it would cause fewer problems gaining access to the site. "I'll go."

As he left, everyone gathered around the briefing board and stared at the red pin that was stuck into the blowup at the end of Barron Street.

Devlin said, "Riley, go to the office and try to run down old man Tome. Get the investigative clerks to make some calls. They have the contacts at the City-County Building." Devlin walked him out the door so the others could not hear. "Steer clear of Fauber. Because you're from the RA, he probably won't know you're with us. But be careful anyhow."

Fifteen minutes later Devlin called the office.

"Anderson."

"Tom, it's Mike."

"What's going on?"

"I think we're close to grabbing Tungworth. Looks like he's staying at a grocery store he used to work at years ago."

"Great. Is there anything I can do?"

"You still have liaison with the utility companies, don't you?"

"Yes."

"How about making some discreet calls to find out if any of them are turned on there?"

"Of course."

Devlin gave Anderson the address of the store. He didn't want to, but he needed the utility information. If electricity or gas was being used, Tungworth had to be there. And if they had to rush the place, turning off the lights at a strategic moment might save someone's life.

Anderson asked, "Are you going to be there long?"

Devlin was suspicious of the question. "Why do you ask?"

"So I can call you back with the utility info. Are you at the same number you gave me the other day?"

"Yes, I'll be here for at least an hour."

"I'll call you as soon as I can get the information."

After his conversation with Anderson, Devlin sat in the warehouse office and considered the call. Anderson knew where his daughter was and might think that by going to Fauber he could rescue her and still be in his supervisor's favor. If he did, the crew would be stopped within hours. Devlin decided there was nothing he could do but concentrate on Tungworth and Vanessa.

As he walked back to the briefing area, Brackoff's voice silenced the warehouse. "Whiskey Hotel Seven to Whiskey Hotel."

Devlin picked up the handset. "Go ahead, Seven."

"I'm set up on the other side of the fence and have a good view of the rear of that location."

"Is there anything there we might be interested in?" Everyone held his breath.

"There's two large sheds at the back end. Between them is our white chopper."

The agents started cheering, shaking hands, and clasping one another on the shoulder. Victory swam warmly up Devlin's spine. He held up his hand for silence. "Can you sit there without being burnt?"

"This location is good. I ran the tag. Came back on an old Chrysler station wagon. The plate was reported stolen a week ago."

"Do you need any help at your location?"

"No. Probably better being alone. Attracts less attention."

"Okay. If he comes out alone, take him as soon as he clears the building. Chances are he won't move until dark, but remember Vanessa is our priority. If he gets away, we can find him later. But if he gets back into that building, we have a serious problem. We're on our way."

"I'll be here," Brackoff said.

Someone asked, "What if he doesn't come out tonight?"

Devlin's mind was in the jungle, charging a fortified bunker. Reluctantly he said, "We'll go in at first light."

The phone rang. It was Riley Smith calling from the office. "Mike, all hell's breaking loose here. Somehow Pilkington found out about Sprinkler. Sprinkler didn't come in to work today, so he sent someone out to his house. They found him dead—suicide—left a note."

"Do they know about Vanessa?"

"I don't know."

"How long have we got?" Devlin asked.

"Not long. They stormed out of here ten to fifteen minutes ago, according to Sue."

"Okay. Get out of there and head to Delray. Gunnar's spotted the car behind the store. If this falls apart, just point your car toward Ann Arbor."

"Sorry, Mike, I can't do that. I've never run from a fight in my life."

Devlin was strengthened by Smith's loyalty. "Okay. Check in with Gunnar when you get down there." He turned to the remaining agents. "We got to pack up and get out of here, Pilkington is on his way."

Ross came out of the office and saw the activity. "What? You didn't like the bagels? I'll get doughnuts."

Devlin took a second to smile and reflect on Ross's friendship. "Jeff, we got to get out of here. They're coming for me. To save yourself a lot of aggravation, you should get out of here too."

"Aggravation! You should have three Jewish daughters. Then you would understand aggravation."

Screeching tires in the parking lot froze everyone. *Sappers in the wire.* Livingston looked out a dusty window. "It's the SAC, Fauber, and about a dozen agents." His words were punctuated by additional arriving tires.

Devlin ordered, "Everybody up on the roof. Jeff will lock you up there until they leave."

The rest of the agents stopped and calmly took their seats. The silent mutiny confused Devlin. Agash spoke. "Mike, we did this for Vanessa, but we also wanted to see if we could prevail over *them*—I guess we have. And none of us are going to run and hide from that. We're proud of what we've done here."

Someone was pounding loudly on the door. Devlin looked at the group and remembered why he had picked these men. He unlocked the door.

Two of the Jedi were first through the door, their hands on their holstered guns. Fauber and the SAC followed. Pilkington seemed to be in a rage. His stride was quick but

long, his face red, his eyes retaliatory. He went to Devlin.
"What the hell do you think you're doing? You were supposed to be investigating a leak, nothing else." Pilkington
watched Devlin's reaction carefully. "That's right, we know
about your attempts to find Anderson's daughter. I have
your supervisor to thank for that. When he noticed all this
secret activity going on, he called me and I authorized him
to use the executive override feature on my telephone."
Devlin remembered the AT&T class, years earlier, when the
new phone system had been installed in the office. The executive override allowed the SAC to listen undetected to
any extension in the office. Devlin had forgotten about it.
"John has been listening to Anderson's extension the last
couple of days."

Devlin recalled his conversations with Anderson. If
Fauber had been eavesdropping, then he had known days
ago about the unauthorized kidnapping investigation and
could have intervened at any time. He, probably at
Pilkington's direction, had monitored the progress of the
case until they felt it was to their advantage to step in and
make the newsworthy arrest. His last call to Anderson had
divulged Vanessa's whereabouts, and now they could make
the rescue and arrest effortlessly. All the glory without any
of the risk. Involuntarily, Devlin shook his head and smiled.

"What's so amusing?" Pilkington asked.

Devlin suddenly felt too tired to answer.

Fauber hung over Pilkington's shoulder like a pilot fish
waiting to clean the shark's teeth. "Well?" he screeched at
the same pitch as the tires that had brought him.

With contrasting composure, which further irritated
Pilkington, Devlin said, "Are you sure you want me to answer that in front of all these people?"

The sureness in Devlin's eyes turned the SAC's rage into
caution. He turned quickly to Fauber. "Get everybody out

of here." Fauber raised his voice and told people to start moving. Slowly, they flowed to the door.

All but Jeff Ross, who stood close to Devlin. Fauber wanted to further demonstrate his command presence to Pilkington, and Ross seemed like the perfect vehicle. "Who the hell are you?"

In a low monotone, Ross answered, "I'm the guy who just called the police because my warehouse has been broken into."

"Well, you can get the fuck out—" With the speed of an angry cobra, Ross's hand found Fauber's throat, cutting off all sound. The creases in Fauber's forehead tipped towards the floor, allowing the gray to run out, leaving a bulging crimson sphere behind. Two Jedi grabbed Ross's arms but could not overcome his strength. The red in Fauber's face darkened with blue. More of the SAC's agents started towards Ross.

Slowly, Devlin said, "Jeff, would you mind going upstairs?"

Ross threw Fauber down with his fingertips, broke the two agents' grip as though they were children wrestling with their father, and walked up the apartment stairs. Fauber sucked in air with a pathetic noise.

Pilkington pointed at all the documents pinned to the board. "Take all of this and anything else concerning this matter. I want all these men in the office immediately. I'll talk to you, there—former Special Agent Devlin." He turned and stalked out. Someone opened the door for him.

It was Duncan Moorehead. Devlin walked to Moorehead and looked at him unemotionally. Moorehead desperately wanted to look away, but his eyes were paralyzed. Devlin's stare was that of a curiosity seeker at a carnival side show. Moorehead's eyes began to ache. They felt as though they would shatter. Devlin leaned over and whispered into

Moorehead's ear, "Duncan, the boss's shoes are looking a little shabby."

Two of the SAC's agents were ordered to drive Devlin to the office and he was "never to leave their sight."

At headquarters, Devlin sat at his desk while his guards kept a respectable distance. One of the Jedi's phones rang. It was Fauber. He wanted Devlin brought to the SAC's conference room.

The SAC sat at the head of a long table, composed. Fifteen of his head-nodders also sat at the table, waiting for orders. "I want you to brief us so we can bring this matter to a logical conclusion."

"This matter is named Vanessa, goddamn it! And if you don't take this thing seriously—"

Pilkington interrupted. "Just the facts. We know how to proceed."

Devlin calmed himself. "First I want your word no action will be taken against anyone but myself."

"You're in no position to bargain. I can call the United States attorney right now and have you charged with obstruction of justice."

"Make the call. I'd like to tell my side of this in an open court where the truth is protected by law."

Pilkington secretly admired the resolve that settled onto Devlin's face. Unyielding resolve. Another luxury of the street agent. He had fought people like Devlin his entire career. Usually, he had lost. The only profit left for him was to rescue the girl. "John, let me see the names of the agents involved in this." Fauber handed him a list.

Pilkington pretended to read it judiciously. "Yes, these are all good men, and they have done an excellent job on this case. They will have no problems from me."

Devlin stared at Pilkington. He knew, because of all the

witnesses in the room, he would not punish the others. Anyway, the real urgency was Vanessa.

Using the confiscated materials from the warehouse, Devlin briefed the group in a half an hour. The last thing he told them was that the building was presently under surveillance by members of the warehouse crew. When he finished, Pilkington said, "Stay at your desk until further notice." Then he nodded to the two men who had walked him over.

"The best time to take him is at dawn. He's up all night and sleeps all day," Devlin offered.

"Thank you. Go back to your desk," Pilkington said in a don't-call-us tone.

ASAC O'Hare walked up to Devlin's desk. "Mind if I sit down?"

Devlin smiled and waved at a chair.

"I'm sorry about all this, Mike. I know you didn't tell me for more than one reason, in part to protect me. The fact that you got the informant list back almost makes me a hero. You've done a helluva job here. On both cases. You would have been out there right now, rescuing Vanessa, if Fauber hadn't intercepted that message you left for Anderson. Fauber knew I was covering for you guys, and he told Pilkington I was allowing the kidnapping investigation in defiance of his orders. Pilkington came to me and asked what your group was doing. I told him about the leak and said I would take full responsibility. He asked about the kidnapping. Naturally I didn't know about it, and told him I had no knowledge of it. Then, as you predicted, he sent people out to Sprinkler's house to pick him up. Remember, at that time we didn't know the list had been recovered. The fool thought Sprinkler would just give it up. Anyway, they found Sprinkler dead. You know the rest."

Out of his inside jacket pocket, Devlin took the list of informants that Sprinkler had surrendered and handed it to

O'Hare. O'Hare quickly looked through the pages and said, "Christ, they really were going to put us out of business." O'Hare handed Devlin a folded sheet of paper he was holding. "It's a copy of Sprinkler's suicide note. There's something in there for you."

Without looking at it, Devlin put it on his desk and leaned toward O'Hare. "John, please do me one favor. Make sure Pilkington doesn't punish any of the others."

"You have my word."

As O'Hare stood up to leave, Devlin asked, "John, just out of curiosity, if I had told you about the kidnapping, would you have given us the green light?"

O'Hare searched his values and his priorities and finally said, "I think so."

Devlin smiled sincerely and said, "I think so, too." O'Hare gave him a nod of appreciation and left.

Again Devlin went over everything. He knew he had missed something. He took the wrinkled card out of his pocket: AT THE AIRPORT. He cleared his mind and stared at the three words. Nothing.

In a noisy crush, the squad area was filled with agents, going into their desk drawers for handcuffs, bulletproof vests, and extra ammunition. The last thing they all put on was a navy blue nylon jacket with large yellow letters—FBI—not only on the back, but on both sleeves and the front. The Bureau called them raid jackets. Devlin called them shoot-me-first jackets. A barricaded gunman with only so many bullets left could be selective and just shoot FBI agents. It was Bureau policy to wear them on raids. Predictably, Devlin never had.

Fauber came out of his office, causing Devlin to laugh. The bulk of Yoda's bulletproof vest and the abundant raid jacket that hung almost to his knees instead of his waist reminded Devlin of a child playing dress-up in his father's suit. Only Fauber's fingertips could be seen at the end of the sleeves. The two agents guarding Devlin visibly suppressed their laughter.

"You go ahead and laugh. While we're out there rescuing the victim, you'll be here spending your last few hours as an employee of the FBI," Fauber said.

"Lucius, I'll bet under that jacket you got some huge handgun. You know what the shrinks say about little guys who carry big guns, don't you? Come on, prove me wrong. Show us."

Fauber's face started to brighten. "Come on, men, let's get out of here and leave *Mister* Devlin with his memories."

"Not going to show us, John? That's all right. While you're out, I'll call your wife and ask her how big your gun is. She'll probably prove me wrong and tell me you've got a derringer—you know, short barrel, big bore."

Fauber was almost at a run when he reached the outer door, panicked, like a man trapped under an ice floe, swimming for an opening.

Devlin looked back at the card in his hand: AT THE AIRPORT. He had to put it out of his mind. He dropped it on his desk and picked up the copy of Sprinkler's suicide note and read it:

To the Living,

I am not asking for forgiveness. What I did was unforgivable. I am asking only for understanding. An alcoholic can drink only so much in a day, a drug addict can spend only so much in a day, but a gambler can lose everything in a day. At first gambling made my routine life not so routine, but like many feel-good things, it soon owned me. The gambling became larger than me, and I became its henchman.

For the past two years, it seems I have been undeservedly punished with this addiction. Now I must punish myself so others won't be further disgraced. It may seem extreme, but sometimes punishment provides the only solution.

For all those I have dishonored, especially you, Mom, I am truly sorry.

John Sprinkler

Mike Devlin—Thank you for treating me like a human being and allowing me some dignity at the end.

Devlin reread the note. Something in it was giving him the same nagging feeling as the card on his desk. He read it again. He wondered if he was not starting to see mirages, little logical oases that were imagined from a distance and whose solutions disappeared as he grew near.

He put the note down next to the card and considered Sprinkler's words: "For the past two years, it seems I have been undeservedly punished. . . ." Devlin thought about his supervisor and how those words described their relationship. Two years ago Devlin had been sent to Seattle to investigate Soundmurs, but unlike with Sprinkler, no solution had accompanied that punishment. And now it had come full circle. But this time, instead of staying three months in a cramped motel room at the airport, he would—

A white-hot burst of recognition went off in Devlin. "That's it!" he yelled. The two agents jumped. Devlin got up, and his guards took a defensive stance. "Relax, I forgot something in the conference room." He walked quickly to the room and could feel the two agents carefully trailing him.

The SAC's group had taken most of the documents from the conference room but had left Livingston's folder. It was organized chronologically. Devlin found what he was looking for—Tungworth's background sheet that Livingston had put together. He took it back to his desk and took out the folder he had kept all his Soundmurs notes in. Side by side, he compared the two.

Tungworth had fled Detroit three months before the first Puget Sound murder. The last known Sound killing had been in the same month Tungworth had returned to Detroit.

Devlin thumbed through the pages of the forty-one victims' profiles. Finally he found what he was looking for: Rebecca Ann Harding, white female, age eighteen, known prostitute, last seen outside Seatac Airport. The airport, located between Seattle and Tacoma, was a notorious pickup spot for the area's young prostitutes.

Devlin flipped more pages. Debra Sue Jenkins, black female, age twenty, prostitute, last seen in vicinity of Seatac Airport. Devlin found two more prostitutes who had last been seen at the airport.

Devlin picked up the phone, dialed the Seattle Division, and asked for Jim Rogers. Rogers and Devlin had both grown up in Chicago, but had not known each other until Devlin was sent to Seattle to work on the Soundmurs case. Rogers, a former Chicago cop and an extremely capable investigator, was the Soundmurs case agent. Because of their similar backgrounds, they became friends quickly. On Friday nights, they would stop after work and, over too many beers, long for Chicago's Home Run Inn pizza and Marge's Italian beef sandwiches.

"Rogers."

"This is the Home Run Inn. Did you order a large with everything?"

"Mike. How the hell are you?"

"Right now the invertebrates are measuring me for a casket."

"Still biting off your nose to spite your face."

"It's an Irish tradition."

"Can I help you with something?"

"A couple of quick questions. Are you sitting at a Soundmurs terminal?" The task force had purchased a half-million-dollar computer to organize the case.

"I'm always sitting at one of the terminals."

"How many of the girls were taken at the airport?" Devlin could hear the plastic clicking of the keyboard.

"Eleven."

"I could only find four in my notes."

"Since you were here, we've developed more information in that regard. Because most of the victims were prostitutes, they weren't tied to anyone. So it's difficult to determine exactly where and when they disappeared. It's funny you ask, because recently we've come up with additional witnesses that have placed more of the girls at the airport. In fact, it's a whole new investigative thrust for us: working the airport angle. The more we work it, the more girls we come up with. Why do you ask?"

"I'll tell you in a minute. Let's finish with the computer first. Run Marion Lee Tungworth on a name query." The clicking stopped, and both men waited. Rogers sensed Devlin was on to something.

"Yeah, we got him. He was called in on two separate tips. Let me pull them up on the screen. Okay. Evidently, he was a cab driver, because the first tip was called in by one of his passengers, saying he resembled the composite we got from that witness in the Carson killing. The second was someone who called in anonymously. Said Tungworth drove a pickup truck like the one we were looking for, and that he was weird. A lot of people here still think it has to be a cab driver."

"Did you guys ever do anything with those tips?"

"The investigative notation on both simply says 'unable to locate.' You were here; you know we have over ten thousand tips. One suspect can take months to eliminate. So we try to find them right away and interview them. If nothing jumps out at us, we move on to the next one. Do you still have your composite?"

Devlin searched through his folder and found the composite drawing. He took Tungworth's mug shot from Livingston's folder. Although composites, because they are drawn from eyewitnesses, can be misleading, this one was close in appearance to the arrest photo. "I've got it, Jim. And it's close."

"How'd you come up with this guy?" Rogers asked.

Devlin explained the disappearance of Anderson's daughter and their investigation to date, including the intervention by the SAC.

"Well, Detroit is one of the bigger offices in the Bureau, so you would want one of the bigger assholes to be in charge."

"If that's how it works, I got a supervisor here that'll be the next director. Anyway, I'll fax you Tungworth's mug shot, so you can make your own comparison. Is there anything else I should be aware of?"

"When was the girl taken?"

Devlin counted on his calendar. "Today is the twelfth day. Why?"

A chilling hesitation interrupted the conversation. "Mike. The Behavioral Science Unit has come up with a new theory in the last six months. They've developed another characteristic of the killer's profile: the victims were held for twelve days and then killed ritualistically."

"How did they come to that conclusion?"

"I don't understand it all, but it's a combination of statistics from all the murders, disappearance dates, dates of discovery, dump site information, and victimology."

Devlin had forgotten the strange language of Soundmurs: dump sites, bones number fourteen, postoffense behavior, sexual hitchhiker, conservative automobiles, strong feelings of inadequacy, proactive investigation, and the most bizarre—victimology. Studying the victims' habits and circumstances to determine characteristics about the killer. "You said ritualistically?"

"They base it on the crosses notched between the breasts. Twelve days probably has some religious significance for the killer. Do you know what religion this guy is?"

Devlin thumbed through Livingston's notes. "Catholic. That's right, I remember his mother saying something about it on the phone."

"On the phone?" Rogers laughed, guessing that under the circumstances Devlin had an illegal tap in place.

"You don't miss much. What about you? Are you Catholic?"

"It's been so long I can't remember. How about you?"

"My wife's the family expert," Devlin said.

"Married to you, she'd have to be. Where is Tungworth now?"

"Half the office is out right now trying to lock him up."

"What do you think?" Rogers asked.

Devlin looked at the wrinkled card and no longer felt its puzzle. He tore it in half. "I think it's him."

||| CHAPTER 18 |||

Devlin stood at the office window and looked down into Canada. Deep in the southwest, he could see storm clouds, inflating like an angry mob, marching toward Detroit. If Tungworth was the Puget Sound Murderer, had he killed since escaping? It had been months.

He called Inspector Wicks at Homicide. The sergeant on the desk said he had just left for home; it was his son's birthday. He could be reached there in half an hour.

The number twelve nagged at Devlin. Did Tungworth hold his victims for twelve days before strangling them? There would have to be some importance, some compulsion about the number for Tungworth. Since this was day twelve for Vanessa, confirming the deadline could prove critical. He called Knox in Chicago.

Because he had not called in the past twenty-four hours, her voice was bound in caution. "How are you, Mike?"

"I'm fine. We're getting close. Hopefully it will be over soon." Devlin did not want to tell her he was about to be fired. Not on the telephone. He had to be with her and hold her, so they would remember what was really important.

"Good. It'll be nice to have you around again."

Devlin explained the twelve-day theory. "Does twelve days have any special meaning in Catholicism?"

"I can't think of any."

"How about the number twelve and a cross?"

"The only thing that's close are the fourteen stations of the cross."

"What's that?"

"It's the events of Jesus's death. The first station is when Pontius Pilate condemns him to die on the cross. The rest are stops on his journey. Three of them are when he falls. Others are people he encounters and so on."

"What's the twelfth station?"

"Let me think a minute. Oh, that's when he actually dies."

Devlin's mind was starting to race. "Then what are thirteen and fourteen?"

"I'll have to get Mom's catechism book." Devlin heard her leave the phone and then flip pages as she returned. "Ahhh, here's fourteen: the entombment of the body."

"And thirteen?"

"Thirteen . . . thirteen is taking the body from the cross."

To himself, Devlin said, "Or taking the cross from the body."

"What?" Knox asked, completely confused.

"Thanks. I'll explain everything when you get home."

Knox sensed something in Devlin's speech pattern, something that was headed for troubled waters.

"Mike—"

"Yeah."

"I told you. I need a man around here."

"Everything is fine."

There's that damn *everything* again, she thought. "Get done soon, Mike," she said and hung up before Devlin could scare her with any more of his vagueness.

Tungworth stood looking out the grocery store transom. A large black Buick with an extra antenna drove by slowly for the third time. The driver looked like a sickly elf, and the passenger's thin, pointed face reminded Tungworth of a

Delray undertaker he knew. They both stared at the store each time they passed. Whoever they were, they were coming for him, to prevent the cleansing. And it was almost time.

At the back of the store, he cracked the door open and searched the area painstakingly. His eyes stopped on the fence that walled off the back of the sewage plant. A small portion of a car's front fender was visible. Tungworth knew the car did not belong there. He thought about slipping away when it got dark, but that would not be for a couple of hours. And whoever these intruders were, they were not going to wait until dark.

A cold wind pushed through the opening. A change of wind direction had caused it. Tungworth watched the sky. Black clouds rushed toward him. In Delray, the rain was always welcome. It brought temporary relief from the foul breath of Zug Island. Additionally, the rain usually kept the thieves at home. A person raised in Delray always knew when the rain was coming.

Detroit Homicide indexed its records three ways: by victim's name, by perpetrator's name, and by location of homicide. Give them any one of the three, and they could provide you with the specific case. However, one of the three was not always available. Devlin remembered one case. The headline had read, "Man in negligée found murdered in doghouse." If someone, a year later, had tried to run down the case without names or an address, he would be unsuccessful. In that event, Devlin had learned, Jerome Wicks had to be called. He had almost total recall for names, locations, and especially MOs.

Devlin dialed Wicks's home phone. "Jerry, I need some help."

Recognizing the urgent tone, Wicks said, "You got it."

"I'm looking for any homicides since April. Victim

would be female, young, possibly a hooker, dumped in water, probably nude and strangled."

"There's only one unsolved case like that. Dawn Marie Clark, white female, early twenties. Found floating in the Rouge River, nude, ligature strangulation. I think a man's sock was used. That was about two months ago."

"Did you see the body?"

"No, I was tied up in court testifying. I read the report. Dr. Zilke handled the autopsy."

"Was there any mutilation?"

"Yeah, that's right. She had a cross cut out of her chest."

Through the front of the store, Tungworth watched several cars, including the undertaker's, parked a block away. He guessed they felt they could not be spotted because the front of the building was boarded up. The rain had started and was intensifying. The agents had scattered when the rain started and now sat in the cars. Tungworth noticed that they did not bother to put on their windshield wipers. "It won't be long now, Miss Anderson, it won't be long."

She stood next to him, rigid with fear. Wide silvery duct tape was wound completely around her head, sealing off her mouth and eyes. A small slit exposed her nostrils. Her hands were taped heavily behind her back.

"As soon as the rain starts coming down hard enough so the pigs on the other side of the fence can't see, we're going to run out of here, past all of those fools. If you hesitate or fight me, it'll just take two fingers to kill you without a sound." He reached over with his thumb and forefinger and pinched her nostrils shut, cutting off her only passage of air. She struggled, finally freeing herself. He laughed and said, "Next time I won't let go."

Of the 10,000 cases a year the Wayne County Medical Examiner's Office investigates, approximately 2,700 bodies get autopsied. Dr. Karl Zilke had become the county's M.E. in 1972 at the age of forty-five. Born in East Germany, his family moved to Palestine when he was seven. He was educated in Switzerland and Israel and served as a medical officer for three years in the Israeli Army. He testified in the Chappaquiddick case and was a member of the House of Representatives Committee on Assassination investigating the deaths of President Kennedy and Martin Luther King. His résumé, being twelve pages long, did not include the most impressive fact about him: without question, he was the world's foremost authority on violent deaths.

While his more famous counterparts from large cities like Los Angeles and New York were at political luncheons, Dr. Zilke was surrounded by the cold, hard basement of the Wayne County Morgue, in blood up to his elbows.

He always had time for a phone call or unannounced visit from some detective who had a new mystery for him. Devlin dialed his number. As always, Zilke answered his own phone. "Wayne County Medical Examiner's Office."

Devlin loved his German accent. *"Karl, wie geht's?"*

"Michael, how are you?"

"Better than your guests in the basement. But just barely. I need a favor. But then, why else would I be calling?"

"Is this an earn-a-free-lunch favor or an I-can-lose-my-job favor?"

"This is an all-you-can-eat-at-the-Ratskeller favor."

"Ugh! I hate German food."

"Why do you think I said the Ratskeller?"

"Okay, big spender, shoot."

"Dawn Marie Clark, white female, early twenties, about two months ago, found floating in the Rouge, nude, strangled. A cross cut into her chest."

"Yes. I remember her. Let me pull the file." Devlin listened to the rain drumming on the window glass like a million excited fingers. The blackness of the storm oozed through the tall office windows, betraying the daylight.

"Yes, let's see. I ruled it a homicide by ligature strangulation. By persons unknown."

"I'm interested in the cross." While Zilke searched the autopsy file, Devlin found his notes from the first day's briefing in Seattle. He had drawn a cross and, like a draftsman, had arrowed in the dimensions: one inch by one and a half inches. In parenthesis were the words "notched out."

"Mike, the cross was an inch and a half high and an inch wide. It wasn't just two cuts. The entire cross of skin was removed through very neat V cuts. The wound was very interesting."

"Why?"

"Well, because the body was in the water less than twenty-four hours, I was able to draw some conclusions about the wound. Because its edges were dark brown, almost black, the indication is that the incisions were made at least one day after death. When the body was recovered, the skin was wrinkled and gray except for the skin around the cross; it was dark and leathery."

"What does that mean?"

"That after the incisions were made, it was another day or so before the body was dumped in the river."

The fourteenth station, thought Devlin. "Anything else?"

"No. The sock used to strangle her was a man's dress sock, black, nylon, knee-high. Nothing to go on there. Wait a minute; there was something else. Her back was coated with grease. Heels, buttocks, shoulder blades, and back of the head. Like she had layed down in grease. The reason I noticed it was when we hosed down the body, the water wouldn't penetrate it. Something heavy."

"Any idea what it was?"

"No, sorry, if I remember correctly, that was a warm weekend. And when we have a warm weekend, the homicide rate goes up geometrically. I think we had sixteen or seventeen that weekend, so I couldn't get as fancy as I would have liked to."

"Thanks, Doctor."

"Whoa! Just a minute. What prize do I get?"

"You get to keep your job."

"Anymore, I'd rather eat German food."

Devlin's brain was recording all the information, but it had become too impatient to analyze it. He needed some downtime to regain his edge, to make sure he was not force-fitting the facts into his theory. He pulled a chair up to the window, loosened his tie, and deliberately surrendered his concentration to the lilting rain. The darkness of the storm had passed. A milk-gray rain continued. It looked like it would last all night.

An hour later, agents started filing back into the office. Livingston and Shanahan were in the first wave.

Shanahan kept his voice low. "Does the *Guinness Book* have a category for clusterfucks? If so, we just set the record. They let Tungworth slip through. We hit the grocery and the apartment upstairs. Nothing!"

The dragon dug its claws into Devlin's chest and considered new targets: Pilkington and Fauber. Devlin calmed the beast. "What about the girl?"

"Well, the Special Agent in Charge of Clusterfucks has once again decreed that Vanessa Anderson has not been kidnapped. Just because the car was there doesn't mean a thing. It's a simple car theft. Mike, I went up inside the apartment. There was a chain with locks on both ends. She was up there," Shanahan said.

"Any idea how long they had been gone?"

"Not long. A candle was still burning. He must have spotted the surveillance and boogied during the storm."

"Was there any blood?"

"I looked it over really well. I didn't see anything. Did you, Ed?"

"No, but I agree with Bill. They were both up there. The place was filthy, thick dust on everything. But the floor where the chain was, was clean. She must have slept on the floor."

Shanahan added, "I checked both locks on the chain. The one attached to the wall didn't have a mark on it, but the other one was all scratched up like someone who didn't know what they were doing was trying to pick it."

"So Pilkington is just going to put his head back in the sand," Devlin said.

"It's what he does best," Shanahan said. "And poor Anderson is wandering around in a daze."

Devlin had had enough. He considered the only possible solution. Livingston and Shanahan both sensed his decision.

Devlin spoke in a low voice. "You've heard of the Soundmurs case." They nodded. "It looks like Tungworth is the killer."

"What?" Shanahan said incredulously.

Devlin explained the serial murders' MOs, Tungworth's coincidental timetable, and the phone calls that had produced the facts about the recent Clark murder.

"Jesus Christ," was Shanahan's only answer.

"The worst thing is that Rogers in Seattle says the killer is on a twelve day cycle."

Livingston counted mentally. "Today is the twelfth day."

Shanahan said, "And we don't have a clue where he is."

Devlin looked at the wet suits the two men were wearing. Like a stubborn tracking dog, Devlin's mind left the conversation. The rain outside transported him back to Chicago. He was seventeen. Every summer, the biggest car dealer in Chicago had sponsored a cross-lake swim. The prize money attracted endurance swimmers from all over the country. While the sponsors partied aboard large cabin

cruisers, lowly Chicago Park District lifeguards rowed with
the swimmers. Four-hour shifts. Devlin rowed through a
milk-gray rainstorm. His swimmer was a beautiful blond
girl from California. Even though she had coated her body
with grease to offset the alien temperature of Lake Michigan, the loss of body heat finally caused her to give up after thirty-six hours in the water. She signaled Devlin and
dog-paddled to the back of the rowboat. She did not have
the strength left to pull herself up over the boat's transom.
Devlin attempted to help her, but was unable to grab on to
her because of the grease. Their combined efforts got her
halfway over the transom. Her dead weight put the back of
the boat low in the water. Ten-foot swells crashed over the
stern. Devlin was being soaked by large gulps of the lake.
The craft was sinking. Finally Devlin ripped a hole in the
back of her suit, wrapped the material around his hand, and
brought her aboard.

"I know where they are," Devlin said.

Livingston and Shanahan asked at the same time,
"Where?"

Ignoring the question, Devlin said to Shanahan, "Go to
the firearms vault and get my black box." He flipped
through Livingston's notes and laid out the map of Delray.

"Where is she?" Livingston asked in a shouting whisper.

Devlin rubbed his fingers together, remembering the im-
pervious grease that would not dissolve after a day and a
half in Lake Michigan. The California girl had covered herself with chicken fat.

"Here," Devlin said pointing at the color-coded location
of the slaughterhouse.

"How?"

"He's worked two places connected with food. He kept
a key for the grocery and pilfered food. He probably kept a
key for the slaughterhouse in case it reopened, so he could
steal from them. You guys forced him out of the store. He's

on foot. Look at the map. He could easily have made it to the slaughterhouse. Now take Dawn Marie Clark. Because of the cross, we know Tungworth killed her. She was dumped in the Rouge River, which is a two-iron from the packinghouse. Zilke said she lay in fat, fat so persistent the Rouge couldn't dissolve it. Animal fat. They're there."

Shanahan walked up, set the black case next to Devlin's feet, and walked away from it.

"Bill, they're at the slaughterhouse. I'm going. There isn't much time. Call Wicks, and then Rogers in Seattle. Let them know everything." Devlin smiled broadly. "Then go and tell Pilkington and Fauber. I don't want them in the way, so I'll need a half-hour head start."

"I'm going with you," Livingston announced.

"I appreciate it, but a dummy hand grenade isn't going to work this time."

In a voice absent of compromise, Livingston said, "I'm going."

When Shanahan saw that Devlin wasn't going to argue with Livingston, he said, "I'm going too."

"With that hand you'd be a liability. I can tell the way you've been holding it, the rain is playing hell with it. Besides, you'll be down there in a half hour."

"Mike. Don't do anything stupid," Shanahan said.

"You're a little late."

Devlin looked over at his guards. They were talking to some of the agents that had returned. They evidently no longer felt it was urgent to watch Devlin. "Ed," Devlin kicked the black box at his feet, "take this down to the car."

Livingston looked at it. It was about the size of a portable sewing machine. He picked it up and strolled out the door.

"Bill, go distract those two."

Shanahan went over to the group and started one of his stories. Devlin slipped out unnoticed.

Devlin drove, but not fast. Livingston was surprised. He had belted himself in, expecting the siren and lights. He could see something gathering inside Devlin; it was as dark as the storm they drove through. Whatever Devlin was about to do, Livingston knew the Bill of Rights was not going to play a major role.

"When we get there, you stay outside. I'll go in. You make sure he doesn't slip out again."

"You can't go in alone."

Devlin laughed a different laugh. "Ever since Vietnam, I've been going in alone."

"Yeah, but this guy is crazy."

"Right now, so am I."

The glaze in Devlin's eyes frightened Livingston. He changed the subject. "Someone told me you got the Navy Cross in Vietnam." Devlin said nothing. "Well?" Livingston asked.

"I got the Navy Cross in Vietnam."

"For what?"

"For being crazy."

"From what I heard, it could have just as easily been the Medal of Honor."

"I wasn't dead enough. Usually the medal is given to a Marine who gives his life for other Marines."

"Well, the Navy Cross is a hell of an honor." Livingston looked at Devlin. The conversation hadn't removed the insanity from his eyes. He couldn't tell if Devlin was in Southeast Asia or a meat-packing house in Delray.

He turned on the "good time" radio. An oldies station was playing "We Gotta Get Out of This Place" by the Animals.

It reminded Devlin of Vietnam. It was the one song all the USO shows had played. He sang along. "We gotta get out of this place if it's the last thing we ever do. Girl, there's a better life for me and you." He looked at Livingston. "You and Sydney could be singing this. Especially now that you're going to be out of work."

Both men sang, "We gotta get out of this place if it's the last thing we ever do—" The rain was sheeting down the windshield faster than the wipers could take it off. Livingston couldn't see the road anymore. Devlin continued at the same speed as if homing in on some invisible signal.

Fauber had never seen Pilkington close the door to his office before. Just the two of them sat in the sealed chamber. Fauber was scared. He had the feeling that if, for some reason, Pilkington could not blame Devlin for their failure, it would somehow become his fault.

Pilkington slowly released a condescending smile as if he were going to offer candy to a child. "John, I assume you would like to be promoted to an ASAC position someday?"

Fauber could not believe what he was hearing. "Yes, sir!"

"Good. That's as it should be if our present management concept is to work." Fauber knew that "present management concept" meant defending each other against all enemies, foreign or domestic. "I suppose you would like me to help you in that direction, if I could. The way I have helped you to become and remain a supervisor."

Fauber keyed on "remain," as though his position had been constantly in jeopardy. "Yes, sir."

"Well, John, everything you want from me is contingent on how you close out this matter."

"Whatever you want, sir."

"The way I see this is, it's nothing more than a car that was apparently stolen—God knows where—and then recovered by us in Detroit. It didn't cross a state line, so we have no jurisdiction whatsoever."

Fauber wanted to show Pilkington that he too understood how to retreat, leaving a maze of deception. "If I may point out, sir, we don't know if the car was actually stolen. The girl was dating a black. She drives to Detroit, and who knows what happened? She could have lent it to someone, traded it for drugs, or anything else."

Pilkington considered Fauber's analysis of the "facts" and said, "John, you're going to make a fine ASAC."

Shanahan knocked on the SAC's door and checked his watch again. It had been half an hour since Devlin and Livingston had left. He had made the calls to Homicide and Seattle. Fauber opened the door. "Can I help you?"

Shanahan was anxious to tell Pilkington and Fauber, to record their response, and to tell the story for the rest of his life.

"Devlin has gone to get Tungworth and the girl."

Fauber's reaction was everything Shanahan had hoped for: panic, pure and intense. He looked at Pilkington, who was unmoved, and said, "Thank you, Agent."

Shanahan was disappointed. He decided to come back in a few minutes, when Pilkington was alone, and give him the "good news" about Soundmurs.

Shanahan left and Fauber closed the door. "What are we going to do? How does he know where they are?"

Composed, Pilkington answered, "Where who is?"

Fauber remembered the "present management concept." "Right, we have a rogue agent who has made up some wild story to prevent his firing."

Pilkington was pleased with Fauber's recovery. "Just to cover all the bases, call that misguided soul on the radio and order him to return to the office."

"But he won't come back."

Pilkington grinned viciously. "I know."

Fauber smiled. "Insubordination on the air."

"Make sure it's recorded."

"Yes, sir!"

Devlin and Livingston sat in an idling car two blocks from the slaughterhouse. The heavy rain continued. Devlin turned off the lights and opened the black case on the seat between them. It was a Thompson submachine gun. Livingston had seen them only in old movies. By current standards for a sleek weapon, it seemed obtrusive, almost counterproductive, like using a dinosaur to level a building. The Bureau had discontinued its use in the early seventies but kept a few in the gun vault for office tours.

Devlin pushed a button on the weapon's receiver and slid the wooden stock off the back end, making the overall length considerably shorter. Livingston remembered being taught in training school that longer weapons are impractical when working in the tight quarters of a building. Devlin took a loaded magazine and snapped it into place. It held .45-caliber ball ammunition, the same he had carried in his sidearm in Vietnam. He had witnessed its stopping power many times and knew the Thompson was extremely accurate. He took a second magazine and slid it into his back pocket.

The radio crackled. It seemed empty inside the sound of the rain. "DE Four-zero to DE Four-one."

Devlin reached to switch the radio off, but Livingston stopped him. "We have to tell him something." Devlin was puzzled. "Four-zero, this is Four-three."

"Go ahead, Four-three."

"Go fuck yourself, Yoda."

Devlin had seen the fear in Livingston as they drove to Delray, but now he saw not only courage, but a transformation. He had become what he had dreamt about: a true Viking Warrior complete with utter disregard for consequence.

Devlin got out of the car and stood in the storm. The machine gun hung from his right hand. He did not seem to notice the pounding rain.

Livingston asked, "Do you have handcuffs?"

"For what?" Devlin answered flatly. Livingston then knew Devlin's intentions. "In case I don't make it, do you know what to do to someone who kills your partner? You don't put them in handcuffs." Devlin's simple statement had made Livingston the executor of his last will and testament. The madness had returned, again creasing itself into Devlin's face. He turned and disappeared into the slanting gray forest of rain.

Fauber ran back to Pilkington's office. He would demand that Livingston also be fired. "Boss, that son of a bitch Livingston—" He saw Shanahan sitting in a chair, looking smug.

"John, this agent has some interesting news. Go ahead, tell your supervisor."

Shanahan turned his full attention to Fauber's face and, like a sadistic flogger, whipped him with each word. "Devlin says that Tungworth is the Puget Sound Murderer."

Fauber looked at Pilkington to see if he should believe it. Pilkington asked Shanahan, "Where is Devlin now?"

"The meat-packing house on Cary Street."

Pilkington told Shanahan to go to his desk and wait. Once he left, Fauber closed the door and asked, "Do you believe them?"

"Of course. Them and their goddamn honesty. It's something they can't help. Never mind that now. We got to get down there. There'll be national coverage. I'm personally going to make the arrest. Have the SWAT team meet us. I'll call the media rep."

● ● ●

Just as Tungworth had used the rain to mask his movements, so did Devlin. The first-floor and basement windows were boarded up. The front double door was also covered with plywood. Devlin followed the shadows around to the back of the brown-brick structure. The second-floor windows were not covered, but were too high to gain entry. In the back, four concrete stairs led up to a small loading dock which stood out under a heavy overhead steel door for freight. An overhang protected the dock from the rain. Next to the overhead door was a thick metal door that had been used as an employees' entrance. At the threshold were clumps of wet mud. Devlin judged them to be from two people. With the lightest touch, he tried the doorknob. Locked. The freight door opened only from the inside. There was no external fire escape for the building. Delray's landscape proved that the fire code had not been a priority of the community.

Devlin stepped away from the dryness provided by the overhang and inspected the building. It was in good shape for an abandoned business. As such, it would attract thieves and vandals.

The building took up enough space to be surrounded on three sides by the downsized streets of Delray. The fourth side snuggled up to a one-story brick building. A narrow passageway, not immediately visible from the street, ran between the two buildings. Three basement windows were evenly spaced along the passageway. They too were boarded over. Devlin set the Thompson down and pulled at the corners of the plywood. It was toenailed in with eight-penny nails. The second window lacked the large nails angled into the wooden framework. Again he gripped the edges and immediately felt the plywood give. It had been set into the frame, but the nails had been removed. The window behind it had been broken out. Devlin looked down into the unending darkness.

Quickly, he climbed into the basement and pulled the Thompson in behind him.

He stood perfectly still and waited for his eyes to adjust. He could hear water slowly dripping into a puddle. The dampness penetrated his nostrils. He listened beyond the dripping water. Nothing. As his nose adjusted to the dampness, he thought he smelled something else. Death. Devlin wondered if it was his imagination. His eyes finished dilating. He could see at about 50 percent efficiency. The room was littered with garbage. A path through it led to a door. When he took his first step, a large, portly rat scurried across his path. Devlin hated rats, a most abundant commodity of his childhood.

Outside the door he found the source of the smell. An old man in filthy clothes stared up at Devlin from a bullet hole where his right eye had previously recorded life. The blood coming from the eye socket had jelled but was not completely dry. Couple of hours, Devlin estimated. Tungworth must have heard him come in and killed him.

Devlin pulled back the bolt on the Thompson and headed for the stairs.

III CHAPTER 19 III

Above him, Devlin could hear one voice. Ranting. Muffled by walls, it sounded like an indecipherable foreign language, but its inflections and volume were unmistakably angry.

Devlin timed the ravings and proceeded up the squeaking stairs as if on cue, keeping his advance unnoticed.

A bar of light underlined a door ahead. He could hear Tungworth clearly now. "You are all that is evil. You fornicate with men and women you bring home. In front of your children! And you have the nerve to have the Holy Cross tattooed between your breasts. The same breasts that nursed me! You are the lowest whore! That cross has become the devil's cross hairs, guiding men and women to your sins of desire. You must be cleansed!"

Noiselessly, Devlin opened the door. Vanessa Anderson was naked, tied to a wooden meat-cutting table. Duct tape was wrapped tightly around her mouth. Her eyes were small spotlights, bright with terror. Tungworth held up what looked like a heavy metal wand with an electrical cord hanging from the handle, so the girl could see it. "I got this 'specially for you. Do you know what a soldering iron does? With it I will cleanse your pit of sin. I shall insert it and then plug it in. It will heat to over 400 degrees, cooking your flesh. Cleansing you forever. You'll want to scream, but you won't be able to. You'll want to die. And I will help you."

Devlin knew he had to get into the room fast. He considered a single killing shot. But the way Tungworth was jumping around made Devlin afraid that if only wounded Tungworth would instantly turn his gun on the girl. He would have to offer himself as Tungworth's first target.

Silently, he stepped into the room and, deliberately aiming the Thompson over Tungworth's head, fired a five-round burst. Tungworth dove through a doorway at the back of the room. Vanessa's eyes reached out of her head, begging Devlin for help. Devlin heard Tungworth thumb back the hammer on his weapon. Now the girl lay between them. Devlin moved to his left, taking the girl out of the line of fire but further exposing himself. Tungworth's 9mm flashed orange from the gray doorway. Devlin felt the slug slam into the plaster wall he was leaning against. Through the doorway, he saw Tungworth's automatic aim at the girl. Devlin stood up and, from the hip, fired the remaining rounds in the magazine, trying to get Tungworth to run. The big, slow-moving slugs pounded the walls with twice the impact of Tungworth's 9mm. Devlin slammed the second magazine into the Thompson and ran at Tungworth's doorway, firing two- and three-round bursts.

He heard Tungworth running toward the rear of the building. Quickly he untied Vanessa and told her to get dressed.

Devlin measured his options. His first priority was getting Vanessa out of the building safely. There were two ways out: the window Devlin and the bum had entered through, and the back door where Tungworth seemed to have headed. If Devlin chose the window, he would have to push Vanessa up through it, leaving her briefly vulnerable outside. The rear door also clearly left Tungworth with an advantage if he felt compelled to wait in ambush and finish with Vanessa. Obviously he did since he had, at great risk, not simply abandoned her at the grocery store. Devlin decided to shift the odds to his favor. With the barrel of the Thompson he shattered the single burning light bulb. As darkness flooded the room, Devlin felt Vanessa grab on to him as if she were drowning. He took a moment to put his arm around her. It seemed to reassure her. Devlin's eyes adjusted to the darkness. "Vanessa, grab the back of my belt; we're getting out of here."

Letting the Thompson lead the way, Devlin walked cautiously to the rear door. Vanessa was silently buried against his back, stepping on his heels. It was exactly where he wanted her.

Ahead, a tall, thin rectangle of gray rain, exposed by the open rear door, beckoned the pair. Vanessa seemed to be pushing. Without a word Devlin stopped, letting the girl know there was still a need for caution. She responded accordingly. Devlin turned his eyes away from the light coming through the door so as not to diminish his night vision. They inched forward.

Finally, at the door, Devlin peeled Vanessa's fingers from around his belt. She could see his face now. He held up his palm to her, telling her not to move. In hopes of drawing fire, he threw the door completely open, causing it to bang loudly. The only sound was the disinterested rain.

He glanced around the doorjamb. Once they stepped through the doorway, there was no cover or concealment for twenty-five yards. If Tungworth was out there waiting, he had a perfect ambush site with a twenty-five-yard-wide kill zone. Devlin had only one option—to expose himself and draw Tungworth's fire. Devlin held his hand up to Vanessa again. She knew what he was about to do and frantically grabbed his hand. Then she looked into his eyes and understood that she had to be brave too; she slowly released him.

Devlin jumped through the doorway and crouched low along the building's back wall. The Thompson and Devlin's head rotated together as if both were directed by some unseen gyroscope.

From behind a large black metal Dumpster, Tungworth's handgun exploded. Devlin's right leg was ripped from under him. He went down, dropping the machine gun. Tungworth stepped from behind the Dumpster and aimed his gun over a sadistic smile.

Before Devlin could react, he heard a long, continuous yell coming around the far side of the building. It was Livingston, running straight at Tungworth, firing his handgun. Tungworth returned fire calmly and hit Livingston in the chest. Livingston went down, and Tungworth turned toward Devlin. Devlin reached for the Thompson, but another shot echoed in the rain. Devlin looked up and saw Livingston on his knees, his gun slowly smoking in the soaked air. Tungworth was hit. Shoulder or chest. He stumbled back into the shadows that lined the river. He stopped, fired one more shot at the kneeling Livingston, and staggered away. The young agent crumpled to the ground, involuntarily losing his gun.

Devlin struggled to his feet and found Vanessa at his side. She helped him to where Livingston was lying face up. A red puddle stained his chest. The rain diluted the edges of it, but the center was kept bright red with each heartbeat. Devlin recognized the shade of red—arterial bleeding.

"Those first shots. I thought he got you, Mike. That's why I came up. I think I hit him. My gun. Please!" Devlin heard the girl moving behind him. She handed Livingston his gun, which he accepted with a sense of relief that Devlin did not understand. Livingston looked at Vanessa and remembered the party on the warehouse roof when he had asked Devlin why he was willing to risk so much. His answer was a question—*What better truth?* Livingston smiled at the girl. "No better truth."

"Thanks to you," Devlin said. "You found her at the grocery. And then saved our lives."

Livingston smiled his crushing white smile. "Tell my mother and Sydney . . . you know," he said, his voice full of fluid.

"I will."

"Mike. You'd have made a hell of a Viking." Devlin could see the life leaving Livingston's body. His face went limp except for a trace of a smile. His chest stopped bleeding.

"And you were a hell of an Irishman."

Ignoring his leg, Devlin picked up Livingston, carried him up the loading dock stairs, and laid him under the overhang, out of the rain. His gun was still clenched in his wet hand. Devlin took off his suit coat and covered his partner's face.

For a moment, he was veiled in a bewildering numbness he had not felt since Vietnam. He thought of the young grunts, who had not seen enough death to consider it a consequence.

For Vanessa Anderson, the hopeless nightmare of the last twelve days rushed forward as she realized the FBI agent at her feet had died instead of her. Breathlessly, her body jerked with sobs. Devlin grabbed both of her arms and shook her. She was unable to make a sound. Like a bullwhip, he shook her again, finally snapping her from her trance. She cried like a sixteen-year-old.

"I've got to go after him," Devlin said and handed her his magnum. "You wait here. Someone will be here soon." She took the gun and backed into the doorway, her eyes burning in the darkness.

Devlin looked again at Livingston. Accelerating rage

burned through him like concentrated acid, his nostrils scorched with the smell of blood.

Devlin walked to the void that Tungworth had escaped into. His ears picked up the faint sound of metal against wood. He hurried in its direction.

Now he could hear gasps ending in small groans. Tungworth *was* wounded. A wounded psychotic who was suicidal could react only one way once cornered. Good, thought Devlin, it will be ended. He no longer cared if he died, as long as Tungworth did. Behind him he heard tires screech and car doors slam. He no longer had to worry about the girl.

He walked forward, feeling he was close. His senses scanned the shadows. The Thompson was held in front of him like a blind man's cane.

Now the only thing he could hear was the rain clicking on the hard coal. He held his breath and listened.

An explosion of light filled the coal yard, then vanished. As in a single frame of film, Devlin saw that Tungworth had been hit in the chest and was losing a lot of blood. His insane face was twisted with pain and confusion.

Devlin's eyes readjusted to the darkness. He raised the Thompson and looked down the barrel at the killer. Tungworth could not move. He stood there, losing strength. Somehow sensing Devlin's advantage, he dropped his gun and raised his hands. "Don't shoot! I give up." Devlin's silence panicked him. "You can't shoot. I'm surrendering. I want a lawyer."

As much as Devlin wanted to pull the trigger and feed the ravenous beast within, he instead thought of Livingston charging Tungworth and, after being mortally wounded, firing the shot that had saved their lives. Devlin decided it should be *that* bullet that ended Tungworth's life.

He lowered the barrel of the machine gun and pulled the trigger. The rounds splattered coal fragments against Tungworth's legs, causing him to run. Devlin limped after him, chasing him through the hills of dark, wet coal.

The throbbing pain in Devlin's leg reassured him that the chase was pumping more blood to his wound, just as Tungworth's was pumping more out of the hole in his chest.

Unceasingly, Devlin's vision tracked him. Every time Tungworth stopped, Devlin sprayed a short burst, being careful not to hit him. Tungworth ran heavily through the quicksand of loose coal.

Finally Tungworth found himself on top of the last coal hill at the edge of the river. With no place left to run, he turned and waited defiantly. His bloodless face glowed white in the dark rain.

Devlin threw down the Thompson and walked to the crest to finish with Tungworth.

As Devlin grabbed Tungworth's blood-soaked shirt, he felt the killer's knees buckle. He knew it would not be long. "Edgar Livingston!" Devlin said. Tungworth stared into Devlin's mouth with confused, lifeless eyes.

Devlin smiled. "He's the man who killed you." Devlin released his grip. Tungworth crumpled and rolled down the back side of the hill, plunging into the Rouge River, the grave he had planned for Vanessa Anderson.

The pain in Devlin's thigh returned, causing him to sit down on the coal. He could hear hard shoes running lightly behind him. It was Brackoff. He looked at Devlin's wound and saw there was no urgency. He walked over to Tungworth's floating body. Satisfied, he helped Devlin to his feet and they walked back toward the flashing lights.

Brackoff steered Devlin toward a waiting ambulance. Tom Anderson stood in the rain, holding Vanessa in his arms, unable to release her. He looked at Devlin and nodded.

• • •

Initially, Devlin had been surprised that the SAC had insisted he stay in the hospital overnight and then take at least a week off. The two guards who had previously failed to contain him now stood alertly outside his door. Brackoff, who refused to leave his side, sat quietly in the corner of his room. Evidently, Devlin was not going to be fired, but Pilkington's apparent concern had puzzled him.

The late news ended all his confusion. The lead story was the Tungworth case. The station went live to the SAC's conference room. Pilkington stood behind a small podium. A large red, white, and blue plastic FBI seal, positioned on the wall behind him, hung over his head like a patriotic halo. He had changed suits since Devlin had last seen him. A small flag pin dotted his left lapel. He spoke with a voice filled with the pain of self-sacrifice.

"Ladies and gentleman, the FBI has been conducting an investigation concerning the kidnapping of a sixteen-year-old Troy girl. She was abducted twelve days ago from the Detroit Metropolitan Airport and held in the Delray area of this city. Our investigation determined that the kidnapper was Marion Lee Tungworth, who escaped from the Michigan Department of Corrections on April 30 of this year. Mr. Tungworth was serving a five-to-fifteen-year sentence for kidnapping. Further investigation led us to the meat-packing house on Cary Street tonight, where Mr. Tungworth was shot to death by an agent of this office. Unfortunately, the FBI has paid the price for this rescue. Special Agent Edgar Livingston was killed during the shoot-out, and another agent was slightly wounded. Additional inquiries by my agents have determined that Tungworth was the individual responsible for the Puget Sound Murders in Seattle." With the condescension of a federal judge, he said, "I'll now take questions."

"How did you identify the kidnapper?" a female reporter asked.

"Through fingerprints." The media accepted the oversimplification. Pilkington, despite Devlin's earlier briefing, could not begin to understand the investigative chain that had led them to Tungworth. But he knew the media would not understand it even if he could explain it, so he didn't expect them to ask anything more penetrating.

The basic questions continued with Pilkington providing the basic answers, always with practiced humility. When a question was asked that he did not have the answer for, he would use one of the standard evasions: "I can't comment because it's under investigation," or "The information is too sensitive to discuss."

Ever the innovator, Pilkington had developed a third deflector—minutiae double-talk. Someone asked about fingerprints again. Pilkington took a noticeable breath, as though organizing data, and said, "Okay. You all know what fingerprint ridges are. In a small portion of the population, the tented arch configuration has irregular directions that produce unusual classifications . . ." And on it went for minutes. Only a fingerprint examiner *would* have known it was double-talk, but by the end of Pilkington's answer, the last minute of which no one heard, the only thing the glassy-eyed reporters wanted to write down was—*Don't ask fingerprint questions.*

By then, the press had enough meat for their articles and reports. Tough questions would just expose gray areas or, even worse, be answered with the SAC's detailed understanding of chickenshit. The few remaining questions were little ground balls, easy for the SAC to field, tying up loose ends for the reporters' stories.

Then Devlin heard a familiar voice, a voice that gave him a twinge of hope. It was Art Nestling, one of the last real reporters. Self-destructively interested in the truth, he was a guy who always let the truth get in the way of a good story. "Mr. Pilkington, isn't it true that this entire investigation was conducted secretly and against your orders?" Someone had tipped Nestling, Devlin thought; then he remembered that Nestling and Shanahan were old drinking buddies.

"Mr. Nestling, a sixteen-year-old girl is kidnapped by a serial murderer and I would order my agents *not* to investigate?"

Nestling shot back, "That's a question, not an answer. Or a denial."

"Sir, let me say one thing in closing, something I want not only all you reporters to remember, but—" Pilkington turned and looked into the TV camera. "All the citizens that the FBI protects. Agents, every last one of us, are witnesses to the truth. Thank you." He started to walk out when Nestling yelled, "Haven't you been out of town the last ten days?"

The rest of the reporters, who were packing up, looked up for Pilkington's response.

The office media agent, another pilot fish, leaned over and whispered in the SAC's ear, "Don't get into a pissing contest with Nestling. He probably knows everything and will let everyone in this room know by asking you questions you won't answer." Pilkington nodded and said, "Ladies and gentlemen, I've just been informed I have an urgent phone call from the director. I'm sure you'll understand if I ask to be excused."

With a shrug, the reporters finished their packing.

Brackoff turned off the television. "You've had enough of that asshole for one day."

"For a lifetime, Gunnar. For a lifetime."

Brackoff rolled the crooked black cigar back into the corner of his mouth and sat down in a chair near the door. "You need anything?"

"No. Why don't you go home?"

Brackoff didn't answer. Devlin knew Brackoff would stay there as long as he was in the hospital.

In the hallway, an argument had started. When Brackoff opened the door, the voices stopped. It was Riley Smith, Al Humphrey, and Theo Agash, trying to get past the two Bureau agents. Devlin invited them in. Agash carried a large brown bag, which he started unpacking on Devlin's bed tray. He said, "Shanahan told us about the slaughterhouse. By the time we got there you were getting loaded into the ambulance. Speaking of getting loaded—" With the flair of a magician, Agash drew a half-gallon bottle of whiskey out of his bag.

Brackoff was filling plastic glasses with ice and whiskey when Bill Shanahan walked in with a case of beer. "Oh, sure, give *me* the job of telling Pilkington and Fauber what dunces they are, but I don't get an invite to the party." Brackoff handed him a whiskey. "Thanks, Gunnar, at least someone around here is civilized." Shanahan fished the ice out of his glass and fired down the whiskey with one hand while somehow cracking a beer with his casted hand. "Mike, Ross went to pick up Knox at the airport." Devlin nodded.

There were no stories, no laughter. Each man drank solemnly, remembering how vulnerable his life was.

When Knox arrived with Jeff Ross, the rest of the crew respectfully cleared out of the room. As Knox held Devlin, he could feel an invisible trembling. He held her at arm's length and watched her confused eyes. "I'm okay. I'm okay."

She refused to cry. Devlin liked that. "Jeff said we could use his place up north for as long as we want."

"Sounds good."

"Mike. Jeff has something to talk to you about. Please listen to him." Now Devlin was confused. Evidently whatever it was, Ross and Knox had discussed it on the way to the hospital, and it was something Knox was very serious about. "Are you sure you're all right?" she asked one last time.

"The shot was through and through, no bone. I'll be out of here tomorrow."

After Knox had left, Brackoff ducked back into the room and sat in the corner on a groaning metal chair.

Devlin turned to Ross. "Okay, Jeff, let's hear it."

"Mike, you did a helluva job."

"We had the help of a good friend."

Ross appreciated being included in the crew's success. He became serious. "Why don't you give up all this glamour and reward to work with me? I'll pay you thirty grand more than you're making now, and all you have to do is hang out with me and check security once in a while. We'll travel, drink beer, and make money. What do you say?"

"Everything except hanging out with you sounds great. Thirty thousand?"

"Think about it."

When Ross left, Devlin leaned back and closed his eyes. He wanted to think about Ross's offer, but the abrupt odor of Brackoff's cigar prevented him. "What do you think, Gunnar?"

"An extra thirty Gs for working with a good guy like that is a hell of a temptation. On the other hand, if you stay you'll get to work with Pilkington and Fauber, or worse yet, their replacements. You may think the Bureau is screwed up, but based on what I've seen at our department, let me give you one piece of advice: Enjoy it now, because it's going to get worse."

Devlin admired Brackoff's ability to get to the bottom line. He was afraid the big cop was right. The crew came back into the room. Shanahan handed Devlin a beer.

• • •

The next day Devlin drove to the Omni Hotel on East Jefferson, where Edgar Livingston's mother was staying. She had arrived the night before to take her son's body back to New England.

"Mrs. Livingston. I'm Mike Devlin."

"Please come in." She waved him into a chair. She was a handsome woman. The blackness was just starting to leave her hair at the temples. Her face had an aged neatness about it, as if it had been designed with an engraver's finest tool. A black suit covered her still trim figure. It was easy to see where her son had gotten his bearing. "I want to thank you for all your help with all of this. Everything has been taken care of. I am a person who appreciates organization."

Devlin smiled. "So Edgar said."

"He spoke of you often. He thought a great deal of you."

"I wish he hadn't," Devlin said almost to himself.

She sensed Devlin's guilt. "Let me tell you something that is giving me strength right now. Edgar believed that everyone has a destiny, and that destiny is in front of you. Not off to the side or behind you. So you pursue life head on, and whatever happens is your destiny. He called me last week and told me that he had reached his destination. You, Sydney, this job. It was where he wanted to be. He had a secret understanding of things. In his short life, he found more than the rest of us ever will. I'll miss him every day until I die, but if he could have picked an ending for himself, I doubt if he would have changed a thing."

"Thank you, Mrs. Livingston. That helps."

After a few minutes of silence, she said, "Would you do me one last favor? I know it will be difficult for you, but it would be impossible for me. I'd like you to clear out Edgar's apartment. I'm only concerned about personal things of his. I don't care what you do with the rest."

"I'll take care of it."

"And I want you to have his boat. I don't sail, and I don't know how I would get it back."

"Would you like me to sell it and send you the money?"

"No. I don't want to remember it that way. Besides, no one would buy that old thing."

"Ed sure loved it, though."

"Yes, he did. He really believed in his Nordic heritage. It was hard growing up in a town where you're the only black male; he sunk his whole being into the Viking image. When they weren't raping and plundering, they had some admirable qualities. It worked for Edgar. When he was on that boat, he traveled back a thousand years and lived as a young man should, full of pride and confidence, desperate to conquer the world."

Devlin thought of Livingston standing at the helm, transfixed, rushing back in time.

A quiet knock came at the door. It was Sydney Jemison. She and Mrs. Livingston embraced warmly, both fighting tears. Mrs. Livingston excused herself to go and regain her composure.

"Mike, I'm going back with Ed's mother."

"That's great. I'm sure she could use the help."

"No, I'm going back there to work. With my CPA, I can get a job easily. And I'll stay with her. I don't know how long it will last, but it's a start. Edgar always wanted me to break out of here."

"I wish there was something *I* could do for him."

She put her hand on his arm and said, "Mike, he felt you did the most."

After the memorial service, Devlin took the two women to the airport and saw them to their plane.

Reluctantly, he drove to Edgar Livingston's apartment and, after identifying himself to the manager, was given a key.

The small, one-bedroom apartment was scantily furnished. A wall in the living room was covered with a taped-together series of posterboards. On them was a thousand years of Livingston tracing his ancestors. Below it, a smaller chart had been started. It traced his mother's family. On a desk directly under the charts was a folder marked THE ROOTS OF LOUISA MAE LIVINGSTON. The handwriting was not Edgar's. He guessed it was Sydney's. They had both changed each other's lives. Real love did that.

Also on the desk was a videotape movie. It was *The Vikings*. Not knowing why, Devlin put it into the VCR and started it. As a stern FBI copyright warning flashed on the screen, Devlin went into the kitchen and brought back an unopened bottle of whiskey and a glass. It was Bushmill's Irish whiskey, probably purchased in case Devlin dropped by unexpectedly. He regretted he never had.

He also regretted, for the first time, his decision to become an agent. Until now, some unseen power had always had a hand on the override button, ready to reverse any blatant injustices; to keep the truly innocent unharmed and, at the same time, somehow punish the disrupters of order. But now disorder was the current triumph, and it promised a long—and probably unending—engagement.

Devlin had always thought of the FBI as the final, unwavering defense, the one thing that would, because of dedication, endure. He thought of Pilkington and Fauber and their bureaucratic descendants. Their self-serving incompetence had almost cost Vanessa her life and, at least in part, had cost Edgar Livingston his. Then, without looking back, they had claimed the successes that Livingston had given his life to ensure.

Devlin again considered Ross's offer. More than money, it was a return to dignity. Dignity had once roamed the great plains of the Bureau with the abundance of the buffalo. Now both, due to poachers, had all but disappeared. Devlin opened the bottle.

The sting from the liquor provided some relief. He watched the movie halfheartedly until he saw a scene in which a Viking is told to jump to his death. He asks for his sword because unless a Viking dies with his sword in his hand, he cannot enter Valhalla. Devlin remembered Vanessa handing Livingston his gun.

Devlin stopped drinking and watched the rest of the movie more closely. In the last scene, the Viking prince is killed and his body is put aboard a longboat and launched unmanned, sails full. As it leaves the shore, archers shoot flaming arrows into it, setting it on fire. It sails out to sea, glowing in the night.

When the movie was over, Devlin sat in the apartment, drinking until dark. He drove home and picked up some things that he put in an old seabag. Then he headed to the dock where the *Valhalla* was docked.

Clumsily, he sailed the boat south along the Lake St. Clair shoreline until he saw the lakefront house belonging to Dr. Zilke. Devlin had gone to a house-warming barbecue there two years earlier. The medical examiner maintained a small floating dock directly behind his house.

A hundred yards offshore Devlin opened his canvas bag and drew out his Marine Corps officer's sword, the symbol of combat leadership for over one hundred years. Its pearl-colored handle was crossed by a brass hilt that was now tarnished. He squeezed it in his hand and took a moment to remember both the good and the bad. He took it to the bow and, with both hands raised over his head, drove it deep into the soft decking. From his pocket he took his Navy Cross and pinned it to the leather lanyard that decorated the sword's handle. He spoke out loud. "Edgar, you deserve more, but this is all I have."

The boat was fifty yards from the dock now. Devlin went

back to the tiller and picked up the seabag. He guided the craft in a 180-degree arc so it would be heading out into open water. When the *Valhalla* touched the dock, he tied off the rudder, aiming the craft straight into the darkness of the lake. He jumped out onto the floating pier and took the last items, three highway flares taped together, out of the bag.

As the boat started to glide away silently, Devlin ignited the flares and tossed them aboard. *Pop!* The sticks ignited and spat out their smoky pink light.

He stood watching. A small glow floated out into the darkness. The farther it reached, the brighter it became, as if it were eternal. The light winds took the *Valhalla* into the calm night, lighting the endless horizon. For the last time, Devlin said good-bye to a Viking prince.

||| CHAPTER 20 |||

For the next two weeks Devlin and Knox hid out at
Schuss Mountain in Ross's ski chalet. There was no television, radio, or newspapers. Devlin's days were spent on the
balcony, gazing across the canopy of the valley below and
occasionally refilling his glass with vodka and tonic. The
wind chased the sunlight through the green-and-silver carpet of treetops.

Knox read books and waited. It had been the same way
when he had come home from Vietnam. No parades, no
dignity, just aching self-doubt. She would awaken in the
middle of the night and find him sitting on the balcony
drinking. He never seemed to sleep. She waited patiently;
she knew no one could help.

One night at the end of the second week, as Knox was
reading in bed, Devlin came in. "We'd better get back."
She searched his eyes.

"I'm okay," he said too abruptly. She could see he was
better but not okay.

"Come to bed."

"You Catholic girls always were easy."

In the morning they left for Detroit. The closer they got,
the more Devlin thought about Fauber and Pilkington.
About L. C. Sanders. About Edgar Livingston and the six
Marines who had claimed their irrevocable truth. Could he
take any more? Why should he? He had done his share.

Knox asked, "Thinking about Jeff's offer?"

"How'd you know?"

"You're doing fifty-five."

"That's the speed limit."

"We're in a sixty-five zone. Anyway, you've never obeyed the limit before."

"You're pretty observant."

"My old man's an FBI agent."

"How do you like that?"

"It's okay."

"Could you live without it?"

"As long as he was around."

"This one worried you?"

"Yep."

"I think I'm going to take Jeff's offer."

Knox did not answer. Devlin glanced at her. The fingers of her right hand appreciatively stroked her wedding band. Knox's vote was in, but first, Devlin had some things to attend to.

When they reached home, he called Brackoff and asked him to meet him at the warehouse in an hour. Then he called the tech room and the Bella Luna case agent answered, "Hey, Mike, how are you feeling?"

"Fine, thanks. How's the tech going?"

"Great now. We shut it down last night at midnight. Didn't really get much against the Pantatellis, not enough to prosecute, anyhow. I know the old man is bad, but that kid of his, Joey, he's the one I'd like to put away."

"What's he doing now?"

"He thinks he's slick. Won't make any calls from the club or his house, but he goes over to his old man's and doesn't have the brains to figure we're on those phones too. He starts making random calls until he gets this little girl on the line and starts all this heavy-breathing bullshit. Then he calls up some slug and is telling about how he almost had a list of our informants and it's just a matter of time until he finds someone who could deliver this time. That little bucket of shit. We now hear he was involved with the old man in the Molini hit."

"It's too bad they're going to skate. I was hoping they would get what was coming to them," Devlin said.

"These guys never get what they deserve. In fact, they'll all be at the Napoli Gardens tonight. Don Scantina's youngest daughter is getting married. They'll be inside drowning themselves in booze, and I'll be out in the surveillance van snapping pictures."

"I suppose the Pantatellis and their wives will be there."

"Hey, it's the Don's daughter. He's invited everyone."

Devlin smiled. "He's invited more than he knows."

When Brackoff arrived at the warehouse parking lot, Devlin was opening the trunk of his Bureau car. He handed Brackoff a suitcase. "Do you know what this is?"

"From the airport?"

"Do you know what to do with it?"

"By when?"

"First thing tomorrow morning?"

"It'll be there."

Then Devlin handed Brackoff a tape cassette and gave him detailed instructions as to its disposal.

When Brackoff left, Devlin went into the warehouse and sat in its quiet murkiness. The naked briefing board still held the staples that Livingston had so surgically inserted. Devlin ran his hand over their neat rows. They felt like precious metals. He went up on the roof and watched the river slip by imperceptibly, remembering the last time he had watched it from there.

At one o'clock he called Lieutenant Stanley Wilson of the Wayne County Sheriff's Office. He was in charge of the Metro Narcotics Unit. Working a hundred or more hours a week, he burned out crew after crew whose drive could not match his own. He was streetwise and unrelenting. He was the best Devlin had ever met. Because of Michigan law, he could execute warrants anywhere in the state. And he did. He piled up statistics that he never took the time to notice.

Devlin's sources had always been productive for Wilson. Time and again he would execute lucrative search warrants based solely on Devlin's information.

"Stanley, how would you like to do Frankie Williams?"

"The last time I arrested him, he spit in my face and called me a 'fucking Tom.' What do you think?"

"Do you know where he's living?"

"Yeah. Up in Oak Park with that mulatto dude, Whitey."

"That's the place. If you knock on his door tomorrow at ten A.M., you'll find he's holding four keys of some dandy Mexican blow."

"How good is this?"

"It's from my ace," Devlin lied. "You've got all his stats from the other search warrants."

"At ten tomorrow, we'll be knocking on Frankie's door with an eighty-pound steel ram."

"I'll call you on your cellular about a quarter to, to make sure you're ready."

"I'll be ready."

At first, Marianna Scantina's wedding gave promise of a typical Mob affair. Too much food, too much liquor, too much jewelry, and, of course, too much hair spray. There was even too much music. The Don wanted the best for his daughter, so he had hired not only an expensive dance band, but also a disc jockey to play music during the band's breaks.

By the third break, everyone was comfortably drunk, so no one noticed the heavyset man in a dark suit talking to the disc jockey. He stood at the doorway until the next tape started. Its jolting volume silenced the large hall. Anthony Pantatelli's unmistakable voice filled the crowded room. "I want you to beg for it, you Guinea whore."

Then came the pleading refrain: "Fuck me, Tony. Please fuck me!" Although he had not heard them in years, Vincenzo Scantina immediately recognized his wife's pleasured groans.

As one of the Don's men started toward the disc jockey's equipment, a new segment of tape played. It was the younger Pantatelli. "There's somebody dirty in your office. They're going to sell my father a list of all the FBI informants in Detroit." Joey Pants remembered the words from the night at the Whitney, when Devlin had taken away his voice-activated tape recorder.

Calmly, Scantina rose without a word and stared briefly at the stunned Pantatelli table. He turned a grinding look on his young wife and then wiped his mouth with a linen napkin as if trying to remove some stinging bitterness. Followed by his scurrying bodyguards, he left.

All eyes turned to the Pantatellis. The old men knew it would be the last time they would be seen.

By 9:30 the next morning, Devlin was dressed in a suit. He was planning to attend a retirement luncheon that afternoon.

Devlin called Brackoff. "Gunnar, is everything cool?"

"Couldn't be better."

"I guess we're square for the pizza robberies."

"Mike, you've got one in the bank anytime you need it."

Devlin dialed Wilson's car phone. When he answered, Devlin said, "This is the American Civil Liberties Union. We understand you're about to violate someone's rights."

Wilson laughed. "Right on time, Mike."

"Are you ready?"

"I'm looking at the house as we speak."

"Okay, let me call the source and make sure you're going to have a good time."

"Go ahead. I'm going to love this. Taking these murdering animals before an Oakland County judge. They won't be buying out of this one."

Devlin smiled to himself—*exactly*. He dialed Frankie's phone and recognized his rude "What?"

In a black voice, Devlin said, "Hey, man, I'm calling about a price for those four—ah—toys you had in your trunk yesterday."

"What the fuck are you talking about, fool? Who is this?"

"Man, you got blow or not?"

"Who the fuck is this?"

"Don't you remember me, I talked to you yesterday. You said you got the four keys from some dude named Stand. Is this Whitey?" Devlin heard Frankie slam the phone down.

Devlin waited five minutes and called Wilson back. "You're all set. He says to be careful because they're both heavily—"

"Mike, we're going in. We got shots fired." The line went dead.

Because Knox knew Danny Holland and liked him, Devlin took her to his retirement luncheon. They arrived late and sat at a table with people from other law enforcement agencies that Devlin did not know. Devlin noticed the other crew members at a table near the bar. They saw him and nodded. Nothing needed to be said.

Devlin had known Danny Holland for over fifteen years. He was a hell of an agent. He was third-generation law enforcement. His grandfather, father, and he, before he came to the Bureau, had been New York City cops. He was Devlin's training agent and had taught him all the basics.

Twenty years earlier, Holland had been severely wounded by a Vietnamese land mine. Within the last year, the trauma caught up to his body, and he developed epilepsy with grand mal seizures. The once ruggedly handsome agent was now pale and thin. His mind, however, remained bright. During polite applause, he stepped to the podium. He spoke with a lonely seriousness.

"This is not the happiest day of my life. Leaving people like you could never be cause for celebration. But leave I must. I am being severed from an important part of my existence. The last eighteen years have been filled with things never deserved in lesser callings, filled with both sacrifice and wonder. When I was offered an appointment to the Bureau, I was reluctant, but felt I owed it to my father to discuss it with him, God rest his soul. It had always been a dream of his to be an FBI agent, but his eyesight was not up to Bureau standards. That night, he told me one of his secrets of life: When it came to the more difficult problems of this planet, only a few were granted the gifts to solve them. And if those few did not accept that responsibility, they were betraying those talents. Which, in the final count, meant they were betraying themselves. He summed it up simply: Many are called, but few are chosen. I cannot believe that tomorrow I no longer will be an FBI agent, no longer will I feel the glow of its exhaustion or taste its wonder. But one thing that can never be taken away is that, for a brief period between the two great darknesses, I was one of the chosen. Thanks, Dad."

For a moment there was not a sound. Everyone, including Devlin, had been swept back to the other side of the myth, when they had hoped to be good enough to be one of the chosen. Danny Holland had never gotten over the honor. At that moment, everyone was jealous of him and angry with their own complacency. Amid the standing ovation, Devlin looked at his wife, who was crying.

In turn she saw a flush in his face that she knew was caused by commitments so deeply rooted, they could never be abandoned. She smiled. "You'll let Jeff know."

"I'm sorry, Knox."

"I'm not."

Devlin drove to Jeff Ross's scrapyard. Ross was in his office on the phone, speaking Japanese to an associate in Tokyo. When he hung up, the two men shook hands warmly.

"Mike, you look great. How's the leg?"

"It's fine. Thanks for the use of your place. It was perfect for R and R."

"Good. Am I about to hear good news or bad news?"

"It's good news for your business."

"So you're going to stay with the Bureau. You hard-headed Mick. Did you watch the news while you were up north?"

"Not even the radio."

"That fucking Pilkington has taken credit for rescuing Vanessa *and* solving the Puget Sound murders. Next thing, he'll claim he's been playing handball with Jimmy Hoffa twice a week. Everything you did, in spite of his efforts to stop you, he's now taking credit for. You Celts just love to beat yourself to death, don't you?"

"Yes, we do. It's what the Irish call victory."

Devlin stood before the cypher lock at the employee's entrance on the twenty-sixth floor of the federal building. A deep breath slowed his surging heart rate. He typed in the combination. It failed to open the lock. He tried it again. Still it did not open. Occasionally, the combination was changed for security purposes, but usually it meant someone had been fired. Devlin hoped it was not him. That surprised him. Two weeks earlier he had almost welcomed the idea.

He went through the reception room and, after showing his identification, was buzzed in. He walked to the squad area and found his desk changed. On it was a picture of an unknown woman in a swimming suit with what Shanahan referred to as tractor-pull thighs. One of the Jedi stretched back in his chair, smiling, evidently aware of something that Devlin was not.

Sue, the squad secretary, got up from her desk and hurried over to him. "How are you, Mike?"

"Just fine. What's going on?" Devlin asked, nodding towards the girl with the smothering thighs.

Sue lowered her voice, "There's been a lot of changes. Pilkington's been promoted to assistant director and is headed back to Washington. Fauber has been promoted and shipped back."

Noting the caution in her voice, Devlin said, "You make it sound like that's bad news."

The worry in her eyes expanded. "There's been one other promotion." Something told Devlin not to ask.

A familiar voice came from Fauber's office. "Sue, I want that Monthly Administrative Report, now!" Duncan Moorehead walked out of the office.

The two men stared at each other. It was not as it had been that last day at the warehouse, when Devlin's stare had humbled him. Because of the title in front of his name, Moorehead, somehow, now thought of himself as superior. Devlin remembered; they always did. But Devlin knew a secret that comforted him now: These self-serving bastards knew what they really were and as a result could never respect themselves. It was an unseen justice.

"Step into my office, please," Moorehead said with polished condescension.

Moorehead shut his door. "I know we've had our differences, but I'm willing to put that in the past. If, however, you feel you cannot overlook those differences and be a productive, responsive member of this squad, I'll be glad to—"

The office PA came on. It was none other than John Wayne. "Your attention, please."

Oh, no, thought Devlin.

"Will Duncan Moorehead report to the ASAC's office immediately. Repeat, the ASAC needs more head, Duncan. I guess you're not dunkin' for apples in there, eh, Pilgrim?"

Devlin didn't bother to deny having any part in the announcement. It would have been to no avail. He just got up and left the screaming supervisor. When he exited the office, he was shocked to see Bill Shanahan sitting at his desk. He looked at Devlin and shrugged, indicating he also did not know the true identity of John Wayne.

On Devlin's desk, he found a new case. He dropped it into his briefcase and headed for the door. As he passed one of the interview rooms, Tom Anderson exited with a strange smile on his face. "Mike, where have you been?"

"Avoiding this place."

"We want you to come to dinner. Saturday night? In your honor Vanessa is doing the cooking. Judy's teaching her."

Devlin was surprised. *"Judy?"*

"Yeah. After you got Vanessa back, we had a long talk about priorities, and I got out of the management program. After all . . ." Anderson's eyes glinted as he finished the sentence with a surprisingly good imitation of John Wayne. "—a man's got to do what a man's got to do."

In the hallway Devlin waited for an elevator. He thought again of Ross's offer. Although he appreciated the Duke's timely announcement, he wondered if things could go on, if there would be as many laughs, or if the only victories were going to be of the Irish variety.

On the hallway wall hung a multi-colored board, three feet high and four feet long. At the top in white letters, it read THE FBI'S TEN MOST WANTED FUGITIVES. As he usually did, Devlin absentmindedly scanned the ten black-and-white wanted flyers for new additions. There was only one. Traditionally, the ten fugitives were wanted for serious crimes such as murder, bank robbery, or terrorism. This one was wanted for "Impersonating an FBI Agent." Devlin recognized the photo and the name—Duncan Moorehead.

In the elevator, Devlin pulled the new case out of his briefcase and decided which lead he would cover first.